The
Secrets
We
Carry

Deanna Lynn Sletten

The Secrets We Carry

ISBN-13: 978-1-941212-67-7

Cover Designer: Deborah Bradseth

For Debbi, Rosanne, Howard, and Donna,
my second family and the ones who helped me
fall in love with Portland, Oregon.

The Secrets We Carry

PROLOGUE

Petrograd, Russia
April 1917

"Maman, I do not understand," Sofiya said softly as she watched her mother's hands shake while carefully packing a suitcase. Maria had been adamant that Sofiya take an older leather suitcase that wouldn't appear extravagant if anyone was watching. "Why must I leave? Why can't I stay here with you and Père?"

Marie's dark tendrils swayed as she shook her head. "Non, non," her mother said in barely a whisper. They were speaking French, as was common among the aristocrats in Russia, despite being born and raised there. "You must leave tomorrow, ma chère. It is not safe for you here now that our beloved Tsar has abdicated."

"But Maman, Père said we will be safe," Sofiya exclaimed. Her father had insisted that he and his family would not be bothered by the incoming government because of the highly regarded position he held at the university.

"Your Père is a good and smart man, ma chère, but he is not being realistic. Once those in power learn we are cousins of the Tsar, we will not be safe. That is why I must send you away. I must keep my last living child alive." Tears filled Maria's eyes as she spoke, and Sofiya's heart clenched. Her brother had died fighting in the war, and his death had nearly broken her mother. At the tender age of sixteen, Sofiya understood how heartbreaking her brother's loss was to the entire family. She missed Mikhail greatly.

Maria smoothed the white shirtwaist with her graceful hand after placing it into the suitcase. "I am packing only the essentials for you, chère. Shirtwaists and dark skirts, undergarments, and practical shoes. One of your white cotton dresses, too. And a warm wool coat. Nothing too extravagant that might make people believe you are from a well-to-do family."

Sofiya's young face crinkled. She was trying desperately to understand what her mother was implying. *Nothing too fancy? Well-to-do family?* Although she had always known her family was related to royalty and had been quite close to her cousins, the Tsar's daughters, Sofiya had not been raised to put on airs. Her father had educated her in several languages, history, science, and mathematics just as her brother had been, and her mother had taught her all the necessities of being a polite young lady. But Sofiya and her brother hadn't been raised as spoiled children. They'd had chores assigned to them around the townhouse, had accompanied their parents to do good works at charities, and had never been given excessive gifts or clothing. Now, her mother was acting strange, as if dressing nicely in this new place Sofiya was traveling to would cause a threat to her life.

"Do not frown, my sweet," Maria scolded. "You do not

wish to scar your beauty with such a face."

Sofiya immediately softened her expression. The young girl knew she was no beauty in any sense of the word with her large features, dark brown eyes, and dark hair. Her dearest friend, Alina Henderson, however, was breathtaking. Alina had a delicate face with a small nose and rosebud lips. Her hair was so blond, it was almost white, and her eyes were the palest blue, like the sky on a summer day. But Sofiya did not contradict her maman because she knew how worried she was at this moment.

After filling the suitcase, Maria laid out a plain dark skirt, a white shirt, and a waistcoat for Sofiya. She turned to her daughter, her expression serious. "You will wear this one outfit as you travel. I've sewn my emerald necklace and diamond earrings into the waistband. You must keep them with you at all times."

Sofiya gasped. "Maman! Why?"

Maria clasped her daughter's hands in her own. "Sweet one, you must listen carefully to me. I do not know what lies ahead for you. I'm preparing you as best I can. Your dear friend, Alina, will travel with you to a place in America where you will be safe and start a new life. Alina's mother has made all the arrangements with a distant cousin of hers who lives in Portland, Oregon. Proper travel papers have been secured for you both. You will travel as Alina's younger sister, and you will use her last name of Henderson and say you're traveling to America from Finland. It is imperative that you never utter the word Russia at any time."

"But why do I need your precious jewels?" Sofiya asked. If all was arranged, why would her Maman give up two of her finest treasures?

Maria's brows drew together in worry. "Because even the

best-laid plans can go awry. If you find yourself in a terrible bind, you can sell the jewels. And if you never need to do so, then they will be a beautiful reminder of me."

Tears filled the young girl's eyes. She did not wish to lose her family. "Maman, I don't want to leave you and Père. Why can we not leave together as a family?"

"Non, we cannot," Maria said sadly. "We can only risk sending you and Alina. If we all try to leave, something terrible might happen. Madam Henderson has worked hard for months to plan your escape. To save you and her daughter. So, you must do as I say."

Sofiya pulled a white handkerchief from her skirt pocket and dabbed at her eyes. She nodded in agreement, although she wished she didn't have to leave. America was so far away, and she was frightened. "Can I write to you and Père, so I know you are safe?" she asked.

A pained expression crossed her mother's face. "Non, ma chère. It is too dangerous for you to write to us. No one must ever know where you are. Ever. Do you understand?"

"Yes, Maman," Sofiya said, but her heart was broken. To cut all ties with her family forever was too much to bear.

"Now, my darling. You must listen to my instructions," Maria said earnestly. "You will go to Alina's home tonight and depart tomorrow for Helsinki, where your journey will begin. It will be a long, arduous trip, but I know you and Alina will do fine. You are both educated young women. And the fact that you speak many languages will help you on your journey. Once you arrive in America, however, you must speak only English. It is imperative you blend in quickly, so no one is the wiser."

"Yes, Maman," Sofiya said, dropping her eyes to the floor.

There was no arguing with her Maman now that she'd made up her mind.

Marie's face softened. "Do not worry, darling one. I trust Alina's mother completely. She is not only our dressmaker; she has been my closest friend nearly all my life, just as Alina has been yours." Marie placed her finger under her daughter's chin and gently raised Sofiya's eyes to hers. "I love you more than life itself, ma chère. Please know that. That is why I'm willing to let you go so far away, far from the danger here. I pray you will have a chance for a better life there, possibly meet a nice man and have a family of your own. There is nothing left for you here."

Sofiya grasped her mother in a hug as tears spilled down her face. She prayed that the turmoil in her beloved country would end so she could one day return and see her parents again. Until then, she would do as her mother wished.

Pulling away, Sofiya once again nodded her assent.

"Good girl," Maria said, smiling through her tears. "Now, let us go to Alina's house before it grows dark, and tomorrow, you begin your new life."

"Yes, Maman," Sofiya said.

CHAPTER ONE

Portland, Oregon
April 2022

Addison Cameron moved slowly through the cramped antique store, carefully studying every piece it held. Addie loved antiques. Antiques, old houses, and everything else that had been cast away and needed to be loved again.

"Look what I found, Addie." Zachery Walker, her boyfriend, sauntered over to her, his brown eyes twinkling. She loved how boyish he looked when he was excited.

Addie looked at the small box he carried. It was an old wooden cigar box, possibly from the early 1900s. Unlike the many she'd seen before, this one wasn't rustic but was polished and shone almost like new. Engraved on the top were the words "CROOKS, Rum Soaked, Portland, Ore."

She grinned up at Zach. "You know me too well. It's beautiful."

He beamed. "Wait until you see what's inside—that's the best part." Zach lifted the tarnished gold latch and opened the lid. Addie swiped her wispy blond bangs from her eyes and peered inside.

"It's empty," she said, disappointed.

"It seems empty, but look again." Zach reached inside and pushed down on one side of the bottom. Up popped the other side. "It has a false bottom."

Intrigued, Addie took the box from him and set it on an antique table. "There are letters inside," she said excitedly.

"That's what makes it so special," Zach said, obviously proud of his discovery.

She chuckled. "You do know me well." Lifting the pile of letters, Addie was immediately aware of how old they were. The yellowed envelopes were tied tightly with a faded blue ribbon. "Do you suppose they're love letters?" she asked.

Zach shrugged. "We won't know until we go through them."

Addie carefully replaced the letters and false bottom, then walked over to the counter. "How much for the cigar box?" she asked Robert, the owner. She'd known Robert for years, having bought many items in his store to decorate the houses she flipped.

"For you, sweetie?" the older man said, winking at her. "Thirty-five bucks."

Addie knew the box alone was worth that price. "What about the letters hidden inside?" she asked. Addie didn't want to cheat her favorite antique dealer. He'd given her such good deals in the past, and she wanted to continue that relationship.

"They were in the box when I bought it, so they go with it," he said, smiling.

"Here, let me buy it," Zach said, taking it from Addie. "It can be an early birthday present."

"Birthday present?" Robert said. "Well, in that case, it's thirty dollars. I have to give the birthday girl a little discount." He winked again.

"Thanks, Robert," she said, touched by his generosity. "You're always so sweet."

"That's me. The local sweetheart." Robert wrapped the box in old newspaper and placed it in a bag. "But in all honesty, those letters won't do you much good. Some are in a different language. Looks like Italian or something. I gave up after looking at a couple of them."

Addie was disappointed to hear that, but she still wanted the box and letters.

Zach paid for the box and carried the bag out of the store as they called goodbye to Robert. Once outside, Addie turned and hugged Zach. "Thank you for the birthday gift. I can't wait to look through those letters."

He kissed her lightly on the temple, his scruffy beard tickling her cheek. "I knew you'd like it. You love mysteries. Maybe we can get someone to translate the letters if they're all in another language. I know a couple of people from the university who studied languages."

A chilly breeze blew up the street, and Addie shivered despite her heavy winter coat. She pulled her knit slouch cap from her pocket and placed it on her head. "I thought winter was over," she said as they walked up the street.

"It's Portland, sweetie," Zach said without further explanation. The words spoke for themselves.

Addie chuckled. "Right. Let's grab a coffee."

Zach wrapped his arm around her as they turned into a small coffee shop on the corner. They ordered their coffees and then sat down at a table. Eagerly, Addie pulled the old cigar box from the bag and retrieved the letters. As she sipped her hot drink, she untied the pile of letters and carefully sifted through them. Most had only one word on the front of the envelope—Maman.

"Isn't that mother in French?" Addie asked, looking up at Zach.

"I think so." He leaned closer for a better look. "It's definitely not Italian."

Growing warm, Addie took off her cap and shook her head to fluff up her short hair. When she was younger, Addie had long blond hair that hung in waves down her back. Now, at thirty-four, she found shorter hair easier, especially with the work she did.

Addie opened a few envelopes, but the letters were written in what she thought was French. Disappointed that she'd have to wait to learn their contents, Addie was about to tie the letters together again when she saw an envelope with no name written on it. Carefully, she opened the brittle envelope and out fell two photos.

"Look at these!" she said, growing excited again. The photos were in black and white on heavy cardboard. One was of a young woman holding a baby and sitting on the front porch of a house. The other was of four people standing in a garden across the street from a neighborhood of houses. "They look like they're from the early 1900s," Addie added.

Zach set down his phone and looked at the photos. "Interesting. Yeah, they do look that old. See if there's anything written on the back."

Addie turned both over, and to her delight, one had writing. It was a photo postcard with a space for a note, a postmark, and a one-cent stamp in the corner.

Zach chuckled. "Look at that. One cent to send a postcard. Crazy."

"It's hard to believe, isn't it?" Addie said. "The postmark says Ketchikan, Alaska, Nov 10, 1919."

"Wow," Zach whistled low. "I figured these were old, but that's over a hundred years old."

Addie nodded as she studied both photos again. "I think the woman with the baby is the same woman standing in the other photo. Look."

Zach studied the photos and agreed. "They must have been friends, and then the other woman moved to Alaska. Is the writing in English?"

Addie turned it over again, and to her delight, it was in English. The writing was in pencil and had faded over the years, but she could still make out what it said in its tiny script.

Dear Sofiya,

I'm sorry I haven't written before this, but you are always in my thoughts. I don't think you would like Alaska. It rains just awful here, even worse than Portland. Ha Ha. Can you believe I am a mother now? Our sweet baby was born October 9th, and my life has been a whirlwind of feedings and diapers. But I am so happy with little Flori-ana Sofiya (Florie) and my husband, Clint. He's working hard, running the factory, and we rent a nice house. It's more than I thought possible after the rough start you and I had. I miss you and wish only good things for you. I'll write more soon.

Love, Alina

"Interesting," Zach said. "It makes you wonder what she meant by their 'rough start.'"

Addie nodded. She studied the other photo again. The two women looked more like young girls. They wore white ankle-length dresses and stood in boy-girl fashion with two men in dark suits. The girls were holding hands in front of one male, despite the distance between them. They weren't smiling; they looked sad.

"What are you thinking?" Zach asked gently. "That frown tells me something about the photo bothers you."

"The girls don't look happy. They look scared."

"Yeah, but those guys aren't that good-looking. Maybe they were set up on the double-date from hell," Zach joked.

"Maybe," Addie said.

They finished their coffee, and Addie carefully placed the photos into the cigar box. After bundling up, they headed outside and made the long walk home.

"Have you found our next project?" Zach asked as they walked toward the house on Seventeenth that they'd just remodeled and sold. It was a 1910 small Victorian that they'd brought back to life after years of neglect. "We have to be out of the house by the end of the month."

"Nothing has caught my eye yet," Addie said. "It's getting harder to find good deals on old houses to flip. Everyone wants so much money for run-down homes. Or many of the large older homes have been turned into apartments. It's sad."

"I'm sure you'll find something," he said encouragingly. "Soon, I hope. Otherwise, we'll be living on the street."

Addie's heart jumped. She knew Zach was kidding, but the thought of living on the street again, even after all these years, scared her.

"It was just a joke," he said, pulling her close to him as they walked.

"I know," she whispered. It always surprised her how intuitive Zach was to her feelings. "We can always stay in one of Valerie's rentals if we don't find a place to flip. I think the house on Stark is still available." Valerie Harding was the woman who'd turned Addie on to flipping houses. Addie had been floundering, working in a coffee shop and trying hard to keep a roof over her head when she'd met Valerie. Noticing the young girl's interest in her designs as she worked at a table in the café, Valerie asked Addie if she'd like to come and work on the house with her on her day off to see what she was doing. Addie had jumped at the chance because it seemed like something fun to do. The two women had a great time discussing house design and decorating. Valerie was thirty when she met nineteen-year-old Addie and told the teen how impressed she was with her design ideas. That evening, Valerie drove Addie home to her dingy apartment over a small corner grocery store in a questionable part of town.

"This is where you live?" Valerie had asked, looking concerned.

"Yes," Addie answered without enthusiasm.

Valerie had looked at her kindly with her pale blue eyes. "Do you feel safe here?" she'd asked gently.

Suddenly, tears burst from Addie's eyes. "No," she'd said, shaking her head. "But it's all I can afford."

Valerie made the offer in that moment that she'd never once regretted. "I have a nice house with an extra room you are welcome to stay in while we work on the other house," she'd told Addie. "Go pack your things."

Addie had been shocked, but even with her deep-seated

distrust of almost everyone, she immediately sensed she could trust Valerie. So, she did as Valerie said and never looked back. They had worked together flipping houses for years after that. Just thinking of Valerie made Addie smile.

"Or maybe we could finally find our own forever home," Zach said, giving Addie a little side-smile.

Addie remained silent. She loved Zach and trusted him completely, but even after knowing him for seven years and living together for five, she was scared to death of settling down. Fortunately, Zach knew that and never pressured her. But little hints like the one he'd just given her made her heart race.

"I'll find a house to flip. One will just come to me like they always do," Addie said.

Zach nodded, looking disappointed.

* * *

Later that evening, Addie curled up in bed with the cigar box and began sifting through the letters. As far as she could tell, they were all in French, and no matter how hard she tried, she couldn't make out enough words to understand what was written. The only thing she could read was the signature—Sofiya.

Puzzled, Addie wondered why Sofiya had written letters that she'd never sent to her mother. The dates at the top of the letters started in May 1917 and continued until 1930, when they finally stopped. Either Sofiya had given up on ever being able to send them to her mother, or perhaps her mother or Sofiya had died.

Opening the envelope with the photos, Addie studied them. The picture of the two women and two men appeared as if they were standing in a park across the street from a row of houses. The houses were large and built close together. Addie knew most of the older neighborhoods around Portland, but she didn't recognize these homes. As she studied the details, it occurred to her that the postcard must have an address written on it.

Excited, Addie turned the postcard over. On the right-hand side—clear as day—was written *Miss Sofiya Henderson, Marshall Street, Portland, Oregon.* Addie knew where Marshall Street was—it ran from The Pearl District up to Nob Hill. She studied the address again. No house number. Addie sighed.

"What's wrong?" Zach strode to the bed, his long legs covering the space quickly. He dropped onto the bed beside her.

"I have an address for the house that Sofiya lived in, but not the house number. It only says Marshall Street," Addie told him.

He frowned. "Sofiya?"

"The woman who wrote the letters."

"Oh, that Sofiya." Zach chuckled.

"Funny," she mumbled. "There are houses across the street from the people in the photo. I don't recognize them. I wonder if one of them was where she lived."

"Let me see." Zach took the photo and studied it. "Hm. There are a lot of houses in that area that look like these. Is there a park on Marshall?"

"Good thinking." Addie grabbed her phone and looked at a map of Portland. "There is a Tanner Springs Park between Tenth and Eleventh Avenues on Marshall."

Zach winked. "Sounds like a good place to start."

* * *

The next day, Addie and Zach drove to Marshall Street and parked near Tanner Springs Park. As they glanced around, they realized they wouldn't find houses here matching the ones in the picture.

"I should have known that there were only apartments and businesses around here," Addie said, disappointed. "It's close to the river, and the property is valuable. I'll bet there were houses here at one time, but they're gone."

"You're not giving up that easily, are you?" Zach asked. "There may have been other parks on Marshall back in 1919 that are now long gone. Maybe the house is a couple of blocks up the hill."

"Or maybe they walked down to this park, and the house Sofiya lived in isn't one of these in the picture," Addie countered. "Without a house number, we have no way of knowing which house it could have been."

"You know the history of real estate around here as well as I do," Zach said. "Even if we had the house number from 1919, all the house addresses were changed in Portland in the 1930s. So don't give up. Let's walk a few blocks and see what's here." He reached for her hand.

"You always look on the positive side, don't you," Addie said, a small smile forming on her lips. She took his hand and let him lead her up the sidewalk. Addie loved that Zach was the optimist to her naturally pessimistic personality. She didn't know how she'd keep pushing through life without him.

The weather was warmer than the day before, and it felt nice walking out in the sunshine. Each block they walked, though, had only businesses and apartment buildings. Old warehouses had been turned into apartment complexes, and new construction was all around. Corner bars and stores dotted the area. From what Addie could see, it didn't seem promising that they'd find any homes until up past Twenty-Fifth Avenue.

They crossed under the 405 Freeway. "We're going to be in Nob Hill by the time we find any houses," Addie complained. "And those are crazy expensive. I just don't see Sofiya living there."

"Let's just go another block or two. Have faith," Zach said.

Addie grumbled but kept walking.

As they neared the corner of Eighteenth Avenue and Marshall Street, Zach smiled and pointed. "I think I spot a house."

Addie rolled her eyes but continued on. "But is it *the* house?"

Zach chuckled.

There were three older homes on one side of the street and three more on the other. Tall ancient oak and willow trees shaded the street. One of the houses looked worn and tired, but the others had been kept up nicely with fresh paint and new landscaping.

Addie studied the colorless photo in her hand, but none of the houses looked like the ones the women were standing in front of.

"Let's keep walking," Zach suggested. "Even if we don't find the house, it's a great day for a walk."

Addie continued walking. Past the homes were more apartment buildings and businesses, and a hospital. No parks were in sight. They passed street after street until they were on block twenty-three. "Finally," she said, letting out a breath. "Here's where they're hiding the houses."

"With all these old trees, they truly are hiding them," Zach quipped.

The neighborhood was filled with older homes from the early 1900s. The street was narrow, and the trees were tall and full. It looked like a peaceful, welcoming neighborhood. Addie studied each house as she also looked at the photo.

"Anything match?" Zach asked, looking over her shoulder.

"Not yet. Let's keep walking."

They slowly walked past several homes, all from the Victorian era but built in different styles. The homes were very close together, with about five feet between them. Many had a garage added to the front where the porch and lawn had once been. The pointed rooftops, bay windows, and old brick chimneys were proof that these homes were from a bygone era.

Addie took her time checking each house for details. While some of the homes were similar to the three in the photo, none matched perfectly. They walked two more blocks before she stopped and stared in wonder. Addie could hardly believe her eyes.

"Look! I think that's it."

Zach stared in the direction Addie was pointing. "The one with the two-pointed rooftop or the one next door?"

"The house to the right of the two-pointed one. It looks exactly like the main house in the photo. And the house with the two-pointed rooftop is exactly like the one in the photo too." Addie's voice rose in pitch with excitement.

Zach turned to her. "How are you so sure the middle house is Sofiya's?"

"I don't know. I just am." Addie studied the house. It had a pitched roof with an arched attic window in the center and below that, a bay window with an outdoor terrace above the first-floor covered porch. A large, three-window bay was on the first floor, and three white columns held up the upper terrace. Both bay windows had stained-glass transoms above the larger windows. A set of steps on the right side of the house led to a door that looked original to the house. An oval leaded-glass window decorated the door. Painted white with dark green trim, the place looked in need of fresh paint. In fact, as she stared at the house, Addie had the feeling it was no longer occupied. Was it abandoned?

"Let's get a closer look," Addie said, already heading across the street.

Zach had to run to catch up with her. "What are you going to do? Just knock on the door and start asking questions?"

She ignored him and did just that. Addie marched up to the door as if she belonged there and knocked. The oval glass in the door was even more beautiful up close. It just needed a good cleaning.

Zach stood behind her. "What are you going to say when someone answers?" he whispered.

"I don't know," she said. "Honestly, I don't think anyone lives here." She knocked again, and when that went unanswered, Addie walked over to the bay window and peered inside. The window took up half the width of the porch. What she saw inside was a generous living room, or parlor as it had once been called, with a fireplace that had decorative tile around it. Ornate moldings lined the floorboards and the ceiling, and the floors were original wood in a beautiful honey color. A wide doorway led to what looked like a formal dining room. A chill of joy went up Addie's spine. As she'd thought, the place was completely void of furniture.

"You won't find anyone at home," a voice called out,

startling Addie and Zach. The couple looked to the right and saw a woman wearing a smart-looking blue suit and tall heels. Her red hair was cut short, and she had serious green eyes. "No one has lived there for a long time."

Addie smiled up at Zach before walking toward the woman. "Do you live around here?" she asked.

"Yes. I live next door. My teenage son has been keeping up the lawn for the owners." She gave Addie and Zach the once over. "I handled the sale of this house for the current owners. I'm a real estate agent."

Addie walked down the porch steps and up to the woman, offering her hand to shake. "Hi. I'm Addison Cameron, and this is my business partner, Zachery Walker."

The woman shook their hands. "I'm Gail Peterson. It's nice to meet you."

"Do you know if the current owners are interested in selling this house?" Addie asked. Out of the corner of her eye, she saw the surprise on Zach's face. Addie never jumped into a sale. She took her time and thought things through before making a commitment. Wanting this house—without even looking it over—surprised even Addie.

"They haven't listed it, but I doubt they still want it," Gail said. "They were going to turn it into a fourplex and sell each apartment, but that never happened."

Addie was thankful they hadn't. Breaking up this house into four apartments, like so many others on this street, would be criminal as far as she was concerned. "Would it be possible to ask them if they'd be interested in selling?"

"Anything is possible," Gail said, breaking into a smile. "Let me get your phone number, and I can let you know."

The two women exchanged numbers, then Gail asked, "Are

you thinking of flipping it? Because to tell you the truth, these homes around here are expensive. That's why so many of them have been turned into duplexes and fourplexes. There isn't much profit in flipping them."

Addie bit her lip and took a deep breath. She knew the woman was right, but from the moment she saw this house, she had to have it. "Let's see if they want to sell it first, and then I can decide from there," she told Gail. "Thank you for your help."

Gail nodded, waved, and headed back toward her house. When Addie turned around, Zach was staring at her with wide eyes.

"Are you serious about buying this house?" he asked.

She shrugged nonchalantly. "Maybe. I mean, we might get it for a good deal." Addie walked around Zach and headed down the street, back toward where they'd parked the car.

Zach caught up with her. "These homes are expensive. It might not even have been Sofiya's house. And we don't know anything about Sofiya other than she lived on Marshall Street in 1919 and took a few pictures."

Addie was usually the voice of reason in their relationship, so it felt strange being the impulsive one this time. She turned and faced Zach. "I know. It's crazy. But I just have a feeling about this house." She drew closer and ran her hands over his sweater, wanting to feel connected to him. "It won't hurt to check into it," she said softly.

Zach took her hands in his and pressed them against his chest. "You're right." He kissed the top of her blond head. "It can't hurt."

She gazed up at him. "Could you check with a friend about having the letters translated? I'd really love to read what Sofiya wrote."

Zach smiled. "Anything for you. You know I can't say no to you."

Addie chuckled softly. "Hold that thought—you may regret it." Still holding hands, she turned and looked at the house again. It felt like it was beckoning her, begging her to buy it. It wasn't odd for Addie to have a special feeling about a house she decided to buy and flip. Houses spoke to her. But this one was different. It was calling her name.

"I think I may have found our next house," she said to Zach.

"You're the boss," he said.

CHAPTER TWO

Sofiya
May 1917

The trip to America was a long and arduous one for Sofiya and Alina. After a tearful goodbye to her maman and père, Sofiya and Alina boarded a small boat with Alina's father and sailed across the Gulf of Finland to Helsinki. There, they had another tearful farewell to Mr. Henderson and boarded a larger boat to Stockholm. Another ship took them to Copenhagen, then they crossed the North Sea to Hull in England. Each step of the way, the girls stayed close together, scared but a little excited. On each boat, an older woman took it upon herself to watch over them, for which the girls were thankful.

From Hull, they rode a train across England to Liverpool, where they finally boarded the large steamship that would take them to New York City. They sailed on the RMS Adriatic, a prominent White Star Line ship. Later, they learned theirs was its last civilian run to America because it had been requisitioned by the military to carry supplies and troops for the war.

The five-day trip across the ocean was an exciting yet scary adventure for the girls. They shared a tiny room with four bunk beds and a wash table with two other women traveling from Norway. Their companions ignored them, so the girls left them alone. During the first two days at sea, Alina and Sofiya were ill from the motion of the ship. When they finally felt better, they were able to join the other third-class passengers in the dining salon and stroll the deck.

The girls marveled at the many different nationalities that were traveling among them. Swedish, Norwegian, German, Dutch, Italian, French, Belgian, Croatian, Hungarian, Portuguese, Scottish, Spanish—the list went on. Sofiya could understand some of the languages spoken and make out a few words from others, but she didn't let on that she spoke anything other than Finnish and English—just as she'd promised her maman. Of all the nationalities, the Russian passengers made her the most nervous. Sofiya was frightened someone would recognize her, and because her maman had warned her to be careful, Sofiya did her best to avoid the other Russians.

"I can't believe we are halfway to America," Sofiya said one evening after they'd eaten and were sitting in chairs on the third-class deck. The outside air was cool, so they were wearing their wool coats.

Alina's blue eyes filled with tears as they'd often done throughout their long trip. She was generally a vivacious, bubbly girl who loved life and having fun. But since their journey had begun, she'd been melancholy, sometimes crying herself to sleep at night.

Sofiya held her friend's hand. "I know you miss your family, as do I. But we must be strong as our parents would want us to be." Alina was the eldest between them, but she was also the more emotional one. Her soft heart and kind ways were what had drawn Sofiya to her when they were children.

Alina nodded, and tendrils of her pale blond hair escaped the hat she wore. "I'm trying to be brave," she told her friend. "But aren't you frightened of what the future holds for us? We won't know a soul where we're going."

Sofiya gave her an encouraging smile. "No, we won't. But we must look at it as an opportunity to meet new people and learn new things. That's what our mothers would want us to do." Despite her optimistic words, Sofiya was also sad and scared. But she knew she had to stay strong for Alina. Sofiya believed her maman would not have sent her away if she hadn't thought it was best for her. Still, her heart ached for her parents.

Excitement filled the ship as they reached America and passed through Ellis Island. No one questioned why these two young girls were traveling alone because many young people passed through this checkpoint. Once they'd been cleared, the girls were put on a barge with the other emigrants that brought them to New Jersey, where they would continue their journey by train across the country.

The girls had been given instructions and an envelope of money to pay for their train trip to Portland. They purchased two tickets to Chicago and, once there, switched trains to one that headed to Portland's Union Station. They had enough money for sleeping berths, so they didn't have to sit up at night.

The trip across America was an incredible adventure for the two young women. Neither had traveled far from their homes, and now they were riding through miles and miles of open country and through large cities. As on the ship, the train was filled with people from different ethnic backgrounds. The girls marveled at the dark-skinned men who worked as porters and waiters in the dining car wearing smart-looking uniforms. In their limited experience, they'd never seen anyone with such dark skin. The small dining car echoed loudly with languages from all over the globe. This, the girls realized, was what it was like to live in such a diverse country, and they both soaked in the experience.

As they neared their destination, they were both nervous and hopeful. Sofiya and Alina hoped their life in Portland would be a happy one.

Their train made many stops along the way. The note in their envelope had informed them to send a telegram at their last stop before Portland so the woman they were to live with, Nora Petrov, would know their arrival time.

Their train pulled into Portland's Union Station along the Willamette River at eleven on a warm June morning. The girls stepped off the train carrying their small suitcases and walked inside the beautiful station, gazing around them. Both were in awe of how grand and busy the train station was.

"What do we do now?" Alina asked, staring over at Sofiya.

Sofiya had no idea. She wasn't sure if they had enough money to hire a cab. The girls walked outside, out of the way of the many people who seemed in a hurry to get somewhere. It was just as busy with automobiles everywhere rushing to and fro. A line of cabs sat on the street near the doors, waiting for fares. Finally, amidst the chaos, they saw a uniformed man standing in front of a large, black motor car, holding a sign with the names Alina and Sofiya Henderson. Tentatively, the girls approached the man.

"Are you the two young ladies I'm supposed to pick up for Miss Nora?" the man asked, a touch of a southern drawl in his voice.

Sofiya nodded. The man was dark-skinned with big brown eyes that seemed to smile at her. "Yes. We're the Henderson sisters," she said.

"Well, it's nice to meet you ladies. Just call me Carter. That's what all the ladies at the house call me."

He took their luggage and placed it in the front passenger seat, then opened the back door and assisted the girls inside. "We best be off. Miss Nora hates to be kept waiting," he said, giving the girls a broad grin.

Alina grasped Sofiya's hand and held on tightly. "Miss Petrov must be well-to-do if she has a motor car and chauffeur," she whispered to Sofiya.

Sofiya nodded. She had no idea what was considered wealthy in this country. She'd grown up with all she needed but hadn't been nearly as well-to-do as her cousins at the palace. Wealth in America could mean something completely different.

Sofiya eagerly gazed around at the businesses and homes they passed as Carter drove the automobile up the road, away from the river. The farther away from the train station they went, the less traffic and noise there seemed to be. The homes looked grand. Large, with front porches, manicured lawns, and flower gardens.

"He said something about other ladies," Sofiya said softly to Alina. "Perhaps she runs a boarding house for women. Maybe we can make new friends." Sofiya hoped that was true. New friends in this strange place would help soften the blow of leaving home.

Alina squeezed her hand tighter. "I hope so," she said, still looking nervous.

It wasn't long before they entered a neighborhood with grander homes than the others they'd passed. Most were built close together. He made a hand signal to turn left, and they pulled into a brick driveway that ran alongside a large house. Carter stopped the vehicle and left it idling. Farther down the driveway was a tall garage where Sofiya assumed he parked the motor car.

Carter pulled their luggage from the front seat and helped the girls alight from the back. "Here we are. Home sweet home," he said with a grin.

Sofiya studied the house. It was tall and built on a hill like the other homes. A brick walkway wound its way to the front entrance and around the house toward the backyard. There was a lovely covered front porch with a bay window. Above that was the second floor with another bay window and a walk-out terrace. Both bay windows had stained-glass transoms above the larger windows. The top floor had a pitched roof with an arched window in the center. The house extended far back onto the property.

Carter must have noticed Sofiya staring down the driveway because he said, "That's the garage back there. It used to be an old carriage house. Miss Nora has two automobiles which she's very proud of. I live in the room above the garage. If you ever need me, you know where to find me."

Sofiya was puzzled over why she'd need a chauffeur, but she smiled and nodded in response to Carter's kind offer.

Carter motioned for the girls to walk ahead of him to the front porch. He set down their bags and knocked swiftly on the door. A moment later, a tall, thin, weary-looking woman answered. Her blond hair was braided and spiraled around her head. She took one look at the girls and sighed deeply.

"Good afternoon, Miss Agnes," Carter said cheerfully. "These ladies are here to see Miss Nora."

Agnes ignored Carter's greeting. "Come in, come in," she said in her thick Swedish accent.

Sofiya and Alina stepped inside onto a thick paisley rug. Carter followed behind them and set their luggage on the polished wood floor next to the staircase.

"I'm sure I will see you ladies around," he said, tipping his hat and heading out the door.

"Go sit there." The woman pointed to a leather-padded bench that sat alongside the staircase. "I just finished cleaning the parlor, and I don't want anyone dirtying it up."

The two girls did as they were told while Agnes walked toward the back of the house. Sofiya quickly inventoried their surroundings. The wooden staircase behind them had a polished railing that swirled at the end and a paisley carpet runner matching the entryway rug. Gleaming wood wainscotting decorated the bottom half of the walls with cabbage rose wallpaper above it. Everything looked expensive and well cared for.

In front of them were wooden pocket doors that opened from each side. They were intricately carved with floral designs on each of the square panels. The doors were partially open, and Sofiya could see a little of the parlor. An upright piano stood against the far wall, and the wood floors were covered in lovely plush rugs of red and gold. Sofiya thought Nora Petrov must be wealthy to own such a beautiful home.

"So, you're here at last," a woman's deep voice said, and both girls turned their heads to see Nora Petrov coming down the hallway. In unison, they stood and stared at the woman in front of them. Nora was not tall, but her large build commanded authority. She wore a burgundy silk dress that hung just above her ankles. It was loose at the waist and decorated down the center with contrasting cream-watered silk. Her auburn hair was piled up on her head, and her cheeks were rouged the same color as her dress.

"Well, let me have a look at you two," the woman said, not bothering to ask the girls their names. Knowing that Nora was originally from Finland, Sofiya was surprised she hadn't a hint of an accent in her speech.

Nora folded her arms under her ample chest as she studied them. She spent more time staring at Alina than Sofiya. The girls fidgeted nervously under her scrutiny. Nora finally looked directly at Sofiya. "You aren't the prettiest girl to look at, are you?" she stated.

Sofiya was dumbstruck. She knew she was plain compared to Alina, but no one had actually stated it to her face. An uneasy feeling crept over her. She felt like a horse being looked over for auction. When she didn't answer, she watched as Nora turned her dark eyes on Alina again, and a chill ran up Sofiya's spine.

"You, however, have potential," the older woman said as she eyed Alina up and down. She reached out and fingered Alina's hair. "So blond, it's nearly silver," she said softly. "And those light blue eyes. They're incredible." She dropped her hand to her side. "Yes, you'll do very well." Nora's nose wrinkled. "Those clothes, however, are dreadful. I thought your mother was a dressmaker. How could she send you both to me in such outdated clothing?"

Both girls glanced down at their outfits. Sofiya bristled. Her mother had insisted she wear her older clothing to not look as if she'd come from money. And when they traveled amongst the emigrants, they had fit right in. But despite her and Alina's skirts being a bit out-of-date, they were still made of the finest fabrics and were not at all shabby.

Nora sighed. "Well, it won't matter for you." She pointed at Sofiya. "You'll be wearing a uniform. But I'll need to find suitable clothing for you, dear." Her eyes turned again to Alina. "All my girls dress appropriately here." She snapped her fingers, and a young woman came rushing down the stairs. "This is Mabel. You and she will share a room, and she and the other girls will prepare you for your coming-out event. Mabel, find her suitable attire for tonight and ensure it fits like a glove."

Mabel nodded her head ever so slightly. "Yes, Miss Nora."

Sofiya frowned. *Coming-out event? Was that like a coming-out season where young girls were introduced to society?* Somehow, she doubted it.

"And you," Nora said, pinning Sofiya with her eyes. "You'll report to Mrs. Jarvi in the kitchen. Do as she says."

"Yes, ma'am," Sofiya said, dropping her eyes.

Nora took a menacing step toward her. "Never call me ma'am. You will call me Miss Nora." Her eyes darted over to Alina. "That goes for you, too. And another thing. No one leaves this house without my permission. I paid good money to bring you all the way here, and I expect you to work that off and do as I say. Understood?"

The woman was absolutely terrifying. Sofiya nodded quickly and saw that Alina did also, but poor Alina had tears pooling in her eyes, and it broke Sofiya's heart. She was such a tenderhearted girl. Sofiya hoped the girls upstairs would be kind to her.

"Go on then. You both have plenty to do." Nora brushed her hand through the air as if they were annoying flies.

Sofiya lifted her suitcase and turned to walk down the hallway, catching Alina's eyes as they passed each other. She gave her friend an encouraging smile but kept silent. Sofiya didn't want to incur the wrath of Miss Nora any more than necessary. Walking toward the back of the house where she supposed the kitchen to be, Sofiya continued to study her surroundings. The hallway was lit with electric lights. Behind the parlor was a room decorated as an office, with a large desk on the far wall covered in paperwork. Hurrying on, Sofiya passed an indoor water closet and was thankful for that amenity.

Agnes was in the kitchen chatting with a woman wearing a white apron over her dress. Both women became silent and stared as Sofiya entered. The cook, Mrs. Jarvi, was a short, stocky woman with dark hair pulled into a tight bun. Silver strands ran through her hair, and lines creased her full face. But it was her bright blue eyes that startled Sofiya. They seemed so out of place on this tired-looking woman.

"Another new one," Agnes said, rolling her eyes. "At least I won't be needed to clean here anymore." She turned her stern gaze on Mrs. Jarvi. "My husband hates when I work here. I hate it too. Good riddance." Agnes took off her full apron, dropped it in a bin, picked up her bag from under the counter, and headed out through a side door.

This left Sofiya and the cook alone to assess one another.

Mrs. Jarvi sighed and walked toward the back of the kitchen. "Come along," she said, motioning for Sofiya to follow. "Your room is in here. It's not much, but it's warm in the winter, and that counts for something." She showed Sofiya to a tiny closet of a room with a small window that looked out to the back yard. From here, Sofiya could see the garage where Carter lived. There was a twin bed against the wall and a three-drawer dresser. "You're allowed to use the bathroom down the hall, but keep it clean because guests use it also."

Sofiya wondered what she meant by guests. The girls

upstairs? Or did Miss Nora entertain often?

"There's a folded uniform, apron, and dark stockings in the dresser," Mrs. Jarvi continued. She looked Sofiya up and down. "It may be too big for you. Can you sew?"

"A little," Sofiya said, wishing now that she'd tried harder to learn to sew. Her mother had tried to teach her, as had Alina's mother, but she'd been all thumbs when it came to tiny stitches and fancywork.

The older woman shrugged. "We can pin it for now. Get changed. We have much work before the evening begins."

Sofiya stood still, feeling lost. This was not what she'd expected when her maman had sent her to America for a better life. She wished she was upstairs with Alina. Her heart ached for her parents and the world she'd left behind.

Mrs. Jarvi turned and raised an eyebrow. "Did you not hear me?"

"Are you from Finland?" Sofiya asked, holding back the tears.

"I was from Finland," Mrs. Jarvi said. "A long time ago. But now I'm an American. Why?"

"It's just nice hearing your accent. It reminds me of home." Sofiya's lip began to quiver, but she stood straight with her hands clasped tightly in front of her.

Mrs. Jarvi's face softened. "You're a young one, aren't you? Well, you'll get used to it here. Believe me when I say you're lucky to be working in the kitchen. The upstairs is not a place you'd want to be."

"Yes, ma'am," Sofiya said softly. She didn't understand why the cook had said that, but she kept her questions to herself.

"Get moving. We have work to do," Mrs. Jarvi said, sounding gruff again. Sofiya did as she was told. What other choice did she have?

CHAPTER THREE

Addie

June 2022

Addie stood in the dark parking lot, staring down the long line of semi-trucks. The sound of the engines idling and the smell of diesel fuel filled the air. She hated that smell—it seeped into your clothes, hair, and even your skin. It was so thick, she could taste it.

Addie glanced around, looking for a way out. Hurrying down the line, she turned and ran between two trucks. If she could make it to the other side of the gas station, she might be able to hitch a ride away from here. Far away from this nightmare of a place.

Suddenly, a cab door opened, and a man jumped out. He reached out a beefy hand and grabbed Addie by the hair before she could squeeze past him.

"Where you going, girl?" he said, staring down at her with dark eyes. "Ain't you working?"

Addie struggled to pull away from his grasp, but he'd already taken ahold of her arm and wouldn't let go.

"I like them wild," he said, laughing. His foul breath assailed her senses, and when she looked directly at him, she saw he was missing teeth.

"No! Let me go!" she screamed, but it was too little, too late. The burly man was already tossing her small body into the truck.

"No! Let me go!" Addie awoke screaming and sat up in bed.

"Sweetie, are you alright?" Zach quickly sat up beside her. His arm was around her instantly, and she fell into his warm body.

"I had a bad dream," she said, her head still thick with sleep. She glanced around, trying to get her bearings. "Must be the new place," she said.

Zach kissed the top of her head but didn't say anything. "It is jarring waking up on a mattress on the floor in a strange room," he agreed.

Addie sighed and sat up straight again while Zach pulled himself up off the mattress and headed toward the bathroom. Sunshine streamed through the side window, promising a warm summer day. They'd purchased the large home on Marshall and had moved some of their furniture into the living room the day before. They'd decided to use the parlor as their bedroom for the first few weeks until they remodeled the master bedroom upstairs. First, though, they still had to decide how they wanted to fix up the house.

She stood and slipped on the pair of jeans she'd worn yesterday. She'd slept in her large sweatshirt, and it nearly hung to her knees as she walked down the hallway to the kitchen to make coffee.

Zach joined her a while later. "Well, it's finally our first day on the job," he said, smiling. "What's it going to be, boss? Are we thinking about turning the house into a duplex, fourplex, or leaving as is?"

Addie set a cup of coffee down on the small table they'd brought over yesterday and then grabbed her own mug off the counter. The kitchen was a good size but needed a complete update. Yesterday, she'd discovered the small room in the back that she'd first thought was a closet. But there was a window in there, overlooking the backyard and the old garage. Her mind was spinning with ideas on how to use the small room's space to its best potential.

"I don't want to split up this house," Addie said as she sipped her coffee. "We'd ruin it if we changed everything."

Zach sat back in his chair. They were old wooden chairs from an antique dinette set Addie had purchased years ago. They were too small for his tall frame, but he never complained. "We could split the house down the middle, using the living room as an entryway. Of course, we'd have to add another staircase somewhere. Or maybe we could use the back staircase here in the kitchen for one side."

Addie shook her head. "I'd hate to ruin anything in that old parlor. The fireplace is gorgeous, and we'd have to tear out the old bay window to create a second door."

"Well, we could split it in two with the front and back sections being separate. That would be much easier than splitting the floors since there are so many bedrooms upstairs."

"I don't like that idea either," Addie said. She fiddled with the handle of her mug.

Zach sighed. "We have to think of some way to get our money back on this house, sweetie," he said gently. "If we remodel and sell it as a whole, we'd never make a profit. Splitting it up is the only way." He took a breath and added, "We've put nearly all our money into this house, Addie. We can't afford to lose it."

Addie stood and walked to the old sink where the window above it looked out over the backyard. An enormous oak tree sat in the middle, a bench that had once surrounded it now broken in two pieces as the tree had grown thicker. She wondered why no one had ever fixed it.

"Addie?" Zach said.

She turned. "I don't want to split up this house. We'll remodel it as is and then see what happens. Maybe someone would like it as a bed and breakfast. It's just too beautiful to split apart."

Zach walked to the sink and put his mug in it. "Okay. We'll do it your way. You're right. Heck, maybe some rich family with eight kids might want to buy it." He grinned.

She hit him playfully on the arm.

Zach glanced out the window. "I'm going to explore that old garage. It looks like it has a room above it. Maybe we could fix that up and rent it as a studio apartment."

She glanced outside. "Hm. That's an idea. Funny, there's a garage back there but no driveway or alley to get to it."

He shrugged. "Maybe there was a driveway, once. The house next door may have been built long after this one and took up that property."

"Probably," Addie said.

"Okay, boss. You search the house and decide how you want to remodel it. I'm going out to the garage. If I'm not back in fifteen minutes, call a group of ghost hunters to save me." Zach chuckled.

A chill went up Addie's spine. "Don't even tease about that. You heard what the real estate lady next door told us. The previous owners stopped working on this house because they kept hearing strange noises. The last thing I need is a ghost."

"Maybe it's a friendly ghost," he teased.

Addie shook her head as she went to shower and dress.

* * *

Addie spent the morning exploring every room of the house. Even though she and Zach had toured it before purchasing the house, she felt like she was learning something new about each room as she explored them. The home had been built in the 1890s, so there was a fireplace in every room. Each one had a beautiful wood mantel surrounding it and inside that was a patterned tile that was also laid on the floor as a hearth. The master bedroom had a beautiful black tile with a red floral design. The other bedrooms had tiles of various colors—red, cream, green, and blue—with a pattern or floral design. At some point, an owner had converted all the fireplaces to gas, which Addie was thankful for. Hauling in wood to heat the rooms would have been impossible.

It was a big house. In all, there were nine bedrooms upstairs and only three bathrooms, two up and one down. Addie thought perhaps a large, wealthy family had originally built this house on the hill for their many young children. Since then, she had no idea how it had been used. Perhaps as a boarding house or a bed and breakfast like Zach had suggested. No matter how it had been used, it had been banged up pretty badly. The original oak woodwork needed refinishing, and the oak floors were covered in many different types and shades of hideous carpeting. Some of the woodwork had been painted white, which was horrifying to Addie. Why someone would paint over woodwork that beautiful was beyond her. Some of the bedrooms had old, dirty wallpaper peeling at the corners;

others looked like someone had painted over the wallpaper. She shook her head at the abuse this house had taken over the last century. But it still had its charm, like the solid oak staircase banister that curled at the end and the oval rose stained-glass window at the foot of the stairs. The stained-glass transoms depicting ivy and roses over the bay windows were beautiful, as were all the tiled fireplaces. The chandelier in the entryway and the smaller lights in the parlor were definitely original. The hallway sconces looked like they were from the Victorian era, as did those in the master bedroom. Addie assumed they'd once been gas lights that were turned into electrical lighting. There was much to admire about this house—but it needed a lot of tender loving care.

Addie studied the master bedroom. It was large by Victorian standards and had an attached bathroom, which had been updated in the 1970s, given away by the harvest gold tub and sink. The room also boasted a huge walk-in closet. As Addie stepped inside and switched on the overhead light, she was surprised by a narrow set of steps that led up to a small door. How had she and Zach missed this on their tour?

Pulling her phone from her pocket, Addie switched on the flashlight and carefully made her way up the steps while steadying herself with her hand on the wall. At the top, she tried the glass knob. It turned easily. The door opened, and she stepped into a large, empty space. Addie's eyes grew wide. The attic room was wide open, with four sides and a window on each side. Light streamed into the room, and despite its emptiness and the slight chill of having no insulation to keep out the dampness, the room was absolutely charming.

"What's this?" a voice said behind her, and Addie nearly jumped out of her skin.

"You scared the bejesus out of me," she said once she realized it was Zach behind her and not some specter from another era.

He grinned. "Sorry. I looked everywhere for you and saw the light coming down that little staircase." Zach glanced around. "This room is amazing, isn't it? Like something you'd see in a Harry Potter movie."

She nodded. "It's magical. This is the type of attic where a child could play pretend for hours on end." Addie walked in a few more steps. Someone had added a hardwood floor up here, apparently decades before, and the many brick chimneys from the rooms below rose through the attic and out through the roof. Each side was slanted and peaked. Each window was rounded at the top and made of old wavy glass from a century ago.

"I wonder what it would cost to finish this ceiling," Zach mused. "This would be an incredible room for someone to use."

Addie spun and smiled at him. "My thoughts exactly." Then she sighed. "Except we should put all our money into the bottom two floors first."

"Yeah. Such a shame, though. This would make a great bonus room."

Addie followed Zach down the stairs and out of the closet. "Maybe someday," she said.

His brows shot up. "Someday? As in, we'll be living here long enough for there to be a someday?"

She shrugged but didn't reply. The business manager in Addie knew that keeping this house after they remodeled it was impossible. But Addie felt connected to this house. She'd never before wanted to stay in a place after they'd finished it. Yet, she hadn't even started working on this house, and she already loved it.

"I need to start in the master bedroom first," she said, ignoring the quizzical look on Zach's face. "Maybe you could do the remodel on the kitchen. We'll need both rooms to be functional since we'll be living here a while."

"Okay," Zach said. "Let's sit down and design the kitchen, then I can get at it."

* * *

A week into their remodel, Zach brought home not only coffee and muffins one morning but also the letters from the cigar box that his friend had translated.

Addie stared at the letters with glee. "I can't wait to read them," she told Zach.

Zach smiled, looking pleased that she'd enjoyed her gift. "Maybe a few before bed each night," he suggested. "You should make them last a while. Unless they're boring, and then they'll put you to sleep."

Addie rolled her eyes, but she placed the letters on the make-shift nightstand she'd set by the mattress on the floor. They were still sleeping in the living room and would be for a while. The work on the master bedroom was going to take her a few weeks—mainly because she'd ordered new fixtures for the bathroom, and they wouldn't be in for some time. Addie's goal wasn't to try to recreate the Victorian look, but she also didn't want a modern look in the vintage home. It needed to feel warm and comfortable yet updated. She was walking a fine line, trying to find the perfect items to fill the space.

Addie had been excited by what she'd found when she began tearing down the wallpaper in the master bedroom. The owners through the years had simply placed new paper over old, and there were several generations of paper peeling off the walls. The top paper, Addie guessed, had been from the 1980s. It had a country cottage vibe to it, with colors of blue and cream—definitely not in tune with the Victorian house or the black-tiled fireplace. As she peeled away the paper, she peeled away the years. Orange paper with large red flowers from the 1960s. Yellowed beige paper with tiny flowers from the 1940s and glossy art deco paper from the 1920s. The very last paper finally made sense. It was black with large red flowers—obviously to match the tile on the fireplace.

Addie stared at the paper for a long time, trying to imagine what type of woman would have chosen this paper for her bedroom. Definitely not a shrinking violet of a woman. It would have been someone bold and vibrant. Someone who hadn't let anyone push her around. Chuckling, Addie began to carefully pull down the old, black paper. Even as a modern woman, this paper was too bold for her. But she planned on saving a piece for the scrapbook she kept of all her home remodels.

That evening, Addie sat on their bed and opened the first of the letters that had been transcribed. Zach's friend had typed up the transcriptions but had put them in order by the dates on the letters. Before reading the first one, she opened the envelope of the one written in French and studied the woman's handwriting. It was definitely that of a woman—with neatly formed cursive letters that flowed in a flowery script. Addie hadn't seen writing like this in years. She remembered her mother's handwriting being slanted and flowing, but most people she knew now wrote bigger upright cursive. If they wrote by hand at all. Everyone typed these days.

With the sound of Zach pounding in the back of the house, taking apart the kitchen, Addie began to read the letters. She became so absorbed in what Sofiya was writing about her and Alina's trip to America that she didn't hear Zach come to bed an hour later.

"Those must be interesting," he said, pulling the covers over him.

Addie jumped. "You scared me." She set the sheets of paper down. "They are really interesting. You'd never imagine how long a trip it was for these two girls to come from Finland to America in 1917. It's incredible."

"Two girls?" Zach rolled onto his side, head on hand, looking interested.

"Yeah. These two girls, Sofiya and Alina, were only sixteen and seventeen when they came to Portland from Finland." She shook her head. "I can't even imagine that. How could their parents have thought that would be safe?"

"Maybe they were really mature for their age," Zach offered. "That would have been during the first world war. The parents may have wanted them to be away from all of that."

Addie nodded. "Sofiya says that in the letters. She and Alina pretended to be sisters because her mother didn't want anyone to know who Sofiya really was. She was related somehow to the Tsar of Russia, but she doesn't say how."

"That's interesting," Zach said. "Maybe she'll explain more later on. Have you run into anything that talks about the house yet?"

"Only that it was on Marshall Street. I'm just at the part where they meet the owner of the house. She's a woman who seems to be running a boarding house or something."

Zach raised his brows. "Or something?"

She laughed. "You know me. I don't trust anyone. And this woman Sofiya is writing about sounds like she isn't the nicest person. I'm going to read a little more before bed. This is too interesting."

"Hey, you have work tomorrow," Zach teased. "No reading past bedtime."

She laughed but went right on reading the letters.

Dear Maman,

Alina and I are now safely in Portland at Miss Petrov's home. She owns a very nice house several blocks from the river. It is decorated very lovely, and she has a cook, a chauffeur, and two automobiles. Père would be impressed. The house seems to be a boarding house for young women, and Alina has a room upstairs. I was given a little room off the kitchen and will be helping the cook and doing a few cleaning chores as well. We both feel lucky to be in such a grand home.

Last night was my first evening of work. Miss Petrov (she told us to always call her Miss Nora, although I feel odd referring to her by her first name) seems to entertain people of wealth quite often, so it looks like we will be very busy. The cook, Mrs. Jarvi, helped me fit my uniform properly, although it is still quite long. It was strange to serve guests instead of being served, and I now have an even greater appreciation for our own servants. But I digress—I will describe the evening to you...

CHAPTER FOUR

Sofiya

May 1917

Mrs. Jarvi did her best to fit Sofiya's uniform to her shape, but it hadn't been easy. "You'll have to cut off a few inches from the hem," she told Sofiya. "It's much too long. And it needs darts in the back. But this will have to do for now."

The uniform was light gray with a full white apron. Once they'd tied the apron over the dress, the fit looked better. Sofiya put on the dark stockings but only had her low-heeled, lace-up ankle boots to wear.

"Maybe you can ask Miss Nora to buy more comfortable shoes to wear with the uniform," Mrs. Jarvi suggested. "You'll be on your feet all day."

Sofiya didn't think she was brave enough to ask Miss Nora for anything, let alone new shoes.

She and Mrs. Jarvi worked all day in the kitchen, which thankfully had all the modern conveniences of running water, electric lighting, and a gas cookstove. First, they cooked a light lunch of soup and sandwiches for the young ladies, then prepared a variety of finger foods for that night's guests.

"Miss Nora entertains every evening except on Sunday," Mrs. Jarvi told Sofiya as they worked. "Guests arrive around eight and stay until all hours of the night. You are only required to serve food in the parlor, and Miss Nora will tell you when you're finished for the night. In the morning, it'll be your job to clean the parlor. In the winter, you'll also need to start fires in all the fireplaces, even in the girls' rooms. Thankfully, it's summer right now."

Sofiya nodded her understanding as Mrs. Jarvi explained her list of duties. The young ladies came down one by one for their food trays, and Sofiya smiled wide when she saw Alina with Mabel. Alina was wearing a flowered cotton day dress with white stockings and shoes Sofiya had never seen before. She didn't speak, though, and her wide eyes told Sofiya that she was scared.

"Take your tray and go upstairs again," Mabel instructed. She didn't acknowledge Mrs. Jarvi or Sofiya. Mabel's behavior and the fear in Alina's eyes kept Sofiya silent. It was as if she knew she shouldn't talk to her best friend.

"All the girls are like that," Mrs. Jarvi said after the pair had left. "They never talk to the kitchen help or even acknowledge us. I think it's because Miss Nora told them to not speak to us."

"Why?" Sofiya asked, feeling confused. "Alina is my..." she was about to say best friend and then caught herself. "My sister."

Mrs. Jarvi shook her head and clucked her tongue. "Then that makes it all the more heartbreaking. She'll be told not to speak to you. It's best to do as Miss Nora says."

Several trays of hor d'oeuvres were ready and being kept

warm on the stove by the time Mrs. Jarvi left for the evening. They had also cooked a roast beef dinner with carrots and mashed potatoes for the girls, who once again came downstairs to take their dinner trays to their rooms. Sofiya thought it was odd that the women didn't eat dinner together. But then she remembered the room behind the parlor where a dining room should be was Miss Nora's office.

After Mrs. Jarvi left, Sofiya had two hours to herself and spent them in her room, sewing her uniform. She did her best at stitching darts into the waist. Because Sofiya was short and also short-waisted, it took a practiced hand at dressmaking to create clothing that fit her perfectly. Unfortunately, Sofiya didn't have that talent. Unlike Mrs. Henderson, Alina's mother, who'd always made Sofiya's dresses. With no one here to help her, Sofiya's awkward stitching would have to do.

Before leaving her tiny bedroom, Sofiya checked the waistband of her black skirt, tucked safely in a drawer, for the jewels her mother had sewn inside. She worried about losing them. Glancing around the room, Sofiya searched for a place she could hide the jewels, but she saw none. She didn't dare hide them under the mattress, but she also didn't want to keep them in the skirt. She'd have to find a safe place so they wouldn't get lost, or worse, stolen.

Miss Nora entered the kitchen a few minutes before eight o'clock. She was wearing a low-cut red satin dress with black lace trim. The dress hung loose—there was definitely no corset underneath—and stopped above her ankles. Her auburn hair was piled up on her head, and gold earrings with red stones hung to her shoulders. A matching necklace circled her thick neck. While the jewelry sparkled and was very beautiful, Sofiya could tell immediately that the stones weren't genuine—they were paste.

"Did Mrs. Jarvi tell you what is expected of you tonight?" Miss Nora asked bluntly.

Sofiya nodded. "Yes."

"I'll buzz for you to start bringing in the first tray when I'm ready for you," she told the young girl. "You will walk around offering the food, then place the tray on the side table and go back for more trays, one at a time. Do not talk to the gentlemen or the young ladies. You're to be invisible. Also, use the entrance from the office. I don't want you coming down the hallway where we greet the guests. Do you understand?"

"Yes, Miss Nora," Sofiya replied.

The older woman scowled and shook her head. "Not that any of the men would even look twice at you. And that dress. You look like you're wearing a potato sack." With that, she spun on her low heel and left the kitchen.

Sofiya swallowed hard and held back the tears that burned her eyes. Nora Petrov was a terrible person. Sofiya's maman could not have known the type of person she was, or she'd never have allowed them to come here. All she could do now was try her best to please Miss Nora and hopefully, someday, leave this place.

From the kitchen, Sofiya heard the male guests arriving one by one. She peeked out the kitchen door and saw Carter, dressed immaculately in a black suit with tails, working as a butler and greeting the guests. After a quick look, Sofiya ducked back into the kitchen and waited.

Around eight-thirty, the buzzer blared, making Sofiya jump. She stood and took a deep breath to brace herself, then lifted one of the heavy silver serving trays and carefully carried it out of the kitchen. Carter caught her eye and smiled warmly at her just before she turned into the office. Sofiya's heart lifted at his kindness. Taking another deep breath for courage, she walked tentatively into the parlor.

The scene she witnessed was not one a young girl brought up in a genteel home could ever have imagined. There were several men—mostly older—wearing expensive three-piece suits, sitting or milling about as young ladies smiled brightly at them or placed a familiar hand on their arms or chests. One young girl was sitting suggestively in a man's lap—a man who looked old enough to be her father. The girls were dressed in beautiful gowns of all lengths, some bearing glass beads that sparkled under the chandelier's light. Except for the familiar way the girls acted around the men, this could have been an ordinary soiree. But despite Sofiya's inexperience, she could sense that something untoward was happening around her.

"Don't just stand there," Miss Nora whispered angrily. "Serve!"

Her sharp words brought Sofiya out of her stupor. She moved around the room, ignoring the girls' giggles as the men touched them familiarly, and stopped only when a gentleman expressed interest in an hor d'oeuvre.

"I see you have a new server tonight," a white-bearded man in a pinstripe suit said to Miss Nora over Sofiya's head.

Miss Nora smiled at the man. "Ah, yes. It's so hard finding and keeping good help." She sighed, and the gentleman nodded his understanding. "But she's not all that's new around here," Miss Nora continued. "Mabel, dear. Please bring down our surprise."

Sofiya had just left the room when she'd overheard Miss Nora call to Mabel. She quickly retrieved another tray from the kitchen and hurried back to the parlor. When she entered, the pocket doors had opened, and Mabel escorted Alina inside.

Sofiya stopped, stunned, as everyone in the room turned to stare at her dear friend. Alina was dressed in a white satin beaded gown that shimmered under the lights. Her pale blond hair was arranged beautifully upon her head with a string of diamonds woven through it. She wore white gloves that went to her elbows, and tiny pearls hung around her neck. She looked like a princess from a fairy tale.

"Gentlemen. Please welcome our newest young lady, Alina," Miss Nora announced.

The men in the room all eyed her like she was the most delicious dessert they'd ever seen. Sofiya watched their reaction with shock. What had Miss Nora meant by the "newest young lady?" And what did these men want of Alina?

Quickly, Sofiya remembered her job and began wandering through the room with the tray of food. She caught Alina's eyes for only a second and saw fear in them. Alina knew something that she did not, but Sofiya didn't dare speak to her in front of Miss Nora.

"Alina, dear," Miss Nora purred. "Why don't you entertain us with a song on the piano?"

Alina nodded, walked gracefully to the piano, and sat down. After a moment's hesitation, she began to play a beautiful, gentle melody.

Sofiya set the food tray down and walked back into the office. She turned for a second to watch her friend play. They both had been taught to play the piano, but Alina had succeeded where Sofiya had not. Music flowed beautifully from underneath Alina's fingertips. Sofiya knew her friend felt each note from deep within. She'd been a natural at learning music, and she had a lovely singing voice as well. Sofiya had been terrible at both. But what Sofiya had lacked in grace, beauty, and talent, she'd made up for by excelling in her studies and languages.

As the evening continued, Sofiya brought in tray after tray of food and cleared away the empty platters and dirty glasses. A side table was filled with crystal decanters of whiskey, brandy, and all types of wine, and the men drank freely. Expensive cigars and cigarettes were provided as well, and much to Sofiya's surprise, some of the women smoked alongside the men. Each time Sofiya entered the room, she saw Alina looking anxious and uncomfortable, standing off to the side. Her heart went out to her friend.

By midnight, many of the girls had disappeared, and the men also had. At least, that was what Sofiya believed. Carter still stood patiently at the door in case he was needed. Stifling a yawn, Sofiya walked into the room to clear away more trays when Miss Nora came up to her.

"You may be finished for the night. Mrs. Jarvi comes in at nine in the morning, but you need to start work at eight. I'll leave a list of duties on the kitchen table you are to perform daily." Her thick brows rose. "You can read, can't you?"

Yes, in five different languages, Sofiya wanted to retort, but she didn't dare. "Yes, Miss Nora."

"Good. Now off with you. You can clean this up in the morning."

Sofiya glanced one last time at Alina as she sat in the corner with Mabel, sent her a smile, then hurried to the kitchen.

She was exhausted. Before going to bed, Sofiya washed the dishes and set the silver trays aside to polish in the morning. She sighed with relief as she finally lay down in bed at one o'clock. Sofiya couldn't believe that just this morning, she and Alina had arrived in Portland. So much had transpired in such a short time. The last thing she did that night was say a little prayer, asking God to watch over Alina and keep her safe. Then she fell into a deep sleep.

* * *

Sofiya awoke with a start the next morning at the sound of a motor running. Shaking her head to clear it, she realized the sun was shining through the window. Quickly, she dressed in a shirtwaist and skirt and pinned up her hair. She hoped it wasn't past eight a.m., or Miss Nora would be furious.

When Sofiya entered the kitchen, she knew immediately she'd overslept. The clock on the wall read nine-thirty, and Mrs. Jarvi was sitting at the table, working.

"I'm so sorry I'm late," Sofiya said, fear rippling through her. But Mrs. Jarvi only brushed her words away with a wave of her hand.

"Don't worry," she said as she continued working on a sewing project. "Miss Nora doesn't usually wake up until ten or eleven, so she'll never know."

Sofiya dropped into a chair at the table and sighed. "Thank you. I'm not used to being up so late at night. I'll do better tomorrow."

Mrs. Jarvi nodded as her fingers expertly pushed the needle in and out of the gray fabric.

"I noticed you washed the dishes last night. From now on, you'll want to wash them in the morning so you can get to bed earlier," Mrs. Jarvi said. "In the winter, you'll be up very early to stoke the fires in every room, so you need your sleep."

"Yes, ma'am," Sofiya said. She watched Mrs. Jarvi sew another minute and then realized what she was doing. "Is that my uniform?"

"Yes. I had a terse note on the table about how sloppy you looked in this dress. So, I trimmed the hem, and I'm sewing it up. I measured it yesterday when we were working on it. It should fit better for tonight."

"Thank you so much," Sofiya said, tears filling her eyes. She had thought Mrs. Jarvi would be a difficult taskmaster, but now she realized she had a kind heart. "You are too kind."

"Ack! It's nothing. I don't want to have Miss Nora on my back, is all," Mrs. Jarvi said but then gave Sofiya a small smile. "Now, off with you. The sooner you clean the parlor, the sooner you can help me in the kitchen. Here." She handed Sofiya the list of chores Miss Nora had left on the table. "This will tell you everything you need to do daily."

Sofiya looked down the long list written in Miss Nora's tight script—it seemed endless. Clean and polish everything in the parlor. Sweep the rugs in the parlor, hallway, and on the staircase. Wipe down the bathroom. Pick up the sheets left in the hallway upstairs from each of the girls' rooms and bring them down for the laundry woman. It went on and on.

"Better get at it," Mrs. Jarvi said.

"Yes, ma'am." Sofiya scurried off to begin her daily chores.

* * *

As the days passed, Sofiya became more efficient with her chores. She was up at eight every morning and spent the first hour of her day cleaning the parlor. It amazed her how messy the finely dressed gentlemen were, spilling wine and whiskey on the carpets and dropping ashes everywhere. Food crumbs also covered the plush rugs. She was thankful Miss Nora had a new carpet sweeper to pick up most of the mess. She lemon oiled the wood furniture and opened the window to air out the room. Sofiya was also responsible for replenishing the cigarette and cigar boxes and liquor decanters. Then, she ran upstairs where the girls had tossed their sheets out their doors in a heap. She gathered those and had them ready for the laundry woman to pick up. Sofiya was grateful she didn't have to change all sixteen beds herself—or wash the sheets. The girls were responsible for changing their own beds.

Delivery men stopped by the house on an ongoing schedule. The iceman replenished the ice in the refrigerator, and the butcher, the bakery, and the milkman delivered items all week long. Fresh fruits and vegetables were also delivered twice a week. Mrs. Jarvi said she had enough to do without going to the market every day, and Sofiya was glad she didn't have to do that either. She had plenty of work to do already.

By Sunday, Sofiya felt she was catching on to her duties, but her biggest worry was Alina. She hadn't spoken to her all week and hoped that since there would be no entertaining Sunday night, she might be able to see her friend. Each night, she'd watched as Alina was brought out like a prized doll and shown off to the men. Sofiya had seen fear in Alina's eyes. She had no idea what Miss Nora was up to. But each night, Alina and Mabel were the only two girls left in the parlor after the men and other girls had disappeared. It baffled Sofiya as to what was happening.

Mrs. Jarvi didn't work on Sundays. Sofiya was responsible for heating the large pot of soup that had been prepared the day before and leaving out the cold sandwiches for the girls' lunch. They ate the same meal for dinner as well. Sofiya, however, didn't get the day off. She cleaned the parlor early that morning and set about doing her other work.

As Sofiya filled the cigar boxes, she studied the sturdy little containers and had an idea. She kept two when she tossed out the other empty boxes and stored them away in her bedroom for later.

Around noon, the girls came one by one to pick up their trays. Sofiya had slowly learned each girl's name and greeted them cheerfully as they entered the kitchen. Rose was a beautiful, dark-haired girl with pale skin, and Lillian was older than the rest, with mahogany hair and a tall, slim frame. Elsie, Nellie, and Lucille were all blondes with blue eyes, and Mae and Marion were shorter, pixie-like girls with impish smiles. Betty was shy, and Velma was quite outspoken and stern, while Essie and Flossie looked very much alike with their red hair and spray of freckles across their noses. Pearl was quiet and exotic-looking and seemed to keep to herself even when all the girls were talking in a group. Mabel was a little rough around the edges, with brown hair and eyes, but she took her job of watching over Alina seriously. Some of the girls smiled and said hello when Sofiya greeted them, others seemed startled, and a couple simply ignored her. Sofiya didn't take it personally. She knew how fearsome Miss Nora was and thought the girls were afraid to get into trouble.

Sofiya waited patiently for Alina to come down. She finally did, dressed in yet another summer frock Sofiya had never seen before. Mabel wasn't with her this time, so Sofiya finally had a chance to be alone with her. As soon as Alina stepped into the kitchen, Sofiya set down the dish she was drying and hugged her.

"I've missed you," Sofiya said. She knew Alina felt the same because she held her tightly, as if for dear life. When finally they parted, there were tears in Alina's eyes.

"I was told not to speak to anyone," Alina whispered. She glanced around nervously. "Especially you."

"Why?" Sofiya asked, shocked.

Alina shook her head. "Miss Nora said not to. She scares me. I don't want to make her angry." She lowered her voice even more. "I've seen her hit the other girls. She grabs them by the hair and pulls them to the ground. She has a terrible temper."

Sofiya's heart lurched. "Has she hurt you?"

"No. Miss Nora says I'm her prized possession—for now. Mabel said I'm lucky, and she is too. Because we share a room, Mabel doesn't have to work right now." Alina's voice cracked. "But Mabel also said that will end soon."

"What did she mean by that?" Sofiya asked, completely confused.

Alina shook her head again. "I'm just supposed to look pretty. That's all they've told me. I do what Miss Nora says. I'm so scared."

Sofiya nodded. She understood because Miss Nora frightened her too. Before they could say another word, the sound of heels in the hallway grew louder. Alina grabbed her food tray and rushed out of the kitchen, nearly running into Miss Nora.

"Watch where you're going!" Miss Nora said sharply. Then her face softened when she saw it was Alina. "We can't have you spilling hot soup on yourself, can we? I'd hate to see you burn that delicate flesh."

Alina looked absolutely terrified. "Excuse me," she murmured, then hurried to the staircase. That was Sofiya's last image of her before the kitchen door shut.

Later that afternoon, Sofiya went to her room and studied the cigar boxes. Both were made of lightweight wood, but one was polished with a small gold latch. She wanted to create something where she could hide her jewels and the letters she'd been writing to her maman. Even though she knew she couldn't send the letters, they were a way for her to spill out her feelings during this trying time. And although Sofiya wrote them in French, she still wanted to be certain no one else found them.

Sofiya decided she'd create a false bottom for the bigger box, like a jewelry box one of her royal cousins had once shown her. But she needed a saw or cutter tool to make it. She walked out to the garage, hoping to find some tools. As she entered, she ran right into Carter.

"Well, good afternoon, Miss Sofiya. What can I do for you?" he asked cheerfully. He wore a heavy apron over his clothing and had been polishing one of the cars.

Sofiya felt comfortable with Carter. He was always quick with a smile and a warm greeting. He came to the house three times a day for his meals, which he took back to his little apartment over the garage. So, she took a chance and confided in him.

"I'd like to make something out of two cigar boxes. But I need a tool to saw out the bottom of one."

"I have just the thing," he said, heading over to a metal box and lifting the lid. "But a lady like yourself shouldn't be doing a project like that. Why don't you bring the boxes out, and I'll do it for you?"

Sofiya hesitated. She didn't want Miss Nora to know about the box. Would Carter tell her?

"I see the worried look on your pretty face," he said. "This is between you and me. No one needs to know what you're making."

The young girl sighed audibly, causing Carter to chuckle.

"I know exactly how you feel," he confided. "Miss Nora can be, let's say, difficult."

Sofiya nodded. "I'll be right back." She hurried to retrieve the boxes and then showed Carter what she wanted done. He studied the larger box a moment, then the other one.

"So, you want a false bottom, huh? Are you going to hide all the love letters your boyfriend is sending you?" He grinned.

"Uh...no," Sofiya said with a stutter. This made Carter laugh again.

"Well, a sweet girl like you should have boyfriends lined up all the way to the river," he said.

Sofiya knew he was teasing her. She wasn't pretty or even considered sweet. Alina always had the boys watching her when they were back home. The only boys that noticed Sofiya were the academic ones who were amazed at her knowledge of literature and languages. But she appreciated Carter's sweet compliment.

"You go on back about your work, and I'll bring this to the house when I'm finished," Carter said. "I have a good idea on how to make it a secure hiding place."

Sofiya thanked him and walked across the yard to the house. It was a lovely summer day, warm with a nice cooling breeze. In the week that she'd been there, she'd barely stepped outside. Glancing around, she noticed what a beautiful yard Miss Nora had. Sofiya knew a gardener came once a week to care for it. There were rose bushes along the back of the house, dogwood trees lining the fence that separated her yard from the house on the left, and small, brick-encircled flower gardens scattered about. The most impressive feature was the very old, tall oak tree that shaded the entire yard. A bench had been built to encircle the circumference of the tree, and Sofiya could picture herself sitting there on a beautiful day like today, reading a book or enjoying a cup of tea.

"Sofiya! Get in here!"

The young girl startled at Miss Nora's stern voice. She glanced up to see her filling the doorway, hands on her hips with a pinched face. Quickly, Sofiya ran to the door.

"Why are you outside? I told you never to leave the house without my permission," Miss Nora said, moving aside to let the young girl inside.

"It was such a nice day, and I hadn't seen the yard. It's so beautiful," Sofiya said in a rush, hoping Miss Nora hadn't seen her come out of the garage.

Miss Nora narrowed her eyes and stared at Sofiya until the poor girl nearly withered under her gaze. "Don't wander off like that again, do you hear?"

Sofiya had been holding her breath and let it out in a whoosh of relief. "Yes, Miss Nora."

Miss Nora turned, headed toward the door, and suddenly spun back around. "Those clothes of yours are atrocious. I cannot have people seeing one of my girls looking so plain and unfashionable. I'll have Mabel take your measurements and go to the dress shop to buy you a few new items."

Sofiya's eyes widened in delight. "Oh, thank you. That's so kind of you."

"It's not out of kindness," Miss Nora said. "I have a reputation to uphold." With that, she left the room. Sofiya nearly fell over from relief after the woman was gone. Miss Nora was a domineering presence unlike any she'd ever known. Even Tsar Nicholas hadn't been as scary to speak to as Miss Nora.

Sofiya went upstairs to collect the lunch trays and dishes that the girls left outside their doors. She washed the dirty dishes and prepared new trays for the girls' dinner. When Carter came inside to pick up his food tray, he was carrying the cigar box underneath his arm.

"I hope you like it." Carter set it on the kitchen table and opened the lid. "Here. Let me show you how it works." He had carved a groove into one side that the false bottom could slide into and then placed a thin rail on the other. If someone was inspecting it, they'd never notice that it wasn't the original bottom.

"You'll have to pry the bottom up with a thin knife or nail file," he told Sofiya.

Sofiya loved what he'd done. Taking a bread knife, she slipped it between the wall and floor of the box and lifted it a little. The false bottom came up easily. It also slipped back in just as easily.

"Oh, thank you so much. It's perfect," Sofiya said. Without thinking, she wrapped her arms around Carter and hugged him.

Carter gently pulled away, looking startled. "You are most welcome, Miss Sofiya. But we best not let Miss Nora see you hugging me like that, or she might get the wrong idea."

Sofiya nodded, although she didn't think anything was odd about hugging a friend. "Thank you. This was very kind of you," she said.

Carter nodded and smiled, then picked up his tray and headed back to his little apartment above the garage.

Sofiya tucked the cigar box into one of the dresser drawers in her room so Miss Nora wouldn't see it and ask her about it.

That evening, Mabel came to the kitchen for her dinner tray and reluctantly took Sofiya's measurements. "At least I get to go shopping," she mumbled. "That will be fun, even if it's not for me."

"Thank you, Mabel," Sofiya said, trying her best to befriend the girl. If she could get Mabel on her side, the girl might tell her what was happening with Alina. "I do appreciate your help. I'm excited to get new clothes."

Mabel stood straighter, her face beaming with pride. "I'm Miss Nora's favorite, you know. She trusts me with jobs like this. The other girls aren't allowed to leave the house, but I am."

"That is quite an honor," Sofiya said. "And I can tell you have good taste in clothing. I like what you're wearing now."

The girl looked down at her sapphire blue dress that had a drop waist and hung loosely to her ankles. "This style is all the rage now. Only old ladies wear what you're wearing."

Sofiya had remembered how her maman had detested the shorter skirts that were becoming fashionable and the loose waists that allowed one to not wear a corset. But if that was the style here in America, then Sofiya had to wear what helped her fit in. "I'm sure I'll love whatever you buy for me," she told Mabel.

To Sofiya's surprise, Mabel smiled. Feeling a little more confident, she asked, "How is Alina? This has been quite a big change for both of us."

"Oh, she's doing fine. She'll get used to this life as soon as she's working. We all do eventually." Mabel left the kitchen, and Sofiya tried to understand what she'd meant.

After all the work was completed that evening, Sofiya sat on her bed with her old skirt, the letters she'd written, and the cigar box. First, she snipped a few threads in the seam of the skirt's waistband and out slid the emerald necklace and diamond earrings.

Sofiya lifted the necklace first, marveling as she always did at the beauty of her maman's beloved necklace. It was a choker style with sixteen emerald cut emeralds set in rose gold. The stones were the deepest color of green and glittered in the light. It felt heavy in her hand, and Sofiya could only imagine what a piece such as this must have cost her père. It had been given to her maman by her père as a gift when Sofiya was born, and Marie had treasured it, wearing it to only the most prestigious events around St. Petersburg.

Next, Sofiya picked up the diamond earrings. Another gift to her mother from her père, they had once belonged to her Père's grandmother. Each diamond was one caret in size set in yellow gold shaped like a flower. They were simple yet elegant, and her maman had treasured them. The fact that her maman would part with such lovely treasures proved to Sofiya that she'd been desperate to ensure her daughter's safety. Now, it was up to Sofiya to care for these family heirlooms and protect them. Sofiya prayed she'd never have to sell them to survive. That would be yet another tragedy.

Pulling the false bottom out of the cigar box, Sofiya first set a handkerchief on the bottom, then placed the jewels inside. She then put the letters on top of them. She reinserted the bottom. It held tightly and looked original to the box. Sofiya set her hairbrush and comb inside the box along with hairpins. She could tell anyone who noticed it that she used it for everyday items. Even if Miss Nora saw the box on top of the dresser and peered inside, she'd never suspect what was hidden underneath.

Placing the cigar box on top of the dresser in plain sight, Sofiya was satisfied her secrets were safe. She went to bed early that night, thankful she didn't have to work late and said another little prayer to keep Alina safe.

CHAPTER FIVE

Addie

Addie sat on the bed in the semi-dark living room with tears spilling from her eyes. A sob escaped her lips, and she quickly grabbed a tissue to wipe her eyes. But Zach had already awakened and turned to see her face wet with tears.

"What's wrong?" he asked, sitting up quickly in bed.

"I know we're in the right house," she said, wiping her eyes. "And now I know why there are so many bedrooms."

Zach's eyes, still looking blurry from sleep, stared at her in question. "Right house?"

"This is the house Sofiya lived in. These letters confirmed it. She describes it perfectly." Addie wiped her eyes again. She hated crying in front of Zach, but her heart was broken for Sofiya and Alina. She knew better than anyone how horrible it was to be held prisoner for someone else's profit.

"But I thought you loved this house," Zach said, looking confused. "Why are you crying?"

"I do love this house. I was drawn to it the moment I saw it. But these letters describe how this house was used."

She stopped a moment, taking a breath. "It was a brothel."

Zach's face fell. "Oh, sweetie. I'm so sorry. I had no idea." He looked worried as he moved closer to her. "I never would have agreed to buy this place if I'd known that."

Addie searched his face, suddenly sorry she'd upset him. "I would have wanted to buy it even if I'd known. I just have to get used to the idea that women were forced to work here, in this very house."

"I never would have guessed there'd be a brothel in this neighborhood. This was and still is a rich area," Zach said.

"Yes. And by the sound of it, this was a place for rich men only." Addie set the letters down beside the cigar box. "The owner trapped girls by making them indebted to her, then threatened them so they wouldn't leave. She was serving a high-end clientele, but she was just as horrible as any pimp on the street." Addie shivered and reached for the sweatshirt she'd worn earlier, slipping it over her T-shirt. Zach wrapped his arms around her and held her tight.

"I'm sorry," he whispered again. "The last thing I want is for you to be reminded of that time in your life."

"I know," she said softly. She'd told Zach about her life before she'd met Valerie and began working with her. But she hadn't shared every detail. From the time her mother had been put in prison for drug and alcohol abuse, and Addie had been thrown into the foster care system in Ames, Iowa, to the moment she'd escaped the sex-trafficking ring, Addie had lived through hell. She could never share everything she'd been through—it was too much to put on one person.

Pulling away from Zach, Addie studied the cigar box. The false bottom no longer held in tightly as Sofiya had described. She saw the grooved line Carter had created, but there was no longer a ledge on the other side for the piece of wood to sit on. That's why Addie had been able to just press on one side to lift it out.

"Are you okay?" Zach asked, cocking his head to study her face.

She nodded. "I'm fine. Maybe I was supposed to find this place and give it new life. Maybe this is the place where I've been meant to be all along."

"Maybe." He didn't look convinced. "But if this house upsets you in any way, please tell me. I don't want you working on a house that reminds you of terrible things."

"I promise. If it bothers me, I'll tell you." She gave him a small smile, and he kissed her lightly on the cheek.

"Are you sure you still want to read those letters? What if they get too," he hesitated. "Too graphic."

"I doubt if a girl brought up in the Victorian era would write something too graphic," Addie said. "I can't stop now. I need to know what happened to them."

Zach sighed and ran a hand through his already-mussed hair. "I feel terrible about finding those letters now."

"No. Don't feel bad," Addie said quickly. "They aren't what I'd expected, but I want to read them." She bit her lip. "Maybe I was meant to read them."

"I don't know about that," Zach said, sliding down under the covers. "But I'll believe you if you want me to."

"You're too easy," Addie said, smiling now. Zach had a calming influence on her that she needed. Especially at times like this when something triggered memories of her old life. She placed the letters back in the box, turned out her light, and slid over next to Zach. "But I'm glad you're easy."

He laughed, wrapped his arm around her, and they fell asleep, curled together.

* * *

Despite feeling safe in Zach's arms, Addie didn't sleep well that night. She awoke early, dressed, and after grabbing a mug of coffee, she wandered into the little room off the kitchen. Today, she was seeing it in a whole new light. This had been Sofiya's room.

It was a tiny room that probably hadn't changed in over a hundred years. The white plaster walls were dingy and had several nail holes. The flooring was hardwood, the same as the rest of the house, but scratched from neglect. There was no closet. Addie tried to imagine a small twin bed against the wall, underneath the window, and a dresser on the other wall. That was all that Sofiya had described. It was hard to picture this room being used as someone's bedroom.

Wandering back into the kitchen, Addie looked over the work that Zach had begun. They were gutting the entire area because someone had painted over the oak cabinets that had probably been added in the 1930s. In Sofiya's era, there probably had been a hutch for dishes and silverware, a worktable in the center of the room, and possibly a cabinet with a sink since they had running water. Built-in cabinets were rare, even in a large kitchen. Now, they planned on updating it with all new cabinets, quartz countertops, and an island in the middle. Very different from when Sofiya had worked here.

Addie left the kitchen, noting that there was no longer a door as Sofiya had described. The small bathroom was still off the hallway, next to the kitchen, and then there was the doorway to the formal dining room. As Addie walked into the room, she glanced around. The last occupants had used it as a proper dining room—she could tell from the low-hanging light fixture in the middle of the room. But in Sofiya's day, it had been Nora Petrov's office. Addie glanced around, imagining a large desk on one side of the room and possibly a Victorian-style sofa in the middle on a fringed rug. The room currently had light wallpaper with tiny flowers, but Addie knew she'd find something flashier underneath. If Nora's office was anything like her master bedroom had been, it was sure to be flamboyant.

The doorway from the dining room into the parlor had been widened at some point, and French doors had been added, but Addie was almost positive she'd find a track for a pocket door behind the moldings. She hoped so. Pocket doors were prevalent in these older homes, and they gave them character.

Addie walked through the French doors into the parlor— the same path Sofiya took as she brought in trays of food for Nora's gentleman guests. Looking around, she pictured an upright piano on the far wall and vintage furniture that men wearing three-piece suits with gold pocket watches on chains sat on. Men who'd been the pillars of the community—bankers, lawyers, business owners. Men who could buy whatever they wanted—even young women for a few hours of pleasure.

A chill ran through Addie, and she set down her coffee mug and wrapped her arms around her. Even after all these years, she remembered what it felt like to be bought and sold like a piece of meat at the market. Her heart went out to Sofiya and Alina and all the girls Nora Petrov had exploited.

"Hey. There you are," Zach said, entering the room. He was dressed in jeans and a sweatshirt, which were already covered in dust and dirt. "Are you okay?"

Addie grabbed her mug again and took a sip of the lukewarm coffee. "I'm fine. I was just imagining how this house looked when Sofiya lived here."

He nodded. "I was out looking over the garage again, and I think it's salvageable. We could shore it up and make a nice little apartment upstairs. Do you want to come look at it?"

"Sure." She followed him outside and down the broken brick path. The air was damp, but Addie knew it would warm up as the day progressed. She reminded herself to open the windows in the house when she returned, otherwise it would get hot in there. No air conditioning had ever been added since there wasn't a central furnace.

They walked inside the old carriage-house-turned-garage. There were two large doors that slid to the side like barn doors. Despite the concrete floor, the room smelled musty. A workbench sagged along one side of the garage underneath a small window, and an old pot-bellied wood stove sat in the opposite corner. Addie followed Zach to the back of the room where the staircase was.

"Is this safe?" She winced when she saw it. The slats of wood were most definitely original.

"I've been up and down it twice, and it's been fine," he said, then headed up two steps at a time with his long stride.

Addie grimaced and slowly made her way up the stairs. Surprisingly, they were solid. When she got to the top, there was a small landing and a door that had been left open. She followed Zach inside.

"It's in bad shape now, but with a remodel, it might be a cute place," Zach said.

Addie looked around. It was larger than she'd anticipated. The kitchen was on the far wall and looked to have been added sometime in the 1950s or 60s. Walls had been added then, too, from what she could tell, creating a bathroom and a private bedroom.

"The windows should be replaced," Zach said. "And that awful paneling needs to be taken down. But otherwise, it isn't bad."

"Those electric baseboards need replacing, too," Addie said. "And the carpet is atrocious."

Zach laughed. "Yeah. I doubt there are beautiful hardwoods underneath. We can put down laminate in the main room and bathroom and carpet in the bedroom."

Addie shrugged. "I thought we were going to finish up the main house first."

"It couldn't hurt to fix this up first so there's a little income coming in while we work on the house," Zach suggested.

Addie sighed as she glanced around the apartment. She thought about Carter and how this place had probably been wide open when he lived up here. There probably hadn't been any wallboard up then, and she'd bet the pot-belly stove in the garage had been his only source of heat. She shook her head just thinking about the unfairness of life.

"Does that mean no?" Zach asked, looking confused.

"What? Oh, no. I was just thinking about Nora Petrov's chauffer who'd lived up here in 1917. I'll bet it was rough then," Addie said.

"I'm sure it was. And cold. Poor guy." Zach looked around once more. "You know, we could turn the lower area into a cute little apartment, too. But we'll have to put a staircase outside for up here and add an outside door."

"That sounds costly," Addie said.

"I'm sure we could easily rent this space for $1500 a month," Zach said. "Especially with this nice, quiet backyard."

Addie's brows rose. "You've really put some thought into this."

He grinned. "It would be an easy moneymaker. And we need the extra income right now. We're going to be soaking a lot into that house."

"Okay. Fine," she said. Addie knew Zach was right. "Can we finish work on the kitchen and master bedroom first, so we have a couple of useable rooms?"

"Don't worry. I'll work on this project around everything else."

Addie nodded. They always had to order items and wait, so Zach could move between projects.

As they walked up the path, back to the side door, Gail from next door waved at them. She met Zach and Addie as they neared the kitchen door.

"Hey, you two," Gail said. "How's the house coming?"

"Really good," Addie said. "I'm working on the master bedroom, and Zach is working on the kitchen. Hopefully, we'll get the mattress out of the parlor soon."

Gail smiled. "It takes time, that's for sure. I just wanted to tell you that I talked to the previous owners the other day, and they said they're still looking for the original abstract title. They know they have it, but it's boxed up with a bunch of paperwork. They'll get it to you as soon as they can."

Addie brightened at the thought of getting her hands on the history of the house. "That's great. I can't wait to see who's owned the house over the years."

"Yeah. Not everyone has kept those old abstracts, so it's nice when they're available," Gail said.

"Say? Do you know the date your house was built?" Addie asked. "We thought the original owner of this house owned your property too, and there would have been a driveway here once."

"Oh, yes. I'm sure there was because of that old carriage house back there. My house was built in 1926. They were a wealthy couple who I think lost all their money in the crash of 1929 because they sold the house for pennies on the dollar in 1931."

"Oh, that's terrible." Addie wondered if Nora was still living here then and what had happened to her.

"It is. But it was kept up nicely by the next owners, so they must have had a little money. Everything is original in my house, although it's been updated. You'll have to see it sometime," Gail said.

"I'd love to," Addie told her.

"Well, I'm off to show some houses. Have a great day." Gail hurried away on tall heels toward her car parked on the street.

"I wonder if she's always a whirlwind," Zach said quietly.

Addie laughed. "She has a lot of energy, that's for sure."

They both went inside the house to work on their projects. Before going into the master bedroom, Addie wandered in and out of each of the other eight bedrooms. The rooms weren't large, except for the two corner rooms at the end of the hallway, but they all were big enough for two beds, one on each side of the fireplace. Addie stopped in the third bedroom from the top of the stairs, and a chill swept through her. Something told her that this had been Alina and Mabel's room. She tried imagining two beds in the room with a curtain in-between for privacy. The girls may have each had a dresser on their side of the room and maybe a washstand to clean up between gentlemen guests. Addie shivered again at the thought of these rooms being used for prostitution. Had Alina known what she was being groomed for? Or, like Addie at fourteen, had she been blindsided by people she thought she could trust?

Addie walked over to the window that looked out toward Gail's house next door. "Maybe Sofiya's letters will answer my questions," she said quietly to herself. Rubbing her hands over her arms to warm the chill she felt, Addie went back to the master bedroom to work.

CHAPTER SIX

Sofiya

Sofiya fell into a routine as the days went by. By the middle of the second week, she knew her schedule well and could complete her chores quickly and efficiently. Mrs. Jarvi was pleased with her performance and told her so.

"I've never had a helper who works as hard as you do," she said one day as they cooked dinner together. "I hope you'll be in the kitchen as long as you're here."

Sofiya wondered what she meant by that. Where else would she be?

Throughout the second week, Sofiya also noticed more of what was going on in the house. She paid attention at night while she was serving and realized the men were being escorted upstairs to the girls' rooms. This unnerved her. As a young woman raised in an upper-class family, she had little knowledge of what transpired between a man and woman in private. But she knew for certain that it wasn't innocent—and Nora Petrov was the person setting these girls up with these men.

Many times, after Sofiya had finished cleaning the parlor,

she'd see Miss Nora in her office, counting money and locking it away. She wondered where the large amounts of cash came from. Sofiya no longer believed the girls were renting rooms from Miss Nora. But she didn't want to believe Nora sold the women to be used in some way by the gentlemen who visited each night. Because if Sofiya believed that, she'd have to admit that would be the fate of her dear friend, Alina. And that thought terrified her.

As far as Sofiya could tell, Alina was just there to entertain the men by playing the piano each night and sharing small talk. She'd never seen Alina go upstairs alone with a man. Sofiya prayed she never would.

On Friday, as Mrs. Jarvi prepared to leave for the evening, Sofiya drew up all her courage and asked the older woman if she knew what happened at night during the gatherings.

Mrs. Jarvi studied Sofiya a moment, her brow creased. "Have you not figured out what type of house this is?"

"I've been to soirees and dances but have never seen anything like this," Sofiya said. "A young woman would never have been allowed to go off privately with a man where I come from."

A long sigh escaped Mrs. Jarvi's lips. "I'm sorry, dear. This isn't a nice place for girls. Men come here for," she hesitated as if choosing her words carefully. "To have relations with the young women. Do you understand what I mean by that?"

Sofiya's heart pounded. "You mean as if they were husband and wife?" she whispered.

Mrs. Jarvi nodded. "Yes. But they pay Miss Nora for the privilege of the young woman's time."

"But what of Alina? I haven't seen her go off alone with a gentleman. Will she be safe from that?" Sofiya had trouble believing Miss Nora would do such a thing to her own relative. To a girl as young as Alina. But then, she realized that most of the girls who lived there were young, too.

"I'm sorry." Mrs. Jarvi's expression looked pained. "I'm afraid Miss Nora is grooming your sister to be one of the girls too. I'm so, so sorry."

Sofiya was so stunned that she dropped into one of the wooden chairs. How could she have been so blind to what was happening around her? Her dear, sweet Alina. Did she know what was to happen to her?

"I can't let her do this to Alina," Sofiya said.

Mrs. Jarvi stepped closer to the young girl. "You can't stop her, Sofiya. There is no end to what Nora will do to protect what she believes is hers. And trust me, she believes she owns Alina and you. Promise me that you won't get in her way. Nora can be a vicious woman if pushed too far."

Tears filled Sofiya's eyes. "What can I do? I have to save Alina from this fate."

The older woman placed a comforting hand on Sofiya's shoulder. "You can't do anything. Otherwise, it will be even worse for you and Alina. Believe me, I know. I've seen Nora toss girls out onto the street with nothing, and they're left to find their own way. It's not pretty. Please, promise me you won't cause any trouble."

Sofiya looked up at Mrs. Jarvi as tears spilled down her cheeks. "I can't promise that."

"Then God help you, dear." The older woman's shoulders slouched as she made her way out of the kitchen.

Weekend nights were the busiest, and Sofiya moved between the kitchen and the parlor multiple times, bringing trays of food to the many men there. It seemed to Sofiya that there were more gentlemen than usual, and she wondered why. But she was too busy to wonder for long.

As she worked, she tried to devise a plan of how she and Alina could escape this terrible place. Sofiya had the jewels, and although she'd hoped not to sell them, she was willing to do so if it meant saving Alina. The toughest part was thinking of a safe way for both girls to escape the house at once. Sofiya didn't know how she would do that yet, but she had to think of a way.

Halfway through the night, Alina was once again introduced to the crowd of men, and she entered wearing another beautiful white frilly dress. Sofiya had stopped a moment, stunned by how gorgeous her friend looked, her hair pulled up in a lovely style with diamonds strung through it, glittering in the light. She looked like a fairy princess, and all the men gasped and stared at her, delight reflecting in their eyes.

Miss Nora walked around the room, speaking quietly to each of the men. Sofiya began serving again, but no one was paying attention to her. All eyes were on Alina.

As Sofiya left the room through the office to collect another tray, Miss Nora followed her.

"You're done for the night," she said sharply. "Go to your room."

Sofiya was surprised. "But there are more trays of food in the kitchen."

"Never mind those. One of the other girls will bring them in. You're to go to your room. Understand?" Miss Nora eyed her sharply.

"Yes, Miss Nora," Sofiya said. She headed for the kitchen as Miss Nora reentered the parlor.

Sofiya wasn't sure what to do with herself. Why had Miss

Nora dismissed her early? Instead of going to her room, she began washing the dirty trays. Mabel came into the kitchen, an angry sneer on her face, and picked up one of the food trays.

"I'm not a kitchen maid," Mabel said under her breath before leaving the room.

Sofiya remained silent as she cleaned the kitchen. She knew she should go to her room as Miss Nora had told her, but she felt too nervous to lie down. Quietly, she peered out the kitchen door and heard Miss Nora laughing with delight in the parlor. Carter caught her eye and put a gloved finger to his lips for her to be silent. He tried to smile, but she could tell he wasn't happy. Something terrible was going to happen, and it seemed everyone knew what it was except her.

After Mabel had come and gone again, Sofiya grew nervous. Suddenly, a loud cheer arose from the men in the parlor, like someone had won a game. The chatter in the room grew louder, and Sofiya couldn't help but look out the kitchen door again to see what was happening. She watched in horror as an older gentleman escorted Alina to the staircase. Alina turned and looked at her friend with large, sad eyes. The realization of what was happening hit Sofiya hard. She pushed open the kitchen door and ran down the hallway with the word "No!" on her lips, but Nora intercepted her, stopping her in her tracks.

"Don't you dare make a scene," Miss Nora hissed, grabbing Sofiya's arm so tightly that her fingernails dug into her skin. "I made a good amount of money on that girl tonight, and I plan to make a lot more."

Sofiya stared up into her hateful brown eyes. "How could you? She's your cousin's daughter!"

Nora pursed her lips and dragged Sofiya back into the kitchen, nearly pulling her arm out of its socket. "I will do as I please," she said menacingly, her face so close Sofiya could feel her hot breath on her cheeks. "I paid your way here, and I own you. Both of you! So do as I say, and maybe I won't sell you to one of the whore houses down by the river."

The young girl pulled out of Nora's grasp and stepped back. The venom in the older woman's voice was so evil that Sofiya believed she meant what she'd said.

Looking satisfied that Sofiya understood, Miss Nora turned and walked out of the kitchen. Once she'd disappeared, Sofiya ran into her tiny room and fell on the bed, sobbing.

* * *

Sofiya awoke with a start in the darkened room. Her face was still damp with tears, and her head ached from crying for so long. She must have fallen asleep as she wept.

The house was silent now, so Sofiya slowly stood up and walked out into the kitchen. It was dark, but a little moonlight made its way through the kitchen window, and she could see the clock on the opposite wall. Three o'clock. Everyone would be asleep, and the men should be gone.

Sofiya had to go to Alina and make sure she wasn't hurt. She didn't care if she was caught or what Miss Nora would do to her. Alina was her friend, and she needed to be with her. Sofiya sat down on a chair and quickly unbuttoned her ankle boots. Then, in her stocking feet, she padded out of the kitchen.

Sofiya hurried down the hallway and glanced into the parlor. No one was there. She slipped up the staircase, thankful there was a rug runner to muffle the sound of footsteps. Once up there, she walked slowly past the master bedroom where Nora slept. Her room was the length of five of the girls' rooms with the doorway near the stairs. Sofiya knew her bed was on the opposite wall from when she'd cleaned Miss Nora's room, so there was a good chance she wouldn't hear her walking by.

Counting the doors, Sofiya stopped at the third one. She placed her hand on the glass knob and slowly turned it, praying the man who'd been with Alina wasn't still in there. Slipping inside, she was thankful the curtain that separated Mabel and Alina's sides of the room was drawn so Mabel wouldn't see her. Sofiya crept over to Alina's bed and peered around the curtain. Lying there, alone and crying softly, was Alina.

Sofiya crawled wordlessly into bed beside her dear friend and pulled her into her arms. Alina continued to weep, her body shaking uncontrollably. Sofiya pulled the covers up around them to ward off the chill despite the warmth of the room.

"I am ruined," Alina said through her sobs.

"Olen niin pahoillani," Sofiya whispered in Finnish so Mabel would not understand them. "I'm so, so sorry that I could not save you."

Alina shook her head. "I knew it was going to happen. It couldn't have been stopped."

"Why didn't you tell me?" Sofiya asked, still speaking in Finnish. "We could have run away."

"No. I couldn't risk it for me or for you," Alina said, pulling away from her friend. She grasped her hands, still needing to feel close to her. "Nora said she was going to make a lot of money off of me, and if I tried to run, she'd sell me to a terrible place. All the girls warned me too. She's done it to other girls. The girls said we are lucky to be in a place where the men are civilized instead of down at the docks."

"Oh, my poor dear." Sofiya gently pushed her friend's

long hair away from her face. "Nora threatened me too. We're trapped. I don't know what to do."

Alina wrapped her arms around Sofiya again and whispered, "We have to stay here. There is no way out. At least until we pay off our debt to her."

"But she'll sell you to men over and over again. Aren't you afraid?" Sofiya asked.

Alina's eyes filled with tears again. "I'm already soiled. It doesn't matter now."

Sofiya held her friend tightly, her heart breaking for her. They had lost everything—their families, their childhood homes, and now, their dignity. What more could they possibly endure?

Sofiya held Alina until she finally fell asleep. She tucked the blankets around her, then tip-toed out of the room, hoping Mabel hadn't heard them.

As Sofiya crawled into her little bed, she couldn't rid herself of the chill that filled her entire body. Was this to be their life for years to come? The thought of men defiling Alina, night after night, made her stomach roll. Sofiya had the jewels she could sell for money to support them, but did she have the courage to run? She was unfamiliar with the laws in this country. What if she and Alina were thrown in jail for not upholding whatever contract their mothers may have signed? All these thoughts plagued her. What could she, a sixteen-year-old girl, do to save her friend? It all felt hopeless.

The next day, Sofiya went about her chores as usual, dark circles under her eyes being the only evidence of a sleepless night. Mrs. Jarvi watched her with sorrowful eyes, but she didn't ask what was wrong. Sofiya knew that the older woman had already guessed the problem, and although she could tell

Mrs. Jarvi felt terrible about it, there was nothing she, or anyone else, could do to help. They were all beholden to Miss Nora in one way or another. They were all trapped.

The days passed in a blur. Sofiya kept her head down and did her work. The weather grew hot, and it was her duty to turn on fans and open windows in the morning to bring in the cool air, then shut them again before the afternoon heat settled in. She and Mrs. Jarvi used fans and opened the outside kitchen door to bear the heat of cooking each day. Despite the heat, the nightly parties continued. Alina was dressed as a beautiful doll each evening and sold to the highest bidder. Sofiya overheard Mabel telling another girl that this would continue until a new, younger girl joined the house. "She's the lucky one for being special," Mabel had said.

Lucky? Sofiya wondered how Mabel could use that word. Sofiya was the lucky one. Her plain looks had saved her from being one of the girls.

Early one August afternoon, as Sofiya finished cleaning the parlor, she heard Miss Nora yelling in the entryway. Sofiya crept to the pocket doors to see what was happening. There stood sweet, quiet Elsie, one of the pretty golden blonde girls, cowering in front of Miss Nora as the older woman's voice echoed down the hallway.

"How could you be so stupid? You know the rules. You get pregnant, you're gone! Why weren't you more careful?" Nora screamed in the young girl's face.

"I'm sorry," Elsie said in a small voice. "I did everything I was told, but it still happened."

"You lazy little twit. You obviously didn't do enough. You're done here! Get out!"

A few of the other girls were standing on the staircase,

watching the scene unfold.

"I have nowhere to go," Elsie said through her tears.

"That's your problem, not mine. Get out and don't come back!" Nora turned and looked up the staircase. "And let that be a warning to all of you. If you aren't careful and get pregnant, you're out on the street. I won't have a squalling brat in my house." Nora stormed down the hallway to her office and slammed the door, leaving Elsie sobbing in the entryway.

Nellie, who roomed with Elsie, ran quickly down the stairs and handed Elsie her small suitcase. "I packed as much as I could for you," she said softly. She hugged her, then ran back upstairs, obviously frightened she might be caught by Miss Nora.

Elsie looked up at the other girls, her eyes pleading with them to help her, but none of them dared. They all turned and walked back to their rooms.

Sofiya watched the young girl walk aimlessly out the front door. There was nothing she or anyone else could do to help Elsie. Even if Sofiya had anything to give the girl, she wouldn't have dared. Miss Nora would seek revenge on anyone who helped.

Sofiya walked to the bay window in the parlor and watched as Elsie stood on the sidewalk, looking confused. Much to Sofiya's surprise, Carter appeared in the driveway with Miss Nora's motor car. He left it idling and walked over to Elsie. After they'd exchanged a few words, he helped her into the front seat and drove off. Sofiya's heart warmed at Carter's generous nature. She hoped he took Elsie somewhere safe.

Later that day, Sofiya sneaked out of the kitchen and headed quickly to the garage. She found Carter sitting at the workbench, cleaning some sort of car part that she didn't recognize.

"Well, hello there, Miss Sofiya. What can I do for you?" Carter said, politely standing because a lady had entered the room.

Sofiya always appreciated how kind Carter was to her. "I wanted to thank you for helping Elsie today. I'm sure Miss Nora would be furious if she knew, so I'll keep it to myself. But I had to let you know I thought it was very kind of you."

Carter smiled. "Thank you. I do what I can. There's a place not far from here that takes in young ladies who are in a delicate condition like Miss Elsie. I took her there. She's safe and will be better off there than here, that's for certain."

Sofiya smiled back, warmed by his kindness.

"Miss Nora is in a tizzy today, so you'd better get back to the house. We wouldn't want her to have a reason to be mean to you," Carter said.

She nodded and walked up the brick path back to the kitchen. Carter was the one bright spot in this dismal place. What Sofiya had seen today had ingrained in her that Miss Nora treated people like they were nothing. And she and Alina would have to be careful not to anger her, or who knew what Miss Nora would do for revenge.

CHAPTER SEVEN

Addie

Addie read Sofiya's words with a heavy heart. Addie had known ruthless people like Nora Petrov. People who used other humans for their own profit and threw them away like garbage. She and Sofiya had lived over one hundred years apart, and still that hadn't changed in all that time.

That night, Addie's nightmares returned. Horrible dreams of when she had no say in her life and men used her, sometimes violently. She awoke in a cold sweat, screaming. Zach sat up quickly and wrapped his arms around her until she was fully awake and aware of her surroundings.

"Do you want to talk about it?" he asked, still holding her. "I'm here for you."

Addie shook her head but held on to him. So much of that part of her life was too horrible to share with anyone. She'd been just a child, really, when her nightmarish life began. She'd trusted the friend who introduced her to the man who claimed he would protect her. That same man sold her to a trafficking ring, and she was stuck for three years selling her body to make money for someone else. Reading Sofiya's experience in Nora's house had brought all her memories to the surface again, memories she'd rather forget.

"It's the letters, isn't it?" Zach asked. "They're reminding you of your past."

Addie pulled away and nodded her head. "Yes. And no. My memories will always be with me whether or not anything triggers them."

Zach shook his head, looking pained. "I should never have bought those for you. You were doing so well before you got them."

She reached for his hand. "I love reading those letters. And they led me to this house. I didn't understand it at first, but I felt a connection to this house. Now, I'm beginning to understand why." She tipped her head to look into his eyes. "This house was waiting for me. I was meant to be here."

Zach's lips tipped into a grin. "Fate, huh?"

"Yeah. Fate. Kismet. Destiny. Whatever you want to call it. I belong here."

"Maybe," Zach said, pulling her close again. "But it's messing with your mind. If it gets to be too much, tell me. Okay?"

She nodded. "I've already been through the worst life could throw at me. I think I'll be fine."

They slid underneath the covers, and this time when Addie fell asleep, she slept soundly in Zach's arms.

* * *

Addie was so busy that next week, she fell into bed exhausted each night and wasn't able to read more of Sofiya's letters. She refinished the ceiling and floor moldings in the master bedroom and then lightly sanded and stained the wood floor. The fixtures for the master bathroom had arrived, and she and Zach spent two days putting them in. Addie had steamed-cleaned and scrubbed the original black and white tile floor and white subway tile wainscotting. They'd ordered a new, white claw-foot tub and added a shower stall with subway tile surrounded by leaded and beveled glass panels. A gorgeous walnut cabinet was set up for the sink, and they planned to order a quartz countertop and sink as soon as they could get it laser measured.

Addie stood back and admired what they'd completed. It was definitely a dream bathroom for anyone who wanted a touch of the old with the new.

The rest of the week, Addie painted the bedroom walls, careful not to ruin the beautiful fireplace mantel. She'd chosen a creamy white to set off the woodwork. By Saturday, the room was ready to be occupied, and she and Zach set up a bed frame and then carried their mattress up the narrow staircase and dropped it on the frame.

"A real bed at last," Zach said, falling on it.

Addie laughed and laid down beside him, admiring her work. "It's beautiful, isn't it?"

He rolled over and kissed her lightly on the lips. "It's perfect. Just like you."

She laughed. Addie hadn't looked in a mirror all day, but she knew there was paint in her hair and dirt smudges all over her face. "Liar."

"I'd never lie." He grabbed her and tickled her until tears of laughter ran down her cheeks.

Afterward, they lay there, holding hands. "Do you think Nora Petrov is haunting this house?" Addie asked.

"Nope. I think she's exactly where she belongs. Six feet

under." He looked over at Addie. "So, what are you lying around for? There are still eight more bedrooms to finish."

She pushed him playfully, and they laughed again. Addie had known this house would be a lot of work and take them months to finish. But she didn't mind. This was what she enjoyed doing.

That night, Addie laid down on the bed and picked up the box of letters. She'd luxuriated in a long soak in the new bathtub and had put fresh sheets on the bed along with their big, cozy down comforter. Zach had headed out to the garage apartment to do some work, leaving her to enjoy the quiet after a long week of work. She was just about to open the cigar box when her phone buzzed. Addie smiled when she saw it was her good friend, Valerie.

"Perfect timing," Addie said, answering the phone. "I just laid down in bed in our newly remodeled master bedroom."

"That's great. You've finished it," Valerie said, her voice chipper.

"How did you find time to call?" Addie asked. "Your kids and work keep you running."

Valerie sighed. "Andy and Amanda are in bed. Finally! So, I thought I'd call and catch up. What's the next room you're going to work on?"

Addie told her about the kitchen remodel and that she was going to work on the parlor first and then tackle all the bedrooms. "It's a labor of love—and money," she said, laughing.

"You've really taken on a big project. I'm happy for you," Valerie said.

"Thanks. Zach thinks we may have taken on too much, but after finding this house, I had to have it." Addie then told Valerie about the letters and pictures and what the house had been years before. "It's almost as if it were calling out to me," she admitted.

"Wow," Valerie said. "That's interesting. How are you handling reading those letters? I'm sure they must be triggering bad memories for you."

Addie had told Valerie her story, little by little, in those first years they'd worked together. Valerie had always listened respectfully and had never judged her. She'd also been the one to talk Addie into going to counseling to manage her PTSD. Addie would always be grateful for Valerie's help, and counseling had helped her greatly. Addie had volunteered many times to share her story with other trafficking survivors and show them there was life after the horror they'd experienced.

"I've been having nightmares," Addie admitted to her friend. "But I have Zach to talk to if they get too bad. I'm so busy with this house, I'd never be able to attend meetings."

"Addie," Valerie said gently. "Remember. Work is never an excuse to ignore your mental health. Please promise me you'll attend meetings if it continues."

Addie knew Valerie was right. But it was frustrating, too. Addie wanted that part of her life to be over. She knew that the PTSD symptoms could return anytime and without any reason. But she'd been doing so well. Yet, she didn't want to go backward, either. "I promise I'll go to meetings if it gets worse."

"Good. Now, tell me more about that amazing house."

Addie heard the cheer return to Valerie's voice. She could practically see her blue eyes sparkling with excitement. Eagerly, she told her everything about the house and what little history she knew from the letters. "I'm sure this house was owned by a family at some point and probably has good karma as well, but I see Sofiya and Alina everywhere in this house." Addie laughed. "Well, I don't actually *see* them. I can picture them here."

Valerie laughed along. "Lady, if you start seeing ghosts, that's it. I'm committing you."

They talked about Valerie's kids and her current remodeling project. Addie always felt lighter after talking to Valerie. They had so much history together—all good history. By the time she'd hung up, Addie's stress had disappeared, and she felt hopeful again.

Addie looked down at the box of letters and almost pushed them aside. They saddened her in a way that made it hard to lift herself up again. Yet, she was so connected to Sofiya and Alina's story. Addie had to know what happened next.

Zach came in and saw her staring at the box. "Are you going to read some of those tonight?" he asked. "Are you sure you want to?"

Addie looked up at him and laughed. He was covered in dirt from working on the garage apartment. "What were you doing? Rolling around on the garage floor?"

Zach looked down at his clothes, then grinned. "Yeah. That's exactly what I was doing. Seriously, though. That room upstairs is filthy. I tore out the old kitchen cabinets and tore down the paneled walls. We need to put up sturdier ones, and the electric wiring is shoddy too. But I got a good start on it."

"You'd better go shower. And don't dirty up our new bathroom."

Zach rolled his eyes. "Really? How can I not get it dirty?" He walked closer to the bed. "Are you really going to read those letters?"

Addie squinted her eyes. "Did you call Valerie and tell her to call me?"

"No, I didn't," he said seriously. "Did you talk to her?"

She nodded. "I told her about the letters and how they were connected to the house. She seemed interested in them. But she was also worried about them triggering my PTSD."

"I'm worried too. You know how hard that is on you. That's why I'm worried about the letters," Zach said.

She smiled. "I'll be fine. I promise. And if I get stressed at all, I'll start going to meetings again. Okay?"

"Okay." He took off his sweatshirt and then his T-shirt as he walked to the bathroom. Turning in the doorway, he waggled his brows. "Want to join me?"

Addie laughed. "Not on your life. You're filthy. Go shower."

He shrugged. "Can't blame a guy for trying."

As Addie opened the box and pulled out the letters, she heard the water turn on in the bathroom. She smiled to herself. She loved Zach so much—he was always there for her no matter what. She hoped Sofiya had found someone to love. Maybe the letters would reveal she had. Lifting the next sheet of paper, she began to read.

CHAPTER EIGHT

Sofiya

Time passed quickly for Sofiya despite the horror of seeing her friend being sold off night after night. By October, Miss Nora had brought in a beautiful young girl named Theodora to take Elsie's place, and she became the new favorite. All the attention was on her. Like little boys in a candy store, the gentlemen stared at her with great excitement in their eyes. The sight of it made Sofiya sick. How could these seemingly intelligent and sophisticated men be so low as to buy favors from young women? If this had gone on around Sofiya all the years she was raised in Russia, she hadn't seen it. But as she thought about the few times she was at the Winter Palace and how the men and women behaved, maybe it had happened. Perhaps people of influence behaved badly everywhere.

Sofiya was glad that the attention had been taken off Alina, but her dear friend still worked night after night, selling her body to these men. Sofiya had noticed that Alina had become colder and more distant from her—possibly as a way to keep her away from it all. Still, it hurt. She missed her fun-loving friend.

One unusually warm Sunday in early October, Miss Nora rushed into the kitchen in a tizzy. "Pack up a picnic lunch," she commanded Sofiya. "For four. And make it nice. You'll need wine and wine glasses, cheese, bread, and some of the roast beef from yesterday."

When Sofiya only stood and stared at her, Miss Nora's hands flew in the air. "Don't just stand there. Hurry!"

Sofiya sprang into action. No one had ever asked her to pack a picnic lunch before. She dug around in the closets and found a basket, then began packing the items as she'd been told. Miss Nora was pacing in her sheer robe, her slipper heals clacking on the hardwood floor. Sofiya was distracted by the fact that the woman wore heels as slippers but tried to concentrate on her work.

"This is ridiculous," Miss Nora muttered to herself. "A picnic lunch? If the young man wasn't the son of a wealthy businessman, I wouldn't even bother." She turned to Sofiya. "It's your sister he wants. Can you imagine? He insisted. But all the girls are tired from last night, and I hate to wake them up."

Sofiya watched as Miss Nora's eyes squinted at her. What could she be thinking?

"Hm. I need someone to chaperone but act like she's interested in the other man who is coming along. I'll have no funny business outside of working hours." Miss Nora placed a red painted fingernail on her cheek as she studied Sofiya. "Do you have a nicer dress than that?"

Sofiya startled. "Well, uh, yes. I do. You had Mabel pick out a couple of nice dresses for me."

"Hm. That might work," Miss Nora said. "After you pack the lunch, put on one of the new dresses. Something cheery." She studied Sofiya another minute. "And straighten your hair.

Pinch your cheeks to add color. I'll be back." She turned and hurried out the kitchen door.

Sofiya's heart raced. She hadn't liked the look on Miss Nora's face. But she finished packing the lunch and changed clothes as she'd been told. Sofiya chose the creamy white ankle-length dress, white stockings, and black leather pumps with short heels. The shoes were snug, but Sofiya hoped they'd stretch as she wore them. Her hair was up in a loose bun, and she pinned up the strands that had come loose. Knowing it was chilly out, Sofiya took her wool coat into the kitchen and sat at the table to wait. A few minutes later, Miss Nora came back with Alina in tow. Alina was also wearing a white dress with her coat hung over her arm.

"The gentlemen are waiting in the parlor," Miss Nora said. "You're to go across the street to the park with them but stay within sight of this house at all times. Do you understand?"

Both girls nodded. Sofiya glanced at Alina and saw that she looked as terrified as she felt.

"This is just a picnic—no funny business. And it ends no later than two o'clock." Miss Nora stared hard at each girl, then pointed at Sofiya. "You will make sure the men behave around Alina. You may be short, but I have a feeling you can be tough."

Miss Nora's words took Sofiya by surprise. Tough? When had she ever displayed any behavior other than submissiveness in this house? "Yes, Miss Nora," Sofiya said, because it was best to just agree.

"Fine. Go on with you now. The men are waiting." Miss Nora shooed them out of the kitchen with Sofiya carrying the heavy basket. They walked to the parlor, neither daring to say a word. Miss Nora watched from the kitchen door but didn't follow. They stopped at the parlor entrance, and two men in brown suits immediately stood up.

"Good afternoon," the taller of the two men greeted them with a smile on his face. The other man smiled and nodded, his hat in his hands.

"Good afternoon," Alina said demurely. Sofiya nodded and studied the men. They were both young, probably no more than twenty years old. The taller one was fair-haired, and the shorter one had dark hair and a funny little mustache. Their suits were expensive, and they looked as if they'd just come from church.

"Shall we?" The taller man walked over to Alina and offered his arm. Alina accepted it, and they walked toward the front door.

The other man walked up to Sofiya. "I'm Gerald. Gerald Carlson," he said, rolling the brim of his hat in his hands nervously.

"I'm Sofiya," she said softly.

"Let me take that for you." He lifted the heavy picnic basket from her hands. He crooked his other arm, and she circled her arm through his. They followed Alina and his friend outside and across the street to the park.

The man with Alina had a large leather satchel over one arm. He stopped a few feet inside the park and motioned to a spot under a large oak tree. "Will this be acceptable?" he asked Alina.

Sofiya watched as Alina nodded. She realized that Alina had been trained by Miss Nora to always be polite to the men no matter what their intentions. It saddened her to see her friend this way. Fortunately, the men had been respectful up to this point.

"I have a blanket to lay on the ground," Sofiya offered. She and Alina laid it out under the tree while the tall man began setting up the contraption he had inside his satchel.

"Here, I'll help," Gerald said. He set the basket on the blanket and helped Sofiya take items out of it while Alina went to see what the other man was doing.

"Who's your friend?" Sofiya asked Gerald. "And what is he setting up?"

"Oh. I'm sorry. He's Clinton Olafson. I believe Miss Nora is a friend of his father's."

"Oh." Sofiya was shocked to hear that Clinton knew of his father's dalliances with other women.

"He loves photography," Gerald continued. "And believe me, his family has the money to indulge his hobbies. He's setting up a camera."

Sofiya frowned. "Why?"

Gerald cocked his head and looked at her as if the question was odd. "To take photographs."

She had no idea why this young man would want to take photographs of them or their picnic. It seemed like a waste of film to her.

The day had grown warm, so the girls put their coats aside, and the foursome sat on the blanket to eat lunch. Sofiya was too distracted to eat her food, though. She didn't understand why these two men would pay Miss Nora just to have lunch with them and maybe take photos. Miss Nora had said to keep everything decent, thank goodness, but did these men have something else in mind? They'd been so polite it was hard to believe they'd suddenly become monsters.

Sofiya also noticed that Alina was warming up to Clinton. He did have a charming way about him. His smile was warm, and his eyes kind. He kept the conversation flowing, asking Alina where she'd come from and about her upbringing. Occasionally, he'd turn and smile at Sofiya in a friendly way, totally disarming her. Gerald also asked Sofiya questions and spoke softly and politely. Sofiya was careful how she answered. She couldn't tell anyone who she really was, and she and Alina had kept up the ruse about being sisters.

After they'd eaten, Clinton jumped up excitedly. "Shall we take some photographs? The light is perfect now." He lined them up with their backs toward the houses across the street. Sofiya stood on the far left with Gerald behind her on her right, then Alina. Sofiya smoothed down her dress and wrung her hands. She wasn't sure if Miss Nora would approve of them taking photographs with these men. She turned to Alina, who looked uncomfortable too. The whole situation seemed strange to Sofiya.

Clinton set a timer on the camera, then ran to pose beside Alina. Seconds before the camera clicked, Sofiya reached across Gerald and grasped Alina's hand. The girls stared into the camera, faces creased with concern, hands clasped, as the photo snapped.

Clinton asked if he could take a few more photos, and the girls agreed. The photos were all dignified and appropriate. Sofiya finally relaxed, feeling this young man had truly wanted to just spend a nice afternoon with his friend and two companions. Nothing improper was expected of them.

Despite that, Sofiya was still concerned. Miss Nora had sold her and Alina for the day to be companions for these young men. Sold. Was Nora moving Sofiya closer to becoming one of the girls? Sofiya wasn't sure she could do what Alina was forced to do each night. But she also didn't know how to escape it.

The two girls were back at the house by two, just as Nora had instructed. Alina hugged her friend and then headed up the staircase, and Sofiya walked down the hall carrying the picnic basket. Once inside the kitchen, she set the basket on the table and went to her room to change. In the doorway, Sofiya stopped, startled. Miss Nora, now dressed properly for the day, was standing in front of Sofiya's dresser, staring at the cigar box.

"Oh. You're back. Good." Miss Nora said, seeing Sofiya standing there. "I came in here looking for you. How was the picnic? Did everyone behave?"

Sofiya nodded, her heart pounding in her chest. If Miss Nora insisted on seeing what was in the cigar box, she might notice the false bottom. How could she have been so stupid as to leave her valuables in plain sight?

"Good. Those young men might want to come back. I guess it was worth the trouble." Miss Nora stared once more at the cigar box. "Why on earth do you have a cigar box in here?"

Sofiya stepped into the tiny space, her hands clasped in front of her so Miss Nora wouldn't see them shaking. "I use it to store my brush and hairpins," she said as calmly as she could manage. "I hope you don't mind. We just throw them away anyway."

"Hm. Not a bad idea." Miss Nora shrugged and brushed past Sofiya. "Well, get back to work. I'm sure you have plenty to do." With that, she left the kitchen.

Sofiya dropped onto the bed, feeling lightheaded. If Miss Nora had found her jewelry, she'd take it away and never give it back. The jewelry was the only thing Sofiya had that could help get her out of this terrible place. She couldn't bear the thought of losing it.

Finally, Sofiya stood and changed into her work clothes. She had recovered from her fright, and she had to prepare the dinner trays for the girls. By the time she started working again, the picnic with the young men was all but forgotten.

* * *

A week after Clinton had paid to have lunch with Alina and Sofiya, he began showing up in the evenings with the other men. Sofiya recognized him immediately, and he smiled and nodded at her as she served food. Gerald, however, never came with him. Sofiya noticed that Clinton never came on the nights his father was there. She found it odd that a young man would want to patronize an establishment such as this. Someone like him, with a wealthy father, should have multiple eligible girls vying for his attention. Why would he pay to spend time with a girl?

The answer became clearer when Clinton requested to spend time with Alina on each visit. After several weeks of this, Alina blushed when Sofiya asked about Clinton's obsession with her.

"He's very kind," Alina said, smiling. "And rather handsome in his own way, don't you think?"

Sofiya feared Alina was falling in love with Clinton. Miss Nora would have a fit if she thought the two were becoming close. "Be careful," Sofiya warned her friend quietly as Alina picked up her dinner tray that night. "You know Miss Nora will send him away for good if she thinks he's sweet on you."

Alina leaned in and whispered, "She wouldn't dare. His father is a regular customer and would be very upset if Miss Nora denied his son. But I will be careful."

Sofiya tried to understand how Alina could feel affection for a man who paid for her attention. It was all so confusing to her. Less than a year ago, they were young girls who only knew how to flirt over their fans with young boys who could only touch them when they danced together. Now, it was unthinkable to Sofiya what poor Alina had to do.

The nights grew colder as November set in, and Sofiya was busy keeping the fireplaces heated around the house. They used coal for heat, and it was a dirty job sweeping out the soot and placing the coals. Every morning Sofiya went from room to room restarting fireplaces that had cooled overnight. The girls maintained the fires once they were started. Between cooking, baking, and cleaning, Sofiya was constantly running.

One brisk morning there was a knock on the outside kitchen door as Sofiya returned from starting fires. Glancing around, she noticed Mrs. Jarvi hadn't arrived yet, so she quickly answered the door.

"My, but it's a cold one out there today," a young man bellowed as he walked inside, right past Sofiya. He carried a large box, and the scrumptious smell of fresh bread and rolls wafted from it. He set the box on the table and backed up near the stove, rubbing his hands together for warmth. His expression changed to surprise when he noticed Sofiya had been the one who opened the door.

"Oh. Goodness," he said, then laughed. "I'm sorry. I thought you were Mrs. Jarvi. Who are you?"

Sofiya closed the door and backed up a step. "I'm Sofiya. I work in the kitchen with Mrs. Jarvi." She rarely answered the door to their many delivery men because she was always so busy cleaning the other rooms.

"I had no idea she had help." The young man smiled, his

blue eyes twinkling. "I'm Harry." He reached out his hand to shake Sofiya's.

Sofiya went to shake his hand but pulled it away immediately when she realized how dirty her hands were. She felt the heat of a blush rise in her cheeks.

Harry grinned. "Using coal for fires sure is messy, isn't it?" She nodded.

"Well, it's nice to meet you, Sofiya. Did you know your name means 'wisdom' in the Russian language?" Harry said.

Sofiya startled and took another step back. "Are you Russian?"

"No, no. Our family is German. But I love to read anything I can get my hands on. And I find the meaning of names quite interesting," he said.

Sofiya relaxed and smiled. "What is the meaning of Harry?"

He gave her a sideways look and grin, then broke out laughing. "I suppose Harry means hairy," he said. "My true name is Harold, which means to wield power or be a leader. Many old-time kings were named Harold."

Sofiya couldn't help but smile at Harry. He was so full of energy and life that he lit up the room like a light bulb.

"I must be off to finish my deliveries," he said, tipping his newsboy cap. "Have a lovely day, Miss Sofiya." He turned and left as quickly as he'd entered just moments before.

"That boy!" Mrs. Jarvi said as she passed him on her way inside. "He's a joker, that one." But her cheeks were red with cheer because Harry had quipped something amusing to her as they passed each other. Sofiya hadn't heard what he'd said, but she could only imagine what it was.

Sofiya set about her day of work and was surprised that long after Harry had left, she was still thinking about his twinkling blue eyes.

CHAPTER NINE

Addie

Addie awoke the next day in a lighter mood. She hadn't experienced any nightmares as she slept and felt calmer and ready to tackle that day's projects.

Sofiya's letters had told of some serious incidents, but Addie tried not to let what happened over a hundred years ago affect her own state of mind. It was imperative she kept her life separate from Sofiya's, despite the similarities. It was the only way she could protect herself from falling into a state of depression.

Still, as Addie began work on the parlor, she couldn't help but picture Sofiya going about her work in there, cleaning and starting the fireplace, tidying up after the previous evening, or serving trays of food to the many gentlemen who frequented the establishment. Addie wondered if Sofiya had felt the same disgust about those men that Addie had over the men who'd used her without a care for her feelings. And to see her dear friend, Alina, having to sell herself to those men had to have been hard for Sofiya. But like so many women throughout the ages, they were trapped in their circumstances.

Addie transferred her anger at those long-ago men to her work at hand, tearing down the eighties-style wallpaper, only to find several other eras underneath. Finally, she came to what she assumed was the very first paper from the 1890s. Again, as in the bedroom, it was bold in color—a red and black medallion-style. She stared at it a moment, trying to imagine this wallpaper all around with the gleaming woodwork and possibly deep red velvet curtains hanging over the windows. Yes, it would be a warm, inviting place for men to sit by the fire and ogle all the pretty young girls, knowing they had the money to buy a night with any one of them.

Addie shivered at the thought. She ripped the paper harder than necessary, causing the plaster underneath to come off with it. Taking a deep breath, Addie backed away from her work. "I guess I'm not as Zen about the letters as I'd thought," she mumbled to the empty room.

Walking out of the parlor, Addie headed to the kitchen and made herself a cup of tea. She glanced around, liking what Zach had accomplished so far. But again, she saw Sofiya standing at the stove or cutting vegetables at the wooden table that had stood in the center of the kitchen where they were going to place an island.

"Done with work already?"

Addie jumped, nearly spilling her mug of tea. "Sheesh. Where did you come from? I thought you were out in the garage."

Zach chuckled. "I came in through the front door. I was talking with Gail's son. He seems like a nice kid."

"Oh." Addie shook her head out of the past and tried to remember if she'd met the boy yet. "How old is he?"

"Seventeen. He was wondering if I'd like help with the

garage apartment. Nice of him to ask, but we can't really afford an extra hand right now."

She nodded. Their money would be tight until they either sold or rented this house. "It was nice of him to ask."

"Yeah." Zach stared at her a moment. "Are you okay? You seem out of it."

She focused on him for the first time since he'd walked in. "I thought I was fine, but I guess I'm not. I keep picturing Sofiya in every room of this house. I guess I'm having more trouble than I thought separating myself from her."

Zach walked over and set his hand on her shoulder. "It's good you're being honest with yourself instead of trying to ignore your feelings."

She nodded. "I think Valerie was right. I need to get back into volunteering at the center. And I need to make an appointment with Laurie. Otherwise, this house, and Sofiya's letters, are going to consume me."

"I think that's a good idea." Zach leaned over and kissed her on the cheek. "And the sooner, the better."

Addie worried her bottom lip with her teeth. "But it'll take time away from my work here."

He shrugged. "The work isn't going anywhere. It'll be here when you are. A few more days here or there won't hurt."

Addie set her mug on their old table and wrapped her arms around Zach. "I'm so lucky to have you," she whispered into his ear.

He hugged her tightly. "I think it's the other way around."

After pulling away, Addie lifted her mug again and took a sip. "Today, though, I'm going to go full-blown crazy on that wallpaper in the parlor. And I'll be thinking about Nora Petrov with every piece I rip off the wall." She grinned.

"Well, there are all types of therapy," he said, laughing.

Addie spent the rest of the day tearing and scraping wallpaper off the walls. It was a tedious job, but she wore her earbuds and listened to her favorite music as she did it. The music kept her mind off Sofiya, and the work was good for her. By evening, she'd cleared off one side of the parlor, and tomorrow she'd do the same with the opposite side and back wall. It would take time because she didn't want to damage the old plaster. Addie didn't mind the work because it helped to keep her mind clear.

That evening, after they'd eaten take-out, Addie sat at the kitchen table and skimmed through her favorite vintage wallpaper website. She wanted to replace the parlor wallpaper with something lighter but from the same era as the house. The site had reproductions of wallpaper from many different time periods.

It was only seven o'clock, and Zach was working on the garage again. Addie sighed. She'd put it off long enough. Scrolling through her phone, she found Laurie Shepherd's number, and after only a moment's hesitation, her thumb hit the call button.

Laurie answered on the second ring. "I was just thinking about you," she said in her velvety voice. "How are you, dear?"

All the stress Addie had felt building up inside her slipped away at the sound of Laurie's voice. "I'm fine. Well, I'm working and happy, but I'm stressed."

"Tell me what's wrong."

The story tumbled from Addie's lips, and every word melted away the tension she'd been feeling. She told Laurie about the letters, the house, and Sofiya's story. "It's so strange, though," Addie said after she'd told her everything. "I feel like I belong here, but on the other hand, it's bringing back the bad memories."

"That doesn't surprise me," Laurie said. "You're a very intuitive person. The fact that you felt drawn to that house means you're supposed to be there. It's your past and your future colliding. That's why it's hard on you."

"So, you believe this place is my destiny?" Addie asked. It surprised her to hear Laurie speaking like this. Generally, Laurie's words were straightforward and tied completely to reality—not mysticism.

"I think it's your purpose. This house will give you a chance to right all the wrongs against you, against Sofiya, and all the other girls who suffered there. This may be your legacy."

Addie sat there in disbelief at what her old friend was saying. "Am I speaking to the right Laurie Shepherd? You don't sound like the down-to-earth counselor I know."

Laurie laughed. "I've always been spiritual, you know that. And I think of us as contemporaries now. You're as knowledgeable as I am about the healing process for those who've been damaged. That's why I was thinking about you earlier. I have a very cynical group of young women who've been put through the wringer by life. They don't believe in anything, let alone changing their paths and their futures. I think you'd be a great inspiration to them."

"I don't feel inspirational," Addie said, her heart sinking. "I've been a bit fragile lately."

"You need to fill up your own well before you can help fill up someone else's. Do you have time to meet for breakfast tomorrow morning? Around nine? We can talk."

"I'd love that. Thank you." They decided to meet at a little coffee shop near the house where Laurie counseled young women. After saying goodbye, Addie thought about what Laurie had said. The house was her purpose. Hadn't she told

Zach the same thing? That this house felt like her destiny? Yet, it was taking as much from her as she was giving back to it. It sounded so strange to think something that happened a century ago could be connected to her. But there was no denying it—she and Sofiya and Alina shared a past despite how far apart in years they'd lived.

As Addie crawled into bed that night, her fingers and hands were sore from pulling down the wallpaper, and her back was tired from standing all day. She glanced over at Zach, who'd already fallen into a deep sleep. She smiled. Zach was doing double time trying to finish the kitchen and update the garage apartment. But he never complained. She loved that about him.

Lifting the cigar box lid, Addie pulled out a few more sheets of paper. She couldn't stop wanting to learn more about Sofiya's life. So, taking a deep breath, she began to read.

CHAPTER TEN

Sofiya

1917–1918

The winter passed slowly for Sofiya as she worked hard every day. She had little to look forward to and felt like she and Alina would be trapped in this house forever. Neither girl was allowed to leave the house except to walk in the backyard. Even then, Miss Nora kept a sharp watch on all the girls. It felt like a prison.

The only bright spot in Sofiya's meager existence was the three days a week when Harry delivered fresh bread and rolls. He appeared at the back door promptly at nine each Monday, Wednesday, and Friday mornings. Sofiya hurried to finish lighting the fires in time to wash her hands just as Harry knocked on the door.

"Well, good morning, Miss Sofiya," he'd say with a bright smile on his face. It didn't matter if it was raining or snowing outside or if the bitter wind was whipping up from the river. His eyes twinkled, and his smile could brighten even her worst day.

Sofiya always offered him a cup of hot tea, and he'd sit and chat with her and Mrs. Jarvi for a few minutes before announcing he'd best be off or he'd be fired.

"But your father would never fire you," Sofiya would say, laughing.

Harry would wink and shrug. "I suppose he could if he really wanted to."

Sofiya treasured those few minutes in the mornings that she spent with Harry. Even Mrs. Jarvi was cheerier after his visits.

"What's going on between you two young people?" Mrs. Jarvi asked after one such visit. "I hope you aren't falling for that boy."

Sofiya had felt the heat of a blush rise to her cheeks. "No, no. It's nothing like that. I just enjoy his cheerful company," she'd said quickly.

"Well, I have no problem with you and him," Mrs. Jarvi had told her with a warm smile. "But don't let Miss Nora see you smiling his way. She'd make sure you never saw him again, that's for sure."

Sofiya thought about that comment often as she cleaned the house and cooked meals. She knew Mrs. Jarvi was right— Miss Nora would be angry if she saw her and Harry talking and laughing. Nora was an angry, bitter woman and wouldn't tolerate it.

The Christmas holiday came, and it was Sofiya's job to decorate the parlor with pine boughs, ribbons, candles, and the beautiful glass ornaments that Carter had brought down in boxes from the attic. Carter also bought a large blue spruce tree the week before the holiday, and the girls came downstairs in a rare appearance during the day and giggled as they decorated it. The house looked warm and festive, but there was little time to enjoy any type of Christmas celebration. The men came each night, as usual, and the girls worked. Even on Christmas Eve, some of the men without families came to cheer themselves up. And Christmas Day was like any other day, where Sofiya worked all day and prepared meals for the girls. There were no gifts or a special meal together.

Christmas Day memories of past celebrations back home brought tears to Sofiya's eyes. She missed her parents dearly, as well as her royal cousins and all the festivities they'd enjoyed. She wished she could write to her maman and père and receive letters from them. Sofiya wondered how they were faring under the new government and if the war was raging around them. She prayed each night that her parents were safe.

The day after Christmas was a Wednesday, and Sofiya worked as quickly as she could so she wouldn't miss Harry's delivery. She'd cried herself to sleep the night before, and she knew she looked a mess from cleaning out the fireplaces, but she washed her hands and face as well as she could in the little water closet and hurried inside the kitchen just as Mrs. Jarvi opened the door.

"Merry Christmas!" Harry bellowed, a big smile on his face. He dropped the box of fresh bread and rolls on the table, and the delicious smell wafted through the small kitchen.

Sofiya's heart warmed as it usually did when she saw him. "Merry Christmas," she said, unable to stop smiling. "But in truth, Christmas is over."

"Christmas is over?" Harry's face displayed shock. "Why, how could such a lovely holiday be over already? I think we should celebrate it every day."

"Amen to that," Mrs. Jarvi said as she took the kettle off the stove. "But then work would never get finished."

Harry chuckled. "There's more to life than work," he said, then lowered his voice. "There's a gift for you ladies inside the box. It's just for the two of you—don't share with anyone else."

Excitedly, Sofiya peered inside the box and saw another smaller box. She lifted it out and opened the lid. Inside were the most beautiful iced cookies she'd ever seen.

Mrs. Jarvi glanced over Sofiya's shoulder. "Ah, your mother's delicious holiday cookies. How sweet of you, dear."

"They look too beautiful to eat," Sofiya said. They reminded her of the type of treats the Tsarina served to the children around Christmas.

"Sit down a bit, Harry, and we'll share some tea and our cookies with you," Mrs. Jarvi said as she poured the hot liquid into cups. They sipped their tea, and each ate one of the sweet treats.

"Heavenly." Sofiya sighed, which made Harry chuckle. "I haven't had anything like this since leaving Russ...Finland," she corrected herself quickly.

Mrs. Jarvi stood and made an excuse of bringing a breakfast tray out to Carter—which Sofiya knew she never did. It left Sofiya and Harry alone in the kitchen, each eating another of the delicious cookies.

"My parents host a small family New Year's Eve party each year. It's mostly just uncles, aunts, and children. All my siblings, too, of course. I was wondering if you'd like to join us this year." Harry watched Sofiya with anticipation in his eyes.

"Oh, my." Sofiya was taken aback. She'd never thought that such a handsome, gregarious man as Harry would even look at her twice. "I would love to meet your family," she said, "but I'm not sure Miss Nora would allow me to go. I'm sure I will have to work that night."

His brows rose. "Work?"

She realized what he must be thinking. That perhaps she was one of the girls in the house, too. He surely knew what type of house this was. "Oh, no. Not like that. I serve the gentlemen food in the early evening in the parlor. I'm so sorry. It sounds like a lovely time."

The smile returned to Harry's face. "Don't worry. It was just a thought. Perhaps we can meet another time. With a chaperone, of course," he said quickly.

"That's so sweet of you," she said. "Perhaps we can." But she knew Miss Nora would never allow her to go on an outing with Harry. She wasn't even allowed to leave the house.

After Harry left, Sofiya's heart was heavy. She was only sixteen, but she felt decades older. Would she ever be free to make her own decisions? She was drawn to Harry—he seemed like a truly good person. But he'd never be allowed to court her as long as Sofiya lived under Nora Petrov's roof.

"Why the long face today?" Mrs. Jarvi asked later that afternoon. "Your sweetheart brought you cookies—you should be happy."

"We're not sweethearts," Sofiya said quickly. "And he brought the cookies for the both of us."

Mrs. Jarvi shook her head and clucked her tongue. "I'm under no illusion that he brought those for me. It was a gift for you because he's sweet on you. Even a blind man could see that."

Sofiya sighed as she set out the trays for the girls' dinner. "What good is it if he likes me or not? Miss Nora would never let him court me."

The older woman stopped stirring the pot of soup on the

stove and turned to Sofiya. "I'm afraid you're right." Her face pinched into a sour expression. "She thinks she owns people. But don't you worry, dear. You can see him on his delivery days, and we'll think of other ways for you two to spend time together. Properly, of course." She grinned.

This made Sofiya smile, but she knew she could never attend any events or go on outings with Harry. Eventually, he'd give up and look for another girl.

The girls came down in pairs to retrieve their trays. Mabel came alone, surprising Sofiya since Alina usually came down with her. Alina was the last to come down. She stood there a moment, looking as if she wanted to speak to Sofiya, but was wary of Mrs. Jarvi. The older woman seemed to take the hint.

"Well, I am off for the evening," Mrs. Jarvi announced. "I will see you tomorrow, ladies." She bundled up in her boots, coat, and scarf, and headed out the door.

"Is something wrong?" Sofiya asked in a quiet voice.

Alina bit her lip. She looked like she was going to cry. "I received a letter from home. Miss Nora allows me to write to my parents as long as she can read each letter first. I've asked about your parents, but I had to be careful that Miss Nora didn't suspect anything, so I called them our dear friends, the Hanikoffs."

This was the first that Sofiya had heard of Alina corresponding with her parents. A wave of jealously swept through her. Her maman had forbidden her to send letters so that no one would ever find her in America. While she understood it was for her own safety, it hurt to know that Alina was able to write and she wasn't.

"What are you so upset about? Are your parents well?" Sofiya asked, despite being sad. She was fond of Alina's parents and wished them no harm.

"Things are growing tense where my parents live. Finland is in a state of change, and my parents fear a civil war is at hand. They are trying to find a way out of there before things get worse, and they'll be forced to stay."

"I'm so sorry," Sofiya said, placing her arm around her friend. "I do hope they're able to leave."

Alina nodded. Sofiya noticed the dark rings under her eyes. Her friend, once the most beautiful girl she'd ever known, now looked colorless and tired. Even her lovely blond hair was not as shiny and thick. Sofiya knew this life was wearing on Alina, and she wished she could help her.

"There's more," Alina said softly. "My mother wrote that your parents were forced out of their lovely home a few months ago—not long after we'd left. They are now living in a tiny apartment, and their house, and its contents, were given to a high-ranking military man and his family. And your father lost his teaching job. The last my mother heard from them was they were trying to escape the country and go to London. My mother hasn't heard anything since."

Sofiya's heart lurched. How would her parents live without her father's income? And the idea that her childhood home had been taken away from her parents brought tears to her eyes.

"I'm so sorry to give you this news," Alina said. "I will pray for your parent's safety."

Sofiya nodded as she brushed away her tears. "And yours, too," she managed to choke out.

"What is going on in here?" Nora's voice boomed in the kitchen. Sofiya looked up, startled by her sudden appearance.

"We were only talking," she told Miss Nora. "Alina was telling me what our parents said in their letter."

"Well, let's do less talking and more work. Alina, go to your room, please. And Sofiya. Get back to work." Nora spun on her heel and headed back out the kitchen door.

With a heavy heart, Sofiya continued her work, but her thoughts were on her parents all evening. Now she understood why her maman was so adamant that she leave. Her maman saw what their world was coming to and maybe understood that things would become tough for them. Sofiya knew the war had been ravaging her country and others around them for years, but it hadn't hit St. Petersburg—which had been renamed Petrograd—until Tsar Nicholas had been forced to abdicate. At that point, her maman must have known things would change quickly.

Once Sofiya was dismissed that evening after serving the gentlemen, she went to the kitchen and picked up the newspapers that Miss Nora placed there when she was finished reading them. Mrs. Jarvi always read the paper early in the morning before bringing it to Miss Nora in the early afternoon, but Sofiya had ignored the news since coming here. She'd been so wrapped up in her own troubles she hadn't thought about the war in Europe or the problems in Russia. She knew the United States had joined in on the war around the time she'd arrived, but it hadn't affected her everyday life. Being stuck inside this house had kept her from the real world outside.

Before going to sleep, Sofiya sat on her bed and read through The Oregonian newspapers. The headlines told of the war in Europe, but there was nothing about Russia and Finland. After reading the papers, she pulled out her writing paper and began a letter to her maman that she knew she'd never be able to send.

Dear Maman,

*I understand now why you felt you needed to send me
away. I have heard what is happening to you and père,
and I am so sad for you both. I hope you are able to leave
and go to a safer place. I also pray that if you do, you will
be able to contact me. Maybe we can be together again.
You do not know how much I wish for that.*

Sofiya went on to write about her life at Miss Nora's, knowing that her mother would never read her words. Because if her
mother knew what type of place Sofiya and Alina were living
in, her heart would be broken.

* * *

As the weeks passed, Sofiya continued to read the newspaper
each night before bed. In early February, she saw an article where
a former military advisor to the Tsar, who was now in prison,
claimed, "Czarism is Gone for Good." It had been almost a
year since the Tsar had abdicated, and the new government had
taken over in Russia. There was constant in-fighting happening
in Russia, and Sofiya's beloved hometown was besieged with
troubles. The article saddened Sofiya, who had fond memories
of the Tsar, Tsarina, and the children. But another article she
read upset her even more. It proclaimed that all Portland residents of German descent who had not become citizens were
ordered to register at the Portland Police Department starting
on Monday.

Sofiya wondered if Harry's parents had become naturalized.
She worried if this aggression toward Germans would affect his

parent's business. She hadn't met his parents, but if they were like Harry, Sofiya thought they must be decent people.

The next day, she noticed that Harry wasn't as carefree and cheerful as he usually was. He joined her and Mrs. Jarvi for a cup of hot tea but then said he must be on his way. As Sofiya walked him to the door, she drew up all her courage and asked, "How are your parents? I read the decree in the newspaper about German immigrants having to register."

Harry's young face grew strained, and his usually bright blue eyes looked dull. "My father went to register today. He's never applied for citizenship, although he did file a declaration of intention years ago to become a citizen. Unfortunately, he never continued the process."

"What does that mean for your family?" Sofiya asked, concerned. "And your father's business?"

Harry nervously fingered his newsboy cap. "I don't know. We've lost some of our regular customers over the past months because they won't do business with Germans. Some people think all Germans are evil." His face tightened. "My father is going to try to apply for citizenship when he registers. He's a good person and a hard worker. If he can begin the process, he believes people will accept him as an American."

Sofiya's heart ached for her friend. She placed a comforting hand on his arm. "I hope he can do that. I'm sorry things have been hard for your family."

Harry's face softened as he looked directly into Sofiya's eyes. "Thank you. You are very kind. But I should be the one asking about your family. How are they faring during this war? From what I've read, there is turmoil in Finland, especially the areas closest to Petrograd."

Sofiya dropped her eyes, unable to lie directly to Harry. "My parents are trying to leave the country, possibly for London. I am praying that they will be able to leave safely."

Taking her hands in his, Harry said softly. "I will pray for your family, too."

"Thank you," she whispered. She liked the feel of his warm hands holding hers.

With that, Harry nodded, placed his cap on his head, and walked out the door to finish his deliveries.

After Sofiya closed the door, she noticed Mrs. Jarvi pretending to have not heard the conversation between the two young people. Sofiya returned to work, putting away the loaves of bread and the rolls, then slicing a roast from the day before to make sandwiches for the girls' lunches. Sofiya was thankful she worked with a kind woman like Mrs. Jarvi and that she had Harry to brighten her days. She hoped her parents would be able to escape Russia, that Alina's parents were able to leave Finland, and that all would work out for Harry's parents. The entire world was sitting on a precipice, and Sofiya's little world felt like it could also fall apart at any moment. All she could do was hope for the best.

CHAPTER ELEVEN

Addie

Addie met Laurie Shepherd the following morning as planned. She arrived a few minutes early and had already been seated when Laurie walked through the café's glass door. Seeing her old friend made Addie smile. Laurie's dark curls bounced as she walked, and her brown skin glowed against the amber-colored T-shirt she wore underneath a white cardigan. When they hugged, the familiar scent of jasmine surrounded Addie, and all the tension she'd been feeling dissipated.

Laurie sat in the booth across from Addie and watched her with deep brown eyes. Addie knew those eyes well. She'd stared into them many times while searching for answers to the hard questions of how to move her life forward after all the pain she'd experienced.

"I'm so happy to see you," Laurie said, smiling. "You look great."

"You do, too," Addie said. "I'm sorry it's been so long."

A waitress came and took Laurie's order for coffee, and both women ordered a light breakfast of two eggs and toast.

After she'd left, Laurie's expression grew serious.

"Now. Tell me what's going on."

Addie sighed. "Everything had been going well the past couple of years. I've been busy flipping houses and so happy with Zach. I thought I'd finally put the past behind me. But then we found the letters, and the house, and my past raced back into my life."

Laurie nodded. "It can happen at any time. PTSD is a fickle character. That's why it's always good to have someone you can confide in when it flares up."

"I know," Addie said. "But sometimes, I wish I could leave it all behind me." She remembered when she'd first gone to Laurie for help. It had been about a year after she'd escaped and a couple of months after she'd started working and living with Valerie. Small things would set her off, like someone coming up behind her quietly or a stranger staring at her a bit too long. Fear rippled through her and paralyzed her. The fear that her captor had found her. The fear that someone would drag her back into the life of selling her body for money—money that she had to turn over to her trafficker. Nightmares had plagued her every night. Even though she'd loved living and working with Valerie, she'd still needed counseling to learn how to live freely again.

The waitress brought their food, and both women ate as they talked. Addie told Laurie more about Sofiya's life and how the house had been connected to her. Laurie spoke about the women she'd worked with and the group she was working with now.

"I have a group of five women living in the safe house, and it's been slow-going trying to get them to believe that their life can get better," Laurie said. "Some of these women have been on the streets for years. And the oldest is only nineteen. They don't know anything else. It's heartbreaking."

"But they must want help, or else they wouldn't have come to you," Addie said. Laurie's safe house was completely voluntary. But if the women wanted to live there, they had to attend counseling sessions, plus go to school to better their lives or work at a job. If they chose to go back on the streets, then they had to leave the house.

"Yes," Laurie said as she spread jelly on her toast. "They did come for help. It's just hard sometimes to help them stay focused on the end game of living a good, clean life. Some went through rehab for drug abuse before coming to me. They've all had a tough road."

Addie nodded. "I can understand that."

This made Laurie smile. "Yes. You can. That's why I think it would be wonderful if you could come to a couple of meetings and share your experiences with them. If the women see how far you've come, it might encourage them to keep working toward a new future."

Addie thought about that as she sipped her coffee. In the past, she'd attended meetings to encourage the women Laurie was counseling. But Addie had felt confident about what she was doing back then. Right now, she was struggling to keep her wits about her with all that was going on in her life.

"It might help to attend a few meetings, too," Laurie said gently. "As a reminder of how to deal with your recent anxiety."

"You're right," Addie said. She trusted Laurie completely, and if her good friend thought going to the meetings might help, then she would.

They parted ways half an hour later after Laurie shared the time for their next meeting. The two women hugged goodbye outside the café.

"Seven o'clock tomorrow night at the house," Laurie said. "I'll see you there."

Addie nodded, then turned in the opposite direction to walk the several blocks to her house. It was early July, and the cool morning temperature was beginning to rise. By the time Addie arrived at the house, she felt quite warm.

Addie worked all day on the parlor, scraping the remnants of wallpaper off the walls, being careful not to harm the plaster underneath. She'd already ordered rolls of wallpaper to replace it with and hoped to have the woodwork sanded and stained by the time the paper arrived. Often, during a remodel, there was a lot of waiting for items to come in. So, Addie always tried to have other projects to do so as not to waste time.

As she worked, Addie thought about what she'd say to the women in the group at Laurie's. It had been at least two years since she'd attended a group session and shared her own experiences. She knew she had to gather her thoughts if she was going to share the darkest days of her life with these women. Reliving it was difficult, but Addie always felt better after sharing her story. She couldn't explain why. It made her feel lighter like she wasn't carrying the heavy load all alone.

Zach found her in the parlor, sanding the baseboard molding. "Hey, there. How did your meeting go with Laurie?"

Addie slowly straightened up, having been bent over on her knees for a long time. "Ugh! I'm getting old," she said with a laugh. Once she was standing, she continued. "We had a good talk. She asked me to come and share my experiences with the current group of women she's working with."

Zach's brows shot up. "Will you be okay with that?"

She nodded. "I've done it many times before. I think it'll

be good therapy for me to share my story with women who understand what I went through. And it'll encourage them to see how well I'm doing now."

"That's great," Zach said. "Maybe Sofiya's letters won't bother you as much after sharing with the other women. You always seem to be less stressed after doing that."

Addie's heart warmed at how well Zach knew her. "My thoughts exactly. I may attend a few meetings, too, just to clear my head. I've missed talking with Laurie."

"That's a good idea," he said. "Whatever it takes to keep your sanity."

Addie laughed. "Are you saying I'm crazy?"

He moved closer and pulled her into a hug. "Well, just a little." Zach kissed her softly. "I mean, you bought this ridiculously expensive house, and now you think you might keep it. That's not normal." He smirked.

This made Addie laugh even harder. "That is a bit crazy. I know in my head that I'll never be able to keep this expensive house, but my heart wants to."

Hugging her closer, he whispered in her ear. "Following your heart isn't such a bad idea, either."

She'd followed her heart right into Zach's arms, so Addie knew he was right.

* * *

The next evening Addie drove across the river on the Fremont Bridge to Laurie's craftsman-style house on NE Hancock Street. When she parked, she glanced around the cute, quiet neighborhood as the sun set. All the homes here were a century old but had been kept up nicely. The fact that the neighbors allowed Laurie to run a safe house here—actually voted one hundred percent at the neighborhood meeting to approve it—made Addie love the neighborhood even more. It was definitely a good, stable environment to change your life.

Taking a deep breath to steel her nerves, Addie stepped out of the car and walked up the sidewalk to the porch steps. The house was warm and inviting. Mature oak trees sat in the front yard, and there was an open front porch that led to the door. Addie knew the interior by heart—four bedrooms upstairs with one bathroom, a master bedroom downstairs with a master bath, and a large extra room on the third floor. There was a roomy living area, dining room, and an open-concept kitchen that had been remodeled since Laurie bought the place. Everything in the house, from the warm brown woodwork to the furniture, was welcoming.

Before Addie could knock, Laurie opened the door with a big smile.

"I'm so glad you came," her friend said, giving her a welcoming hug.

"Were you afraid I wouldn't?" Addie asked, surprised.

Laurie's brows rose. "Well…you never know. You were a bit hesitant."

Addie let out a sigh. "I'm here. I need to be here. So, let's meet the other women."

Laurie smiled and led Addie to the living room on the right. The five other women were already seated on the two sofas that sat in an L-shape around the square coffee table. Laurie offered Addie a big, cushy chair and then sat in a dining room chair next to her.

"Ladies, this is Addison Cameron, but you can call her Addie. She's the woman I was telling you about who has built up a house flipping business over the past fifteen years," Laurie said. She turned to Addie. "This is Latisha, Tonya, Melanie, Izzie, short for Isabella, and Wanda." She pointed to each girl as she introduced them.

"Hi," Addie said. "It's nice to meet all of you." It didn't surprise her how young they looked or the wary expressions on their faces. She'd once looked that suspicious of strangers, too.

"You don't look like a successful businesswoman," Izzie said from her spot on the sofa.

This made Addie laugh. She'd dressed casually in jeans, a T-shirt, and sneakers. She rarely dressed up since all she did was get dirty working anyway. "No, I guess I don't. I actually work on the houses myself, so I'm always sanding, scraping, or painting something. Dressing up isn't my thing."

"How did you learn to flip houses?" Melanie asked shyly. Her long blond hair practically hid her face from view, but she looked interested.

"A very kind woman saw my interest and offered me a job helping her," Addie said, talking about Valerie. "I was nineteen and about a year out of *the life* living in an unsafe neighborhood and working as a waitress in a café. She gave me a chance, and I'll be forever grateful."

Latisha grunted, her arms crossed over her chest. "That's great for you. But who's going to offer any of us opportunities like that?"

"I don't see why you can't have the same opportunities," Addie said seriously. "I came from the same place as all of you. It takes work to get back into a mainstream life, but it can be done."

"So, what's your story?" Tonya asked. Her brown eyes were lined with dark eyeliner, and she wore bright red lipstick, but underneath the thick makeup, she had a pretty face.

Addie took a deep breath and let it out slowly. Then she began.

"I grew up in Iowa. In a town named Ames. We weren't rich, but we had a place to live and food on the table. I was an only child. My mother had always been a drinker, but my father kept things together. He worked for UPS, packing trucks. He also picked up any odd jobs he could find. He was a good guy.

"He was killed in a car accident one night as he and my mom returned from being out for the evening. My mom was driving drunk and only got scratched up, but my dad died on impact. I was ten years old when that happened."

"That's messed up," Izzie said. "I lost my dad too. Sorry."

Addie's heart warmed at Izzie's words. "Thank you," she said softly. She cleared her throat and continued.

"Things went from bad to worse over the next couple of years. My mom couldn't hold down a job, and her drinking grew worse. She had one DUI after another until she'd had one too many. They locked her up, and I was placed in a foster home when I was twelve. We had no relatives to take me in—I'd never even met any of my grandparents. So, for two years, I was in and out of foster homes. My mom got out once but was put back in for breaking parole. It was like she'd given up on life—and me."

"She couldn't take care of herself, let alone you," Laurie said gently. "It's sad, but unfortunately, it happens."

Addie nodded, and Melanie spoke up. "My mom wouldn't stop doing meth. She did it until it killed her."

"I'm sorry," Addie said, her heart going out to the girl. Melanie couldn't have been more than fifteen.

Melanie shrugged. "Thanks."

Addie continued. "At fourteen, I was in a foster home that I hated. The foster parents' son kept coming on to me, and they wouldn't do anything about it. So, I ran away and ended up on the streets. I was this naïve girl from Iowa. I knew nothing about living on the streets. A couple of other teen girls befriended me, and we did our best to stay alive. What I didn't know was they were working with a trafficker to pick up young girls. After a few days of helping me and gaining my trust, they took me to a hotel where they said we'd be safe. That's when they turned me over to him."

All the girls nodded except for Latisha. They understood what Addie was saying. "Him" was the guy who'd sell her to make money. But Latisha's story was different.

"I wasn't taken to anyone," Latisha said. "I left home because it was a terrible place to live, and I chose to sell myself for sex to earn money. It wasn't until later that someone pushed their way in and stole my independence."

"No matter how we got there, we're all still victims of a crime," Laurie spoke up. "None of us asked for the cards we were dealt."

The girls sat silent, as did Addie. Addie knew Laurie spoke from experience. Laurie didn't just happen to start helping young women—she'd been one of them once, a long time ago. Addie knew her story, and it was even more horrific than her own. She had a lot of respect for how far Laurie had come since her days on the streets.

Laurie nodded at her, and Addie continued her story. "I wasn't a particularly tough girl or strong-minded, so it didn't take much persuasion from the guy to pull me into *the life*."

"By that you mean he only beat you up a couple of times, right?" Tonya said seriously.

Addie nodded. "Yes. We all know how they persuade you. I didn't have it in me to fight back. I was too young and too green. So, I just did as I was told. A group of five girls, including me, were put in a van and taken to a large travel center gas station on the fringes of Des Moines. The other girls knew what their job was, and they were the ones who taught me what I was supposed to do. If the trafficker was around, I never saw him. He kept a low profile." She stopped a moment, remembering the very first time a trucker paid her for sex. All the disgust she'd felt then washed over her now. Memories like that never went away. They were the ones that gave her nightmares despite the years that had passed.

"Are you okay," Laurie asked, placing her hand on Addie's arm. Addie turned to her and again found strength in her warm, brown eyes. Addie nodded, swallowed hard, and continued.

"Well, I won't go into the details. It was awful. For three years, it was hell. As you all know." Addie took another deep breath and let it out slowly. "Every few weeks, I was moved from one truck stop to another. It became so routine that I was able to blank out and not think when I was with a guy. It was my way of protecting myself. Because if I'd thought about what I was forced to do, I would have fallen to pieces."

"Did you do drugs?" Latisha asked.

Addie shook her head. "No, but they were always readily available. In fact, my trafficker preferred the girls do drugs—it kept them indebted to him. But I refused, and he didn't push it as long as I did what I was told." Addie never called her captor by name because he didn't deserve to be acknowledged as human. That was something that Laurie had taught her. He was her captor or trafficker. She never wanted to think of him as anything other than that.

"When I was seventeen, I started thinking of ways to escape. It wasn't easy, though. If he wasn't around keeping an eye on the girls, there was always a lead girl who collected the money and made sure you were doing your job. One night, I saw my chance. I had serviced two guys and still had the money in my pocket. The girl who was supposed to take it had been busy that night too. I saw the back of a truck where the tarp that hung over it was slightly torn. It was flapping in the breeze, just calling to me. It was dark, no one was around, and the back of the truck was out of view of the gas station. The engine was running, so I knew he'd be taking off soon. I casually walked up to the truck, looked around, and then pulled myself up into the back. My heart was pounding as I waited for someone to come after me. But a few minutes later, the truck took off. I was free."

The girls had moved forward in their seats, enthralled by her escape.

"No one saw you or came after you?" Tonya asked.

Addie shook her head. "No. But I'd only jumped one hurdle. I knew I'd have to get far away, and with only $200 in my pocket, I doubted I could get far. That's when the truck pulled over on the side of the road and parked. I panicked. I slid as far back in the truck as possible, but it was empty, and there was nothing I could hide behind. Suddenly, the tarp was pulled up, and a flashlight shone on me. I was so scared, I didn't know what to do.

"The trucker waved me toward him. 'You can come out now,' he said. 'Don't worry. I saw you climb inside. I won't tell anyone.' This guy had paid me for sex a couple of times. I thought for sure he'd take me back to the truck stop. I was prepared to jump out and run, but I didn't know where to—it was dark, and there was nothing around. He kept assuring me he wouldn't take me back or tell. I finally had no choice except to believe him."

"Wow. That must have been scary," Wanda spoke up for the first time. "What happened?"

"He let me sit in the cab and didn't say much. He asked me where I was headed, and I told him I wanted to go to a bus station. He acted kind of shy, like he was suddenly embarrassed that he'd paid me for sex and hadn't thought of me as a person. He said he was headed for Minneapolis, and I could sleep up in the bed behind the cab until we got there if I wanted to. I finally gave in and did that because I was exhausted. By morning, he'd pulled into a place near a Greyhound Bus Station outside of Minneapolis. I thanked him for helping me, and before I could walk away, he handed me some cash—two hundred dollars. I was shocked. 'I'm sorry,' he said. Then he walked away."

Addie sat silent a moment, remembering that day as if it were yesterday. Even though that man had been one of her customers, he'd had the decency to help her. She'd forever be grateful for the money he gave her because she'd never have made it to her life here without it.

"So, you came to Portland?" Izzie asked.

"Yes," Addie said. "I went as far away as I could. I never wanted to run into my trafficker again. I was free, and I planned on staying that way."

"And then you met that lady, and you started working for her?" Tonya asked.

Addie nodded. "I met her a year later. And it was the best thing that could have happened to me."

"How did you know you could trust her?" Latisha asked, looking cynical.

Addie ran a hand through her short hair and shook her head. "Believe me, I didn't know I could trust anyone yet. But she took me out of an unsafe apartment and brought me to her home. She always lived in the houses she remodeled, then moved to the next. She had a couple of rentals, too." Addie laughed. "The first couple of weeks, I slept with my clothes on and my backpack packed in case I had to run away. Valerie, my friend, knew I did that but never judged me. She made me feel wanted and needed and trusted me. After a while, I finally did feel safe with her. We've been friends ever since."

"Thank you for sharing your story," Laurie said. "This gives us all something to think about. Even when things seem their worst, something good can happen."

Latisha snorted. "Right. We all have a savior waiting right around the corner."

"Actually, you all do," Addie said. "And she's sitting right here." She pointed to Laurie. "She's here for you."

Latisha dropped her eyes. Addie knew that all the girls realized she was right. Laurie was there to help them when no one else would.

After the meeting, Laurie walked Addie out onto the porch. "Thank you for sharing. I know it isn't an easy story to tell. But it will give these girls something to think about."

"I'm glad I did. I hope it helps. I always feel better after sharing my story. Maybe, someday, telling it will really set me free," Addie said.

"Sweetie. It already has. You have a great life. Remember that." Laurie pulled her into a hug. "And you are always welcome here, even if you just want to sit in on a session."

"Thanks. I may take you up on that."

As Addie walked the short distance to her car, she realized

that her life had changed considerably since her days of being trafficked. She trusted people easier than she did before. And she no longer looked over her shoulder when she was out alone. She was still careful but not paranoid. Realizing that tonight made her heart feel lighter.

CHAPTER TWELVE

Sofiya

1918

That spring, Sofiya noticed that fewer young men were attending Miss Nora's salon in the evenings. She'd learned from reading the paper that a draft for men ages twenty-one to thirty had been put in place that past June. But since Harry was only eighteen, he hadn't been expected to go to war. Clint—Alina's favorite customer—hadn't gone either because of his age. But the older men still came, and Miss Nora didn't worry about losing a few young men because the mature clientele had the bulk of the money to spend.

Three times a week, Sofiya saw Harry as he delivered bread, but his demeanor continued to decline. He was desperate to help his father, but he didn't know how. He spoke to Sofiya about their struggles and how he wished he could change things for his parents. And as he confided in her, the two grew closer. Sofiya wished she could tell Harry all her secrets, but she knew she couldn't. She'd promised her maman never to utter a word about who she really was. And what she'd read about what was happening in Russia, Sofiya knew her maman had been right to worry. It was too dangerous for anyone to know her secret.

That March, Sofiya turned seventeen, but she didn't mention her birthday to anyone. Alina had made her a pretty, hand-drawn card and given her a lovely lace handker- chief she'd saved from a few she'd been given, but that was the only recognition of her turning a year older. As Sofiya stared into her small mirror, she saw only a slight change in herself from the year before. Her face wasn't as round with baby fat as it had been, and she'd lost weight from worrying about her parents and Harry. Still, in her eyes, she was no beauty by any standards. But that was what had saved her from working upstairs with the girls, and she was thankful for that.

The weather warmed as spring came, and in early April, Harry appeared at the kitchen door on a Sunday afternoon. Sofiya had just finished handing out the lunch trays to the girls and was surprised to see him at the door.

"What are you doing here?" she whispered, fearful that Miss Nora would hear them and come to investigate.

"I need to speak to you," Harry said. He looked so sad and desperate that Sofiya couldn't deny him. Miss Nora was in her office, eating lunch and working on financials. Sofiya thought she might be able to sneak out for a short time, and Nora wouldn't notice.

Grabbing her coat from the rack by the door, Sofiya waved for Harry to follow her. She led him to the bench under the large oak tree. They'd be out in the open, so it wouldn't look like Sofiya was hiding anything if Miss Nora saw her. It was the best she could do.

The two young people sat, and Harry immediately took

Sofiya's hands in his.

"I just signed up at the recruiting office. I'm going to war." Harry looked into her eyes, waiting for a response.

"Oh, Harry." Sofiya was speechless. She didn't want to lose Harry. She understood that was selfish, but he was the only person in her life who brought her happiness. Now, he was leaving her too. "Why would you do that?"

Harry squeezed her hands tighter. "I have to do it for my family. My father will lose everything if he can't prove we are loyal to America. If I go to war and fight for this country, people will know we're dedicated to America."

Her heart sank. She understood but didn't want to let him go. "You don't have to go to prove that. Your father can get his citizenship. That will prove he's an American."

The young man shook his head. "He did apply, but it's a slow process. Besides, I've heard they will be drafting men my age very soon. It's best if I go now. Then my parents can proudly display my photo in a uniform at the bakery. Hopefully, customers will see that as the ultimate gift to this country."

"Oh, Harry." Tears filled her eyes, and she dropped her head. "I can't lose anyone else. I just can't."

Harry wrapped his arms around her, and she let him hold her. He smelled of freshly baked bread and wool from his coat. She wished she lived in another time—a time when war wasn't prevalent around the world. Her whole life was taken from her when she came here, and now, she was losing yet another friend.

"I'll come back," Harry said softly. "I will come back, and you and I will be together." He pulled away and looked her in the eyes. "I care so much for you, Sofiya. I want to take you away from this terrible house and take care of you. Please believe me. I'll be back."

She stared at him, stunned. This beautiful young man cared about her. Her—the plain girl who worked in a kitchen because she wasn't pretty enough to be seen. Sofiya smiled at him, and her heart filled with love for him. "Promise me you'll be careful. I couldn't bear for you to die in this terrible war."

He smiled at her. "I will. I'll stay as far away from danger as I possibly can." He hugged her again and then walked her back to the house. Sofiya stood on the stoop and watched him walk down the driveway. The only man who had ever cared about her. Harry had always made her feel special; he'd made her feel seen. Now, she was losing yet another person in her life.

* * *

A different young man delivered their bread after that, and a few weeks after Harry had left, there was a photo of him in the newspaper as a local boy who was being sent overseas. Sofiya cut out his photo and slid it into one of her maman's letters for safe keeping. She prayed the war would end soon and Harry would return safely.

By summer, new news was spreading across the United States that was even scarier than the war abroad. The Spanish Influenza was attacking soldiers in Europe, causing more than half of the French, British, and even German soldiers to become ill and die. Sofiya didn't know where Harry was stationed, but she prayed he was well. Cases were slowly seeping into the United States too. A soldier in Kansas was diagnosed with the Spanish Flu in March, and Sofiya feared it would spread quickly. But Miss Nora ignored her concerns.

"It'll pass. Our door will remain open no matter what happens," she told Sofiya when the young girl mentioned her fear of the deadly flu. Sofiya thought that was dangerous, especially since so many of the men who came to the house had sons or younger brothers who'd been to war and had come home. They could have been infected. But the young girl had no choice but to do as she was told.

Throughout the warm summer, Miss Nora was raging. Fewer men were attending the evening events, and money wasn't flowing in as it once had. A few girls had run away, some with young men they'd fallen in love with. Nora was having a tougher time getting girls to work at her house, and this put her in a nasty mood. With less money coming in, she began cutting expenses—mainly from the kitchen budget. The girls were fed leaner meals—less meat, cheese, and other expensive items. The bread deliveries were halted, and Mrs. Jarvi and Sofiya were expected to bake bread and rolls in the summer heat. Sofiya worked late at night after serving, preparing the bread to rise overnight, and then baked it early in the morning before the heat of the day. With fewer other foods to eat, the girls ate more bread, and it was hard to keep enough in the house.

One morning in early August, as Sofiya entered the kitchen after cleaning the parlor, she noticed Mrs. Jarvi shaking her head sorrowfully while reading the paper. The younger girl wondered what was wrong and glanced over Mrs. Jarvi's shoulder. The bold headline made her blood grow cold. "Czar Nicholas Dead."

"Such a terrible thing," Mrs. Jarvi said. "They killed him in cold blood."

Sofiya grabbed a chair and sat, afraid she might faint. How could they have killed him? And what had happened to the Tsarina, the girls, and young Alexi? Finding her voice as she choked back tears, Sofiya asked, "What about the family?"

Mrs. Jarvi glanced up from the paper. "My goodness, dear. You're white as a sheet." The older woman studied Sofiya a moment, her brows furrowed. Then her expression softened. "I suppose this is a blow to you since you've only been away from Finland for a short while. It says the family is safely hidden away. Unfortunately, how are we to believe the same monsters who killed the Tsar?"

Sofiya dropped her head, trying hard not to cry in front of Mrs. Jarvi. She could only pray that the Tsarina and the children were safe. And what of her parents and all the other Romanov family in Petrograd? Would they be imprisoned, or worse, killed?

Mrs. Jarvi folded the paper and stood, placing a kind hand on Sofiya's shoulder. "I'm so sorry, dear. There is so much death happening all over Europe and Russia, and even our beloved Finland. It's as if the world has gone mad. And here you are, stuck in this horrible place." She glanced around in disgust. "Life will get better, I promise you. It has to."

Sofiya swallowed hard and nodded. She felt like her entire world was falling in around her. But even when things were growing worse, she still had work to do, or there was hell to pay from Miss Nora.

All that summer and into September, as Sofiya worked in the kitchen, she'd gaze out the window at the bench that surrounded the oak tree and remembered the last time she'd seen Harry. He hadn't written to her, but she hadn't expected he would. He would have been fearful that Miss Nora would get the letters first. She wondered how he was faring and how his parents were doing at the bakery. Since she hadn't left the house since arriving there, she had no way of knowing what was happening around town. As the days passed, her hopes for a better future faded. Sofiya felt she'd die in this house and never get a chance to marry or have a family of her own.

In October, the dreaded Spanish Influenza hit the city of Portland hard. It came by way of a soldier passing through and spread very quickly. The mayor immediately ordered businesses to shut down early each day and churches, schools, and other meeting places to close completely to prevent the spread of the flu. But residents balked at being told what to do, and despite the efforts of the city leaders, the deadly flu continued to spread.

Miss Nora's house was not left untouched. She kept her parlor open, despite the girls coming down with the dreaded illness. By early November, nearly all the young girls were sick, and men stopped coming to the house. Miss Nora also became ill and took to her bed.

News of the war ending on November 11th didn't even phase the household. They were fighting their own war against the flu, and what should have been a happy celebration was altogether ignored.

Sofiya began wearing a mask over her face at the first sign of illness in the house, despite Miss Nora yelling at her about it. Now, she was thankful she had. Her life became even more challenging when Mrs. Jarvi sent a note to Sofiya apologizing for not coming to work. Her husband was ill, and she couldn't leave him. Sofiya understood, but she needed help. She, Mabel, and Carter were the only ones in the house who hadn't succumbed to the flu, so Sofiya recruited them into service. Carter came into the kitchen to help Sofiya prepare soups, tea, and anything else they could get the young women to eat. He also ran around town for necessary supplies because the delivery men wouldn't come near the house.

Sofiya insisted Mabel wear a mask as she tended to the sick. "You can't risk getting sick too," Sofiya told her. "I need your help. I can't do this on my own."

For once, Mabel didn't fight back. The two women worked tirelessly, bringing cold compresses to the girls to lower fevers, blankets for those with the chills, and then placing warm poultices on their chests when the virus worked its way into their lungs. Miss Nora refused to send for a doctor until she became deathly ill. Finally, Carter went in search of a doctor who could look in on Nora and all the girls. But there was little the doctor could do except give them instructions on how to care for the sick.

Sofiya and Mabel worked night and day caring for the girls. Alina was the weakest one, her fever high and breathing ragged. Whenever she had an extra moment, Sofiya sat with her dear friend, holding her hand and praying she'd get well. Sofiya had lost so much that she couldn't lose Alina.

As the days passed, Sofiya was impressed by how seriously Mabel took her work in nursing all the young women. She'd feared that Mabel would use this opportunity to leave, but she'd stuck it out with Sofiya, and she worked just as hard.

"I couldn't have done this without your help," Sofiya told her one evening as they were boiling water in the kitchen to make warm compresses for the girls and Miss Nora. "Thank you for staying and helping."

Mabel had actually smiled. "Where else would I go?"

Sofiya had a newfound respect for Mabel.

Finally, weeks after the flu hit the house, the girls began to feel better. Fevers broke, lungs cleared, and the women were eating better and regaining their strength. Miss Nora slowly felt better, too, but continued to rest to regain her strength. All the women had lost weight and needed nourishment.

To Sofiya's relief, Alina showed signs of improvement. Her breathing was less strained, and she could finally keep down a few spoonfuls of soup. She was very thin, but Sofiya was sure her dear friend would get well.

"I thought I would lose you," Sofiya told Alina one evening as she helped her wash up and change her nightgown. Tears filled her eyes as she thought of what life would have been like without Alina.

"I was afraid I'd leave you here alone," Alina said softly, her voice still hoarse from coughing. "But I'm not going anywhere, thanks to you. We all owe you so much for the care you gave us."

Sofiya smiled even as tears rolled down her cheeks. "And Mabel and Carter, too. They helped every step of the way."

Mabel usually attended to Miss Nora, but when Sofiya would go into her room to check on her, Miss Nora stared at her strangely. Finally, one day, Sofiya asked her if something was wrong.

"You had the opportunity to leave while I was sick," Miss Nora said, narrowing her eyes. "Why didn't you?"

Sofiya was stunned by her question. "I couldn't leave knowing that the girls needed my help. *You* needed my help," she said pointedly.

Miss Nora smirked and shook her head. "You're a stupid girl," she said, then closed her eyes.

Sofiya sighed as she left Nora's room. She hadn't expected gratitude, but to call her stupid for not leaving everyone to die was terrible. Yet, what else had Sofiya expected of someone as conniving and selfish as Miss Nora?

There was no Christmas celebration in the house that year. Everyone was still too worn out from their illness to bother, and Mabel and Sofiya were drained from working so hard to keep all the women alive. The house was quiet, with no guests crossing the threshold. People had died all over the city by January, and despite quarantines and businesses closing across Portland, the flu continued to spread. By the end of January 1919, over 1,100 residents had died, but the flu was finally waning. Sofiya was just thankful that no one in their household had perished.

* * *

Mrs. Jarvi returned to work in late January. Her husband had almost died, but she'd worked tireless to keep him alive, and he was finally strong enough to be left alone while she worked. The older woman had noticed immediately that something had changed in the household since she'd been gone.

"Everyone is actually being nice," she said to Sofiya after her second day back. "The girls are talking when they come to the kitchen and thanking us for their meals."

Sofiya smiled. "We all grew close during those weeks everyone was sick. You should have seen Mabel. She worked hard to care for the girls and Miss Nora. I couldn't have done it without her and Carter."

"Carter? What did he do?" Mrs. Jarvi looked shocked.

"He helped with meals, laundry, and even making poultices for the girls. He was a Godsend."

"Well, my, my," Mrs. Jarvi said. "What a dear soul he is." She grinned. "I don't suppose Miss Nora saw the light and became sweeter after you saved her life."

Sofiya made a face. "No. She's as mean as ever. She just

wants to reopen and make money again. But thankfully, she realizes no one will come until they're sure the influenza is gone for good."

"I suppose we have to take the little miracles as they come," Mrs. Jarvi said.

One miracle that Sofiya prayed for each day was to see Harry walk through the kitchen door, smiling and joking as he used to now that the war was over. But each day, she was disappointed not to see him or hear of his return. Mrs. Jarvi went to the bakery to check with his parents but returned, shaking her head.

"They haven't heard from him," she told Sofiya. "But we'll continue to believe he'll return."

As the weeks passed, Sofiya soon lost hope that Harry had survived the war. Between the Spanish Influenza and the dangerous conditions of war, the chances of him returning were slim.

In late February, Miss Nora opened her doors with only eight girls working the parlor. All the others had run away, and finding young girls up to Miss Nora's high standards was difficult. The men returned, but the parlor wasn't as busy or boisterous as it had once been.

Alina's young man, Clinton, arrived the first night they opened, eager to see for himself that Alina was well. Sofiya saw Miss Nora watch the young couple with narrowed eyes as she served meager food trays. Sofiya knew that Alina and Clint would have to be careful. Nora had lost too many girls who'd fallen in love with the young men who came to the house. She wasn't about to lose Alina too.

One afternoon in late March, Alina's face looked strained as she walked into the kitchen to retrieve her lunch. In her hand was a letter. Sofiya stared at the letter, and her heart pounded. She knew there must have been bad news from home.

"We need to talk a moment," Alina whispered.

Sofiya glanced over at Mrs. Jarvi, who was busy making food for the evening's guests. She trusted the older woman but wanted to speak privately with Alina. "We'll be in my room for a moment," Sofiya said to Mrs. Jarvi, who glanced over her shoulder and nodded.

Pulling Alina into the tiny room and closing the door, the two girls sat on the bed. "What's happened? Are your parents all right?" Sofiya asked.

Tears ran down Alina's beautiful face. She took a deep breath and spoke in barely a whisper. "My parents are fine. They've already left Finland and are now living in London, at least for the time being."

"Then what is it?" Sofiya asked.

"Before leaving, my mother inquired of a mutual friend about your parents. Everything in Petrograd had been kept quiet, but the people knew what was happening. My mother learned that in August of last year, your parents were found in their apartment, murdered."

"No!" Sofiya's hand flew to her heart. "That can't be! Why would anyone hurt my parents?"

Alina's tears fell faster. "I'm so sorry. I am." She handed Sofiya the letter.

Sofiya tried to read the words written in Finnish through her tears. Alina's mother explained how after the murder of the Tsar last July, the Bolsheviks went on a rampage throughout the area, killing anyone they believed was related to or had worked for the Tsar. No one knew how many members of the Romanov family were murdered, but many were missing.

Sofiya's hand shook so hard that she couldn't continue reading the letter. Her parents were gone. Dead. She'd lost them forever.

Alina wrapped her arms around her friend, and the two girls cried together. It was the biggest blow that could ever have befallen Sofiya. Her parents were gone, and she no longer had anyone she could hope to return to. All that was left for her was her dear friend, who she clung to now. In her heart, Sofiya felt her life was no longer worth living.

CHAPTER THIRTEEN

Addie

Tears streamed down Addie's face as she read Sofiya's letter. The poor girl had lost everything. Addie understood what that felt like, and her own feelings of past loneliness crept over her. The same feelings she'd had after her father died and then her mother went to jail, leaving Addie to live with strangers.

She wiped her tears and glanced over at the Zach, a sleeping lump in the bed beside her. This made her smile, despite her tears. Zach was her family. He was the one who helped her to no longer feel lonely.

Setting down the letter, Addie dug through the box to the original letters and glanced through the envelopes. Finally, a small scrap of yellowed newspaper fell out. Addie looked at the photo of the handsome young man wearing a uniform. This was the clipping of Harry that Sofiya had saved.

Addie studied the clipping, understanding why Sofiya had fallen for this young man. Even though he looked serious in the photo, Addie could picture him coming into the kitchen each day with a broad smile and teasing banter. There was something in his eyes—despite how old the photo was. A twinkle or devil-may-care look about him. She wondered if Sofiya ever saw him again or if she ever married and was happy. Addie's curiosity made her keep reading the letters, no matter how sad they were.

The days went by quickly as Addie finished work on the parlor, then set her sights on Miss Nora's office, which had been turned back into a dining room. She spent days peeling off the many years of wallpaper, then painted the walls a pale aqua-blue. The color offset the beautiful wood wainscotting on the bottom half of the walls. The cream-colored tile around the fireplace was a nice contrast to the rest of the room. She also purchased a new dining room light for over the table—one that looked like it had come from the Victorian Era. Changing this room that had once belonged to the nasty Nora gave Addie immense satisfaction. Nora's spirit, if it was still here, could be as angry as she wanted about the changes. The house was coming back to life as a happy home, and Nora couldn't do anything about it.

In late July, as Addie placed a coffee mug into the new dishwasher in their freshly remodeled kitchen, she glanced out the window and saw a teenage boy surveying the broken bench around the old oak tree. Curious as to who he was, Addie went outside.

"Hi," Addie said, watching the teen warily. He didn't look menacing in a blue T-shirt and tan cargo shorts. But Addie was always careful around strangers—especially men.

"Oh, hi," the kid said. He was tall and slender and looked a bit awkward. But he had thick blond hair and blue eyes and seemed friendly.

When he offered no more information, Addie asked, "What

are you doing?"

The kid jammed his hands in his pocket, looking guilty, even though he hadn't done anything wrong. "Sorry. I was looking at this bench. It looks like the tree outgrew it, and it's broken."

"Yes, it does," Addie said, still confused. "But why are you here?"

"Oh. Sorry. My mom is Gail, next door. She told me I should come over here and help you two since I'm not doing much this summer. I talked to your husband, Zach, a while back, but he said you couldn't afford to pay for help. I hadn't meant he'd have to pay me."

Addie's brows rose at the word "husband." She supposed she and Zach looked like an old married couple to him. That thought made her smile. "We wouldn't want you to work for free."

He ran his hand through his hair. "I really have nothing to do. My friends are all working or gone for the summer. So, if you don't mind, I thought I'd fix this bench for you."

Zach came out of the garage and smiled when he saw the kid. "Hey, Matt. I see you've met Addie."

Matt seemed to relax when Zach came over. Addie thought it was funny that he'd been nervous talking to her. "Matt is offering to fix this old bench for us. For free," Addie said.

"Really?" Zach turned and looked at the broken bench. "That's really nice, but we couldn't let you do it for free."

"That's what I said," Addie added.

"Have you ever worked with wood before?" Zach asked.

Matt nodded. "My dad has a workshop in the backyard. He likes making things—sort of as a hobby. He's taught me how to build benches and chests and stuff."

Zach turned to Addie. "What do you think?"

"It would be nice to fix Sofiya's bench," Addie said. Whenever she looked at it, she thought of Sofiya and Harry. "Are you sure you want to do this?" she asked Matt.

His face lit up. "Yeah. It'll be fun."

"That's really nice of you," Addie said. "Thank you. We'll think of some way to repay you."

"Come in the garage," Zach said, waving for Matt to follow. "I have a bunch of boards that might work.

Addie watched as Matt followed Zach. The two were talking as if they were old friends. Zach was a natural around teens and kids. It was yet another thing that made her love him so much.

* * *

Some evenings, Addie attended Laurie's meetings with the other women. It helped her to listen to their stories, as well as share more of her own. Addie felt more balanced and in control of her life. She felt so much better that she started working at the hotline Laurie had set up to help those who wanted to get off the streets. After a refresher course in answering the hotline, Addie took an occasional shift. In most instances, they received calls from people looking for resources available. But the occasional reporting of suspected trafficking did come in, as well as a victim calling, asking for help. Those were the calls that tore at Addie's heart.

One August evening, Addie answered one such call that took her off guard.

"Trafficking hotline," Addie said when she answered the phone. "How may I help you?"

"Please, will someone come get me?"

Chills ran down Addie's spine. The voice was a mere whisper, but she could tell the girl was young. "Yes. Where are you?"

"I'm in the women's bathroom at Gandy's Corner Superstation. The one on highway 84 and 99E. Please," the girl pleaded. "I need help now. I'm using this lady's phone, and he'll be back any minute looking for me."

Addie was writing the information down and waved Laurie over. She placed her hand over the receiver. "We need the police sent here now. This girl is in danger."

Laurie nodded. "Get her name. Try to get the name of her trafficker, too. I'll call 911."

"We're sending help," Addie assured the girl. "Can you give me your name?"

"Please hurry," the girl pleaded. "Please."

In the background, Addie heard another woman's voice. "You need to give me my phone back. I have to go. I don't want to be in the middle of this."

"You can't leave," the girl said to the woman. "If you open that door, he'll get me. Please. Just another minute."

"Hello?" Addie said. "Hello!"

"I'm still here."

"What's your name?" Addie asked.

"It's Katie. Katie Abrams."

There was a sudden pounding on metal, and Addie heard a male voice yelling, "Come out now!"

Addie looked over at Laurie, who was still on the phone with 911. "Her name is Katie Abrams."

Laurie repeated that to the 911 operator. Then she turned back to Addie. "Ten minutes. Tell her to stay locked in the bathroom."

"Ten minutes!" Addie heard the man pounding on the door through the phone. "Katie! Are you still there?"

"Yes," Katie said, but she was crying now. "He'll get inside. He'll take me away again. Please help me!"

"The police are coming. Sit tight. Keep the door locked, and don't let him in."

"I'm so scared," Katie whispered, sobbing.

Addie was fighting back tears of her own. She turned to Laurie. "I can be there in five minutes if I leave now."

"What? No! You can't go there. It's dangerous!" Laurie looked horrified.

"No more dangerous for me than for that girl." Addie stood and handed Laurie the phone. "Keep her calm, and don't let her open that door."

"Don't go!" Laurie yelled. "You can't help her. Let the police do their job."

"I can't sit here and wait when I know I can help her," Addie said, her heart pounding. "Don't you understand? If that guy gets ahold of her, he'll beat her, maybe even kill her. If the cops can't get there in time, then I need to go." She grabbed her bag and ran out of the upstairs room, down the stairs, and outside to her car.

Addie drove so fast, she was shocked she wasn't pulled over. In less than five minutes, she was at the gas station. Addie parked far away from the building so she'd be out of range of the security cameras. She knew how this worked from her own experience. The station manager was usually paid off to look the other way and would help the trafficker if asked. She didn't want anyone to see her license plate number so they could identify her and track her down.

Running to the building, past where the truckers filled

their tanks, Addie saw no sign of police cars. Swearing under her breath, she glanced around for someone who could help her. That's when she saw the sticker on the window of a big truck. "TAT – Truckers Against Trafficking."

She ran up to the tall, muscular man beside the cab. "Did you put that sticker on your window?" she asked hurriedly, pointing to it.

He looked startled. "Yeah. Why?"

"Do you believe in that cause?"

"You bet. I have a teenage daughter. No grown man should ever touch a young girl."

"Come with me," she said, waving at him to follow her.

He caught up with her as they entered the gas station. "What's going on."

"There's a girl in trouble in the restroom. I need you for backup."

"Are you a cop?" the guy asked.

"No. She needs help now!"

The trucker stopped, and Addie stopped too. "What?"

"We're not supposed to get involved. We're supposed to wait for the police," he said.

"Then you stay here. I'm going to help her," Addie retorted. She ran through the aisles toward the back, where the bathrooms always were. Behind her, she could hear the thud of the trucker's boots following her. Relief flooded through her. She knew she couldn't do this alone.

The sound of a man banging on a metal door echoed down the narrow hallway. He was screaming to open up. He'd managed to dent in the door but not break it down. No one was coming to the girl's aid. The guy wasn't tall and had little weight on him. But his dark eyes and black hair made him look menacing.

The trucker moved ahead of Addie and stood between her and the guy. "What are you doing?" he asked the smaller man. "Leave the girl alone."

"This isn't your problem," the guy yelled at the trucker. "Get out of here." He reached for something in his back pocket. Addie held her breath, hoping it wasn't a gun.

"I don't think so," the trucker said, his deep voice echoing in the hallway. He grabbed ahold of the trafficker's shirt and slammed him into the metal men's bathroom door. The trafficker hit hard and slumped into a pile on the floor.

Addie turned to the ladies' room door. "Katie? It's Addie from the hotline. You're safe now. You can come out."

From inside the bathroom, Addie heard a girl crying and a woman saying in an anguished voice that she wanted out. But the door remained closed.

"How do I know it's you?" the girl asked through her sobs. "This might be a trick."

Addie sighed. She knew how the girl felt. Fear made you trust no one.

"Police!" a voice called down the hall.

Addie and the trucker turned and saw two officers coming toward them. *Finally,* Addie thought.

She quickly explained who she was and what had happened and pointed to the trafficker.

"What happened to him?" the officer asked upon seeing the small man lying unconscious on the floor.

"Karma," the trucker said with a grin.

An hour later, they were all allowed to leave. The officers took the trafficker to their car and said he'd be in jail for a long time. He was wanted in several states for trafficking young people. The woman whose phone Katie had used was let go, too, after Addie shared her appreciation for helping Katie. Since Katie was eighteen years old, she was free to go home or to a shelter. After discussing it with her, Addie offered to bring her to Laurie's safe house.

The trucker walked Addie and Katie to her car.

"Thank you," Addie said to him. "This could have ended badly without your help."

He shrugged. "Happy to help. He had a knife in his back pocket, nothing I couldn't handle."

She smiled. "Well, I appreciate it. I'm Addie, by the way."

He grinned. "I'm Mark. Nice to meet you." Then his smile faded. "Promise me you won't ever do anything like this again. It's too dangerous."

She nodded. "I'm sure I'll get an earful from my boyfriend and friend. I promise. It was stupid of me to think I could do this. But I'm glad we got here in time."

Mark nodded and headed back to his truck.

Addie turned to Katie. The young girl's mascara was smudged down her cheeks from crying, and her thick red lipstick was smeared. She was definitely dressed in the 'uniform' with a skimpy tank top, short skirt, and tall heels. But there was an innocence still in her eyes.

"Let's take you somewhere safe," Addie said.

* * *

"Don't you ever do anything like that again! You could have been killed!" Laurie said in a low, menacing tone to Addie. "Do you know how scared I was for you? Do you realize how insane what you did was?" Before Addie could say a word, Laurie pulled her into a hug, squeezing the breath out of her. Addie hugged her back. She knew her friend cared about her, and that was why she was so mad.

"I'm sorry," Addie said, still in Laurie's arms. "I know it was a stupid thing to do." The two women finally parted. "But Katie is safe now, and that's all that matters."

Laurie let out a long sigh and glanced into the living room where Katie was sitting with Melanie. The two girls were talking quietly. Laurie thought Melanie would be the best one to help Katie feel at ease.

"Did she share any information about herself?" Laurie asked Addie.

Addie nodded. "A little. She ran away two years ago from a foster home. Her parents are dead, and no one in her extended family wanted her. She said she lived on the streets for a few months, but then that guy recruited her with the promise of a place to live. All this happened in Idaho. He was moving her from a place in southern Oregon up to a new station in Seattle. I guess the guy was sort of a middleman, moving the girls around."

"I'm glad she's safe. How did she get our number?" Laurie asked.

"Off a poster in the women's bathroom. I guess it does work to have those everywhere." Addie smiled. She had been one of the many people who put up posters in every gas station in Portland.

Laurie nodded. "Yes, it does. So, I've been calling around, trying to find a place for Katie to stay. I haven't had any luck yet."

Addie's brows rose. "I thought she could stay here."

"I'm only licensed for five girls, max. I can't take her in.

I'm trying to find her another safe house or a shelter for abused women. No luck so far."

Addie dropped into one of the dining room chairs. "Can't she just stay on the couch? At least until tomorrow? I'd hate for her to be taken somewhere else after all she's been through."

"Sorry, Addie, but I can't risk breaking the rules and losing my license. This work is too important," Laurie said.

Addie understood, but she was afraid if Katie was sent off to some other place, she would end up running again. A thought struck her. "What if she comes home with me? Just for a day or so, until you can either get permission to host another girl or find her a safe place."

"You?" Laurie's eyes grew wide. "Are you kidding?" She lowered her voice. "You don't know this girl, Addie. Would you want her in your house?"

"I know this girl," Addie said quietly. "I was this girl. And if Valerie hadn't taken a chance on me, I wouldn't be where I am today. Besides, she risked her life to get away from her trafficker. I really don't think she's dangerous."

Laurie frowned and paced a moment. Then she turned back to Addie. "What will Zach say?"

Addie smiled. "Leave Zach to me."

CHAPTER FOURTEEN

Sofiya

Sofiya no longer cared about anything after learning the news of her parents' fate. The day Alina told her, she lay on her bed all afternoon crying, unable to move. After Alina left her, Mrs. Jarvi came to check on her. She asked her several times what was wrong and if she could help, but Sofiya only sobbed. The older woman made her lie down and covered her up, hoping Sofiya would finally fall asleep.

That evening, before Mrs. Jarvi left, Sofiya was awakened by loud voices in the kitchen. Miss Nora's voice was angry, and Mrs. Jarvi snapped back to her.

"Leave her be. She's had a shock and needs to be left alone," Mrs. Jarvi said as Miss Nora pushed open Sofiya's bedroom door.

"Get up, girl! I don't care what happened, you need to work tonight," Miss Nora said sternly, her hands on her hips.

Sofiya didn't move except to pull the blanket up higher. She didn't care what Miss Nora did to her. She couldn't have moved even if she'd wanted to.

Miss Nora came up to the bed and roughly shook her. "Get up, do you hear? Get up, you stupid girl."

"Enough!" Mrs. Jarvi said from the doorway. "Enough, or I'll never come back here again, do you hear?"

Miss Nora spun on her heel. "How dare you? After all I've done for you?"

Mrs. Jarvi snorted. "All you've done for me? Like what? Pay me too little and expect twice the work in return? I mean it. Leave her be. Make one of the other girls serve tonight. It's not like it matters anyway. The men aren't here to eat food—they're here for the girls."

Miss Nora's face screwed up so tight, Sofiya thought for sure she'd hit Mrs. Jarvi. Instead, she pushed past the cook and headed out the door in a huff. Mrs. Jarvi closed the bedroom door quietly, and that was the last thing Sofiya remembered until morning.

The next day Sofiya forced herself to get up and work and was surprised when Miss Nora didn't reprimand her. But Sofiya no longer cared what Miss Nora thought or what she'd do. The distraught girl went about her work in utter silence, ignoring everyone and barely even speaking to Mrs. Jarvi. Nothing mattered anymore. She no longer read the newspaper or conversed with the girls when they picked up their meals. Everyone noticed how griefstricken she was, but no one knew why. Sofiya had lost her will to live.

Some afternoons, between Mrs. Jarvi leaving for the evening and the men arriving, Sofiya went outside to the backyard and sat on the bench under the oak tree. She thought about her parents, about Harry, and sometimes even about Tsar Nicholas and her beautiful cousins. Her heart ached over everyone she'd lost. What was the point of her continuing without anyone who cared about her?

One evening, Miss Nora came outside wearing her gown and heels and glared at Sofiya. "Why are you out here? You're not allowed to leave the house."

Slowly, Sofiya raised her eyes to the older woman's. "I'll sit out here if I please. I'm not hurting anyone, and I'm still on the property."

Nora's brows shot up at Sofiya's impertinence. Then her eyes narrowed. "Don't think because you saved my life during the bout of flu that I won't cuff you for speaking back to me."

Sofiya shook her head. "Do what you like. You already own me. What more do you want?"

The younger girl's tone was so broken, even someone as hard as Miss Nora saw that it wasn't worth fighting with her. "Just make sure you're inside on time for the evening's guests," Miss Nora said sternly, then turned and left.

There was no sense of jubilation in Sofiya for winning this battle because there was no more joy inside her. She may as well have been a rag doll because she felt as empty as one.

* * *

"I need to talk to you," Alina whispered to Sofiya in late April when she was in the kitchen, picking up her lunch.

Sofiya's eyes darted up to her friend. "No more bad news, please," she said sorrowfully.

Alina bit her bottom lip. "Meet me in my room tonight after everyone has left. Please?"

A long sigh escaped Sofiya's lips, but she nodded.

Sofiya worked as usual, serving drinks and food to the gentlemen. Clint was there to see Alina, and the two sat in one corner, speaking softly to each other. With only eight girls working now, each had her own room—which meant more privacy. But Sofiya knew that Miss Nora hated having so few girls. She made much less money.

The evening began to wind down as each girl brought a man up to her room. Alina and Clint were walking toward the staircase when Miss Nora stopped them. Sofiya had stepped out of the kitchen door just as Miss Nora intervened.

"Not tonight," Nora said to Clinton. "You've been monopolizing all of Alina's time. It's against the rules."

Clinton looked shocked. "But I've paid you."

Miss Nora handed him his money. "Take it and leave. And don't come back."

Sofiya watched as Clinton seethed, and Alina's eyes grew wide.

Clinton straightened his back and lifted his head high. To Sofiya, the usually gentle-looking young man looked intimidating. "If you make me leave, I'll tell my father, and he'll stop coming here too. And so will his friends," Clinton threatened.

Miss Nora laughed. "So be it. But I truly doubt your father will stop coming. He has a favorite of his own. Now go."

Clinton glared at Nora, then must have decided that fighting her was not an option. He turned, bowed to Alina, and headed out the door.

Alina moved to go upstairs, but Miss Nora grabbed her arm and turned her around to face her. "No more playing favorites. Tomorrow night you'll more than make up for the money I lost tonight. And he'll no longer be allowed to spend time with you. Understand?"

Sofiya could see that her friend was holding back tears. "Yes," Alina said softly. After Nora let her go, Alina walked slowly up the stairs.

Miss Nora spun around and saw Sofiya watching. "Get back to work!" she yelled.

Sofiya turned back into the kitchen. She felt bad for Alina but wasn't surprised by what Miss Nora did. Nothing surprised Sofiya anymore.

Later that evening, after Sofiya had finished her work and was sure Miss Nora had gone to bed, she crept up the stairs and let herself into Alina's bedroom.

There was a light on beside Alina's bed, but she had fallen asleep. Sofiya stood quietly for a moment, staring at her beautiful best friend. They had known each other since they were mere children and played together while Alina's mother fitted Sofiya's maman for new dresses. They truly were like sisters, and Sofiya had never begrudged her friend for being so beautiful and petite, the complete opposite of her. Now, as she watched her, sadness crept over Sofiya for the loss of innocence they both experienced at the hands of Miss Nora. It broke her heart to know that they would never be as carefree and happy as they'd been as children.

Alina's eyes fluttered open, and she raised a hand to her chest. "Oh! I must have fallen asleep," the blonde beauty said, sitting up against the headboard. She patted the bed, and Sofiya sat down beside her.

"What did you need to tell me?" Sofiya asked, speaking quietly in Finnish. Even though they were alone in the room, they never knew who might be listening.

Alina gently took Sofiya's hand in hers. "I'm leaving this place. With Clint."

Sofiya's eyes grew wide. "What?"

"We've been talking about it for a while. Now, it's finally the time. His father has purchased another fish canning factory in Ketchikan, Alaska, and he's sending Clint there to run it. Clint wants me to join him." Alina's blue eyes watched Sofiya expectantly.

"Do you love him?" Sofiya asked. She hadn't expected her friend to run away with Clint—at least not yet. Sofiya had known they were close but hadn't understood the real nature of their relationship.

A sweet smile lit up Alina's face. "Yes. I love him. And he loves me. Imagine that? Despite what I've been doing in this terrible house, he still loves me. He wants me to be his wife."

"I don't know what to say." Sofiya stood and walked to the window. She knew she should be happy for Alina, but this meant another loss. Another person she'd never see again. Sofiya wasn't sure her heart could take it.

Alina came over and stood behind her. "Please be happy for me. I'm happy. I never thought I'd have anyone who'd love me after I'd been…soiled." Her voice cracked.

Shame fell over Sofiya for only thinking about herself. She turned and hugged her friend. "I am happy for you. I'm sorry. It was a shock to hear you're leaving. But I want you to be happy. I know you've endured so much more than I have living in this place. I can't even compare our experiences because yours is so much worse. I want you and Clint to be happy."

Alina smiled as tears filled her eyes. "Thank you. It's been a nightmare, but since Clint came into my life, it's been much more bearable."

Sofiya forced herself to smile. "I'm glad you have him in your life. I'm sure you two will be very happy."

Her friend dropped her eyes a moment, then lifted them again to Sofiya. "It will be three of us. I'm expecting a baby."

"A baby?" Sofiya stared at her friend. "Clint's baby?"

"Clint says it's his. He won't believe it's anyone else's. He's promised me he'll treat the baby as his own no matter what. He's that good of a man, Sofiya. He will take care of me and our child."

"When are you leaving?" Sofiya asked. She walked back to the bed and sat down. She might as well give in and face the fact that she was losing her friend for good.

Alina smiled down at her. "The day after tomorrow. I only have one more night here, and then I'll sneak out early in the morning before anyone is up. Clint has purchased three tickets for the train to Seattle. Then we'll take a ship the rest of the way to Alaska."

Sofiya frowned. Had she heard right? "Three tickets? Why three?"

"Because I want you to come with us." Alina's face brightened with excitement. "I could never leave you behind. We came to this country together, and we'll stay together. Clint is completely fine with it. We'll all be a family."

Sofiya was stunned by Alina's generous offer. "I don't know what to say."

"Say yes, of course," Alina said, laughing. "We can finally be free of this place. Don't you want to leave here?"

"Yes. More than anything," Sofiya said. Could she really walk out of here with Alina? As she thought of escaping, she remembered Harry. Even though she hadn't heard from him since he'd left for the war, she still hoped he'd walk through the door someday. But the war had ended over five months ago, and still, there was no sign of him. Was it realistic to stay and wait here for him to return?

"Well? What do you say?" Alina asked. "You'll come with us, won't you?"

"I want to leave this place," Sofiya said. "But I'm not sure I can just yet. Alaska is so far away. I've been waiting for someone to return, and he'll never find me if I go with you."

The pale blonde stared at her in disbelief. "I didn't know you knew any young men."

Sofiya nodded. "His father owns the bakery we used to purchase bread from. He delivered it, and we became quite close. His name is Harold—Harry—and he asked me to wait for him to return from the war. I'm still hoping he'll come home."

"Oh." Alina's expression grew solemn. "Could you not ask Mrs. Jarvi to tell him where you are? If he's serious about you, he'll come for you."

"I don't know," Sofiya said, suddenly confused over what she should do. "And you're starting a new life with Clint. Where would I fit in there? I...I just don't know what I should do."

Alina's face softened. "This was a lot to drop on you at once. Think about it tonight and let me know tomorrow. I'm sure once you've had time to think, you'll want to come with us."

Sofiya gave her friend a wan smile. "Yes. Maybe. But whatever happens, know that I wish only the best for you. I want you, Clint, and the baby to be happy."

Alina hugged Sofiya. "I will be happy. I can't wait to leave with him."

Sofiya pulled back and smiled brightly. "A baby. Think of that. You're going to be a mother."

Her friend's eyes lit up. "I know. Doesn't it seem strange? But I'm so happy. I hope I have a little girl. Then I can name her after my mother and you. Floriana Sofiya Olafson."

"I'd love that," Sofiya said, truly touched.

The two hugged once more, and Sofiya quietly left her room and went back downstairs to her tiny bedroom. She was so torn as to what to do. Should she take this chance to escape? Or was there something else waiting for her in the future? She felt so confused as she crawled into her bed and tried to sleep.

The next morning, Sofiya knew what she had to do. She did her usual morning work and handed out the lunch trays to the girls in the early afternoon. After Miss Nora had left the house for an appointment with her dressmaker, Sofiya rushed upstairs to speak to Alina.

"I can't go with you," Sofiya told her sadly in Finnish. "And I don't want you to worry about me. I'll be fine. I want you and Clint to have a wonderful life together."

Alina was sad her friend wasn't coming with her. "I understand. But what will you do? How will you leave this place?"

Sofiya smiled. "I still have my mother's jewelry to sell when I decide to leave. If Harry doesn't return soon, I'll find another position, somehow, and leave this place."

"Do you promise? I hate to think of you being here longer than you have to."

"I promise." Sofiya hugged her dear friend. "I also want you to not have to entertain one more man before you leave. So, I have a plan."

Alina's pale brows rose. "What?"

Sofiya grinned. "People are still scared about catching the Spanish Flu. You should complain about a stomachache, pretend to vomit in the bathroom—very loudly—and wear extra rouge to make it look like you are feverish. If Miss Nora still makes you come down to entertain, then cough loudly while you're downstairs and pretend to be dizzy. Not a man in the place will want to go to your room with you."

Alina's face brightened. "That's a wonderful idea. Miss Nora might get mad, but it might work. Even she won't want to risk becoming sick again."

Sofiya hugged her friend again, knowing she might not get another chance to say goodbye before Alina left. Then she hurried back downstairs before Miss Nora returned.

That evening, as Mabel retrieved her dinner tray in the kitchen, she mentioned she'd heard Alina being sick in the bathroom. "You don't think she's pregnant, do you?" she whispered to Sofiya.

Sofiya wrinkled her forehead. "She hasn't mentioned it. I hope she isn't getting sick." She turned toward Mrs. Jarvi. "Can a person get the Spanish Flu more than once?"

Mrs. Jarvi turned from her spot at the stove, looking horrified. "Oh, heavens. I hope not. Someone should check on Alina to see how she's feeling."

Mabel shook her head. "Not me. I haven't had that horrible flu, and I don't want it." She hurried away, and Sofiya couldn't help but smile. She hoped her plan worked.

By evening, all the girls had heard that Alina was ill, and no one wanted to go near her. Miss Nora didn't believe it, so she checked on Alina. After only a minute upstairs, she came hurrying down and quickly washed her hands in the bathroom sink before entering the kitchen.

"Alina is as red as a beet, coughing, and perspiring. I don't want her anywhere near me or the men tonight," she told Sofiya. "Do whatever you did before to care for her but do it quickly before you're needed this evening."

"Yes, Miss Nora," Sofiya said. She quickly gathered a few towels and poured cold water into a bowl, adding ice she'd chipped off the block in the icebox. She retrieved the mask she'd worn during the pandemic and headed upstairs to tend to Alina.

Sofiya entered Alina's room, closed the door behind her, and set the tray with the bowl and towels on the desk. Taking off her mask, she placed a finger to her lips so Alina wouldn't say anything that would incriminate her. In a concerned voice, Sofiya said, "Miss Nora is afraid you're ill. You're to stay up here tonight, away from everyone."

Alina smiled brightly but didn't respond. After all, she was supposed to be delirious with fever.

"Keep this cool towel on your forehead and rest," Sofiya said lovingly as if Alina was actually sick. The two smiled at each other. It was the last time they'd be alone before Alina left, but they didn't dare say a word. Their eyes said it all, though. They would miss each other, but they would always be friends, even when they were apart.

Later that night, once the men had left and everyone was sound asleep, Sofiya slipped into her bed. She knew by the time she awoke, her dear friend would be gone, on her way to a new life. She said a little prayer for Alina, Clint, and the baby.

The next morning, Alina was gone.

CHAPTER FIFTEEN

Addie

Addie called Zach before leaving Laurie's house and asked him to go to the closest store that sold mattresses and buy one for the guest bedroom.

"We're having a guest?" he asked, sounding confused.

"I'll explain as soon as I get home. Sorry to make you run so late at night."

"I'll do my best. I'll have to figure out where to find a mattress this late," he said.

Addie smiled. Zach didn't sound upset by her request. There was an amused tone to his voice. She knew how lucky she was that he was so easy-going.

After Laurie spoke with Katie alone for a while, the girl followed Addie to her car.

"I hope you don't mind staying with us for a day or so," Addie said. "The house is a mess since we're remodeling it, but you'll have your own room, and you'll be safe. No one except Laurie and me knows you'll be there."

Katie looked over at Addie, her brown eyes wide. "Us? Who

else lives there?"

"Oh, sorry. My long-time boyfriend and business partner lives there too. He's the sweetest person alive, so you don't have to worry about him. He's buying you a mattress as we speak since we barely have any furniture in the house."

Addie glanced over at Katie as they sat at a red light. She hadn't thought about the girl being nervous about Zach living there too. Of course this girl would be worried. She didn't know Addie, and now there would be a strange man around too.

"Everything will be fine," Addie said gently. "Zach is a dear. And if his being in the house upsets you, we can send him out to the room over the garage for the night."

This brought a smile to Katie's lips. "You'd actually send your boyfriend to the garage just for me?"

"Yes," Addie said. "I've been in your shoes. I ran away from my trafficker after three years of captivity, and I was scared to death the first few months I was free. I kept looking over my shoulder, and I didn't trust anyone. Then a very kind lady invited me to work with her, and my fear slowly subsided. I learned to trust again—although tentatively. So, believe me when I say I completely understand if having Zach in the house will upset you."

Katie tipped her head and stared at her for a moment. Her long, auburn hair was thick and shiny under the streetlights and framed her oval-shaped face. She really was a pretty girl, and despite being eighteen, she looked so young. Addie wondered if she'd looked just as young to Valerie.

"I wondered why someone like you would risk your life to save me," Katie said.

"Someone like me?" Addie asked as she parked the car in front of her house. "What do you mean by that?"

Katie shrugged. "You just look so pretty and normal, you know? Like someone who has it all figured out. Knowing we come from the same background makes me think I can survive this after all."

Addie smiled. "Sweetie, you risked your life to leave that horrible person. You're a survivor already."

Her words made Katie smile.

Addie led Katie up the side of the house and through the kitchen door. When she turned on the lights, Katie looked around in awe.

"This is your house? The entire building?" Katie asked.

"Yep. The whole thing. We're remodeling it right now. That's what Zach and I do—we flip houses."

"You mean like those people on TV?" Katie asked. She dropped her faded, ripped backpack on a kitchen chair and walked out of the kitchen and down the hall.

Addie followed her. "Yeah. Except it's a lot more work than they show on TV. It takes months to finish a remodel, and this house may take a year by the looks of it."

Katie eyed the curved staircase, then turned toward the parlor. She wandered into the big room where Miss Nora and the girls once entertained gentlemen. "This place is huge." She spun around. "I love this room. Did you do all this work?"

"Yes, I did," Addie said proudly. "Zach did most of the kitchen remodel, but it was all my design. I also remodeled the master bedroom and bathroom upstairs. After I'm finished with the dining room, I've got eight bedrooms upstairs to work on."

"Eight! That's crazy. This is like a hotel." Katie looked amazed.

"It's big, that's for sure," Addie said.

A noise came from the kitchen, and both women jumped.

"Addie? Are you here? I need help carrying in the mattress box," Zach hollered. He walked down the hallway and stopped in the parlor's doorway. "Oh. Hi," he said to Katie.

Addie watched Katie take a step back and thought it was more of a reaction than fear. She walked over to Zach and put her arm around him. "Zach, this is Katie. She'll be staying with us a day or so. Katie, this is Zach."

Zach smiled and offered his hand to shake. "Hi. It's nice to meet you."

Tentatively, Katie shook his hand, then stepped back again. "Hi."

"Let's get the mattress and bring it upstairs," Addie said. "Make yourself at home, Katie. There's pop and water in the fridge if you're thirsty and snacks in the cupboard. We'll be back in a bit."

Zach and Addie went out to the car to get the mattress. It was the kind that was rolled up in a box, so the two of them could manage it.

"What's her story?" Zach asked as he pulled the box out of the back end of his truck.

Addie spoke quietly. "She escaped her trafficker tonight. Laurie couldn't find a spot for her in a safe house or shelter, so I offered one of our rooms."

"Really?" Zach frowned. "I'm sorry she's been held captive, but can we trust her to be in our house?"

Addie's face dropped. "Do you trust me to be in the same house as you?"

He sighed. "It's not the same thing, Ads, and you know that. She just got off the streets. Does she do drugs? Does she have a weapon? We don't know anything about her."

"She called the hotline to save her life. That's all I need to know," Addie said sharply. She pulled on the box to drag it inside, but Zach stopped her. He wrapped his arms around her.

"I'm sorry. I know this is a sensitive subject for you. And I'm not trying to be mean or judgmental. It's my job to keep you safe," Zach said gently.

Addie melted in his embrace. "I know you're not a judgmental person. And I know you mean to keep me safe. But this girl wouldn't have risked her life to escape just so she could kill us in our sleep. Believe me, I trust her. She needs someone to help her." Addie looked up into Zach's brown eyes. "She needs someone to keep her safe."

He gave her a small smile. "Okay. I trust your judgment." They lifted the box, one on each end, and walked toward the front door. "Do you know how hard it is to find a mattress this late at night?" He chuckled. "I bought a frame too. I can put it together quickly while the mattress flattens out."

"Thank you," Addie said. "For believing in me, and for everything else."

He smiled.

"Oh, and you might have to sleep in the garage tonight." She grinned mischievously.

"What?"

Addie laughed.

An hour later, Zach had finished putting the frame together, and he and Addie lifted the mattress on top of it. Addie had chosen a bedroom farther down the hallway from theirs, closer to the bathroom, hoping Katie would feel more comfortable there.

"Wow. This is nice," Katie said when Addie showed her the room. "Do all the rooms have fireplaces?"

Addie nodded as she set the sheets and blanket on the mattress. Zach had left to give the women privacy. "Yes. And thank goodness someone before us changed them all to gas. I'd hate to have to chop that much wood."

Katie smiled. "That would be work."

Together they tucked the sheets on the bed and smoothed out the blanket.

"It's pretty warm since we have no air conditioning. You might want to crack the window for a cool breeze. We're on the second floor, so it's safe to do that. If you'd like a fan, I could bring one up."

"I'll be fine," Katie said. She dropped onto the mattress. "This is soft. Thanks so much for putting me up. It was nice of Zach to buy this just for me."

"You're welcome," Addie said. "And it's no big deal. We have the room, obviously."

Katie sighed. "I haven't slept in a real bed for months. We had a van where we'd sleep but no bed. This is going to be heavenly."

Her words stabbed at Addie's heart. She remembered feeling that way once. "If you need anything at all, holler, okay? I know how hard the first few nights can be. I hope you'll feel safe here."

The younger girl smiled at her. "I already do."

Holding back tears, Addie said goodnight and headed down the hallway to her room. It was midnight by the time she crawled into bed beside Zach, who still hadn't fallen asleep.

"Okay. Tell me how you ended up bringing Katie home. I know there's more to the story," Zach said.

Addie took a deep breath and let it out slowly. She'd always been honest with Zach, and she wasn't going to stop now.

"Okay. But let me finish the story before you have a fit."

His brows rose. "I'm going to have a fit?"

"Just listen first." She explained what had happened, starting with the phone call and her rushing out to help Katie. Addie could tell Zach wanted to interrupt her several times, but he held his tongue. She ended her story by saying, "I promise I won't do anything stupid like that again, so please don't be mad. Laurie already read me the riot act. My gut instinct was to help her. I'm glad I did, but I know it was a dangerous thing to do."

Zach stared at her but didn't say a word. His silence was worse than if he'd started yelling.

"Aren't you going to say anything?" Addie asked.

"What can I say? You've already said it was a stupid thing to do. You promised not to do it again. There's nothing left to say."

Addie bit her lip as she watched him slide down under the blankets. "If you're mad at me, tell me. Don't leave me hanging here, or I won't be able to sleep."

When he looked at her, he seemed more disappointed than angry. "You risked your life for a stranger without giving any thought to what might have happened. Without considering what my life would be like without you if you'd been killed. I get that what you did was a good thing for Katie. But if things had gone bad, I might have lost you. Then what?"

Addie frowned. "So, I shouldn't have helped her? I should have left her there so her trafficker could hurt her, or worse?"

"No." Zach sat up, running a hand through his hair. "That's the problem. It's hard for me to be selfish when you were saving someone's life. But I just wish you'd think of me—of us—before doing something dangerous like that. After all these years, I still come last in your thoughts. That's why I'm upset."

Tears filled Addie's eyes. He was right. They were a couple and a team. And she should have thought about him and their life together before rushing out and not waiting for the police to do their job.

"I'm so sorry," she said. "You're right. Sometimes I just do what I want and forget to think of how you'd feel. Like buying this expensive house. I bought it even though you had reservations. And now I'm remodeling the way I want—which is not the smartest way to get our money back out of it. I'm sorry. I'll try to do better."

Zach reached out and hugged her tightly. "I don't care about the house or the decisions you make for it. I trust your judgment on things like that. Your safety is all I care about." He pulled back and looked into her eyes. "I love you, Addie. I don't know how I can make that any clearer. I love you, I care about you, and I want to be with you for a long, long time. So, if you love me too, please think before doing anything dangerous."

She nodded and hugged him again, holding on as if her life depended upon it. Addie didn't know what she'd do without Zach. He was the rock that kept her steady, even when her world was falling in emotionally. She hadn't always put their relationship first, and she knew that. "I'll try to do better. You deserve that," she whispered.

"Thank you," Zach said. "That's all I want. Now," he pulled back and gave her a mischievous grin. "What was that about me sleeping in the garage?"

Addie laughed. This was the Zach she loved.

* * *

Addie awoke early the next morning, eager to get back to work on the house. By the time she'd showered and dressed, Zach was up and groggily heading toward the bathroom. "Another workday," he said, passing her on the way.

"Every day is a workday," Addie said with a grin.

She went downstairs, made a cup of coffee, and then stared out the window over the sink. They'd put in a larger window than the original to brighten up the kitchen. Addie thought about Sofiya standing in this same spot, staring out into the yard at the bench around the tree, praying for Harry to come back. So much had happened in this house, and so much more would in the generations to come.

"Good morning."

Addie jumped at the sound of a girl's voice. She turned and was surprised at the sight of Katie. The young girl had scrubbed her face free of makeup and wore her long hair up in a high ponytail. She wore jean shorts, a T-shirt, and a pair of high-top sneakers. She looked all of fifteen years old.

"Hi," Addie said. "Did you sleep well?"

Katie nodded. "I haven't slept that good in years. A bed makes all the difference."

Feeling safe makes all the difference, too, Addie thought. "Would you like a cup of coffee? We have tea, too. And I have cereal in the cupboard or eggs if you'd like them."

Katie smiled. "Don't go to any trouble. You've done more than enough already. I can make my own breakfast." She walked past Addie, put a coffee pod in the Keurig, and found a mug in the cupboard to fill the machine with water. "So, what are you working on today?"

Addie sat down at the kitchen counter. "I'm starting on the first bedroom upstairs. Today is tear down wallpaper day."

"Can I help?" Katie asked.

"Sure. If you want to." Addie was surprised she'd offered.

"Great." Katie smiled and picked up her coffee, placing it on the counter beside Addie's. "Which cupboard is the cereal in?"

Addie pointed and then told her where to find the bowls, too. The young girl poured her cereal and milk, then sat beside Addie while she ate. "How do you take down wallpaper?"

"I usually wet it with some solution and then scrape it off. But I want to see what other paper is underneath, so I'll try pulling up a corner or two first. I've found this house has many layers of wallpaper," Addie said.

"I suppose because it's old, huh?"

"Yeah. Many families have lived here over the past hundred years. There are so many styles of paper on the walls. It's kind of cool."

"I'm off to get the shelving for Sofiya's room," Zach said, sauntering into the kitchen. He headed for the coffee maker. "Morning, Katie. Was that mattress any good?"

Katie smiled, and Addie noticed she didn't look tense around Zach. That made her happy.

"Good morning," Katie said. "It was perfect. The most comfortable mattress I've slept on in years."

Zach smiled over at her. "That's great to hear."

Katie looked over at Addie. "Who's Sofiya?"

"Oh." Addie glanced over at the little room off the kitchen. She didn't know how Katie would react to knowing this house was once a brothel. "Sofiya was a teenager who lived here in the early 1900s. She worked in the kitchen and lived in that little room over there."

Katie glanced to where Addie had pointed. "Wow. It looks

so small. How do you know this?"

"Through some letters we found in an antique store," Addie said. "They're what led me to this house in the first place."

"Wow. Really? That's dope," Katie said.

"Yeah, man. Pretty dope," Zach said with a grin, making Addie laugh. She saw Katie frown.

"He's not making fun of you," Addie said quickly. "We're just old compared to you, but at least we know what dope means."

"Oh." Katie chuckled. "I didn't think of you two as old. The guys that bought me, they were old." She shivered.

Addie went quiet and sipped her coffee. Katie looked worried.

"I shouldn't have said that. Sorry." Katie stared down at her now-empty bowl.

"I want you to feel comfortable saying whatever you're thinking," Addie said. "Your life has been different from a regular teenager. There's no shame in it. You are not to blame for what they did to you."

Katie nodded, but the air had grown heavier in the room.

"Let's go upstairs and start peeling wallpaper," Addie said brightly. "When Zach comes back, we can start working on the shelving. I'm making Sofiya's room into a laundry room and pantry."

"Okay," Katie said, sounding like she'd perked up. She glanced out the kitchen window as she rinsed her bowl. "Who's that out in the yard?"

Zach stepped over and glanced out the window. "Oh. He's up early for a teenager. That's Matt from next door. He offered to fix the bench wrapped around the oak tree."

"Oh." Katie watched him a moment, and Zach turned to

look at Addie as if to ask, *will this be a problem?* Addie shrugged.

All morning, Addie and Katie worked on the bedroom, peeling off years of wallpaper. Some of it was pretty, and some was dark and ugly. Addie knew that in some high-end brothels, the madam allowed the girls to pick their own wallpaper for their room. But she couldn't picture Miss Nora letting the girls re-paper when a new girl started working there. She was too mean and cheap. Still, there were layers and layers on the wall.

By noon, Addie had a call from Laurie.

"I thought Katie would like to join us for our group meeting tonight. You too, of course," Laurie said.

"I can ask her. She's helping me work around the house today."

"That's great. How is she doing?" Laurie asked.

"Quite well, actually," Addie said, keeping her voice low. "But I remember when I first escaped, I kept telling myself I was fine. I wasn't. I think the meetings will be good for her."

"I agree," Laurie said. "And I'm still working on getting permission to add another person to my house. It might take another day or two."

"That's okay. She'll be fine here." Addie felt she was bonding with the girl, and she wanted to spend more time with her.

After hanging up, Addie went to the kitchen where she'd left Katie to tell her about the group meeting. But when she entered the room, it was empty.

"Katie?" she called. No answer. Addie peeked into Sofiya's room, but the only things in there were the shelves and brackets that Zach had picked up. Addie wondered where the girl had gone. She hoped Katie hadn't had a panic attack and run away. It happened to girls who survived trauma all the time.

Walking to the kitchen sink, she glanced out the window. A sigh escaped her. Katie was holding a board for Matt while he worked on connecting them with his electric screwdriver. The two teens were talking and laughing—a typical everyday scene. But Addie knew differently. Katie hadn't been able to act like a normal teen for years.

"Looks like those two are getting along," Zach said as he entered the kitchen. He was wiping his hands with a rag.

"Yeah." Addie looked up at Zach. "She's been a real help today, too. She's a hard worker."

"That's great," Zach said. "Do you think at some point her past will hit her?"

She sighed. "I'm sure it will, eventually. I'll know more tonight. Laurie invited her and I to a meeting with the other girls."

Zach nodded. "As hard as that is, it's what helped you get through the tough times."

"It still does," Addie said. She glanced outside again. The two teens were laughing. Addie hoped Katie's transition into a regular life would be easier than hers had been.

Chapter Sixteen

Sofiya

Miss Nora went on a rampage once she realized Alina was missing. She ran from room to room, shouting at each girl, asking what they knew about the missing girl. Of course, no one knew anything. Even Mabel shook her head and shrugged.

"I never heard a thing last night. She must have snuck out while we were asleep," Miss Nora's one-time ally said. Since the days when they'd all been sick, Mabel had stopped being Nora's spy. She'd even told Sofiya that someday she'd disappear like many of the other girls had.

Nora cornered Sofiya in the kitchen, standing over her menacingly as Mrs. Jarvi watched. "Where did your sister go? I know you were in on it."

Sofiya was no longer afraid of her captor. She ducked around her and walked to the other side of the kitchen table where she and Mrs. Jarvi were preparing lunch. "Don't you think I would have gone with her if I'd known she was leaving?" Sofiya asked. "I have no idea where she went."

Miss Nora's face turned red with anger. "You're lying." She stopped a moment and frowned as if a thought had come to her. "Clinton. That's where she's gone. She's run off with him." Nora swept out of the room as quickly as she'd entered.

"This won't make her any easier to live with," Mrs. Jarvi said, but grinned. "Do you know where your sister has gone?"

Sofiya trusted Mrs. Jarvi completely but didn't want to give away Alina's secret. "Far away from here, where she'll be safe and happy."

"Good." Mrs. Jarvi winked. "We must make sure you leave soon too."

Sofiya didn't know where she'd go, but she did wish to escape.

Life in the house became unbearable, just as Mrs. Jarvi had predicted. Once Miss Nora learned that Alina had run off with Clinton, she had a terrible fight with Clint's father and lost not only his business but that of several of his friends. She lost a considerable chunk of money from those men deserting her. Finding replacements for the girls who'd left was also becoming increasingly difficult. She was desperate to find more girls and bring in high-end clientele once more.

Throughout the summer, the guests became fewer and fewer at Miss Nora's parlor. Nora grew desperate and began bringing in girls she'd recruited from establishments on the waterfront. She tried to pass them off as younger and less experienced, but the men didn't buy it. The women weren't of the quality that her customers were used to, and her client list continued to dwindle. Nora's reputation for running a high-end brothel was fading, and nothing she did helped her rise back to the top.

As Sofiya cleaned the parlor one Friday morning, she saw Mabel, dressed in a prim suit and carrying a suitcase, coming down the stairs. Mabel looked startled for a moment but quickly regained her composure. She set down her suitcase and walked up to Sofiya.

"You won't tell, will you?" Mabel asked.

Sofiya shook her head. "No. Of course not. But I'm surprised to see you leave."

"I've had it with this life," Mabel said. "Believe it or not, I want more. Miss Nora took me from the streets when I was only fifteen. I haven't known anything else. I was grateful to her, but now, I can hardly look at her. I don't want to become her."

"What'll you do?" Sofiya asked.

Mabel grinned. "I'll find something. I'm tough. I can do just about anything I set my mind to."

Sofiya believed her. "Good luck. I mean it."

"Thanks." Mabel walked across the foyer, lifted her suitcase, then turned back to Sofiya. "Get out of here as soon as you can," she said. Then Mabel walked out the door.

Sofiya knew Mabel was right. She needed to leave this place soon.

Mabel's betrayal set Miss Nora into a tailspin. She began drinking heavily and was usually quite sloshed by evening when the few men showed up. They were low on funds, so Sofiya no longer served food trays. The type of men who frequented the place weren't used to that kind of entertaining anyway. A good stiff drink and a girl were all they wanted. Miss Nora sat in the corner of the parlor, intoxicated, and collected the money from the men. No longer was there any pretense of entertaining. The girls didn't chat politely with the men while someone played the piano. Miss Nora's house had become a low-end bordello in a high-end neighborhood.

Instead of greeting gentlemen, Carter stood at the door to act as a protector of the girls. He was careful not to let drunken men into the house, and if a man was deep into his cups and causing trouble, it was Carter's job to toss him out. Many a night, Carter, looking tired and disgusted, would nod for Sofiya to stop serving drinks and go to the kitchen. He was on constant alert, protecting her from the rabble that now frequented the household. Sofiya felt sorry for him. He'd been so proud of his job, but now, he looked defeated.

With money growing tighter, Mrs. Jarvi's hours were cut down along with the budget for food and other supplies. Miss Nora sold one of her prized cars to pay the bills. Sofiya overhead a conversation between Miss Nora and her banker about a possible sale of some of her property. While all the country was celebrating the end of the war and the beginning of a new decade, Miss Nora's world was crumbling.

As Sofiya prepared a meager lunch for the girls one chilly October morning, Mrs. Jarvi came inside the house with a bright smile on her round face. She only worked from noon to five these days, but she still was the first one to pick up the post.

"I have a letter for you," the older woman said. She handed Sofiya a small postcard.

Sofiya's heart pounded with excitement. The front of the postcard had a photo of her dear friend, Alina, holding a small baby. They sat in a rocking chair on the porch of a nice-looking home. "It's Alina and her baby," Sofiya said, smiling brightly. "Look at how beautiful she is."

Mrs. Jarvi looked over her shoulder and nodded. "Well look at that," she murmured. "She's had a beautiful baby." Mrs. Jarvi knew by now that Alina had run away with Clinton, but the baby was a surprise to her.

"She had told me she was expecting before she left. I'm so happy for her," Sofiya said.

The older woman patted her shoulder and set about working on the lunch, leaving Sofiya to read the postcard. Sofiya turned the card over and read the neat script.

Dear Sofiya,

I'm sorry I haven't written before this, but you are always in my thoughts. I don't think you would like Alaska. It rains just awful here, even worse than Portland. Ha Ha. Can you believe I am a mother now? Our sweet baby was born October 9ᵗʰ, and my life has been a whirlwind of feedings and diapers. But I am so happy with little Floriana Sofiya (Florie) and my husband, Clint. He is working hard, running the factory, and we rent a nice house here. It's more than I thought possible after the rough start you and I had. I miss you and wish only good things for you. I'll write more soon.

Love, Alina

Tears filled Sofiya's eyes. She was so happy for her dear friend. "She's fine, and so is the baby. She and Clint are happy together," she reported to Mrs. Jarvi.

The cook smiled. "I'm glad to hear that. She deserves a good life after having lived here." Mrs. Jarvi's expression turned serious. "And so do you. We must find a way for you to leave this place."

"And go where?" Sofiya asked. "I don't know anyone in this town. And Harry never returned. Where would I go?"

"We'll find something for you," Mrs. Jarvi said with certainty.

Sofiya went to her small bedroom and hid the postcard in the false bottom of the cigar box. She did want to leave. But she was afraid she'd end up somewhere worse than here.

Two weeks later, Mrs. Jarvi arrived with a newspaper under her arm. She laid it out on the kitchen table and pointed to an advertisement she'd circled.

"This is your chance," she told Sofiya.

The young girl read the small ad.

Looking for a young single woman to work as a travel companion and ladies' maid for an elderly woman. Must be literate, and the ability to speak multiple languages is preferred. Bring references to the address listed below.

Sofiya looked up at Mrs. Jarvi. "I have no references. I doubt this woman would appreciate that I've worked in a house like this."

Mrs. Jarvi brushed her protest aside with a sweep of her hand. "We'll make up a story. You can be an orphan whose parents died during the pandemic. Or your parents died in the civil war in Finland. There are a multitude of stories we could come up with."

"You want me to lie?"

"No, no. Not lie, exactly. Exaggerate. Anything to get you that job. After all, you are literate and educated and speak several languages. You'd be perfect for this job."

Sofiya had no idea how Mrs. Jarvi knew she spoke several languages. "I don't know," she said.

"Dear. This is your best chance to leave. Obviously, this

woman is wealthy, or she wouldn't be able to afford a travel companion. It'll take you away from this place, and she'll take care of you. You must at least try," Mrs. Jarvi said.

Sofiya thought about the job throughout the day. It was tempting. But she had no idea how she'd get away from here long enough to apply without Miss Nora becoming suspicious. Mrs. Jarvi had a plan for that, too.

"Tomorrow, you'll dress nicely, and Carter will drive you to the address to apply for the position," the cook said. "I'll pose as your great-aunt and write a letter of recommendation, boasting of your many accomplishments as a young lady and your education. You only need to say that your parents have passed, and you are in need of a respectable position to support yourself."

Sofiya wasn't as sure of this plan as Mrs. Jarvi, but she was willing to try.

The next morning, as Miss Nora slept off her drinking spree and the girls slept upstairs, Sofiya dressed as nicely as possible. She wore one of the newer dresses Mabel had chosen for her the previous year with stockings and low-heeled pumps. Mrs. Jarvi brought a suit jacket that she'd altered to fit Sofiya. It was long, and the light gray color went nicely with her flowered dress. Sofiya pinned her hair up and wore a small, gray hat and white gloves. She looked as respectable as was possible.

"You look perfect," Mrs. Jarvi said, beaming at her. "Now, here is the letter I wrote for you. I introduce myself as your great-aunt Olga Jarvi and state that although we enjoy having you with us, it is time you made your own way in the world. I mentioned how organized and resourceful you are and how pleasant your personality is."

"Thank you, Mrs. Jarvi," Sofiya said, her heart filling with gratitude for all she had done for her. "I'll do my best."

"I know you will, dear," Mrs. Jarvi said, patting her arm. Taking a breath, she said, "Well, it's time. Carter is waiting for you at the side door. Luckily, Miss Nora doesn't think twice about him going out on errands with the car."

Sofiya walked out the kitchen door, and there was Carter, wearing his chauffeur's uniform, waiting to open the car door for her.

"Good morning, Miss Sofiya," Carter said, smiling. "Quite a big day for you today."

"Good morning." She stepped inside the car. When Carter slid in behind the wheel, Sofiya scooted forward. "Thank you for this. I hope you won't get into trouble."

"You are more than welcome," Carter said, giving her his best smile. "And it's no trouble at all. Miss Nora never knows where I'm off to." He chuckled, then they took off.

The address wasn't too far from their house, so in what seemed like only moments, the car was parked in front of a respectable, two-story home. Sofiya smoothed her skirt and tugged at her gloves. She knew nothing about applying for a position and was fearful she'd do something wrong.

Carter stepped out and opened the door for her. "Good luck, Miss Sofiya," he said.

Taking a deep breath, Sofiya slipped out of the car and walked stiffly up the sidewalk. There was a beautiful oak door that gleamed in the morning sun. Not seeing a doorbell, Sofiya used the brass knocker to announce her presence.

A woman wearing a gray maid's uniform answered the door. She was older, her brown hair streaked with silver peeking out from under her white cap. She stared at Sofiya a moment, then past her to where Carter was waiting at the curb. Frowning, she looked back at Sofiya. "May I help you?"

"Good morning," Sofiya said, her voice trembling. "I'm here to apply for the traveling companion position."

The woman looked her up and down. "A bit young, aren't you?"

Sofiya was taken aback by her comment. "Yes. I suppose I am. But I have a letter of recommendation." She handed the woman the neatly folded letter Mrs. Jarvi had given her.

"Fine. Come inside," the maid said.

Sofiya followed her into the neatly appointed foyer. The area was much like Miss Nora's home, with the staircase on the right and closed pocket doors on the left. Sofiya assumed the parlor was behind the wooden doors.

"Take a seat," the maid said, pointing to the padded bench that sat along the paneled wall of the staircase. "I'll inform Mrs. Dawson you are here."

Sofiya sat, crossed her legs at the ankles as she'd been taught, and folded her gloved hands in her lap. She tried to look calm, but her stomach was a twist of nerves. She hated lying above all else, but she knew she'd have to lie to secure this position.

Muffled voices could be heard in the parlor, and a moment later, the wooden pocket doors slid open. A woman not much taller than Sofiya stood there, smiling at her.

"Good morning. I'm Mrs. Marion Dawson. Please, come in and sit awhile." The older woman led the way into the tastefully decorated parlor. She directed Sofiya to sit on the striped cameo-backed sofa while she sat across from her in a green tufted chair.

"Would you like a cup of tea?" Mrs. Dawson asked. An oak table sat between them with a silver tray holding a china tea set.

"Thank you. That's very kind." Sofiya took off her gloves

and laid them on her lap. She was so nervous, she wasn't sure if she could hold the cup steady. But Sofiya accepted the cup and saucer with a smile and took a sip before setting it down.

"Well," Mrs. Dawson said, sitting back in her seat. She wore a simple white blouse tucked into a navy and white striped skirt that hung just above her ankles. Her salt and pepper hair was cut to shoulder length but was thick and curly, and her face was round with prominent features. She smiled, and her brown eyes looked kind as she watched Sofiya. "You've come to apply for the traveling companion position?"

"Yes, ma'am," Sofiya said, feeling even guiltier for having to lie to this motherly-looking woman.

"I read your aunt's glowing letter of recommendation. You sound quite accomplished. Exactly what I am looking for," Mrs. Dawson said.

"That was very kind of her. I've never held a real position, but I've assisted my aunt in many ways around the house," Sofiya said. Basically, it was true. She'd been assisting Mrs. Jarvi.

"And you speak several languages? Which ones are you fluent in?" Mrs. Dawson looked intrigued.

"Finnish is my native language," Sofiya said. "I also speak German, French, Russian, and English, of course."

The older lady smiled. "Wonderful. May I pry and ask how a young woman such as yourself learned to speak so many languages?"

Sofiya took a breath. She'd try to stick as close to the truth as possible. "My father was a language professor at the University of Helsinki, where I grew up. He was a true believer in women's education. We left the country before the Finnish civil war and uprising with Russia."

"Oh, I'm so sorry, dear. I shouldn't have brought your history up. I'm sure it is upsetting to you. Your aunt's letter mentioned how your parents both died during the Spanish Flu pandemic. How awful for you."

"Thank you," Sofiya said softly, lowering her eyes.

Mrs. Dawson took another sip of her tea while assessing Sofiya. She set down her cup and spoke. "You would not believe the type of women I've had applying for this position." The older woman sighed. "Women older than I am. Spinster teachers. And women I'm sure who worked in the underbelly of society if you know what I mean," she said, lowering her voice. "You, however, are a breath of fresh air. Refined and educated."

Sofiya knew Mrs. Dawson would be shocked to learn she'd also lived in a house of the "underbelly of society."

"I've put off leaving Portland long enough. I am eager to return home and prepare for my trip abroad."

"Yes, ma'am," Sofiya said, confused by this explanation.

Mrs. Dawson's face softened. "Would you come work for me, dear? You will receive a monthly income, and all your necessities and travel expenses will be paid for. I believe you and I would have such fun traveling together."

The younger girl's heart beat faster. "You're offering me the position?"

Mrs. Dawson chuckled. "Yes, dear. For as long as you can put up with me."

"Oh, ma'am. Thank you. I'd love to work for you," Sofiya said.

"Wonderful." Mrs. Dawson sat back again in her chair. "Can you start tomorrow? I know that is quick, but truthfully, I'd like to leave on the train as soon as possible. I want to begin my next trip."

Sofiya nodded. "Yes. I can start right away."

Mrs. Dawson stood, a broad smile on her face. "That's wonderful. I will see you bright and early tomorrow morning. We can start packing and make our train reservations right away."

Sofiya shook hands with her new employer and thanked her again, hardly able to believe she had found her way out of Miss Nora's clutches.

Carter was thrilled to hear that Sofiya had secured the position, and Mrs. Jarvi was ecstatic.

"Oh, I'm going to miss you, dear, but I'm so happy for you," Mrs. Jarvi said. "What a wonderful opportunity for you—traveling all over, even to Europe, with this fine woman." The cook sobered. "You do believe she will be kind to you, don't you?"

Sofiya nodded. She'd changed back into her gray uniform for the last time and had carefully put away her clothes so she could pack them in the morning. "She seems very kind. I think she will be a good employer."

"Oh, you lucky girl. I will miss you terribly. But I will also be relieved knowing that you will never have to put up with that horrible Nora again."

All day, she and Mrs. Jarvi were careful not to speak of Sofiya's new opportunity in front of the other girls and especially Miss Nora. Sofiya worked as usual, cleaning and cooking and then serving liquor in the evening now that they no longer served food. By one o'clock in the morning, she fell into her tiny bed for the last time to get a few hours of sleep.

As she lay there, she thought of everything that had happened over the past two years. She had taken a few moments to write a letter to Alina telling her about her newfound job and promising to write more later. Mrs. Jarvi had taken the letter to post it, so there was no chance Miss Nora would find it. All that was left was to pack in the morning, and Carter would drive her to Mrs. Dawson's house.

Finally, Sofiya would be living a life she could be proud of. One that her mother would be proud of her for. The young girl couldn't wait for her new life to begin.

CHAPTER SEVENTEEN

Addie

That evening, Addie brought Katie to the meeting at Laurie's house. The teen girl had been hesitant about going at first but finally agreed when Addie told her she didn't have to share if she didn't feel like doing so.

"Sometimes it just helps to be around others who understand what you're going through," Addie had told Katie.

"I'd rather just forget it all," Katie had said. "It was a nightmare."

"I understand. I really do," Addie had told her. "That's exactly what I did when I first escaped. I thought I could push all the bad memories down and start my life over. But I soon learned that it didn't work. I was scared, angry, and always having nightmares. After I sought help, I was finally able to let some of it go."

Katie had nodded but didn't agree to share. When they arrived at Laurie's, the other girls were already sitting in the living room, chatting. Melanie waved Katie over to join them, and she did so, smiling at the girl she'd already met.

"How's she doing?" Laurie asked quietly as they stood in the entryway.

"Pretty well, actually," Addie said. "She helped me work around the house today and then helped the boy who lives next door with a project outside."

"That's good to hear," Laurie said. "Do you think she'll share tonight?"

Addie shrugged. "She was against sharing her experience when we discussed it earlier. She just wants to forget everything. I think you and I both know how that feels."

Laurie nodded solemnly. She led the way into the living room, and Laurie and Addie sat down in chairs that faced the sofa.

The meeting was casual. Laurie spoke a little to all the girls about letting go of the past, and then Wanda, the quietest one, talked a little about her experience being trafficked. Addie watched as Katie seemed to fold into herself as Wanda spoke. She wondered if Wanda's experiences brought back bad memories for Katie. But Katie didn't offer to speak throughout the meeting.

Latisha spoke about her progress with the classes she was taking at the local beauty college. "The teachers there are cool, and I really like coloring hair and learning to do the acrylic nails. It's right up my alley," she said, flashing her own brightly colored nails.

The other girls laughed, and Laurie complemented Latisha on the good job she'd done on her nails.

"Thanks," Latisha said, smiling widely, which was unusual for her. "I can't wait to do the makeup course too. I never thought I'd be able to learn real job skills, but I'm really enjoying this."

"I wish I knew exactly what I wanted to do," Wanda said. "I like going to the junior college, but I haven't found anything yet that sparks my interest."

"How were you able to get into college?" Katie asked. "Didn't you have to finish high school first?"

"I got my GED," Wanda said. "I always did well in school until I was taken. I studied for my GED and was able to pass those tests easily. Melanie is working on doing that right now."

Katie turned to Melanie. "Really? Is it hard?"

"I'm not a very good student, so it's a lot of work for me," Melanie said. "But the online courses I'm taking to prepare me for the tests are really good."

Katie nodded. She looked intrigued. As Addie watched her, she hoped the girl would consider studying for the GED as a starting point.

Later, after arriving home from the meeting, Addie casually asked, "What did you think of the group meeting?"

"It was interesting. Hearing some of their stories is sad—but like you said, I can relate."

They were sitting in the kitchen snacking on store-bought chocolate-chip cookies. Addie had a cup of tea while Katie drank a Coke.

"Do you think I could get my GED?" Katie asked. "I was talking to Matt today, and he's going to be a senior this year in high school. I don't think I could do the whole high school thing now, but I think I could study for the tests."

"I don't see why not," Addie said. "We can look into it tomorrow and see if we can get government assistance to help pay for it."

"That would be great," Katie said.

Later, once they were in bed, Addie caught Zach up on

what happened at the meeting and Katie's interest in getting her GED.

"That's good," Zach said. "She's really adjusting well for someone who's lived in hell for the past couple of years."

"It seems that way," Addie said. "But I'm not sure everything has sunk in completely for her. It's a relief to be free again, but then it becomes overwhelming. I'm sure at some point, she'll crack."

"And then what?" Zach asked.

"That's what the meetings are for. They're a safe place to get all the pain out. It just takes time."

Later that night, Addie was awakened by a strange noise. She glanced over at Zach, but he was sound asleep. Just as she settled in again, a scream broke the silence. Addie got up in a flash, ran out of the room, and headed straight to Katie's room. She stopped for a moment outside the door and listened. It was quiet, but then Katie screamed, and Addie rushed inside.

Katie was crouched on the floor in the darkened room, grasping her old backpack in her arms. "Get out! Leave me alone!" she screamed. It took a moment for Addie to realize that the young girl wasn't looking directly at her. She was staring at some unknown nightmare she was in the middle of.

"Katie. It's okay. It's Addie. You're okay," Addie said in a calm voice. She knew to never wake up a person during a nightmare, but she couldn't bear to see the frightened look on the young girl's face.

"Get out! Don't touch me!" Katie yelled. She turned her back to Addie, still clutching her backpack.

Addie took a chance and flicked on the light. She hoped the bright light would wake Katie up. But the girl continued to huddle on the floor with her back turned to her. Gingerly, she walked toward her. "Katie. It's okay. You're safe here," Addie said soothingly.

Katie turned toward Addie. Her eyes were wide open but blank. Addie could tell she was still asleep.

"Why don't you lay down and rest?" Addie said calmly. She drew closer to Katie, and the younger girl seemed to relax. Carefully, Addie reached out and guided Katie back to bed. Katie curled up on the bed, still hugging her backpack, and Addie covered her with the blanket. Katie hadn't awoken during the entire exchange.

As Addie turned off the light and quietly closed the door, she began to shake. She remembered the nightmares she'd experienced directly after running away, and even to this day. The fact that Katie was keeping her backpack close, even as she slept, told Addie that even though she said she was doing fine, she wasn't. Katie was clutching her possessions as if she'd have to leave at any moment. Or as if someone might take them from her. It was the same fear Addie had experienced the first few months after she'd escaped.

The nightmare proved to Addie what she'd already suspected. Katie wasn't doing well, and she had a long way to go.

The next day, Addie didn't mention the nightmare to Katie. The girl looked tired when she came downstairs but never said a word about having bad dreams. After talking to Laurie about the possibility of Katie working for her GED, Addie relayed what she'd learned to the girl while they continued scraping wallpaper in the bedroom.

"Laurie said there's a state-funded program that allows young people to study for their GED for free. All you have to do is sign up. She's sending the link to my computer," Addie said.

"That's great." Katie wasn't wearing makeup again, but she was such a pretty girl, she didn't need it. Her hair was piled up with a clip, and she wore a T-shirt and jean shorts.

"Maybe we could go shopping and pick you up a few things," Addie offered. "My treat."

Katie immediately looked wary. "I don't want you to spend money on me after everything you've already done."

"You've been working around here without pay. And you were helping Matt make the bench yesterday. I think of it more as something you've earned," Addie said casually, trying not to make a big deal about it. She realized why Katie was cautious about taking things. In the trafficking world, if someone gave you something, it was never free. You were obligated to give something back. Addie didn't want Katie to feel obligated.

"Oh. Okay," Katie said after she'd thought about it. "Thanks. I could use some things."

After lunch, Matt appeared in the backyard to work on the bench, and Katie asked if she could help him.

"That's fine," Addie told her. "I'm sure he enjoys the help." She watched as Katie ran outside and greeted Matt. The boy had a goofy smile on his face.

Zach came inside a while later and nodded toward the two teens. "How's that going?"

Addie smiled. "Like it should. Two teens getting to know each other the old-fashioned way. Katie seems to enjoy Matt's company, and Matt looks shy. It's cute."

Zach reached around her from behind as she stood at the kitchen window. He placed his chin on her shoulder. "Are you being nostalgic?"

"Certainly not. My teen years were a nightmare. But I'm hoping Katie will get a chance to be happy again like I did."

He kissed her cheek and went to the refrigerator. "How are the bedrooms coming along?" he asked.

"Ugh." Addie turned around to watch him. "Bedroom. Singular. Wallpaper takes a long time to get down. But Katie's been a big help. I think I'll paint that room once we get it all scraped off. Or maybe we could add some wainscotting on the bottom half. I know how much you like extra work." She grinned.

"You're evil," he said as he set the fixings for a sandwich on the table. "But if that's what you want, you know I'll do it."

Later that afternoon, Katie came back upstairs to help Addie. "We're almost finished with Sofiya's bench," she said happily. Her cheeks were pink from being out in the sunshine. "I told Matt about Sofiya, and he said you should get a small plaque with her name on it for the bench."

"That's a good idea," Addie said. "Matt seems like a nice kid."

"He is. He said he wants to go to college to become a lawyer. That's big. I have no idea what I'd want to go to school for."

"You have plenty of time to think about it. Once you get your GED, you could try a few classes at the college and see what interests you," Addie said.

Katie grew quiet, which drew Addie's attention.

"Is something wrong?" Addie asked.

Katie sat crossed legged on the floor. "It just hit me that I've never thought about my future before because I never thought I'd have one. It's weird to finally have the freedom to make my own decisions. And it's a bit scary."

Addie walked over and sat across from Katie. "I get it. It is scary. When I first ran away, I didn't know what to do. I got a job at a café, and a girl there had a room I could rent. It was in a crappy apartment in a scary part of town, but I could afford it, so that's where I lived. That first year, I didn't change anything because I didn't know what I wanted to do. I just worked and lived in that little apartment. It's like I froze. Then I met Natalie, and she changed my life."

"Like you're changing mine?" Katie asked. She looked at Addie with watery eyes. "How will I ever repay you for all you've done?" Tears fell down her cheeks.

Addie hadn't thought of it that way. She'd been happy to help Katie get away from that terrible life. "Hey. You don't owe me a thing, okay?" She took Katie's hands in hers. "I'm happy to do whatever you need to help you restart your life."

Katie's shoulders shook, and the tears came faster. "It's all so much. I thought I'd die in that life. I can't believe anyone would care enough about me to help me like this."

"Oh, sweetie." Tears filled Addie's eyes as she scooched over next to Katie and wrapped her arm around her. "You deserve all of this and so much more. I know it feels overwhelming. But don't feel like you don't deserve it because you do."

The younger girl swiped at her tears. "I feel so stupid falling apart like this. I guess I'm not doing as well as I thought I was."

Addie smiled at her. "It's normal, believe me. It's only been a couple of days since your life changed. It'll take time. That's why the group meetings are so important. It's where you can let this all out, and everyone understands."

Katie nodded, then pulled Addie into a hug. "Thank you for everything."

"You're welcome. And you can stay as long as you want until you get on your feet. I'm not going anywhere," Addie said.

Katie drew back and sniffled. "Especially if you don't finish this house." She chuckled despite her tears.

Addie laughed. "Then I guess we'd better get back to work." They found Kleenex in the bathroom, and both women wiped their faces and blew their noses, which brought giggles from them. Addie knew from that moment on that Katie—after a lot of hard work—was going to be okay.

CHAPTER EIGHTEEN

Sofiya

Sofiya's new life as Mrs. Dawson's companion began after many tears and hugs from Mrs. Jarvi and a goodbye hug from Carter when he dropped her off at her new employer's home.

"You take good care of yourself, Miss Sofiya," Carter said with tears in his eyes. "You know where to find me if you ever need anything."

"Thank you, Carter. I wish only good things for you," Sofiya said, trying hard not to cry.

"Do you have your cigar box with its hidden treasures?" Carter asked, glancing at her suitcase.

Sofiya beamed as she remembered the day Carter helped her make the box with the secret compartment. "I do. It's packed away in my suitcase."

He nodded and waited until she was safely inside the house before driving away for the last time.

"Your great-aunt must be wealthy to have her own chauffeur," the maid said with a sniff as she led Sofiya into the dining room.

Sofiya thought it best not to respond. She hoped the maid wouldn't travel with them. She seemed a bit mean-spirited.

"Ah, there you are," Mrs. Dawson said from her seat at the dining room table. "Please join me for breakfast, and we can begin planning our trip to New York."

Sofiya's eyes grew wide. New York. She wondered if that was where Mrs. Dawson's other home was.

Sofiya set down her suitcase and sat at the table. There was tea, toast, and scrambled eggs, all with silver covers to keep them warm. Out of the corner of her eye, she saw Mrs. Dawson glance at her one suitcase.

"Please, help yourself," Mrs. Dawson said. "Do you have only the one suitcase, dear?"

Sofiya placed eggs and a piece of toast on her plate. "Yes, ma'am." When she saw Mrs. Dawson's brows lift, she continued. "We left Finland with very little. And I don't like to speak badly about my great-aunt, but she never offered to help us in any way other than sharing her home."

"Ah, I see. A bit of a tightwad, is she?" Mrs. Dawson smiled. "Well, you'll find I'm not so tight with my money. We'll do some shopping while in New York before we leave for London. Have you ever been to that part of Europe?"

Sofiya shook her head, having just taken a bite of the toast with jam. Swallowing her food, she answered, "No, ma'am."

"Then it will be a joy to share it with you," Mrs. Dawson said. She moved in closer and whispered, "And don't worry about the surly maid. She works for the owners of the house, not me. She won't be coming along."

Sofiya was shocked—it was almost as if Mrs. Dawson had read her mind. "This isn't your home?"

"Oh, no, dear. It's the home of a friend of mine. You'll find

I have friends all over the world who are more than happy to let me stay in their homes. The flat we'll be using in New York City belongs to a former senator I know. He's off on a winter vacation of his own."

A senator? Sofiya thought. She wondered how Mrs. Dawson knew someone so prestigious but was too polite to ask.

After breakfast, Mrs. Dawson called for the maid to show Sofiya to her room. "I'd take you myself," the older woman said, "but I don't navigate stairs like I used to. My bedroom is down here on the main floor."

The upstairs didn't have as many rooms as Miss Nora's place but there looked to be four bedrooms, and the maid showed her to one.

"There's a necessary room down the hallway," the maid said as she turned in the doorway to leave. "And towels and other items in the cabinet." With that, the maid left, shutting the door.

Sofiya stood in the large bedroom, hardly believing this room was all hers. There was a four-poster double bed with a beautiful burgundy counterpane, a vanity table and mirror where she could do her hair, and a tall dresser. Two curtained windows looked out over the side garden and the house next door. A small closet had space for her to hang her few dresses and store her suitcase. After the past two years of living in the tiny room off the kitchen, this room made Sofiya feel like a princess.

Sofiya was quite busy the next two days as she made reservations at the train station for her and Mrs. Dawson and ran errands for items they'd need before their trip across the country. She was given taxi fare and additional money to buy necessities she'd need. The young girl was surprised at how generous

Mrs. Dawson was to her—a literal stranger—so she was frugal with the money. She wanted Mrs. Dawson to never feel taken advantage of.

They left from Portland's Union Station on a chilly day in late October with a heap of luggage for Mrs. Dawson and two small bags for Sofiya. The older woman promised that by the time they left New York City, Sofiya would be drowning in luggage.

"One cannot go through a winter season in London and Paris without the proper clothing," Mrs. Dawson said haughtily with her nose up in the air. Then she smiled widely and laughed. "But truthfully, it's so much fun!"

They had two sleeping compartments with connecting doors on the train to Chicago and even nicer rooms on the train that took them into New York City. Compared to Sofiya's last trip across the country when she and Alina had first arrived, this one was luxurious. They ate in the first-class dining car for every meal, and there was even a car with entertainment—a small band playing music to dance by on a tiny dance floor. Mrs. Dawson loved listening to the music and chatting with the other travelers, and Sofiya sat quietly, watching everyone. This was the style in which she'd been raised, but after two years of working at Miss Nora's, she felt uncomfortable in the upper-class environment, as if she no longer belonged.

"Now, dear. You must enjoy yourself on this trip," Mrs. Dawson chastised her. "There are so many interesting people to meet and things to do. Enjoy life while you're young."

But it was hard for a shy girl like Sofiya, especially after all she'd been through. She'd seen men at their worst at Miss Nora's—men in the upper echelons of society buying favors from young girls. It was difficult for her to trust these men now, wearing their best evening attire and gold chains across their bulging bellies. They might be just as terrible as the ones she'd served hor d'oeuvres and drinks to each evening.

"May I have this dance?" a young gentleman asked, standing beside Sofiya with a smile.

The girl looked around her, wondering who he might be speaking to. She looked so plain compared to the many young women in the entertainment car. Her dress was a black drop-waist that she'd bought at the last minute at Mrs. Dawson's insistence, and she wore a long string of fake white pearls around her neck. He couldn't possibly be speaking to her.

"Go along, dear," Mrs. Dawson urged. "Dance with the nice young man."

Sofiya looked up into the man's blue eyes and clean-shaven face. He was young—at least he looked young—and he seemed harmless. She accepted his hand and let him lead her to the crowded minuscular dance floor. The music playing was slow, so he held her respectfully at a distance, and they began to move in time with the other couples.

"Have you ever danced on a train before?" the man asked, grinning. "It's quite an odd feeling, don't you think? Dancing as the train rattles beneath us."

His words made her smile. "No, I haven't. But you're right. It feels like one cannot keep their balance."

"My name is Adam," the man said. "I'm traveling with my father as his assistant. He says I must learn the family business from the ground floor up." He rolled his eyes.

"I'm Sofiya. I'm Mrs. Dawson's traveling companion." She nodded toward her employer.

"I guess we are both saddled by the older generation," Adam said.

The music's beat turned faster, and Adam moved Sofiya around the floor at a quicker pace. Sofiya wasn't familiar with the new dances that were becoming popular since the end of the war. She followed along as best she could, laughing at herself when she tripped over her own feet. The two young people were laughing by the time Adam escorted her back to her table.

"Thank you for the dance. I'm sure I'll be seeing you around," Adam said. He nodded to Sofiya and headed off into the crowd.

Sofiya took a long drink of the water she'd ordered. Mrs. Dawson had tried to get her to order something stronger, but the younger girl had refrained. She wasn't used to such extravagances.

Her employer leaned over and spoke softly in her ear. "Do you know who that young man was? That's Adam Ackerman. His father is a wealthy industrialist. They are what you'd call old money."

Sofiya forced herself not to smile, but Mrs. Dawson's words tickled her. Not because a wealthy young man had asked her to dance, but because of the term "old money." In America, old money was decades old, possibly a century old. But where she was from, her Russian cousins' old money was centuries old. She wondered what Mrs. Dawson would say about that.

"He was very kind," Sofiya said. "He had many pretty girls to ask ahead of me."

Mrs. Dawson's expression turned serious. "He did ask a very pretty girl. He asked you, my dear. Never, never think of yourself as anything less." She squeezed Sofiya's arm affectionately and then turned back to her conversation with the other women.

Tears filled Sofiya's eyes. Mrs. Dawson said exactly what

her own mother would have told her. She felt grateful to have found this position and such a lovely woman to work for.

After three and a half days of living on trains, they pulled into Grand Central Station in New York City. Porters pulled out their many bags and helped them find a taxi to take them the short distance to their apartment.

Sofiya looked around her as they rode along in the large black automobile. There were autos everywhere, and people dressed in fine suits and dresses walked quickly along the sidewalks. The driver took them around the lower half of Central Park and then followed along the western side of it. The leaves were still tinged with fall colors of red, orange, and amber. It was heavenly.

"It's beautiful here," Sofiya said excitedly. "This isn't at all what I'd imagined."

Mrs. Dawson nodded. "Yes. This is what wealth and privilege can buy. The innermost parts of the city are probably more of what you were thinking."

Sofiya understood. She had always lived in the nicest area of St. Petersburg—now known as Petrograd—but she hadn't been shielded from the poverty areas. Her parents had taken her along to volunteer in the poorer areas so she would understand that wealth was a privilege but also must be shared.

The auto pulled up in front of a beautiful, large apartment building—the only building in the area. To Sofiya, it looked like a castle standing tall over its kingdom.

"What is this place?" Sofiya asked.

"Our home for the next few days," Mrs. Dawson said, smiling. "This is where we'll be staying. It's called The Dakota."

"The Dakota?" Sofiya questioned as the two women were helped out of the car by the driver. "Didn't we pass through a state by that name?"

The older woman chuckled. "Very observant. Yes, our train went through South Dakota. The apartment building was aptly named as it was the only living quarters built so far west of the city in 1884. Everyone teased the owner that it might as well be in the Dakota Territory because of its distance. Hence, the name."

A parade of uniformed porters came outside and began carrying Mrs. Dawson's luggage to the elevators. The building manager greeted the two ladies and personally escorted them up to the third floor, where they'd be living.

"Please let me know if you need anything," the manager said, bowing to Mrs. Dawson. She thanked him, then took Sofiya's hand and walked her to the large window.

"This view," was all the older woman said, and Sofiya was suddenly mesmerized. This was what the residents paid for. A lovely view of the park with the tops of the city buildings in the distance.

"It's stunning," Sofiya said.

Mrs. Dawson turned toward her. "It is, isn't it?"

Their stay there was short—only a couple of weeks—but eventful. They were treated like royalty the entire time. There were kitchens at The Dakota and meals could be requested and brought up to their apartment, much like a restaurant. Maids came daily to clean, and coal for their fireplaces, which were in every one of the eight rooms, was delivered daily as well as the ashes being swept away. It was like living in a castle. Even in the lovely home Sofiya had grown up in, she hadn't been as spoiled as here.

Then there was the shopping. Mrs. Dawson loved to shop, especially when she was buying for others. They entered a waiting automobile, as motor cars were always available to the guests, and were taken downtown to all of Mrs. Dawson's favorite department stores. Bloomingdale's, Macy's, and B. Altman. At each store, they'd go to the second floor where women's wear was located and spend hours choosing new outfits and buying piles and piles of clothing.

"Where would I ever wear so much clothing?" Sofiya asked her employer one day on yet another shopping trip. "I do appreciate it all, but it seems excessive."

Mrs. Dawson laughed. "Humor me, my dear. I was never blessed with children, especially a daughter, so I find much joy in buying you all these things. Besides, we'll have teas and luncheons, dinner parties, operas, ballets, and balls to attend while in Europe. You must have clothing for it all."

Sofiya graciously accepted the purchases but felt guilty. She did very little work for Mrs. Dawson, yet she was rewarded daily with free meals, clothing, a grand place to live, and soon a trip to Europe. "I feel I'm doing nothing but spending your money," she said to Mrs. Dawson one afternoon as they ate lunch in a lovely little restaurant near Bloomingdale's. "I should be earning my keep."

"You will be earning your way soon enough, Sofiya," Mrs. Dawson said. "Believe me, tagging and keeping track of our luggage as we travel around Europe, making travel reservations, and keeping our schedule straight will be all up to you. My dear husband used to do all that for me, and now I depend on my travel companion for that."

Sofiya was relieved to hear that she would eventually be earning her way. She had never been one to sit and enjoy leisure, so keeping busy would be perfect for her.

On a Friday evening, Mrs. Dawson announced they'd be

having supper with old friends of hers. "You should wear that lovely royal blue dress with the drop waist we purchased the other day. And those beautiful blue satin T-strap shoes that match." Mrs. Dawson's eyes twinkled. "And definitely wear that adorable little barely-there hat with the sparkle to it and the peacock feather."

"Are you sure you want me to wear that to supper?" Sofiya asked. She loved the small hat, but it seemed like something one would wear out dancing.

"It will be perfect," Mrs. Dawson declared.

Sofiya did as she was asked, also wearing the royal-blue wool overcoat. The women were driven downtown and helped out of their motor car by a lavishly dressed doorman at the high-end restaurant.

Once inside, Sofiya was impressed. The interior was opulent with black satin curtains over the walls, black leather padded booths that stood in large half-circles, and enormous chandeliers spreading glittering light all over the polished wood dance floor. A full orchestra sat on stage playing soft dinner music, and a few couples dressed beautifully were dancing to the tunes.

The maître d' greeted Mrs. Dawson warmly. "Ah, Madam," he said with a French accent that didn't sound French to Sofiya. "Your party is here. I will take you to them."

After checking their coats, they followed the maître d' across the dance floor to the far end of the dining room. An older couple, looking close to Mrs. Dawson's age, sat there, smiling warmly at them.

"How wonderful to see you again, Marion," the woman exclaimed as she stood to hug her friend. "And who is this lovely girl you have brought with you?"

Mrs. Dawson introduced Sofiya to the couple. "She is

quite accomplished and comes from a distinguished family in Finland," she said grandly.

Sofiya stared at her employer in wonder. Did the woman make that up, or did she know more about her past than Sofiya had shared?

"Sofiya," Mrs. Dawson continued. "These are my oldest and dearest friends from my hometown of Syracuse, Mr. and Mrs. Edgar Burton."

"It's nice to meet you," Sofiya said demurely. Mrs. Burton was the same height as Sofiya, with a thicker build, but she was dressed impeccably. She had the most beautiful porcelain skin with barely a line on it and lovely auburn hair done up in a French roll. From the diamonds on her hands, neck, and ears, Sofiya was completely aware that this couple came from money.

"Oh, dear girl," Mrs. Burton said, shaking her hand warmly. "You must watch out for this one." She nodded toward Mrs. Dawson. "She's already married off two of her former travel companions. If you aren't careful, you'll be next."

"Hush, hush," Mrs. Dawson said, waving her hand in the air. "The matches were just a coincidence. I had nothing to do with them." She grinned, her eyes sparkling.

"Very nice to meet you, young lady," Mr. Burton said, nodding his head. He was tall and lean with salt and pepper hair and a nearly silver beard and mustache. His eyes were steel gray, yet not cold at all. He looked at her kindly when he smiled.

The group sat in the booth, and a smartly dressed waiter came and took their drink order. Mrs. Dawson urged Sofiya to try a glass of wine, and not wishing to be rude, she did.

"Adelaine. I thought your handsome son was joining us

this evening," Mrs. Dawson said once their drinks arrived.

"Ah, yes. Edgar Jr. will be here soon. You know how these young people are today. They are always so busy and lose track of time," Mrs. Burton said, sighing.

"He does keep busy with his business concerns," Mr. Burton said proudly. "We mustn't be too hard on him."

Mrs. Burton rolled her eyes. "You only say that because you would work all the time, too, if I'd let you." She chuckled softly.

"You know me too well, dear," Mr. Burton responded.

"The Burton family has held land north of Syracuse for generations and done extremely well," Mrs. Dawson told Sofiya. "They are also very active in the community."

Sofiya nodded, not quite sure how to respond. Money was never a topic of conversation when she was growing up. It made her uncomfortable the way Americans spoke of it so freely.

"Well, we'll see how well we do in the coming years," Mr. Burton said, his expression turning serious. "We've always sold our crops of wheat, barley, and hops to the local breweries, but with prohibition coming our way in January, that will all change. We might have to find places up north that will purchase it."

Mrs. Burton shook her head, clucking her tongue. "Whoever in their right mind thought prohibition was a good idea? People who want to drink alcohol will find a way to continue, legal or not."

"Spoken like a true Burton," a handsome gentleman said as he approached the table. "But don't worry, Mother. Our family will do just fine."

"Edgar!" Mrs. Burton beamed at her son. "It's about time you joined us. Come, sit down beside the lovely Sofiya, and we can finally order our food."

Edgar Charles Burton, Jr. smiled a warm hello at Mrs. Dawson and his parents before turning his attention to Sofiya. "Do you mind if I sit beside you?"

Sofiya nodded her permission, unable to speak. Edgar Jr. was an attractive man with a quick smile and deep brown eyes. Dressed impeccably in a navy pinstripe suit, he cut quite the handsome figure.

Introductions were made between Sofiya and Edgar Jr. He smiled widely at her, his clean-shaven face giving him a boyish look, and she suddenly felt her face heat up in a blush. Other than Harry, she'd never spent time sitting so close to a man her own age.

"Mrs. Dawson isn't trying to marry you off, now, is she?" Edgar Jr. asked with a devilish grin. "If so, I envy the lucky man."

The young girl's heart beat faster. She'd never been considered attractive in her life other than by her mother, whose love for her caused her to be blind to Sofiya's plainness. But here was a handsome young man, flattering her. "No, no," she said quickly. "I'll be traveling with Mrs. Dawson to Europe this winter."

"Oh, I envy you. I'd love to go there again now that the war is over. But I have much work to do here, preparing our business for its next phase, now that our government has gone insane," Edgar Jr. said.

"Gone insane?" Sofiya asked, confused.

"With all this 18th Amendment nonsense. But our family holdings will do just fine. I just need to shift things around a bit." Edgar Jr. smiled at her again.

"Edgar has come up with some new business ventures for

the coming years," Mr. Burton said proudly.

"And luckily, our government gave us a year's notice about prohibition so that businesses could prepare," Edgar Jr. said with a wink to his father.

The men chuckled, leaving Sofiya completely confused as to what they were talking about.

They ordered dinner, with Mr. Burton suggesting the best meals, and then visited among themselves while they waited. After a time, Edgar Jr. turned to Sofiya again.

"Would you care to dance while we wait for supper?" he asked.

"Oh, yes, dear," Mrs. Dawson chimed in. "Do go dance."

Feeling she had no choice, Sofiya accepted Edgar's extended hand and let him lead her to the dance floor. There were several other couples out there, so she didn't feel self-conscious.

Edgar Jr. held her at a respectable distance, and they danced slowly to the music. He was shorter than his father, yet it didn't bother Sofiya. Being short herself, she fit better with someone closer to her height.

"Mrs. Dawson holds you in high regard," Edgar Jr. said as they danced. "I've known her my entire life, and I have great respect for her opinions."

"She's a dear," Sofiya said. "I feel lucky to have found this position with her."

Edgar Jr. drew back and looked at her quizzically. "She says you're educated in multiple languages. Could you not have taught instead?"

Sofiya shook her head. "I had to leave my homeland before I could continue my education."

"May I ask how old you are?"

She hesitated a moment, then thought there was no harm

in telling him. "I'm eighteen."

"Really? Someone as intelligent as you, and you're so young."

Sofiya turned serious. "Are you mocking me?"

"Oh, no. Not at all," Edgar Jr. said quickly. "I meant it when I said you're intelligent. And you seem so grown up compared to other women your age. I like that."

They danced in silence for a time, flowing to the music. Sofiya had been trained to dance alongside her cousins in the palace and was quite accomplished. But Edgar Jr. was the perfect partner—light on his feet and easy to follow.

"May I ask why you left your homeland?" Edgar Jr. said, breaking the silence.

"There were many reasons, but mostly because of the civil war erupting and the changes in Russia. We knew that eventually, the fighting there would hit our land as well," she said, trying to be as vague as possible.

"Ah, yes. The war," Edgar Jr. said.

"Did you serve?" she asked innocently, assuming all young men had gone.

"Well," he seemed to be fishing for an answer. "I was fortunate. The war was over before I could be shipped abroad."

"Oh, yes. You were lucky," Sofiya said.

The music ended, and Edgar Jr. escorted Sofiya back to the table. They all had a lovely evening of lively chatter, a little too much imbibing, and delicious food. By the time they were ready to depart, it felt like Sofiya was saying goodbye to old friends.

"You have a lovely time in Europe," Mrs. Burton told Sophia as she hugged her. "But don't let my friend marry you off to the first prince she finds."

Sofiya laughed. No prince would even look her way.

"I hope to see you again when you return," Edgar Jr. said, holding her hand. He gave her a smile and a wink as he handed her into the motor car beside Mrs. Dawson, and then they were off.

"What a wonderful night, don't you agree, Sofiya?" Mrs. Dawson said, sitting back against the seat.

"Yes, it was. Thank you for including me." Sofiya had enjoyed the Burtons' company and had especially enjoyed talking with Edgar Jr.

"That young Edgar," Mrs. Dawson said as if reading her mind. "He's a go-getter, that one." She turned to Sofiya. "And he seemed quite taken with you, dear."

Sofiya's cheeks heated up. She highly doubted that Edgar Jr. found her anything but amusing. With his good looks, he could have had any woman in the room. She knew her limits, and she was no great beauty.

"He's a nice man," was all Sofiya could manage to say.

"Well, in a couple of days, we'll be on our way to England. I must say, I'm getting excited," Mrs. Dawson said. "We're going to have a wonderful time."

Sofiya nodded. She also was excited. Her life had changed so much in such a short time, and it was all for the better. She couldn't wait to return to the apartment and write down everything that had transpired that evening.

CHAPTER NINETEEN

Addie

Saturday morning, Addie and Katie drove to the closest mall to do some shopping. Addie hadn't gone clothes shopping for herself in a long time, so both women had a great time trying on different styles and buying new items. They quietly laughed together at some of the styles, and Katie's eyes grew wide when she saw jeans that were ripped all the way down the legs.

"Who would wear these?" she asked Addie.

"Uh, just about everyone your age," Addie answered with a chuckle.

Katie shook her head. "No, thanks. I'd like to be able to wear my jeans long enough to put my own holes in them."

Katie had great taste in clothing and picked out a couple pairs of new jeans, a few tops and T-shirts, and two cute casual dresses. "Are you sure this isn't too much?" she asked Addie when she saw the amount tallied up.

"It's fine," Addie assured her. "I haven't spent anything on myself in a long time, so this makes up for it." Addie also picked up new jeans, tops, and a fall jacket she fell in love with.

After that, they hit Target and bought necessities that both women needed.

"I haven't had so many nice things in so long, I won't know what to wear first," Katie said with a big smile on her face. "You have no idea what this means to me."

Addie smiled back but stayed silent. She knew exactly what it meant to Katie.

They brought home Mexican takeout for dinner, and the three of them sat at the picnic table outside, enjoying the evening breeze in the shade of the big oak tree.

"Is Matt finished with the bench?" Katie asked Zach, looking a little disappointed. The new bench rounded the tree perfectly and looked complete.

"He finished it today but said he's going to add a water-proof stain so it doesn't rot," Zach told her.

"Oh, that's good," Katie said.

Addie noticed she didn't look happy, though. "I'm sure Matt would enjoy hanging out with you even if you don't have a project."

Katie's cheeks turned red. "Oh, I didn't mean it that way. It was just fun helping him."

Addie chuckled. "Well, he's right next door. I'm sure you'll be seeing him around."

Katie nodded and focused on her food as Zach and Addie looked at each other with brows raised. Both were thinking the same thing—Katie really did like Matt.

On Monday, Katie signed up to start her online studies for the GED. They had purchased some notebooks, a calculator, and a few other supplies she might need for her studies. She sat at the kitchen table with Addie's laptop that afternoon, staring at the screen but not starting.

"What's up?" Addie asked, coming in to wash her hands. She couldn't wait for Zach to set up the utility sink in Sofiya's room. She hated cleaning her brushes and rags in the new kitchen sink.

"I'm all ready to start studying," Katie said.

"That's great. Work on that as much as you want, and don't worry about helping me. Getting your GED is more important than scraping wallpaper."

Katie looked over at Addie. "I'm scared. What if I'm too stupid to do this? What if I was never meant to finish school? This seems like such a big commitment." Tears filled the young girl's eyes.

"Whoa, wait a minute." Addie dropped into the chair next to her. "Just take it one step at a time. It can be overwhelming if you think of it as a whole big project."

Katie swiped at her tears. "I don't know why I'm crying. It just suddenly hit me that if I do this, I can actually have a decent future. I stopped dreaming of a future while I was in *the life*. I never believed I'd get out alive."

Addie scooted her chair over and wrapped her arms around the shaking girl. "I totally understand. Believe me. And if this feels like too much right now, you can always take it slower." She pulled away and looked into Katie's eyes. "Your life has changed completely in just a few days. It's natural to feel overwhelmed."

Katie sniffled and nodded her head while Addie handed her the box of tissues. "I had a nightmare the other night. I thought for sure that guy had found me and was going to take me back."

"I was with you during your nightmare," Addie said. "I was

the one who calmed you down and put you back to bed."

"You were?" Katie's eyes grew wide. "I don't remember."

"You were yelling in your sleep. I knew instantly what was happening," Addie said. "It happens. I still have nightmares, occasionally."

"Do they ever stop?" Katie asked in a hushed voice.

"They come less and less. You just have to continue to move forward in your life and trust people again. It takes time. Talking about it helps. That's why I started visiting Laurie's group again—I was having nightmares."

"I really want to feel normal again as fast as possible," Katie said. "I don't want to miss out on any more of my life. I just don't know if I can do it."

Addie stared the young girl in the eyes. "You had the strength to borrow that phone that night and call for help. You knew that guy would kill you if he knew what you were doing, but you risked it. I'd say you have the strength to do anything."

Katie wiped her tears. "Okay." She turned back to the computer. "One step at a time, right? Like how you remodel an entire house. One step at a time."

Addie smiled. "Exactly." She patted Katie on the back and left the room to give her some time alone. As she went up to the bedroom where she'd been working, Addie thought about Sofiya and all she'd endured in this house and how she'd found a new life with Mrs. Dawson. "Good things come to those who are willing to work for them," she said aloud. It was true. She'd worked hard to succeed in what she was doing—flipping houses. And Katie would succeed too. That made Addie very happy.

* * *

Katie worked hard on her studies the next two days and excitedly shared what she was learning with Addie and Zach. Tuesday afternoon, she took a break and found Matt in his yard, mowing. The two kids talked for a long while, sitting in the August sunshine drinking Cokes. Addie sneaked a peek out the bedroom window into Matt's yard, and it warmed her heart as she watched the two teens.

"They're so cute together," Addie told Zach when he came upstairs to measure the bedroom walls so he could buy wood for the wainscotting.

"Are you playing matchmaker?" he teased.

"No. But it's nice to see Katie having a normal friendship with a boy her own age. Men frightened me that first couple of years. I'm glad she has him for a friend."

"Katie seems very centered, considering what she's been through," Zach said as he went to stand beside Addie at the window. "You're really making a difference in her life."

Addie looked up at him, surprised. "I'm just helping her the way Valerie helped me. She's a good kid."

Zach dropped a small kiss on her lips. "So are you," he said, then laughed. "Except that you're making me create wainscotting on these walls."

"You complain too much," Addie said with a grin. But it made her feel good she was helping Katie restart her life.

That evening found Addie and Katie at the meeting at Laurie's home again. This time, Katie seemed more comfortable with the girls. She was joking and laughing with them before the meeting began.

Laurie started the meeting by asking if any of the girls had something good happen to them that week. Melanie rose her hand quickly.

"I passed my Math and Reading GED tests!" the girl said excitedly. "Two down and three to go."

"That's wonderful," Laurie said. "Were they difficult?"

"Not as hard as I'd thought," Melanie said. "I'm a little scared of the Science test, but I've been practicing pretty hard with that one."

"Congratulations," Addie told her. She smiled over at Katie, who was taking all the information in.

"I had a good week at business school," Izzie spoke up. "And my manager at work said I was doing a great job and is going to give me a small raise."

"Yay. Two accomplishments for the week," Laurie said.

"Where do you work?" Addie asked.

"At a little thrift store not far from here," Izzie said. "They always have a ton of fun stuff coming in and are super affordable. The owner is really nice, too. He's good about setting my hours around my school schedule."

Tentatively, Katie raised her hand. "I started studying for my GED yesterday."

"That's great," Melanie said, smiling over at her.

"Girl, you're going to be glad to get it," Latisha said. "I didn't need it to start beauty school, but I did it anyway. It builds your confidence."

"Good for you," Tonya said. "I haven't started working on mine, but I really should."

Addie watched Katie beam with pride as all the girls encouraged her.

The girls continued talking about the one or two good things that happened to them that week. After that, Laurie opened it up to any questions the girls might have. Addie watched Katie to see if she'd speak and was surprised when she shyly asked a question.

"Do any of you have nightmares about your past lives?"

The group grew somber, and each girl nodded solemnly.

"I do," Wanda said, nervously pushing her red hair behind her ears. "I had a bad one last night. It was a guy who beat me up regularly. The trafficker never cared how the girls were treated. All he cared about was getting paid."

"I'm sorry," Katie said softly. "I had a dream the other night that my trafficker found me. I was so scared."

Melanie moved closer to Katie and held her hand. "That's scary. I've had that dream too. Losing your freedom again is the worst nightmare of all."

"I have nightmares all the time," Latisha said matter-of-factly. "But I try not to let them bother me."

Tonya gave her side-eye. "Really? You think we don't hear you yelling in your dreams?"

The other girls laughed, and Latisha finally joined in. "Yeah, there are a lot of nightmares going on in this house," Latisha said.

"The nightmares do come less often as time goes on," Laurie said. "I still have them, but only when I'm feeling stressed or insecure. It will get better, girls."

"Then you must be having nightmares all the time," Izzie said. "Because working with us is stressful."

The girls laughed, and so did Laurie and Addie. It broke the tension in the room.

Later, on the way home, Addie spoke up. "I'm proud of you for speaking up tonight. It's good to know you're not alone in this."

Katie nodded. "I know I'm not alone. I have you and Zach." She smiled over at Addie.

Her words warmed Addie's heart.

As Addie joined Zach in bed that night, he looked over at her curiously.

"You haven't mentioned anything new about Sofiya lately. Have you read any more letters?" he asked.

"Yeah. I've just been so busy with Katie and the house I haven't had a chance to tell you. And you've been so preoccupied with the wainscotting." She gave him a mischievous grin.

"Forget the wainscotting," he said, acting grouchy. Then he smiled. "Tell me about Sofiya."

Addie filled him in on Alina leaving to marry Clint and Mrs. Jarvi helping Sofiya find a new job. "As of right now, Sofiya is living the good life, and it seems Mrs. Dawson is going to try to set her up with a young man."

"Oh, a busybody, huh?" Zach asked.

Addie shrugged. "Mrs. Dawson sounds like a nice woman. She seems to know people all over the world. I should look her up and see if she was in high society or something."

"Well, I'm glad things are finally going well for Sofiya and Alina. Let's hope their lives turned out to be wonderful," Zach said, yawning. "Just like ours."

As they lay cuddled in bed that night, Addie thought about Sofiya and how her life had changed to be so much better. It was much like Katie's life. One day she was being held a prisoner, the next she was free to live whatever life she wanted. It was a strange coincidence, especially since they were living in this house. She couldn't wait to read more of Sofiya's adventures.

CHAPTER TWENTY

Sofiya

Sofiya's life was a whirlwind of activity as they prepared for their journey across the ocean. The apartment manager had taken care of their ship tickets and London hotel reservations. Sofiya was thankful for that because she had so much else to do. She packed the clothes they would need while on the steamship in separate trunks from those they'd wear in London. The ship could store the extra trunks below so they wouldn't take up space in their cabins. She also wrote a quick note to Alina to let her know she'd be away for several months. Sofiya told her she'd send a permanent address once they arrived back in the states.

The young girl marveled at all the clothing and accessories she had to care for just to go on a trip. She thought of her first trip across the Atlantic with only one small suitcase, and it made her laugh in comparison to now. Although she understood they'd be gone for three months, and from the sound of it, they'd be attending several events, so a large wardrobe was necessary. Even as a girl in Russia, she'd never owned so many dresses, shoes, hats, stockings, and coats. She felt as if God had smiled down on her after all the loss she'd suffered over the past two years.

Finally, the day arrived, and their trunks were taken away to the harbor to be loaded. They carried only their personal bags and coats as the two women entered the car that took them to the harbor.

Excitement bubbled up inside Sofiya. Although she and Alina had made this trip from their homeland once before, this time would be different. She'd be traveling in grandeur beside Mrs. Dawson instead of as an immigrant coming to America.

When they pulled up to the building where they'd check in and board their ship, she looked around her in wonder. People were coming and going in all directions. Sofiya knew she had to keep her wits about her in order to help Mrs. Dawson navigate the crowd.

To Sofiya's surprise, Mrs. Dawson was greeted by a uniformed agent who escorted them to the front of the line to check in and then personally escorted them up the gangplank to the ship. From there, a ship's porter took over the job of showing them to their first-class compartments.

As they walked down the carpeted hallways, Sofiya was once again taken aback at the special treatment given to Mrs. Dawson. Who exactly had her husband been, and how did she manage to be treated like a VIP everywhere she went?

"Your rooms," the porter said, bowing as the women walked past him into one of the compartments. The porter followed them inside. "There's a connecting door between your rooms here," he said, opening the door to the other bedroom. "And your luggage has already been brought up. Would you like me to send a maid to unpack for you?"

"Thank you," Mrs. Dawson said, handing the young man a tip. "But that won't be necessary."

The porter bowed and left the room.

Sofiya gazed around the room. Compared to the tiny compartment she and Alina had shared in third class, this room was enormous. They were in the sitting area, where there was a table they could dine at and a fireplace. Another door led to Mrs. Dawson's bedroom, which was large and held a double bed. She peeked inside her room, and it too was comfortable looking with a double bed as well. She noticed that they each had a small bathroom of their own as well.

"Quite luxurious for a ship, don't you think?" Mrs. Dawson said, smiling at Sofiya. "I remember the days of public bathroom facilities." She shuddered. "It's nice to be able to afford luxury."

"This is extremely nice," Sofiya agreed. She went into her own room and checked to ensure her trunks had arrived. Then she checked Mrs. Dawson's. "And they are quite efficient. Everything is here."

"Wonderful," Mrs. Dawson said. Sofiya helped her off with her coat and hung it up in the wardrobe.

"Would you like me to unpack your belongings now?" Sofiya asked.

"Don't worry about it now, dear," Mrs. Dawson said. "I believe I will take a short nap while the ship disembarks. They serve supper quite late on these ships, so I need to refresh myself a bit."

"All right," Sofiya said, heading for her own room. She was so excited about the trip, she didn't think she could nap. "Perhaps I'll unpack my own things and do yours later."

Mrs. Dawson grinned. "Or you could go to the main deck

and watch the ship disembark. It's always very exciting, with everyone waving and cheering."

"You wouldn't mind?" Sofiya asked, already growing excited.

"Not at all. Wake me at six so we can get organized and go to eat."

"Yes, Ma'am," Sofiya said. She hurried out of the room, buttoning her coat tightly. She reached the railing just as the ship was being escorted by tugboats through the harbor. The sound of people on board yelling goodbyes to their loved ones was deafening but exciting. She waved along with everyone else, even though she was leaving no one behind. It was just so much fun being a part of this celebration.

That night she and Mrs. Dawson went to the dining room to eat, but the next two nights, they ate in their cabin. Both were a little green around the gills from being out to sea, so they stayed inside their rooms and slept. By the third night, both women felt better and were invited to eat at the captain's table, which was a great honor.

Dressed in their new evening gowns, Sofiya and Mrs. Dawson joined the other guests at the special table. Only eight were invited, so it was an intimate group. The captain arrived a few minutes late, apologizing profusely, and the waiters began to serve their first course.

Sofiya had no idea who the people at the table were, but by the size of the women's jewels, she suspected they were all people of great importance. Mrs. Dawson had several nice pieces of jewelry, but she was prudent in not displaying her wealth as flamboyantly as other women her age. She wore a simple pair of sapphire earrings and a small sapphire pendant to compliment her conservative black dress. Sofiya liked that about her. She was down to earth, yet obviously a woman of high esteem.

"Mrs. Dawson," the captain said, turning his attention to their side of the table. "I'm so honored you and your traveling companion were able to join us. Your husband sailed on another of my ships years ago, and he was such an interesting man. I'm sorry to hear that he has passed."

"Thank you, Captain," Mrs. Dawson said. "He had a fascinating job and loved every minute of it. I usually traveled with him, but sometimes he had to go alone."

"He and I spoke extensively on the subject of foreign affairs. I was impressed by his knowledge. How many presidents did he work under?" the captain asked.

"Three. McKinley, Roosevelt, and Taft. He was very proud of his service." Mrs. Dawson smiled warmly at the captain as everyone at the table stared at her in wonder. Even Sofiya was shocked to hear that Mrs. Dawson's husband had been working for the government. But then, that explained all her high-ranking connections.

After supper, the captain made a point of inviting Mrs. Dawson and Sofiya to join everyone in the lounge for music and dancing. She thanked him but told Sofiya she wished to return to their suite of rooms.

"I hope you don't mind us not taking the captain up on listening to the entertainment and dancing, my dear," Mrs. Dawson said as they entered their cabin. "I'm just too tired for all that."

"Not at all," Sofiya said. She actually preferred the quiet of their room to a ballroom full of people and noise. "Your husband sounded like an interesting man," she continued, hoping it didn't sound like she was prying.

Mrs. Dawson's face glowed. "He was. And we were so happy. We traveled all over the world and met so many interesting people. I still count many of them as my friends. We were very lucky." The elderly woman walked into her bedroom and returned with a small silver frame that folded closed. She opened it and handed it to Sofiya. "That was my Franklin. We married when we were both older, and he'd already built a nice practice as a lawyer and was becoming involved in politics."

Sofiya studied the photo. Franklin looked very distinguished with dark hair that was graying at the temples and a clean-shaven face. His eyes seemed to sparkle with mischief in the photo. "He was a very handsome man," she said.

"He was," Mrs. Dawson said, accepting the photo back from Sofiya. "He loved being around people and learning new things. Franklin worked as a special envoy for all three presidents. He'd carry important documents and messages to United States Ambassadors around the world—messages that couldn't be trusted in a telegram or letter. He was an advisor to Teddy Roosevelt, too. It was quite an interesting life."

Sofiya helped Mrs. Dawson change for bed and hung her dress carefully in the wardrobe. After saying goodnight, Sofiya padded to her own bedroom. She had learned so much about her employer, and she wanted to write it down in a letter to her maman. As she wrote in French, she felt a tinge of regret for having lied to Mrs. Dawson about her past, although much of it was true. Her parents had passed, and she had left Russia via Helsinki. Still, keeping the secrets of her past life weighed heavily on her. But she'd promised her maman never to tell the secret of her family ties, and she was determined to keep that secret. No matter what.

* * *

Three days later, their ship docked in Southampton, and Sofiya was in charge of ensuring their luggage was transferred to the Savoy Hotel in London. She found a cab to take them to the train station, and they boarded first class to London. By the time they arrived and a car brought them to their destination, Mrs. Dawson was extremely tired. Sofiya was too, but she knew it was her job to check into their rooms and ensure their luggage had arrived.

Upon entering The Savoy Hotel, Sofiya was mesmerized. The main lobby was beautiful, with marble floors and columns that shone under the gorgeous chandeliers. They checked in and were escorted by smartly dressed bellhops to the lift, where an attendant pushed the button to their floor. Everything in the hotel was extravagant, from the plush rugs on the floors to the lighting overhead. To Sofiya, it was like visiting a palace.

Once in their suite—connecting bedrooms with a sitting room in-between—Mrs. Dawson tipped the bellhops and went to look out the heavily curtained window. Sofiya was counting their trunks that had been delivered just moments before their arrival when Mrs. Dawson sighed.

"Is everything all right?" Sofiya asked, hurrying to Mrs. Dawson's side. She hoped the day hadn't been too strenuous for her.

"It's wonderful," Mrs. Dawson said. "Look at that view."

Sofiya turned her attention to the window and gasped. From the crowded street where they'd entered The Savoy, she'd never have imagined the back of the hotel would have such a glorious view. Stretched out in front of them was a lovely grassy area and walkway, and beyond that was the River Thames, sparkling in the winter sunshine.

"I had no idea we were on the river," Sofiya said, delighted. "How wonderful."

"I never thought I'd see this view again," Mrs. Dawson said in a shaky voice. "During the war, I feared London had been decimated by the bombs dropped by the Germans. I'm so happy to see so much of this beloved city is still intact."

Sofiya understood precisely what she meant. She, too, had lived in areas affected by war before leaving for America. She reached out and held the older woman's hand in solidarity. Mrs. Dawson smiled over at her. "I know you understand," she said.

Sofiya nodded, and together they enjoyed the view as the sun set over the river.

* * *

The next day, cards and letters began to arrive at their suite with invitations to luncheons, dinner parties, teas, and even the ballet. Mrs. Dawson had so many invitations from friends that Sofiya had to act as her secretary and go through each one to organize the dates. Sofiya wrote out the responses to each invitation, and her employer signed them personally. After a couple of days, their time in London was filled with many events.

"Now you understand why we needed so many outfits," Mrs. Dawson said with a wink. "We'll need to organize our wardrobe closets by casual to dressy, so we don't have to think about what we'll wear each day."

That in itself was a daunting task, and soon Sofiya found she had to call up a maid to help her organize the clothing. Under

Mrs. Dawson's supervision, the two women pulled dresses, skirts, jackets, hats, and all manner of clothing from the trunks and separated them by style, placing the outfits together in the wardrobes. Tea gowns in one section, day dresses in another, and evening gowns in yet another spot. The maid looked over each item for any snags or wrinkles. But when they were finally finished, Sofiya understood why Mrs. Dawson had wanted it done. It would save them time when choosing outfits.

The following two weeks were a whirlwind of activity for the ladies. They started the first day with a quiet luncheon at the restaurant in The Savoy with two close friends of Mrs. Dawson's. Their husbands had been in public service in Britain, and the three women chatted and visited easily as Sofiya sat quietly, enjoying their stories. Mrs. Winifred Chambers, a lively, slender woman with silver hair piled on her head, seemed to be Mrs. Dawson's closest friend. She suggested several events they might enjoy attending.

"I can get you tickets to anything," she promised. "And you must join my husband and our friends for the Christmas holiday. We always have a lovely Christmas Eve party that you are sure to enjoy."

Later, back in their rooms, Mrs. Dawson confided in Sofiya. "Winnie can be quite bossy at times, but she does know how to open doors for anyone in London."

So, taking Mrs. Chambers' lead, the women attended banquets given for illustrious people, quaint dinner parties at some of the most lavish homes in the city, and watched the Ballets Russes perform Le Tricorne at the Alhambra Music Hall.

"The program says the artist Pablo Picasso designed the sets and costumes for this ballet," Mrs. Dawson whispered to

Sofiya in their box seats. "So interesting."

Sofiya watched the ballet in wonder. She'd seen the Russian Ballet as a child, but this was different from anything she'd ever experienced. The ballet was influenced by Spanish dancing, making it an interesting and intriguing combination.

By early December, Sofiya felt as if she'd been in every dining room and parlor in the city. She was surprised that Mrs. Dawson could keep up with their busy social schedule as she, a young woman, was exhausted by it. But seeing all her old friends animated Mrs. Dawson, and she appeared years younger. Sofiya was happy her employer was enjoying her holiday in London.

Being in Europe brought back memories of the short time Sofiya had spent with Harry before he'd been shipped here to fight. He hadn't returned to Portland by the time she'd left, and she continued to wonder what had become of him. She found herself looking at the faces of young men all over London, wondering if she'd see him. But of course, she didn't.

"Why the long face, dear?" Mrs. Dawson asked her one afternoon as they returned from yet another luncheon with old friends. "Are you not having a good time?"

"Oh, no. It isn't that. I'm having a wonderful time here," Sofiya was quick to say. "I've been thinking a lot of a young man I knew in Portland. He went into the service in the last months of the war, but he was never heard from again. I often wonder what became of him."

Mrs. Dawson motioned for them to sit on the settee. "I see. I had no idea you had a young suiter."

Sofiya felt her face heat up. "Oh, no. It wasn't as serious as that. He and I were good friends. But he did ask me to wait for him. I did for a year, but no one ever heard from him. And his parents were never notified of his death. I still wonder about him."

The older woman sat thoughtful for a moment, then a smile crept up on her face. "Dear. Over the past several weeks, you've been in the company of the wives of many prominent men who work for the government. All I need is to ask, and they'll do a thorough search for him."

"Really? Would it be that easy?" Sofiya hadn't even thought to ask before.

"I can't promise we'll find him," Mrs. Dawson said. "But we can certainly try."

Sofiya jumped up and hugged the older woman, shocking them both. "Thank you so much. I would be greatly indebted to you for this."

Mrs. Dawson pulled back, smiling. "Your happiness is gratitude enough, dear. Everyone loves a happy ending."

Sofiya knew that happy endings weren't always possible, and she braced herself for the possibility of not finding Harry, but the chance of finding him made her heart sing.

That evening at dinner, Mrs. Dawson set the search for Harold Meyer in motion, and all of her dearest friends were thrilled to help Sofiya find her lost love. It became a mission for them all, which tickled Sofiya immensely.

* * *

As the days passed, Sofiya became comfortable around Mrs. Dawson's friends and enjoyed herself immensely. They planned on staying in London through the New Year and then were heading to Paris for a few weeks before returning to the states. Sofiya looked forward to seeing Paris as she'd never visited there before.

One afternoon, as Mrs. Dawson visited with a table of her closest friends in an elegant tearoom, Sofiya froze when she caught the eye of a woman sitting in the back corner with two younger ladies. Her heart pounded as she recognized the dark-haired woman with the large dark eyes and solemn expression. There was no doubt the woman was a Romanov.

Sofiya turned away suddenly to break the gaze with the older woman. Her movement caught Mrs. Chambers' eye, and she turned in her seat to see who Sofiya had been looking at.

"Ah, I see you've noticed our local celebrity in the corner," Mrs. Chambers said in a low voice to Sofiya. "That is none other than the Grand Duchess, sister of the late Tsar of Russia."

Sofiya had immediately known who it was and was shocked to see her in public. Grand Duchess Xenia Alexandrovna was the younger sister of Tsar Nicholas II. Sofiya had played with the Duchess's children while at the palace for family celebrations.

"Is she not fearful of being recognized in public?" Sofiya asked. "Her life could be in danger."

Mrs. Dawson watched Sofiya curiously as Mrs. Chambers gave a small laugh.

"No, dear. She's in no danger here," Mrs. Chambers said lightly. "There are no Bolsheviks around that I know of who are looking to assassinate random Romanovs. Plus, she's living under the protection of the Crown, so no one would dare touch her—it would be considered an attack against Britain." Mrs. Chambers grew serious. "In fact, the Grand Duchess is quite a nice woman. I've met her at several fundraising events over the past year."

At that moment, one of the young women sitting with the Duchess came to their table. "Excuse me, please," the young woman said. "The Grand Duchess asked if the young lady would like to come to her table and speak with her."

All eyes went directly to Sofiya. Her heart beat wildly. Had the Grand Duchess recognized her? What would she say? Sofiya couldn't give away her relationship with the Romanov family in front of all these people.

"Well, isn't that nice," Mrs. Dawson said directly to Sofiya. "Imagine, an audience with royalty." She turned to the young lady. "May I accompany her to meet the Grand Duchess?"

The woman nodded politely.

"Come, Sofiya," Mrs. Dawson said, her eyes sparkling with excitement.

"I can't," Sofiya said, staying seated.

"But dear. When will you ever have a chance to meet a Grand Duchess again?" She smiled down at Sofiya. "Don't be afraid. I'll be right next to you."

Sofiya's body shook as she stood. She was not afraid of the Grand Duchess. She was fearful of being called out for who she really was. On trembling legs, Sofiya walked beside Mrs. Dawson across the room to the table. The Grand Duchess was dressed nicely—nothing too extravagant and with very little jewelry—and sat straight-backed as a lady should. She gave a small smile to Sofiya as she approached the table.

Once there, Sofiya immediately curtseyed and bowed her head as she'd been taught to greet royalty. Mrs. Dawson gave a slight curtsy also. Both women stood politely, waiting for the Grand Duchess to speak first. Finally, the Duchess spoke up in a clear voice.

"Thank you for humoring my curiosity," she said. "I saw this young woman across the room and was so taken by her looks." The Duchess reached out her hand to Sofiya. "What is your name, child?"

Sofiya swallowed hard and held the Duchess' hand. "Sofiya Henderson, ma'am. Of Helsinki, Finland."

Disappointment shadowed the Duchess' face but then disappeared quickly. "So, you're from Finland, not Russia?"

"Yes, ma'am. Finland," Sofiya said, dropping her eyes so the Duchess couldn't continue to study her face. "This is Mrs. Marion Dawson, my employer. We've traveled here from America for a visit."

Mrs. Dawson smiled at the Duchess. "Sofiya is quite a lovely traveling companion. So bright and knowledgeable."

The light faded from the Duchess' eyes as she let go of Sofiya's hand. "I'm so sorry to have bothered you. Sofiya's large eyes and round face reminded me so of my brother's daughters, especially young Tatiana. But I see you have brown eyes, not blue. I guess it's my deep longing to find my young nieces that made me see things that were not there."

Sofiya felt Mrs. Dawson's gaze upon her before the older woman returned her eyes to the Duchess. "There's still no word on the fate of the Tsarina and her children?"

The Duchess shook her head. "No. But we keep praying for their safe return."

"I will pray for them also," Mrs. Dawson said warmly.

"Thank you. You are very kind," the Duchess said. She turned back to Sofiya and spoke softly in French. "Je ne te souhaite que du bonheur." *I wish you nothing but happiness.*

Sofiya's eyes rose to the Duchess' eyes. In them, she saw recognition. Did the Grand Duchess truly know who she was, or was she only being kind? "Merci," Sofiya responded. "chaptr." *May God bless you.*

The Grand Duchess gave a slight nod, and Sofiya once again curtseyed before taking her leave. Mrs. Dawson followed

Sofiya back to the table.

"What did she say to you?" the older woman asked.

"She wished all the best for me," Sofiya answered.

Mrs. Dawson cocked her head and stared at her. "Why?"

Sofiya knew why. The Grand Duchess recognized her and wanted her to be safe in her life. She hadn't given up Sofiya's secret, which meant that the Duchess still believed there might be danger in the world for a relative of the Romanovs. It proved to Sofiya that her mother had been right to warn her never to trust anyone with her true identity.

"She was just being kind," Sofiya told Mrs. Dawson, giving her a smile. Her employer looked as if she would question it but then decided not to.

"How nice of her," Mrs. Dawson said. Then they rejoined their table, where the women were eagerly awaiting to question them.

CHAPTER TWENTY–ONE

Addie

As September began, the household fell into an easy routine. Katie spent her mornings studying online for her GED tests while Addie and Zach worked on their many house projects. After lunch, Katie helped scrape wallpaper, painted, stained, or worked on whatever project needed to be done. They'd finished the first bedroom—the wainscotting had turned out amazing—and began working on the next bedroom.

Pulling up the hideous carpeting in the next bedroom was a challenge. Addie pulled up a corner, and the two women grabbed hold. The shag carpeting had been stapled to the floor in two long lines, and it took all their strength to pull it up. The padding underneath had deteriorated so badly that dust flew up all over the room. Addie ran to get face masks before they returned to ripping up the rest of the carpet.

Zach came upstairs and helped them roll up the mess and toss it out the window into a dumpster they'd rented. Dust flew everywhere as they picked up the padding that fell apart in their hands.

"Yuck. Just think of what might have been living in that horrible carpet," Addie said after they'd cleaned it away. She shuddered, and Zach laughed.

"Worse yet, look at the mess they made of these beautiful floors," Zach said. "All those staples have to be pulled up by hand. And I think we have to sand and re-stain this floor."

"First, I'm going to vacuum up all this dust," Addie said. "Then I guess we'll spend the rest of the day pulling up these staples."

"Sounds like fun," Katie said with a wry grin.

"That's the glamour of flipping houses," Addie said.

After Addie vacuumed the room, the two women poured glasses of iced tea and began the slow process of pulling up all the staples and nails. From what Addie could tell, this floor had been carpeted at least two separate times because there were so many staples. The best way they found to pull them up was to pry them carefully with a flathead screwdriver first and then pull them up with plyers. It was tedious work.

"At least it's cooler out now," Katie said as a breeze came through the bedroom window. "Are you thinking of putting in some type of air conditioning system?"

"That's a tough one," Addie said. "There's no central system, and to add ductwork now would cost a fortune, not to mention ruin the ceilings downstairs. We could do mini-splits, but one in every room would also be expensive. We might have to add air to the main rooms downstairs and maybe one or two in the hallway upstairs. We'll see how long the money lasts."

"It must be expensive doing all this work," Katie said. "How do you manage it?"

Addie grimaced. "Usually, we're done with a house in three to four months and sell it. This time, we have to make the money last longer. To tell the truth, I'm not sure how we'll manage. Zach wants to rent the room above the garage for extra income. It's a good idea."

Katie's expression turned serious. "Am I costing you money by living here? I don't want you to spend money on me that you need for the house."

Addie stopped working and looked Katie directly in the eyes. "You aren't costing us a thing. Don't even worry about that. Plus, you've been a big help around here."

Katie nodded and went back to pulling up staples.

Addie's phone rang just then, and she smiled when she saw it was Laurie. "Hey, Laurie. How's it going?"

"Great," Laurie said, sounding happy. "I just got the okay from the state to house another girl. So, Katie can come to live at the house now."

Addie's smile faded. "Oh. Okay. She's right here. I'll let you talk to her." Addie handed her the phone. "It's Laurie for you."

Katie put down her tools and said hello. She was quiet as she listened to Laurie, then said a soft, "Okay." After she hung up, she handed the phone back to Addie.

"Laurie said I could live at her house with the other girls," Katie said.

Addie pocketed her phone. "Yeah. She told me."

"What do you think?" Katie asked.

"Well," Addie hesitated. She knew she should encourage Katie to go there, but she would miss her. "You'd be with other girls your own age who understand what you're going through."

"I already see them at the meetings," Katie said.

"True."

"And I'm already working on my GED. And after that, I thought I might sign up for a couple of college classes," Katie said. "Would I have to live in a safe house to qualify for college grants?"

Addie shook her head. "No. You're eighteen. You can apply based on your income."

Katie snorted. "What income?"

"Exactly," Addie said, laughing along.

Katie's expression grew serious. "I'd really like to stay here with you. I mean, if you and Zach don't mind."

"I wouldn't mind at all," Addie said. "In fact, I'm kind of getting used to having you around."

The younger girl smiled. "Then can I stay?"

"I don't see why not."

Katie slid over and hugged Addie. "Thank you. I promise I'll keep helping around here, so I'm not a bother."

"I'd like that," Addie said. "But I want you to finish your GED and start college. So maybe we can come up with some way to help you as payment for helping us. I'll talk to Laurie and see what we can do."

"Great." Katie picked up her tools again and began plucking staples from the floor with even more vigor. For the rest of the day, the two women worked side-by-side with music blaring, pulling up those pesky carpet staples.

Later that evening, Addie called Laurie to tell her that Katie was staying with her.

"I hope she'll still come to the meetings," Laurie said, sounding worried. "It seems like she's handling everything well, but we both know that PTSD can crop up at any time."

"She said she still wanted to attend meetings," Addie said. "And you know, this seems to be a good fit for her. She has occasional nightmares, but she feels safe here. And I have plenty of work that will keep her busy. Plus, she's even talking about taking college classes after she completes her GED. She's on a good path."

"That's wonderful," Laurie said.

"I'd really like to pay her for her work here at the house, but we're pretty strapped. Do you know of any type of apprenticeship program we could apply to for funds to pay Katie? I know it's a long shot."

"Actually, I might know of a program that will pay her for working for you. Give me a few days, and I'll check into it. The state is working hard to help kids who've been trafficked, so there might be something."

"Thanks, Laurie. I appreciate all your help," Addie said.

"You're welcome, but to tell the truth, you're doing a great service, taking Katie in. You know, with that big house, you could start your own safe house," Laurie said with a chuckle.

"Oh, yeah. Right." Addie didn't have the educational background that Laurie did to do this as a permanent thing.

That night as she got ready for bed, Addie told Zach what Laurie had said about making this place a safe house for trafficked kids.

"Was she kidding?" Zach asked, brows raised.

"Of course she was kidding," Addie said, laughing. "I don't have a degree in social work or psychology. But she's right about the house. It's the perfect size to house people in need."

"Could a person afford to keep a house like this to use as a safe house?" Zach asked, looking interested.

Addie walked across the room and sat on the bed near Zach. "Are you asking seriously?"

He shrugged. "Maybe. I mean, you're right. It's the perfect size to hold a lot of people. And there's enough space to have meeting rooms and such. Could a person rent it out to a group to use for a safe house, and they could hire the staff?"

"You are serious." Addie was shocked that Zach would even consider it. "I don't know anything about it. I'm not sure if someone would buy it to run a safe house or if the state would be involved. Either way, I doubt we'd get enough money back to make it profitable."

"Or get this neighborhood to agree to allow a safe house here," Zach said. "Well, it was just an idea."

Addie went back into the bathroom to get ready for bed. As she washed her face, she wondered about turning this big house into a place for young people. Would it be a crazy idea? It was large enough, like Zach had said, and the parlor downstairs would be perfect for meetings. Eight girls could live here, although they'd probably have to add another bathroom.

Staring at her face in the mirror, Addie thought about the day she ran away and how scared she'd been because she wasn't sure where to go or what to do. She'd never heard of a safe house back then and hadn't thought to look up such a place. But what a difference a safe house would have made in her life. Even though she loved what she did and would be forever grateful to Valerie for taking her in and teaching her a skill, maybe her first year would have been easier and less stressful if she'd had a place like Laurie's to live in.

Walking back into the bedroom, she crawled into bed beside Zach.

"Are you okay?" he asked, rolling over in bed to look at her. "You look like a zombie."

"I was just thinking about that first year after I'd run away. I wish I'd known about safe houses for teens back then. Maybe I wouldn't still be so messed up if I had."

Zach reached over and pulled her to him. "You're not

messed up. You have nightmares. You sometimes freak out. We all do. Your memories are definitely more intense than the average person, but you're not messed up."

She curled in closer. "That's because I had Valerie to help me, and then I met you."

"Someone was looking out for you," he said softly.

"You know, maybe a safe house is a good idea for this place," she said. "Yet, just saying that sounds like it will be a mountain of work."

"Well, let's fix it up first, and then we'll climb that mountain when we get to it."

Addie agreed. The house still had a lot of work ahead of it before they decided what to do with it. "One thing at a time, right?" she asked.

"Yep. That's how I stay so calm. One thing at a time." He chuckled.

Addie thought it was truer than Zach realized.

* * *

Two weeks later, Addie was upstairs painting the bedroom walls after days of scraping down wallpaper when she heard Katie scream. She dropped her paintbrush and hurried downstairs. "What happened? Are you alright?"

"I passed the Math test!" Katie yelled excitedly. "I can't believe it."

It took Addie a moment to comprehend that Katie was okay and digest the good news. "That's wonderful," she said, hugging the young girl. "I'm so proud of you."

"I kept putting it off, thinking I'd fail, but I did it," Katie said. "It feels so good to accomplish something."

Addie smiled at her. "Every day, you've been accomplishing something positive. This was an added bonus."

"Thanks," Katie said, suddenly looking shy. She turned back to her computer. "I think I'll do one more practice test for the English Literature course before trying the real test. I want to do well."

"That's smart. Good for you," Addie said. "Let me know how it goes." As she headed back upstairs, she couldn't help but smile. She was so proud of Katie and how hard she was working to move forward in her life. It wasn't easy, Addie knew.

That night at group, Addie shared her good news. "I passed both the math and literature tests today for my GED."

All the girls and Laurie congratulated her. They then shared the positive things that were going on in their lives. Izzie brought up something that had happened at work that had triggered her.

"I had this really nasty customer come in the other day, and she was so rude to me," Izzie said. "She said all the items in the shop were overpriced, and it was all junk. It's a thrift shop, lady. Did she expect things to be brand new?"

"How did you handle it?" Laurie asked.

"For a moment, when she just wouldn't stop getting in my face, I wanted to slap her. You know, when a girl did that in my old life, you'd kick her butt. But I walked out the back door for a moment and took a breath. It kind of scared me that I still had that much anger in me that I might actually hit a customer."

"You did the right thing, Izzie," Laurie said. "Anger is a normal emotion. Controlling it is what we all work at doing. I'm so proud of you for not reacting immediately."

Izzie smiled. "Well, I still wanted to slap her, but I went

back in, and thank goodness she'd left. It's hard, though. When you live a certain way for so long, where everything is a primal reaction, it's hard to change."

"But you are changing," Latisha said. "I mean, the other day, I was in your face about taking my nail polish, and you didn't slap me." She laughed.

"Yeah. You and I could have really gone at it," Izzie said, also laughing. "But I didn't take your stupid polish, and I also don't want to get kicked out of here."

"I know you didn't take it, now," Latisha said. "I was in a mood that day."

"Tell me about it," Izzie said, and the whole room erupted into laughter, even Latisha.

"We can all change if we try," Laurie said after the laughter subsided. "And it's for the better. You'll see."

"What about nightmares?" Katie asked. "I had another one the other night. I know the guy who took me is in jail now, but I'm still scared I'll be found and taken back."

"That's a legitimate fear," Laurie said, leaning forward in her chair. "And, we as women are always looking over our shoulders to make sure someone isn't following us. Unfortunately, that's the way the world is. You have to build a safe space around yourself to alleviate some of that fear."

"I feel like I'm in a safe place," Katie said, smiling over at Addie. "But I still freak out at night sometimes."

"One thing I tell the girls here is to have a safe routine every night," Laurie offered. "Check all the windows and doors and check your own space before going to bed. That might ease your mind when you sleep. It seems simple, but it's effective."

"It helped me," Melanie said. "I don't have as many nightmares as I used to. I feel safer if I do that routine each night."

"And I feel safer knowing you're doing that routine each night," Tonya said. "Then I don't have to do it." She laughed, and the other girls did too. Even Katie laughed along.

"It's about controlling your own space," Laurie said. "You feel safer if you know you're in control."

"I'll try it," Katie said.

On their way home, Katie asked Addie if she thought having a nightly routine would help alleviate her nightmares.

"I do," Addie said. "When I lived in that awful apartment with those girls, no one locked anything. I was always scared someone would get in. Then, when I moved to Valerie's house, I saw she would go around locking everything when it got dark out. I started to help her each night, and it became routine. I felt safer that way."

"Do you mind if I do it at your house? I don't want you to think I'm checking everything behind you," Katie said.

"I don't mind at all. You can never be too careful."

That night before bed, Katie walked around the house checking all the doors and windows before going to her own room. Addie said goodnight to her as she walked into her bedroom and closed the door.

"What was that all about?" Zach asked. He'd just walked out of the bathroom, fresh from a shower.

"Katie is trying something new to see if it helps lessen her nightmares." Addie explained what they'd talked about in group.

"That's a good idea," Zach said. "But do you think it'll help?"

Addie shrugged. "It can't hurt. I want her to feel safe here."

They both crawled into bed, and Zach turned out his light. Addie left hers on.

"I think I'll read more of Sofiya's letters," Addie said, reaching for the box. "So far, she's having a great time in London, and she's hoping the ladies can help her find what happened to Harry."

"It's starting to sound like a soap opera," Zach teased.

"Go to sleep, or I'll find another room where you can build wainscotting," she teased.

"Ugh. Good night."

Addie curled up under the covers and opened a letter from December 1919.

CHAPTER TWENTY–TWO

Sofiya

December flew by, and soon, it was Christmas Eve. That afternoon, Mrs. Dawson hired the ladies' maid who worked at the hotel to come to their rooms and style their hair. Mrs. Dawson asked the maid to style her shorter hair in a swept-back fashion and place a beautiful pearl-encrusted headband around her head, much like a tiara. She insisted Sofiya allow the maid to style her long hair as well. She piled it high on Sofiya's head, creating a loose chignon, and made tiny braids from each side that were swept back and wrapped around the bun. Tendrils of hair were left to hang down her neck, giving the style a soft appearance.

"Lovely," Mrs. Dawson said upon seeing Sofiya's hairstyle. "But it's missing something." The older woman dug through her jewelry case and produced several hairpins with diamond clusters on the ends. "These should be placed around the chignon to give it some sparkle."

Sofiya immediately knew that these were not fake diamonds. "Oh, I couldn't," she protested. "What if I lose one?"

"Don't worry about that, dear," Mrs. Dawson said, handing the pins to the maid to place. "If you do, you do. These things must be used, or else what's the use of owning them?"

After the maid had placed them in her hair, she handed Sofiya the hand mirror. Sofiya looked at her hair and had to admit that the sparkle from the pins added to the beauty of her hairstyle.

"Thank you," she said to her employer. "You've been more than generous to me."

Mrs. Dawson swiped away her words with a flick of her wrist. "Pretty girls need pretty things," she said with a smile.

The two women donned their most elaborate dresses and wraps and then went down to the waiting motor car that would take them to the party. When they pulled up in front of the Chambers' four-story townhouse, Sofiya took in a sharp breath. The place was lit up with Christmas lights, and pine boughs encircled the hand railings and large double doors. Autos were ahead of them, waiting to drop off exquisitely dressed guests.

"It's beautiful," Sofiya exclaimed. She'd seen the palace decorated for Christmas, and it was gorgeous, but this was just as much a delight to Sofiya.

"Wait until we go inside. I'm sure Winnie has pulled out all the stops."

A smartly uniformed man helped them out of the car and escorted them up the carpeted steps, delivering the women to the butler at the front door. After taking their wraps, another man escorted them to the second floor, where they heard music playing and people chatting.

"Ah, there you two are," Mrs. Chambers said, greeting them both at the top of the stairs with two air kisses each. "Darling, come out here and greet my dear friend Marion and her companion, Sofiya."

Mr. Chambers walked down the hallway behind her and smiled at the two women. He was a short, portly balding man, wearing a black suit with tails with a white shirt and vest underneath. Sofiya couldn't help but think he looked like a penguin, and she had to cover her mouth with her gloved hand to keep from showing her smile.

"It's so nice to see you, Marion," Oliver Chambers said, greeting her with a warm handshake. "And how nice that you have a traveling companion." He smiled at Sofiya and held her hand. "It's a pleasure to meet you."

Sofiya nodded and smiled. Mr. Chambers did seem like a very nice man.

"Please go into the parlor and enjoy yourselves. I'll catch up with you both as soon as I've greeted all the guests," Mrs. Chambers said.

Mrs. Dawson walked ahead of Sofiya into a room that looked more like a ballroom than a parlor. There were decorated Christmas trees on each end of the room and lovely pine boughs over the two fireplaces. Two large chandeliers hung from the ceiling, and a long row of floor-to-ceiling windows covered one wall. A four-piece band played quietly in the corner of the room as guests mingled while drinking wine and eating hor d'oeuvres from silver trays circulated by waiters.

"This seems to be more than just a few close friends and family," Sofiya whispered to Mrs. Dawson.

Mrs. Dawson laughed. "Winnie does enjoy overdoing everything."

A few of the other women Sofiya had met were there, and they soon all gathered together to chat while sipping wine. Mrs. Dawson pointed out Winnie's son and wife to Sofiya, as well as her daughter and her husband. Sofiya also met a few of the other women they hadn't had a chance to visit with yet. She hoped she wouldn't have to remember names because there were too many to keep straight.

Once everyone had arrived, they were escorted to the dining room that held a long, beautifully decorated table. From what Sofiya could count, there were forty-two people sitting at the table. She'd been to large formal dinners in her past life, but they usually didn't have this many people in attendance.

There were name tags at each seat, and Sofiya found hers across the table from Mrs. Dawson and between two younger men. She saw from the look on her employer's face that Mrs. Dawson found it amusing that Mrs. Chambers was so blatantly matchmaking.

Both gentlemen were pleasant, one better looking than the other, but neither seemed to find Sofiya interesting. She thought it might have to do with the fact that she shared so little of herself. One of the men was Mrs. Chambers' nephew, Andrew Waverly, and the other was the son of a business associate of Mr. Chambers. Getting through the seven-course meal became an ordeal for Sofiya as she tried to be polite yet avoided talking about herself.

After the meal, there was dancing in the parlor. Sofiya was surprised when Andrew came over and asked her to dance. She accepted, not wanting to be rude.

"Are you having a good time," he asked as they danced a slow waltz.

"Yes. Your aunt is quite nice to have invited me," Sofiya said.

He grinned. "My aunt is a busybody who thinks she's a matchmaker."

Sofiya startled. "Should I be offended by that comment or amused?"

"I'm sorry. I didn't mean to offend. I always find it funny when she places all the single men and women together," Andrew said while keeping up perfectly with the timing of the music. "I thought myself very lucky being placed next to you."

"Thank you," she said as the song finished. She wasn't sure if he really meant it, but it didn't matter. They'd be leaving soon for Paris, and she'd never see him again.

The night grew late, and Mrs. Dawson began to tire, so the two women made excuses and left the party. As they stepped outside, exactly at midnight, church bells around the city rang, welcoming Christmas Day.

The two women stood a moment under the clear night sky, listening to the bells. It was a magical ending to a lovely evening.

"Merry Christmas, Sofiya," Mrs. Dawson said warmly as their motor car drove up.

"Merry Christmas," Sofiya said. Then she helped the older woman into the automobile, and they headed back to The Savoy.

* * *

Sofiya and Mrs. Dawson spent a quiet night in their hotel room on New Year's Eve, exhausted from all the celebrating leading up to Christmas. After a round of luncheons to say goodbye to Mrs. Dawson's friends, Sofiya began the process of packing their things so they could travel to Paris. Before leaving, however, Mrs. Chambers stopped by the hotel one last time to give Sofiya news.

Sitting in the cozy tearoom at The Savoy, Mrs. Chambers addressed Sofiya. "I'm so sorry, dear, but we were unable to find your young man. My husband had his secretary dig through records and call in favors, but he was nowhere to be found. His service records were found, but it shows nothing after his troop was sent to Paris. We have no idea if he went back to the states or became missing in action."

Sofiya tried to absorb the news Mrs. Chambers was giving her. How could there be no record of him? "Could he have been killed in action?" she asked. Surely, if he were alive, he would have written to his parents to let them know he was fine.

"That is a possibility, but it was never recorded," Mrs. Chambers said. "Many young men stayed in Paris and London after the war. Maybe he was discharged and did that. His discharge papers would be in the states, not here."

"I'm so sorry, Sofiya," Mrs. Dawson said, looking sad. "I had hoped we could find your young man."

"Thank you for searching for me," Sofiya told Mrs. Chambers. "And please thank your husband for me. Maybe I'll still be able to find him. As you say, he may have remained here in Europe."

"It's a possibility," Mrs. Chambers said. "I hope you find him, dear."

Sofiya thought about Harry often as she prepared the trunks for their travel to Paris. Could he have just disappeared and not cared to tell his parents? Or maybe he'd been injured, and it took him months to heal. For all she knew, he may even have returned to Portland by now. With a heavy heart, she finished her work and tried to look forward to the rest of their trip.

They arrived in Paris the first week of January and went

directly to the apartment on the Champ de Mars where they'd be staying. Yet another friend of Mrs. Dawson's had loaned them his luxury apartment on the third floor of a grand old building. They had a beautiful view of the Eiffel Tower as well as the entire city.

"These views never get old," Mrs. Dawson said once their luggage had been brought up by the apartment building's concierge staff.

"It's incredible," Sofiya said, gazing out into the late afternoon sky. She was tired from their traveling but not so much as to not enjoy their lovely view.

They spent the next day settling into their new living space. The apartment had been built in the 17th century but had been updated with all the modern conveniences. The ceilings were tall and chandeliers hung in every room. The bathrooms had marble floors and large, luxurious bathtubs. It was a delight to stay in such a historic place with spectacular views.

Just as in London, cards and letters soon arrived with invitations from old friends of Mrs. Dawson's. They spent the first week at luncheons and suppers with friends. But this time, Mrs. Dawson was adamant about putting aside time for sightseeing.

They visited the Louvre Museum, spending two days admiring the many works of art. Sofiya was especially captivated by the Egyptian collection. To think these items had survived thousands of years seemed incredible to her. They also visited Notre Dame Cathedral, admiring the many religious relics and the beauty of the large stained-glass windows.

At all the sites they visited, Sofiya found herself searching the faces of young men in the hope of catching a glimpse of Harry. Young American men were everywhere in Paris since the end of the war. Perhaps Mrs. Chambers had been right—maybe Harry stayed in Europe. She became obsessed with watching crowds for a familiar face.

The day they visited the Eiffel Tower was a chilly one, and Sofiya and Mrs. Dawson bundled up in wool coats and wore their most comfortable shoes. After a brisk walk, they arrived at the tower, where they took their turn on the lifts to go up to the top. People were bustling about, and once they were high above Paris, Sofiya gasped at the magnificent view of the city.

"This is incredible," she exclaimed, standing at the rail.

"It makes me a little dizzy," Mrs. Dawson said, standing back a few feet. "I've never been one for heights."

Seeing that it made her friend uneasy, Sofiya backed up a step from the railing and ran directly into a young man. She turned quickly to apologize and found herself looking up into a pair of kind blue eyes. The young man had dark blond hair and a heavy beard, but something about him tugged at her heart. Before she could utter a word, the man limped away with the use of a cane to the other side of the tower.

Feeling confused, Sofiya hurried after him. She heard Mrs. Dawson calling for her, but she couldn't stop. Quickening her steps, she rushed through the crowded tower to catch up with the man. Could it be Harry? The man's eyes looked so much like his.

Sofiya circled the tower, but there was no sign of the tall, blond man. Her heart dropped. Was she seeing things that weren't there? Crestfallen, she made her way back to Mrs. Dawson, who'd found a bench to sit on.

"Where did you go?" Mrs. Dawson asked, looking concerned. "You ran away so quickly."

The concern on her employer's face was more than Sofiya could bear. Tears filled her eyes as the crowd moved around them.

"What's wrong?" Mrs. Dawson asked, pulling a handkerchief from her coat pocket and handing it to Sofiya. This only made the young girl cry harder.

"I'm so sorry," Sofiya said through her tears. "I feel like I'm falling to pieces." She wiped her tears, but they just wouldn't stop.

Mrs. Dawson placed her arm around her and patted her back. "It's all right, dear. We've been so busy on this trip. Perhaps I've worked you too hard."

Sofiya shook her head. "No. I've enjoyed this trip so much. You've been nothing but kind and generous."

"Then what is it?" Mrs. Dawson looked confused.

"I thought I saw Harry. I bumped into a man, and his eyes reminded me of him. But he got away from me, and I ran to find him." She wiped her eyes again. "But it couldn't have been Harry. I want so badly to find him that I'm seeing him where he isn't."

"Oh, my dear. I'm so sorry. I knew you wanted to find him, but I had no idea he meant that much to you," Mrs. Dawson said tenderly.

Sofiya looked directly at her friend. "He was the only man I felt had ever actually seen me. The real me. He'd known me at my worst and still professed how much he cared for me."

Mrs. Dawson stared at her in amazement. "I know exactly what you mean, dear. That was how I felt about my Franklin. He knew me through and through. He saw me."

The two women sat on the bench for a while as Sofiya pulled herself together. After a time, Mrs. Dawson said, "I think I've had enough of this vacation and the endless luncheons and suppers. It's time we went home."

Sofiya looked at her, her lashes still damp with tears. "I

have no home to return to," she said sadly.

"Oh, dear. Of course you do," Mrs. Dawson said. "Didn't I make it clear when I hired you? I need a companion not only for travel but on a regular basis. You'll come home to Syracuse with me."

"Really?" Sofiya was stunned.

"Yes, dear. Really. And no more calling me Mrs. Dawson. After all this time, I consider us friends. Call me Marion from now on. Please."

"Thank you," Sofiya said, giving her a small smile. "You don't know how much this means to me."

"I think I do, dear," Mrs. Dawson said with a kindly smile. "Now. Let's get down from this tower and make plans to return home."

Sofiya was only too happy to begin the journey home.

CHAPTER TWENTY-THREE

Addie

As Addie continued her work on the house, Katie finished testing on her GED, passing all the courses. The night she passed her final test, the three of them went out to eat to celebrate Katie's accomplishment.

"I'm so proud of you," Addie said as they ate pizza in a restaurant overlooking the Willamette River. "Now, you can move on to even greater things."

"Maybe I can apply to community college for the winter term," Katie said, looking hopeful. "I was looking at it online, and I could take some of my basic classes before deciding if I want to try to transfer to a state college."

"That's a great idea," Zach said. He'd been more than happy to have a night out and not work on the house for a change. "Any idea what you might want to major in?"

Katie shrugged. "No, not really."

"You don't have to know right away," Addie said. "You can take a few classes and see what interests you."

"Do you think it's a waste of time?" Katie asked.

Addie shook her head. "Not at all. Any type of education is never a waste of time."

Katie brightened. "I'll have to apply for grant money. Until I can start, I can help you finish the house."

"We need all the hands we can get," Zach said. "This project is so much more than I'd first thought."

"We should go to the campus and walk around," Addie suggested. "You could make an appointment with an advisor."

"That sounds like a good idea," Katie said. "There are several campuses, though. I'll have to see which one would be the closest to the house." Katie's excitement faded quickly. "Oh. But I don't have a driver's license or a car. How will I get to school?"

"I forgot about that," Addie said. She tapped her fingers on the table as she thought. "I guess the first thing you're going to have to do is study for your driver's test."

That week, Katie downloaded the driver's handbook and studied it while Addie worked on sanding the bedroom floor so she could stain it. They'd pulled up old carpeting from this room as well, and it had left hundreds of carpet tacks just like the previous room. Zach took down the trim and brought it to the garage to sand and stain while Addie worked in the bedroom. Throughout the weekend, when Katie grew tired of studying, she helped Addie.

By Monday, the third bedroom was finished except for the molding, and Addie hauled all of her supplies down to Katie's room which was the next one. She'd dreaded this room. Someone had painted over the wallpaper, and the paper had bubbled underneath. It looked terrible. And it would be a mess to pull down without harming the wall beneath. The room had no carpeting, which was a relief, but the floor was badly scratched, so Addie would have to sand and stain it.

The three of them moved Katie's furniture to the third bedroom. "I hope you'll like this room," Addie said, nervous the change might trigger her nightmares.

"Are you kidding? This room is great," Katie said. "And I like the fact that I helped you remodel it."

That made Addie feel better.

While Zach worked at tearing apart the upstairs bathroom, Addie and Katie worked in unison to get the painted wallpaper down. First, Addie carefully removed the floor moldings so she wouldn't harm them and left them for Zach to stain. Then, Katie used a tool to score the wallpaper while Addie used a solution to spray on small sections of the wall, then scraped through the paint, so the wallpaper ripped off easier.

"Oh, wow. This is going to take forever," Katie said, wiping her forehead with her sleeve.

"Welcome to the fun of remodeling," Addie said, chuckling.

They worked all day, with both women scraping the walls after Addie had finished scoring the paper. It looked like it would be a two-day project just getting the old paper down.

"We should see if we can visit the college on Thursday," Addie said that evening as they all ate dinner at the kitchen table. "It'll give our arms a break."

Later, Katie emailed the advisor's office to see if they could make an appointment for Thursday. She'd decided to go to the Sylvania campus, which was southwest of the house.

The next morning, she had a response saying a campus advisor could meet with her to talk about Katie's options at one o'clock on Thursday.

"Great," Addie said. "We can go a little earlier and walk around the campus before the meeting.

"What if I decide to go there, and then you sell this house? What will I do then?" Katie asked, looking stressed.

"It'll be a while before this house is ready to sell," Addie assured her. "So, I wouldn't worry too much. And we're not going to kick you out. You can also live at Laurie's house, which will be a longer drive, but it shouldn't be too bad."

Katie nodded, biting her lip.

"Hey," Addie said gently, sitting closer to Katie. "You really don't have to worry. I'd never tell you to leave. I'll make sure you have somewhere to go first, okay?"

"Okay," Katie said.

"I know you aren't used to people making guarantees and sticking to them," Addie said. "But Zach and I keep our word."

This seemed to quell Katie's anxiousness.

On Thursday, Addie and Katie drove to the campus and found a parking place. It was noon, so many of the students were eating lunch or had left between classes. Katie mentioned that she liked how it was in a quiet area and not downtown Portland where it would be teaming with people.

"It's a nice campus," Addie agreed. They made their way to the offices in time for their appointment with the advisor.

An hour later, carrying a folder full of information and applications for the college and funding, Addie and Katie joined the throngs of students making their way through the building to get to their next class.

"Wow. This place is super busy," Addie said, glancing around. She'd seen in the college brochure that there were thousands of students attending at any one time, but it hadn't seemed real until she was in the crowd of people. She glanced over at Katie and was immediately worried. The poor girl looked pale, and her eyes were wide.

"Are you okay?" Addie asked.

Katie glanced around like a trapped animal looking for a place to flee. Suddenly, she ran down the hallway and through a door.

Addie tried to follow her, but there were too many people. She made her way to the door where Katie had escaped and saw it was the women's bathroom. "Katie? Are you okay?" Addie asked as she walked into the small bathroom facility. There were only four stalls, and two of them were closed. "Katie?"

From inside one, Addie heard heavy breathing. "Katie. Let me know you're okay," she said, her voice echoing in the tiled room.

One of the doors opened, and a blond girl wearing shorts and a T-shirt carrying a heavy backpack stared at Addie like she was crazy. The girl left immediately.

"I'm okay," Katie said in a small voice. Tentatively, she opened the stall door. Tears streamed down her face.

"What's wrong?" Addie asked. "Why did you run away?"

Katie cried harder. Addie pulled some paper towels from the machine and handed them to her.

"It's okay," Addie said gently. "I'm here."

"There were so many people," Katie wailed. "I didn't feel safe. It was like anyone could have grabbed me in that hallway. I could just disappear."

"Oh, sweetie." Addie hugged her close. "I'm so sorry. I should have thought of that. I guess I didn't realize the halls would be so crowded."

"But it's so stupid," Katie said, wiping her face and blowing her nose. "I was okay when you took me shopping. But today, it was like something snapped. How will I ever do anything normal again if I'm always scared?" Her tears started again, and no matter what Addie did or said, they wouldn't stop. Finally, Addie wrapped her arm around Katie and led her through the now nearly empty hallway and outside to their car. She drove the still-crying girl to the one person who'd know how to calm her down. Laurie.

By the time they'd pulled up in front of Laurie's house, Katie had stopped crying but looked so desolate that Addie was worried about her. "Let's visit with Laurie for a few minutes," she told Katie gently. "She can help you."

"No one can help me," Katie said, shaking her head. "I'm a mess. I'm useless."

"You had a setback. It sucks, but you'll be fine. Let's talk to Laurie."

The minute they walked inside, Laurie came to the girl's aid. It was as if she knew immediately what had happened. Katie broke down in tears when Laurie put her arms around her. Addie waited in the living room while Laurie took Katie into the kitchen so they could talk privately.

"Is Katie okay?" Melanie asked, coming into the living room. "I saw her crying when she came in." She sat on the sofa next to Addie.

"She'll be fine," Addie assured her. "She had an emotional moment that took her by surprise. Laurie's with her."

Soon, Izzie and Tonya came home from their jobs and joined the two in the living room. Everyone was worried about Katie.

"Let's not make a big deal about it when she comes out," Addie suggested. "I don't want to upset her even more."

The girls nodded. Izzie started talking about her day at work, and then Melanie shared that she'd passed her GED tests. Addie congratulated her. Katie had already shared that she'd passed her GED at the last meeting.

"She really lit a fire under me," Melanie said. "I started studying harder and finished. I'm glad to hear she's checking out the college now."

"Who's going to college?" Latisha came into the room with a new hairstyle and bright blue nails.

"Whoa, girl. What's with the hair?" Izzie asked with round eyes.

"Hey! Don't you like it? I love it," Latisha said.

"It's so red!" Izzie said.

Latisha narrowed her eyes at the other girl. "So!"

Izzie started to laugh. "I'm just messing with you. I do like it. But it is really red."

Latisha sat down with the group, asking what was going on.

"Katie had a bad day," Melanie said. "We're just here for support."

"Oh. That sucks," Latisha said. She settled in, and the group of girls started talking about things they were doing and wanted to do. Addie sat and listened to their banter. They were a great group of girls, and she felt lucky that she'd had a chance to get to know them.

A while later, Katie and Laurie came out of the kitchen. Katie looked better but was surprised to see the girls there.

"My goodness," Laurie said, her tone upbeat. "If Wanda were here, we'd have a full meeting."

"The girls were keeping me company," Addie said. She rose and went to Katie. "Everything alright?"

Katie nodded. "Is it okay if we go home now?"

Addie caught Laurie's eye and saw her nod. "Sure. Let's pick up something for dinner and head home."

Melanie walked up to Katie. "If you need anyone to talk to, I'm here," she said softly.

"We're all here for you," Izzie said. "Anytime."

Katie looked like she was going to cry again. But she said a heartfelt "Thank you" to the group.

When they got into the car, Katie reached over and placed a hand on Addie's arm. "I'm sorry I fell apart at the college."

"There's no reason to be sorry. It happens. I'm glad you're feeling better," Addie said, giving her a smile.

"Laurie said that too. We had a good talk. She suggested I have a few private sessions with her to work on these issues."

"I think that's a good idea," Addie said. To her surprise, Katie began to laugh. "What's so funny?"

"It seems you're always saving me in bathrooms," Katie said.

Addie gave a small chuckle. "It's my pleasure. Come on, let's go home."

The younger girl sobered. "Home. You don't know how much that word means to me."

Addie looked Katie in the eye. "I do know. Believe me." She put the car in drive, and they headed to get food and go home.

CHAPTER TWENTY-FOUR

Sofiya

At the end of January, the two women sailed into New York harbor, and after a night at The Savoy, they took the train up to Syracuse.

"I hope you like snow, dear," Marion said. "Because in Syracuse, we get a lot of it."

Sofiya was used to snow and cold temperatures, having lived in Russia. "I come from snow," she told her employer. "I'm used to it."

"Used to it," Marion said, laughing. "Not quite the same as liking it, but I know what you mean."

They were greeted by a driver and car at the train station and arranged for the rest of their luggage to be dropped off at her house.

"Welcome home, Mrs. Dawson," the young man driving said as he helped the ladies into the back seat. "It's so nice to have you back."

"Thank you, James," Mrs. Dawson said. "How's your mother?"

"She's doing nicely," James said. "She was a bit sick a while back but is well now. She was excited to hear you're coming home."

"I can't wait to see her," Mrs. Dawson said. She turned to Sofiya. "Mrs. Prescott has worked for us for years. She's a lovely woman. I've known James since he was just a young boy."

Sofiya smiled and nodded, then glanced out the window at their surroundings. Marion had been right—Syracuse had a lot of snow. They drove through the downtown area and onto West Onondaga Street. The business buildings soon disappeared, and they entered a quiet neighborhood with impressive homes and large yards. When James pulled up to a well-kept-up Victorian house with a large turret on the right side, Sofiya's eyes grew wide.

"What a lovely home," she said to Marion. "Is this yours?"

"Yes, it is, dear. Franklin and I bought this in 1902 as a summer home. We ended up spending our last years together here when he moved his law practice to Syracuse. With all the traveling we did, it always felt good to come home."

Sofiya could believe that as they entered the home. Warm, polished wood covered the walls in the large entryway, and the staircase was magnificent. It ran up the right side of the wall, then took a sharp left. Decorative spindles filled in the open space where the stairs turned. A warm fire greeted them in the entryway fireplace as Mrs. Prescott approached them on the burgundy paisley carpet runner.

"Welcome home, Marion," Mrs. Prescott said, opening her arms to give her employer a warm hug.

Sofiya watched the two women greet each other like old friends. She liked that about Marion. She had all the grace and style necessary to visit dignitaries but was warm and caring about the people she was closest to.

"And who is this young lady?" Mrs. Prescott asked, smiling over at Sofiya. She was of medium height and very slender. Her dark hair was piled on her head, and she wore a day dress with a white apron over it. She looked like someone's mother just coming from the kitchen.

"This is my traveling companion, soon to be social secretary, now that we're home," Marion said with a broad smile. "Sofiya Henderson, this is Mrs. Ardith Prescott."

"It's so nice to meet you," Sofiya said, reaching out to shake the woman's hand.

"And it's very nice to meet you too, Miss Henderson," Mrs. Prescott said.

"Please, call me Sofiya," she said.

Mrs. Prescott nodded as James entered the house with the few bags the women had brought along.

"Where would you like these?" he asked.

"These two are mine," Marion said. "Please place them in the bedroom down the hallway." She glanced at Mrs. Prescott. "Ardith, which room have you prepared for Sofiya?"

"Top of the stairs on the right," Mrs. Prescott said. "The washroom is next door to it."

"Wonderful," Marion said. "That's a lovely bedroom, Sofiya."

"Thank you," Sofiya said.

James took off up the stairs with Sofiya's luggage as Mrs. Prescott led the ladies into the parlor. Much like Miss Nora's house, there were two wooden pocket doors that opened to expose the large room. A cozy fire was lit, giving the room a soft glow. The room was done in the same burgundy colors as the hallway rug, with browns and greens mixed in.

"Would you like some tea before settling in?" Mrs. Prescott asked. "I've also prepared a light dinner for later tonight."

"Thank you, dear, but I think I want to go to my room for a while and change out of these traveling clothes," Marion said. "Would you show Sofiya to her room, please?"

"Of course," Mrs. Prescott said.

"And dear," Marion said, looking at Sofiya. "This is your home now, so please make yourself comfortable. Anything you need, just ask."

"I will," Sofiya said. "Thank you."

"My room is down this hallway, past the dining room. I can't manage the stairs anymore. If you need me, just knock," Marion said. She walked slowly down the hallway toward her room.

"Follow me," Mrs. Prescott said. James had already deposited their luggage and had disappeared.

Sofiya followed Mrs. Prescott up the beautifully paneled staircase. On the right, where it turned sharply, was a doorway into the second floor of the turret.

"The turret rooms on all three floors are extra little nooks," Mrs. Prescott said. "Marion loves sitting in the first-floor room where she grows plants and sunlight streams in each morning. Each nook has a small stove you can light a fire in. They're perfect for curling up with a book."

"Sounds lovely," Sofiya said.

"Marion turned what used to be the morning room into her bedroom downstairs a few years ago. She never really used the room. She liked sipping coffee in the turret room each morning with her husband. She said it was much cozier," Mrs. Prescott said. "Well, here we are."

They had arrived at the top of the stairs, and Mrs. Prescott opened the first door on the right. "I aired out the room and changed the linens. I hope you'll be comfortable in here."

Sofiya entered, and immediately loved it. The furniture was white French Provincial. The double bed had a thick cream and pink coverlet on it, and there was a dressing table with a mirror and a matching dresser. The walls had been papered in a soft sage and pink striped and flowered design, and sage curtains hung over the large window.

"It's perfect," she told Mrs. Prescott. "Just beautiful."

Mrs. Prescott smiled. "Marion had telegraphed me that you two were coming home, and she suggested this room. She knew you'd love it."

"I do. It's like a room for a princess."

"It certainly is," Mrs. Prescott said. "This room has a nice closet. Hopefully, there will be plenty of room for your things. If not, we can store extra items in the guest room closets. If I know Marion, she bought too many clothes for the European trip."

Sofiya laughed. "She was quite generous. We have trunks of clothing coming from the train station."

"That doesn't surprise me. Perhaps you and I can go through them tomorrow and sort the clothing and accessories."

"Thank you. That would be nice. It's a big job going through everything," Sofiya said.

"The washroom is the next door down. There are towels and other necessities in the cabinet in there." Mrs. Prescott moved to the door. "I hope you'll make yourself at home."

"Thank you so much," Sofiya said.

After the other woman left, Sofiya sat down on the bed. It was comfortable, and the coverlet was soft and fluffy. Sofiya stood and walked to the window. Outside, there was a large lot between this house and the next one. The driveway pulled up alongside the house, and when she looked toward the backyard, she caught a glimpse of a garage or perhaps an old carriage house.

Her mind wandered back to the day she'd arrived at Miss Nora's house and how happy she and Alina had been. They'd thought they'd been lucky to live in a nice house in their new town. And then all had gone sour from there. Sofiya felt so fortunate to have found the job with Marion and had escaped that terrible place. Now that she had a permanent address, she could write to Alina and even Mrs. Jarvi at her house. Maybe Mrs. Jarvi had heard something of Harry by now.

Feeling content and safe in her new surroundings, Sofiya changed into a more comfortable outfit so she could meet Marion downstairs later.

* * *

For the next few days, Sofiya was busy going through the trunks and sorting the clothes that needed mending and cleaning. Marion went through her closet to donate some of her older clothing to make room for the new. Mrs. Prescott was true to her word and helped Sofiya go through Marion's trunks and her own.

"Are you good with a needle?" Mrs. Prescott asked Sofiya. "There are seams and some beadwork on a few of these gowns that need mending."

"I'm average," Sofiya said, laughing. "My mother had a heck of a time teaching me to sew. But I can manage."

After all was sorted and Sofiya had a pile of clothing to fix, Marion asked if she'd help her send out notes to friends in the area informing them that she was home. Sofiya sat at a small desk in the parlor and wrote addresses on envelopes from Marion's address book and then wrote notes Marion dictated. Marion would sign them, then Sofiya would prepare them to post.

Sofiya's days started to fall into a routine. She'd breakfast with Marion in the small turret room on the main floor, then they'd work a bit on correspondence. In the afternoon, Sofiya sat in the second-floor turret room where the light was good and sew a few of the dresses. After supper, the two women usually sat and read quietly in the parlor. It was a nice change from their traveling days when each day was a flurry of activity.

A week after they'd returned, Adelaine Burton dropped by for afternoon tea to see her dear friend.

"How lovely to see you both," Mrs. Burton said, greeting Marion and Sofiya. "I see you haven't yet married off this dear girl, Marion. Your skills are slipping." She laughed, and Marion laughed along.

"No, no. Sofiya was the belle of the ball on our vacation, but no one caught her eye," Marion said. "Sofiya's a smart girl. When she finds the right man, she'll know."

Sofiya's face grew warm with embarrassment as they spoke about her, but she knew it was all in good humor. She sat in as the women visited and served the tea, leaving Mrs. Prescott more time to do her own work.

"You both must come to the house next Friday for dinner. I insist," Adelaine said. "Edgar Jr. will be home for a change, and my daughter Amelia and her husband will be home too. We must celebrate your return to town."

"That's very sweet of you," Marion said. "We'd love to come."

"Wonderful. I'll send a car around for you at six that

evening. We always dress for dinner," Adelaine gently reminded them. "But then, what well-bred family doesn't?"

Sofiya found her words amusing. While she'd been raised in a family that dressed for dinner, she knew that most families did not. Only the rich or the wannabe rich did.

After she left, Marion addressed Sofiya, "I hope you don't mind my accepting a dinner invitation for the both of us. I don't want you to feel you must do everything I do."

"I don't mind at all. I'm curious to see their home."

"Oh, yes. You'll be amazed," Marion said. "It's a mansion compared to my house. I think they would have built a castle if they could have." Marion laughed. "It was actually Edgar Senior's father who built up the wealth in the family. But through the years, Edgar has added to the house. Amelia, her husband, and children have a wing of their own, and young Edgar will most likely live there with his wife when he finally has one."

"My goodness. This will be interesting," Sofiya said. They sounded like they thought themselves American royalty.

The evening of the dinner, Sofiya dressed in a lovely royal blue satin dress with a drop waist and hemline that hung mid-calf. It had a bit of beadwork that sparkled under the lights. She put her hair up and placed a beaded headband around it. Blue stone drop earrings hung from her ears, and she had a warm coat that matched the dress. As Sofiya looked at herself in the full-length mirror, she thought she didn't look too bad. She was short, and dresses tended to make her look dumpy, but these new straight styles gave the appearance of height, especially with the heels she wore. Sofiya knew she'd never be considered a great beauty, but she felt beautiful in all this finery.

A car arrived precisely at six and drove the women north of town, where there were acres of farmland and houses dotting the landscape. After a time, they pulled down a long driveway. Sofiya could see part of a house surrounded by oak and pine trees. The driveway curved, and Sofiya gasped when she saw the entire house.

"Oh, my goodness," she said under her breath.

Marion smiled and nodded. "That's one way to put it."

The house was rectangular in shape and four stories high. The shallow front porch displayed six heavy pillars, creating a walk-out balcony on the floor above it. Lights gleamed through the many windows, with black shutters accenting the white exterior. It was an imposing structure, sitting in the middle of so much land.

The motor car stopped in front of the wide double doors, and the driver ran around to help Marion, then Sofiya out of the car. As they walked up the four steps to the door, it opened wide, and a finely dressed butler invited them inside.

After taking their coats, he escorted them to the parlor on the left side. "Mrs. Marion Dawson and Miss Sofiya Henderson have arrived."

The people in the room all turned to look at them with smiles on their faces. Sofiya took in the large room, the vast burning fireplace, and the beautifully dressed people sitting on the sofas and chairs. The scene was so elegant that she suddenly felt as if she didn't belong.

"Welcome, welcome," Adelaine exclaimed as she approached the women. "My, don't you two look lovely. Edgar, come say hello to our guests."

Mr. Burton walked over, looking stately in his black tails and tie. He greeted Marion warmly, then took Sofiya's gloved hand. "It's so nice to see you again, Miss Henderson," he said. "I see Marion hasn't married you off yet." His eyes twinkled with mischief, making Sofiya's face grow hot.

"It's nice to see you again too, Sir," Sofiya said. "Thank you for inviting me to your home."

"Oh, my dear," Adelaine interrupted. "You are always welcome here." She turned to her son. "Edgar, darling. You remember Sofiya, don't you?"

Edgar Jr. walked over and greeted first Marion with a kiss on the cheek, then held Sofiya's hand. "How could I forget such a lovely young woman," he said with a devilish grin.

Sofiya smiled back, feeling nervous under Edgar's gaze. He looked handsome in his black tails, despite being shorter than his father. His brown hair was swept back, and his face was cleanshaven, which Sofiya liked. He looked young, but his intense brown eyes showed he was deeply intelligent.

"Come meet the rest of the family," Adelaine said, sweeping the two women along with her. "Edgar, dear, please get the ladies a drink. Sherry for you, Marion?"

"Yes," Marion said. "You know me too well."

"We've been friends for nearly a lifetime," Adelaine said. "I should know you well."

"And what would you like?" Edgar Jr. asked Sofiya, his brows raising suggestively.

She glanced around and saw that his mother was drinking red wine. Sofiya knew that prohibition had become law while they were in Europe and wondered how they were able to serve spirits. Not wanting to appear rude, she said, "Whatever wine you've been serving is fine."

He nodded and went to the mirrored bar cart near the grand fireplace.

"Sofiya," Adelaine said. "This is my daughter, Amelia, and her husband, Christian."

"It's nice to meet you both," Sofiya said. Christian stood and gave a slight nod of his head while Amelia sat and smiled up at her. Amelia appeared to be tall and very slender, and she had the most beautiful auburn hair cut in a swingy bob. Her hazel eyes glittered in the light when she smiled. Even without saying a word, she seemed like a warm person, much as Mr. Burton was. Sofiya felt an instant connection with her.

"Your wine," Edgar Jr. said, handing her a glass.

"Thank you," Sofiya said.

"Come sit with me," Amelia said to Sofiya. "I rarely see anyone close to my own age anymore."

Sofiya accepted a spot on the settee next to Amelia. Her burgundy dress with a black lace overlay was gorgeous, and she wore a garnet necklace and earrings.

"I highly doubt Sofiya is as old as you, dear sister," Edgar Jr. said with a smirk.

"You're so mean," Amelia admonished her brother. She turned to Sofiya. "How did you enjoy your European trip with Mrs. Dawson? Is everything over there still beautiful after the war?"

Sofiya told her of the places they'd visited and the many places they'd eaten or met friends for tea. "It's a magical place," Sofiya said. "I enjoyed the trip immensely."

"Sofiya and I met the Grand Duchess Xenia Alexandrovna, Tsar Nicholas's sister," Marion said. "She invited us to her table because she thought Sofiya looked like one of her brother's daughters."

"Really?" Amelia's eyes grew wide. "That's incredible. How lucky you are to have met a duchess."

"She was very kind," Sofiya said, hoping the subject would change.

"So, was she right?" Edgar Jr. stared at her from the other sofa. "Are you a long-lost princess from Russia?"

Sofiya's heart pounded as she looked up at Edgar Jr. "No, of course not," she said, harsher than she'd intended.

"Ignore him," Amelia told her. "He's always teasing."

Sofiya tried to relax and place a smile on her face, but her heart still thudded in her chest. She didn't understand why she'd been scared. She was no princess. But she'd kept her relationship with the Tsar's family a secret for so long that she was terrified of it coming out.

"Dinner is served," the butler announced.

"Escort me to dinner, will you?" Amelia said to Sofiya. She ran her arm around Sofiya's and led her out of the room. Sofiya saw Edgar Jr. offer his arm to Marion as they all walked across the hallway to the dining room.

Like the parlor, the dining room was immense in size. Another large fireplace, surrounded by a beautiful maple mantel, was on one wall, and a long sideboard sat on the opposite wall. At the very end of the room were large floor-to-ceiling windows with luxurious draperies over them. Sofiya guessed the dining table was maple underneath the tablecloth because of the gorgeous matching chairs.

"Here you are," Amelia said, stopping at the spot with Sofiya's name. She whispered in her ear. "Mother put you next to Edgar Jr. on purpose." Then she went to the other side of the table to sit with her husband.

"May I?" Edger Jr. asked. He pulled out Sofiya's chair, and she sat. Then he sat next to her. "It looks as if we're being set up," he said with a grin.

Sofiya didn't know how to respond. She wasn't used to anyone being so brazen. She was relieved once the food was served, and she could concentrate on eating.

They sat through a five-course meal, which was delicious but more food than Sofiya could eat in one sitting. She was used to her small meals with Marion. By the time dessert was served, she was happy her dress was loose, and she no longer wore a corset.

The women returned to the parlor while the men disappeared to Mr. Burton's den for brandy and cigars. Sofiya was thankful for the respite from Edgar Jr. He had been polite and often funny as they dined, but he unnerved her. She never knew how to respond to some of his quips.

Amelia poured them each a small sherry, and the women sat and talked for a while. Adelaine and Marion caught up on all the latest gossip while Amelia asked Sofiya a hundred questions.

"Have you a suiter?" Amelia asked. "I do hope not." She lowered her voice. "My parents have been going on and on about you since they first met you, telling Edgar he needs to find a woman like you to marry." Amelia grew serious. "I would love to have a sister-in-law living here. I get so lonely for female friends."

Sofiya was stunned that Amelia would share such a thing with her. It all seemed so personal for having just met. "I believe your mother said you have two children," Sofiya said to change the subject.

Amelia's face lit up. "Oh, yes. We have a son who's five and a daughter who's three. They are both little dolls. Jonathan, our son, is a quick learner, and Edina is the sweetest little girl ever. But our nanny takes care of them much of the time, leaving me too much time with nothing to do."

Sofiya found that odd. Her maman had spent a great deal of time with her, and she knew the Tsarina had been very hands-on with her children as well. Sofiya couldn't imagine letting a nanny raise her child.

The men returned, and Edgar Jr. came over to Sofiya. "Would you like to see the conservatory? My mother has a penchant for roses and also grows fruit trees all year long."

"Oh." She glanced at Marion, and the older lady nodded her approval. "Why yes. That would be nice," Sofiya said.

He offered her his arm, and they walked out of the room and down the hallway toward the back of the house.

"You have a lovely home," Sofiya said as she glanced around. The main staircase was in the center of the entryway and split into two staircases at the top, turning left and right. It was quite grand. They walked past the morning room and what appeared to be his father's den, and then the library.

"Thank you. My grandfather built it decades ago when he first became prosperous, and my father has added on through the years. The conservatory was built especially for my mother. She has a green thumb."

"Your father's farm must be quite prosperous," Sofiya said.

"Yes, it has been. But now, with prohibition in place, the breweries we used to sell our wheat and hops to have all closed down. Christian is speaking with a few breweries in Canada to sell to, but I've spread out into other business ventures that will do well."

"That's wonderful," Sofiya said. She was about to ask about his business, but they'd arrived at the door to the conservatory.

"After you," Edgar said, opening the door.

Sofiya entered and was immediately surprised at how warm

the room was. Down the middle were rows of roses in white, red, yellow, and pink. Along the glass walls stood trees, and in planters all around, there looked to be some berry vines. "My goodness, this is like having your own hidden garden," she said, turning to Edgar.

"It is. We have orange, plum, and apple trees. And over here," he pointed to the berry plants, "we have strawberries, raspberries, and blueberries. My mother likes to have fresh fruit in the winter, so we grow our own."

"It's so lovely." Sofiya followed the brick path around the plants. She stopped a moment to smell one of the roses. "So fragrant."

Edgar led her to a bench among the flowers and invited her to sit. "Look up," he said.

She did, and she saw the night sky through a raised glass ceiling. It was so clear out that the stars shone brightly. "Simply beautiful," she said.

Edgar nodded. "Another perk of being wealthy. And I don't say that to brag. I know we're a very lucky family to live in such a house and have the lifestyle we do."

Sofiya smiled at him. "It's rare to hear someone with money be so humble."

He grinned. "I'm probably more realistic than humble."

Sofiya sat quietly, staring at the night sky. It was so quiet and peaceful in there among the flowers and trees. When she turned back to Edgar, she saw he was watching her.

"I'm sorry my mother is blatantly trying to push us together," Edgar said. "Although, I admit I'm enjoying your company very much."

Sofiya felt her face grow warm with embarrassment. "I...I didn't feel that your mother had been pushing us together."

"Ah, but she is," Edgar said, then smiled. "But as I say, I don't mind. In fact, I wondered if you'd be so kind as to let me take you out to dinner tomorrow night. It will give us a chance to spend time together without my family watching our every move."

Sofiya was pleasantly surprised. She hadn't expected to come to a family dinner and be invited out by Edgar. But as she gazed at him, she had to admit that she thought she'd enjoy spending an evening out with him. "Yes. I'd like to go to dinner with you."

"Wonderful. I can pick you up at seven. There's an excellent dining establishment downtown that I'm sure you'll enjoy. It's all the rage, even for our small town."

He walked her back to the parlor, and soon she and Marion were taken home in the motor car. As they rode along, Sofiya blurted out, "Edgar asked me to dinner tomorrow night."

"He did? Wonderful!" Marion said, clapping her hands. "I knew he couldn't resist your charms."

"You didn't set this up with Mrs. Burton, did you?" Sofiya asked, her stomach suddenly turning at the thought. "Amelia said her parents were pushing me on Edgar."

"No, dear. I had no hand in this," Marion said. "Edgar asked you on his own."

A sigh of relief escaped Sofiya's lips.

"You did say yes, didn't you? To his invitation?" Marion asked.

"I did. Now I'm nervous as can be."

"You'll have a good time, I'm sure," Marion told her. "Edgar is a wonderful young man. I think you two will get on brilliantly."

Sofiya looked out her window as the motor car drove along.

Edgar wasn't anything like Harry, but then, Harry never came back for her. It was time she moved on, and maybe, as Marion said, they'd get along well. She hoped so.

CHAPTER TWENTY-FIVE

Addie

September faded into October, and Addie's days continued with scraping wallpaper, sanding and staining floors, and painting. She was thankful to have Katie working with her most days. The work progressed quicker that way, and it was nice having someone to talk to.

Katie studied the driving handbook at night after they worked. She hoped to pass the written test and then practice driving as much as possible so she could pass that test soon too. Katie told Addie that she wanted to be as independent as possible so she wasn't always bothering them.

"We don't mind helping you or driving you places," Addie assured her.

"But you have to stop working on the house every time I need to go somewhere," Katie responded. Addie always drove her to group meetings and now drove her to weekly sessions with Laurie. "I feel like I'm keeping you from your work."

"I really don't mind," Addie said. "I like going to the group meetings too, and taking you over there for sessions with Laurie isn't a problem. But I get it. You want your independence."

Katie dropped her head. "Yeah. As long as I don't have to live alone or go anywhere by myself," she mumbled. "I hate being afraid of being out in public alone. I don't know how I'll ever shake that."

"Eventually, you will. Believe me," Addie told her. "And I don't mind you living with us until you're able to be on your own. I like having a helper around here."

"Thanks." Katie bit her lip. "I'm going to have to get a job at some point so I can save up for a car and someday move out. I know you guys can't afford to pay me, and I don't expect you to. Room and food are more than enough payment for what I do around here."

"I wish we had more funds," Addie said. "And the grant I applied for didn't come through, unfortunately. Do you think you'd be able to work somewhere and feel safe?"

"Maybe if I work at an all-female place. Or a smaller place." Katie laughed. "Like, what kind of place would that be? A convent?"

Addie chuckled. "Let me think about it. Maybe I can find something for you."

That week, they finished painting and staining the next bedroom, which was one of the two large corner bedrooms in the back of the house. They had three bedrooms left. Then Addie had to do something with the hideous wallpaper in the upstairs hallway. Zach had remodeled the upstairs bathroom, and it had turned out great.

"I've been looking at our budget," Addie told Zach one day at lunch. "Since the corner bedrooms are so large, do you think we could add a small bathroom with a shower stall next to the room over the kitchen? It would be long and narrow, and it would make the bedroom smaller, but another bathroom might be a good selling point."

"Bathrooms are expensive," Zach said, looking thoughtful. 'We'd have to tear out that room's closet to use that wall. Are you sure you want to put the money into it?"

"I figured we could cut the closet in half in the bedroom next door and make a half closet in the other bedroom. Most houses this old don't even have closets, so it wouldn't seem strange. As for the cost, I think we'd get our money out of it in the end."

Zach studied her. "Are you still thinking of finding a way to turn this into a safe house?"

Addie sighed. "No. Like you said, we'd never get our money out of it. I just think an extra bathroom is a good idea with all these bedrooms."

"You're the boss," he said, giving her a quick kiss on the lips. "Draw it up and tell me what you want to buy for it. I'll start looking at how the plumbing is run in the kitchen and see where I can cut into it."

Addie stood and wrapped her arms around Zach. "Thank you for always being so willing to make changes. It makes my life easier."

"I trust your judgment," he said. "You haven't led me astray yet."

She laughed. "There's always a first time."

The following week, Katie passed her driving exam with flying colors, and Addie took a little time each day to let her practice driving. "You're doing really good," Addie told her after a few lessons. "Valerie taught me to drive, and I think I drove her crazy."

When they arrived home one afternoon from their driving

lesson, Gail waved from her yard. "How's the remodel going?" she asked as she met them in-between their houses.

"Really good. I have three more bedrooms upstairs to finish, and I talked Zach into creating another bathroom upstairs," Addie said.

"That's a good idea," Gail told her. "With that many bedrooms, having an additional bathroom will be good for resale."

"Exactly what I told him," Addie said.

Gail turned to Katie. "Matt's in the backyard shooting hoops if you want to see him. With school and his part-time job, he's rarely home."

"Great. I haven't seen him in a while," Katie said. She turned to Addie. "I'll be back in a little bit."

"Okay."

"She's a nice girl," Gail told Addie. "She's been over a few times to hang out with Matt, and they get along really well."

"She's pretty special," Addie said, smiling. "Say, speaking of part-time jobs. Do you know anyone who's hiring, like maybe a hair salon or women's clothing store? Somewhere that's smaller and, well, safe."

Gail's brows lifted. "For Katie?"

"Yeah. She's applied at a few places, but she doesn't have any experience, so it's tough getting anything," Addie said.

"Well, to tell you the truth, I have a job available. It would be in my office, part-time. I need someone who can create the house flyers on the computer, file, and do other things I don't have time for," Gail said. "Matt said Katie was going to college winter semester. She could easily do the job around her schedule."

"Really? That sounds perfect," Addie said, happy she'd

asked. "She's good on a computer, as most kids her age are, and she's a hard worker. She's been helping me with the remodeling, but we don't have enough money to pay her."

"Oh. Well, you can run it by her, and she can come talk to me. We can figure out something." Gail cocked her head. "I figured she was your younger sister, and she was working for you."

Addie hesitated before answering. She didn't feel she had the right to tell Katie's story to others, but she didn't want Katie to be ashamed of her past either. "Katie is a friend I made recently. We're helping her out," she finally said. She'd talk to Katie first to see if she was comfortable sharing her past with Gail.

"Oh. Well, tell her to drop by. I'd be happy to talk to her about the job," Gail said. She waved and headed back to her house.

Zach was in the kitchen getting a Coke when Addie walked in. "Was Gail being nosey again?" he asked with a smirk.

"Again?" Addie asked.

"Oh, she drops by occasionally when I'm in the yard or garage to ask how things are going. She's friendly enough, but I think she's dying to see what we've done so far," Zach said,

"Oh. Yeah, I suppose she is. She's probably hoping we'll hire her to sell it," Addie said. She grabbed water out of the refrigerator. "No, she said she might have a job for Katie. It sounds good, working in her office. I just wasn't sure if I should mention Katie's past or let Katie do that. Or not say anything at all."

"Does it matter if Gail knows her past?"

Addie shook her head. "No, not really. I don't know what Katie has told Matt. It's really not for me to say to anyone."

"You said in the letters, Sofiya kept her past secret from her employer, even though they grew really close. It didn't matter then where she came from, and it doesn't matter where Katie came from either," Zach said. "It only matters how she lives her life now."

"That's so true." Addie sat at the counter. "Most people don't know my past either. All that matters is I've worked hard to move forward. And Katie's a lot like me. She's honest and a hard worker."

"Yep." Zach sat down next to her. "I feel bad that I questioned her living with us at first. She's proven to be a great person."

Addie reached for his hand. "It's good to be cautious. We never know if it's safe or not when someone comes from a situation like hers. I think you've been pretty good about it."

Zach drew closer and kissed Addie softly just as the kitchen door opened.

"Oops. Sorry. Should I leave?" Katie looked embarrassed.

Addie laughed. "No. Come in. We can control ourselves."

Addie told her about the job Gail mentioned.

"Yeah. She came into the backyard and talked to me about it. It sounds perfect," Katie said excitedly. "And she has a small office and said there are only two other women who work with her. I told her I'd have to check with you to see when I could stop by and have her show me around. She said she'd be in tomorrow morning if that works."

"Great. Yeah. I can drop you there," Addie said. "We should talk, though."

"My cue to go back to work," Zach said. He left the kitchen, and they heard his footsteps on the staircase.

Katie sat in Zach's abandoned seat and looked at Addie curiously. "What's up?"

"I think Gail's job offer sounds perfect. But I wanted to let you know that she questioned me about you. She said she thought you were my little sister. I told her you were a friend. I didn't want to tell her your story—I wanted to leave that up to you."

"Oh." Katie let out a long breath. "I haven't mentioned anything about my old life to Matt. I thought it might freak him out. And I like having him as a friend. I don't want to scare him away."

"You have the right to tell or not tell anyone you want," Addie said. "It's no one's business. So, if Gail asks, you tell her as much or as little as you want."

"Okay."

"I just don't want you to be ashamed of your past," Addie said gently. "You didn't do anything wrong. If people judge you, it's their problem, not yours. But that doesn't mean everyone needs to know everything about you, either. Who you let into your circle is up to you."

Katie grinned.

"What?" Addie asked, surprised by her reaction.

"It's just that you sound like Laurie. She says the same thing."

"Oh. Well, that's a compliment. Laurie helped me through some tough times," Addie said.

"Thanks for caring enough to look out for me," Katie said. "I want to be like you. Only the people closest to me can know my business, but not the whole world. I like how you've handled your life."

"That's sweet. I haven't always handled it well," Addie admitted. "But I keep trying."

Katie got the job at Gail's office and managed to politely

avoid any personal questions. Addie was proud of her. She was making another step forward, and Addie hoped that working at the office would give Katie the confidence to become more independent and not be scared when she went to the college again.

"Baby steps," Addie told herself. That's what it takes to move forward, for Katie and for her.

* * *

Katie started her new job, working about fifteen hours a week for Gail, and continued helping with the house as well. Addie had picked out the tile, shower stall, and sink cabinet for the new bathroom upstairs, and Zach started creating the new space. He was able to connect with the kitchen plumbing to run new pipes upstairs, but he had to cut out part of the floor upstairs to do it. Addie chose tile for the floor for when he finished it.

Addie skipped working on the other corner bedroom until Zach finished the bathroom and moved on to the next bedroom. She actually liked the old wallpaper in this room. It was a soft pastel sage and cream stripe on the upper wall and cream wainscotting on the bottom half. Addie was sure the wainscotting was the same as the original woodwork, but since it had already been painted, she'd just freshen it up with a new coat of paint. The wallpaper needed a good cleaning too. What she loved about this room was the fireplace. The insert was like all the others, but the ceramic tile between it and the mantel was cream with a vine of pink wild roses painted around the insert. Addie thought the room looked perfect for a little girl's nursery. She imagined pale sage curtains over the window and maybe a white crib and dresser. It would be adorable.

"Daydreaming?" Zach teased as he walked up behind her. Addie jumped. "Hey! You scared me. I thought you were working in the other room."

"I am. But I wanted to ask what you thought about something." He glanced around the room. "This is a cute room. Are you stripping the wallpaper?"

"No. I like this room exactly as it is. I just need to wash the paper and add a coat of paint over the woodwork," Addie said.

"It looks like a little girl's room," he said offhandedly.

"That's what I thought," Addie told him.

Zach caught her eyes with his. "Were you thinking about what it would be like to have a baby?"

"What? Where did that come from?"

"I saw the dreamy look in your eyes when I walked in. The look you get when you're imagining how to decorate a space," Zach said.

Addie shook her head. "What in the world would I do with a baby?"

Zach shrugged. "I don't know. Maybe what everyone else does with babies. Snuggle them, feed them, raise them to be responsible citizens." He chuckled. "Stuff like that."

She rolled her eyes. "I wasn't thinking of having a baby." Although, she had to admit that she'd been thinking of how to decorate the room for one. "Show me what you want me to look at."

"Okay."

They walked down the hallway to the new bathroom. "We have the shower stall at the end. Do you want a cut-out for a shelf in the shower?" Zach asked.

"Sure. That would be handy."

"Since this room is so long, we could put in a double sink.

Would you rather do that or have a single?"

"Oh." Addie studied the room. She could do a double sink or maybe have a floor-to-ceiling cabinet next to the sink for towels and supplies. "Let's keep the single sink. I'll look for a tall cabinet to place next to it." She turned to the other wall. "And we can place the towel rack on this side."

"Okay," Zach said. "You know, it wouldn't be so bad thinking about it."

Addie frowned. "Thinking about what?"

"Having a baby. We're not getting any younger." He grinned.

"Are you kidding me? I'm only thirty-four. You're the old guy here."

Zach laughed. "True. Thirty-six is pretty old."

Addie sighed. "I'm not ready to have children. Or get married. Or settle down in a permanent house. I might never be ready."

"I know. I just thought maybe it was on your mind, that's all. You're so good with people. Look how you've been with Katie. You'd make a great mom," Zach said sweetly.

"Maybe someday," Addie said softly. "Let's get this house done and see where we end up first."

"Yes, ma'am." He saluted.

"You're a goof."

As Addie worked on the bedroom, cleaning the wallpaper and wainscoting, she thought about their conversation. If it was up to Zach, they'd get married, have children, and buy a forever home. They'd still flip houses but not move constantly while doing it. In many ways, it appealed to her. In other ways, it scared her to death.

Not wanting to even think about the future, Addie went back to work on the bedroom.

CHAPTER TWENTY–SIX

Sofiya

The night of her evening out alone with Edgar, Sofiya was nervous. She'd never gone out alone with a man before. Years before, a chaperone would have been necessary, but things had changed. That's what made Sofiya jittery. After having seen the way the men at Mrs. Nora's acted around women, she feared how Edgar would behave. Would he be the gentleman she thought he was, or would he make unwanted advances?

She dressed in an emerald-green sequined dress with a scalloped hem from which matching satin flowed down past her knees. The waist was loose, giving her the appearance of height with the help of her emerald pumps. As Sofiya turned in front of the mirror, she thought she looked lovely. She'd pulled her brown hair up into a chignon and wore a simple headband wrapped in emerald satin with a black netting flower design that held a large pearl-type stone in the center.

You look lovely, dear," Marion said as Sofiya came downstairs.

"Thank you." Sofiya fingered her black satin handbag. "I'm

a little nervous."

"I'm sure you'll have a wonderful time. Edgar is the perfect gentleman. And if he isn't, well, he'll have heck to pay with me and his parents." Marion smiled at her. "Just enjoy yourself, dear. You're only young once."

Sofiya nearly laughed. She didn't feel young. At nineteen years old, she felt three times her age after all she'd been through.

Edgar arrived on time, driving a sleek black car himself. When he saw Sofiya, he smiled broadly. "You look enchanting."

"Thank you." Sofiya felt a blush warm her cheeks. She thought he looked nice too in a black suit with tails and a snowy white shirt.

He chatted a little with Marion before helping Sofiya slip on her wool coat and escorting her out to the front seat of the car.

"Are you warm enough?" he asked. "I have a fur blanket if you're cold."

"I'm fine, thank you," she told him, appreciating his thoughtfulness.

He drove downtown to a nice restaurant. After pulling up to the front door, under the portico, a valet appeared to park the car after Edgar helped Sofiya out. "This is the nicest place in this town. It's not quite New York City, but it's good."

They walked inside and checked their coats. A smartly dressed maître d' greeted Edgar warmly and immediately took them to a padded booth.

Sofiya studied the room as she sat. The place was beautiful, with burgundy tufted leather semi-circular booths and tables with crisp white cloths over them. The booths sat on tiers on the floor so everyone could see the stage where the full band was playing music. Chandeliers hung from the ceiling, casting glittery light upon the dance floor.

"It's a lovely place," Sofiya said, smiling over at Edgar. He sat a little straighter, obviously proud that she appreciated it.

The waiter took their drink orders—Edgar asked for a beer, and Sofiya ordered tea—and then left them to look over the menu.

"Do they serve alcohol here?" Sofiya asked in a hushed voice.

Edgar chuckled. "No, although many restaurants still do, under the table. They serve near-beer. It has very little alcohol in it."

Sofiya found his words interesting. "Under the table?"

"Yeah. If you know the password, many restaurants will spike your drink for you. But I figured on our first date we should behave and not break the law." He grinned.

"I appreciate that," she said, thinking he was teasing her.

The waiter returned with their drinks and took their order. Edgar had suggested the steak dinner, so Sofiya said she'd have that.

"You'll love the food here. They have an excellent chef," Edgar said. "I eat a lot of meals in New York City, and I think this place is just as good."

"Your mother said you travel a lot for business," Sofiya said. "May I ask why?"

Edgar looked pleased that she was interested in his work. "My new business takes me to several places between here and New York City. I keep many establishments flush with the supplies they need to stay open."

"Is this different from the farming side of your father's business?" Sofiya asked, not entirely understanding what he meant.

"Very different. Let's just say I've expanded our business to sales. I get what the other businesses need and sell it to them. It's very profitable."

"You must be quite the businessman," she said, impressed. "How smart of you to find a need and fill it."

He smiled broadly. "Yep. That's what I did."

They were served a light soup first, then their meal came. Edgar asked Sofiya about her life before meeting Marion, and they talked a little about her life in Finland before moving to Portland.

"My parents were fearful the war would come to our country," Sofiya explained, trying to be as honest as possible. "So, they sent me away to live with a relative. My good friend, Alina, came with me. My mother's fears came true. A civil war erupted in Finland, and then they fought the Russians. It all seems so far away now."

"And what of your parents?" Edgar asked.

"They moved to Portland, too, a bit after me. But they died during the Spanish Flu pandemic." She hated lying, but what else could she do?

"I'm so sorry," Edgar said sympathetically. "My family is the foundation of my life. I can't imagine living without them."

"Thank you," Sofiya said. "You're very lucky to have them. They are all so kind."

They stayed a while after dinner and danced a few times as the band played slow romantic tunes. Finally, Edgar escorted Sofiya to the door, where they retrieved their coats. His car was brought around the front, and they stepped inside.

Even though the car had a full top and side windows, Sofiya accepted the fur blanket to cover her legs on the drive home. The night had become brisk, and she was chilled. "Winter does last a long time here in Syracuse," she commented.

Edgar laughed. "Yes, it does. The snow seems to stay forever. And then one day we'll wake up, and spring will finally be here."

Sofiya had a lovely evening and no longer felt nervous around Edgar. He'd been the perfect gentleman the entire night. When they arrived at Marion's house, he escorted her to the door.

"I had a wonderful time," he told her. "Thank you for accepting my invitation."

"Thank you for inviting me. I enjoyed it immensely," she said.

"I hope we can do this again," Edgar told her. "I'll be traveling a bit, but when I come back, will you allow me to take you out again?" He looked hopeful.

"I'd like that very much," she said, trying not to sound too desperate.

Edgar reached for her gloved hand and kissed it gently. "I'll look forward to seeing you very soon," he said. Then he opened the door for her and, once she was safely inside, bid her farewell.

Sofiya quietly closed the door and turned to go upstairs when she caught a glimpse of Marion asleep on the sofa in the parlor, sitting up, a book in her lap. Smiling to herself, Sofiya walked into the room. "Were you waiting up for me?" she asked.

Marion awoke suddenly, looking started. "Oh, dear. I didn't hear you come in."

Sofiya laughed softly. "I saw you in here asleep. I think you'd be more comfortable in your room."

Marion rolled her neck this way and that. "Yes. I think

you're right." She smiled. "How was your evening with Edgar."

"He was the perfect gentleman. We had a wonderful time."

"I'm so happy to hear that. Nothing would make me happier than to see you two get together," Marion said.

"Oh, my," Sofiya said. "I'm not sure about that, but he did say he'd invite me out once he returns home again."

"Perfect." Marion stood and stretched. "It's time for this old lady to go to bed." The two walked out of the parlor, turning off the lights. "Goodnight, dear. I'm happy you had a good time."

"Goodnight," Sofiya said. As she climbed the staircase, her heart felt light. She was looking forward to spending more time with Edgar and getting to know him better.

* * *

Spring did finally come, as Edgar had predicted, and throughout the spring and summer, Sofiya and Edgar spent many afternoons and evenings together. They had picnics beside Onondaga Lake and visited the Burnet Park Zoo, where they saw retired circus bears, exotic birds, and a pond of beautiful waterfowl. Sofiya became a regular Friday night dinner guest at the Burton home, along with Marion, and was always treated warmly by the entire family. She met Amelia and Christian's children, Edina and Jonathan, and adored them both. Sofiya was also invited to the house for afternoon tea with Adelaine and Amelia and sometimes some of their area friends. Everyone was always kind to her, and soon Sofiya felt as if she were a part of the family.

Sofiya had her own car and driver for the times she visited the house, to the point where she got to know her driver, Noah

Scott, quite well. He was a young man whose parents were tenant farmers for the Burtons, and because he was skilled with machines, he was hired to help care for the cars and drive the family members. The Burtons had a large garage full of motor cars and three men always at their disposal as drivers. But Noah was different. He was always proper and polite, but he'd answer Sofiya's questions as they rode along, and they always had a friendly conversation.

As their courtship continued, Sofiya grew to care deeply for Edgar. While she wasn't madly in love with him, as she'd felt for Harry, she had a deep respect for his intellect and enjoyed his quick wit and candor. And the first time he kissed her, she felt a sweet warmth fill her that she'd never felt before. It had been on a Friday night, after dinner at the house, and they'd gone to the conservatory to see how Adelaine's flowers were progressing. Sitting on the bench with the sweet smell of roses, honeysuckles, and peonies surrounding them, Edgar slowly lowered his lips to Sofiya's. A soft, chaste kiss turned into one of desire, and when they finally parted, Sofiya knew she'd felt something deeply delicious run through her.

After that first kiss, they stole kisses from time to time, but Edgar was never aggressive in any other way. By fall, Sofiya thought she must be in love with Edgar, for she desired to do more than just kiss. In her letters to Alina, she asked her friend how she'd known she was in love with Clinton, and Alina responded that he'd brought out the best in her and made her so very happy. It wasn't much to go on, but Sofiya felt that happiness too.

One fall evening, after dinner at the Burton home, Edgar and Sofiya walked around the outside garden in the fading light enjoying the colorful leaves and the last of the summer flowers. Standing underneath a tall, thick maple tree, its red leaves full and bright, Edgar pulled a small box from his jacket pocket and turned to face Sofiya.

"This has been a memorable summer," he said, reaching for her hand. "And I'd love for it to go on forever." He placed the red velvet box in her hand.

Sofiya stared at the small box and then up at him. "What is it?" she asked.

He chuckled. "Open it and see."

With trembling fingers, Sofiya unsnapped the gold clasp and lifted the lid. Inside sat the most beautiful diamond ring set in platinum.

"Will you marry me?" Edgar asked, his dark brown eyes watching her intensely.

She looked again at the lovely ring, a cushion-cut diamond surrounded by several tiny diamonds. It was the loveliest ring she'd ever seen. When she raised her eyes to his, she thought of her life and how she'd come to America, hoping for a new beginning. How her mother had wanted her to find a fine man and marry. And how lucky she was to be standing here, in this garden of this grand home with Edgar. It was everything her mother would have wanted for her.

"Yes," she said, smiling brightly. "I would be honored to be your wife."

He smiled and took the ring from the box and placed it on her finger. Then, pulling her into his arms, he kissed her in a way he never had before. Sofiya knew in that moment that she'd made the right decision. She loved Edgar and his entire family. They would raise a family and grow old together. For the first time since leaving Russia, she felt completely safe.

CHAPTER TWENTY–SEVEN

Addie

By November, Katie had passed her driver's test and could now drive alone in a car. Addie let her use her car since Zach's truck was available if she needed to go somewhere. Katie had signed up for two college courses—Freshman English and Algebra I—starting after the winter break in January. Working in Gail's office had given her more courage to be alone in public, and she told Addie she thought she was ready to try the college campus again.

Addie thought Katie's sessions with Laurie had helped her a lot too. Laurie had the ability to build up a person's self-confidence, which Addie knew from experience.

Zach had completed the new bathroom, and Addie had finished the bedroom next to it, so she went back to the other bedroom to work on it. Addie thought that bedroom had been last remodeled in the 1970s because there was cheap brown paneling on the walls, and all the original moldings had been replaced with inexpensive ones. There was orange shag carpeting in there too. Addie couldn't believe that someone hadn't torn it up by now.

"Sofiya married a wealthy man who lived in a big house that she didn't have to remodel," Addie grumbled to Zach as they pulled up the ugly carpeting. "And here I am, tearing out the worst carpeting on the planet that has heaven-knows-what living in it."

Zach laughed. "You could marry me—a poor guy who owns half of a big house that's almost totally remodeled. Would that work?"

"Would I have to finish remodeling it?" she countered.

"I can't do it without you," Zach said. They pulled and pulled on the carpet until it finally gave, and they both fell back onto the floor with the carpet falling on top of them.

"Eeew," Addie yelled, scrambling to get up on her feet. The padding underneath was so old that it had turned to dust and was flying all around them.

Zach let out a laugh, then clasped his hand over his mouth when he realized carpet dust was getting into it. "Time to get the masks out," he said behind his hand. He left the room and returned with masks, and they both put them on.

"Well, that was fun," Addie said.

"The good part is we can use the shop vac to vacuum up most of the padding since it's just dust," Zach said. "The bad part is we'll be pulling up carpet tacks the rest of the day."

Addie sighed.

"Do you think they lived happily ever after?" Zach asked.

"What? Who?" Addie asked, completely confused.

"Sofiya and Edgar. You said they were rich and had nothing to worry about. Is that the end of Sofiya's story?"

Addie shrugged. "I don't know. There are still several more sheets of paper for me to read. I guess I'll find out."

"Do you believe in happily ever after?" Zach asked.

"What? You don't think all this is us living happily ever after?" Addie teased.

He chuckled, which sounded more like a muffled grunt under his mask. "I'll get the shop vac," he said.

Katie came home from work, and after they ate dinner, she helped Addie pull up carpet tacks.

"This floor is pretty beat up," Katie said. "Maybe you can teach me to use the big sander, and I can help you stain it this weekend."

"Sure," Addie said. "That would be great. Every young girl should learn how to use a floor sander."

"Ha ha. Seriously, though. It can't hurt to know how to do things. Maybe someday I'll buy a house and will need to remodel it," Katie said. "It's a good skill to know."

Addie stopped working and looked up at Katie. "Is that what you want? To buy a house someday?"

Katie shrugged. "Isn't that what everyone wants? Their own home, maybe someone to share it with. Kids." She studied Addie. "Don't you want that someday?"

"I don't know," Addie said truthfully. "I've never put that much thought into it. Zach does, though. I keep putting off commitment to him and a forever house, though."

"Why?" Katie asked. "I mean, I shouldn't pry, but he's such a great guy. And you'd make a pretty neat mom. It's not like you'd have to give up flipping houses just because you have kids."

Addie cocked her head. "Did Zach put you up to this?"

The younger girl laughed. "No. I've just been thinking of everything I want out of life. It's something Laurie suggested I do. Like a wish board. She said if I can imagine the life I want,

I can make it happen."

Addie nodded. "That's a good idea. I guess my wish list never got past starting my own business flipping houses and finding someone kind to share my life with."

"You've done both," Katie said. "Now what?"

"Good question," Addie said.

The next day they rented a floor sander, and Addie taught Katie how to use it. Once the floor was smooth and they'd vacuumed up all the dust and grit, Addie showed Katie how to clean the floor with paint thinner to prepare it for the stain.

"I didn't realize so much went into refinishing a floor," Katie said after the first day. The floor was cleaned and drying, so they had to wait until the next day to stain it.

"Tomorrow is the fun day," Addie said. "The floor will come alive once we put the stain on. Every wood floor is different in how it reacts to color. That's what's so cool about old wood floors."

"You really love doing this, don't you?" Katie said, smiling at her. "It's a lot of work, but you enjoy it."

"I do," Addie said. "I love making old things new again and bringing them back to life."

"It's kind of like therapy, isn't it?" Katie asked. "You put in the work and chip away at the old, then bring out the best of it to make it new again."

Addie was surprised at Katie's analogy. "You're so right. I think that's why I loved helping Valerie when she was teaching me how to flip houses. I felt like I was fixing my own life while I fixed up houses. It was therapeutic."

"Is it still?" Katie asked.

Addie smiled. "It is. It's how I make a living, but it's still how I deal with my past, too."

"Do you think at some point you'll get bored with doing this?" Katie asked.

"Wow. I don't know. I never really thought of it," Addie answered. "I've been doing this for so long, I haven't thought of doing anything else."

"I just wondered," Katie said. "I'm not sure what I want to do with my life yet, but I want to make sure I choose a profession that will always challenge me, so I don't get bored."

"That's something to keep in mind," Addie said. She and Katie decided what to get for dinner, and Katie went off to the kitchen to order it while Addie put things away. But as she worked, she couldn't stop thinking about Katie's words. Why hadn't she gotten bored with flipping houses all these years? It was no longer a challenge, yet she never thought to do anything else. And her life hadn't changed much since meeting Zach. Valerie had married, moved away, and started a family. And Katie was already talking about her goals in life. Addie wondered if she was in a rut. Was she using her business to hold herself back from moving ahead with other things in her life? All of that bothered her throughout the evening.

* * *

Later that night, as she lay in bed, Addie asked Zach a question. "Am I stuck in a rut?"

He looked at her with brows raised. "What do you mean?"

Addie sighed. "I've been thinking all evening about a conversation I had with Katie. I started flipping houses as a way to heal. Making old houses new again made me feel I was rebuilding my life along with them. But I've been doing this for years now, and I haven't moved forward with anything else in my life. I just flip houses."

"You don't just flip houses. You've built up a business flipping houses. You earn more with each house. You have a savings account and are saving for retirement. And you're turning old, run-down neighborhoods into nice places to live again. Basically, you're saving history. How can that be 'just' flipping houses?"

Addie stared at him in disbelief. "I've done all that?"

He chuckled. "Yes, you have. And you did it while maintaining a relationship with the love of your life."

This brought a smile to Addie's lips. "Very true," she said. "But I haven't wanted to settle in a house, get married, or have children. I'm thirty-four years old, and I still don't know what else I want out of life. I'm stuck."

Zach moved over closer and wrapped his arm around her. "You told me when we met that you weren't sure if you would ever commit to marriage or children. I told you then that it didn't matter to me, and it still doesn't. If you want to marry, I'm all in. If not, I'm okay with it as long as we can be together."

"I know. You've been really good about it. But shouldn't I want to move on with my life? Am I using my business to avoid trying other things? Am I moving forward or standing still?"

"That's a lot to think about so late at night," Zach said. "I don't think you're going to get all your answers at once. What I do know is not only are you flipping houses, but you're helping a young woman rebuild her life. If that brings up questions about your own journey, that's not a bad thing. But don't feel like you have to constantly be moving forward to enjoy your life. We have a good life as it is."

"We do," Addie said, snuggling in closer to him. "Maybe Sofiya's letters have been influencing me too. They brought me to this house, and now they're making me think that I'm not doing enough with my life. It's all so weird. I feel like I know Sofiya so well, and yet I've never met her and never will."

"Well, you've sort of met her. You've read all her thoughts, hopes, and dreams," Zach said.

"Yeah. It's strange. I feel like I could be doing more with my life, but I don't know what," Addie said. "Who knows. Maybe because I'm getting older, I'm thinking of all this, or maybe I just feel like the world is passing me by." She looked up at Zach. "What if this is all I'm doing in thirty years? What would I have to show for it?"

Zach smiled down at her. "I really think you're overthinking this. Once we're finished with this house, maybe you can be more involved in helping Laurie and the girls she works with. That's rewarding."

"It is. I feel a connection to the girls she helps." Addie sighed. "It's a start, I suppose."

As Addie lay in bed, trying to fall asleep, her mind raced with ideas of how she could be more involved in something other than house flipping. She loved what she did—it would always be her business—but there had to be something more. Somehow, she'd find it.

CHAPTER TWENTY–EIGHT

Sofiya

Sofiya and Edgar were married in a small chapel not far from the Burton home on an unusually warm November day. Sofiya wore a beautiful white satin dress with lace overlay that fell to a scalloped hemline almost to her ankles. Her hair was done in a French knot, and she wore a pearl-encrusted headband to which her floor-length lace veil was attached. Everyone commented on how lovely she looked as Edgar Burton Sr. walked her down the aisle toward her future husband carrying pink roses from Adelaine's conservatory.

Sofiya and Edgar made a handsome couple. Her short stature complimented the fact that he wasn't a tall man, and her young, radiant complexion gave her a blissful glow. Although only family and very close friends attended the ceremony, everyone there agreed that it was a lovely, intimate wedding.

A wedding breakfast was served after the ceremony, including many more family and friends. The gathering was large but tasteful, and everyone toasted the new couple multiple times, wishing them the greatest happiness.

Marion was thrilled that Sofiya had married Edgar. She took Sofiya aside for a moment to congratulate her. "I'm going to miss your company at home, but you have made a fine match," Marion told her. "I couldn't be happier for you both."

Sofiya hugged her friend. "I'll miss seeing you every day too, but you're like family to me and the Burtons. I'm sure we'll see each other often." She thanked Marion for taking her in and for all she'd done for her. "I wouldn't be here if it weren't for you."

"My dear. Didn't you know this was my plan all along?" Marion winked and smiled, but Sofiya couldn't help but wonder if what she said was true.

After the breakfast, Sofiya quickly changed into a plum-colored suit and cloche hat, and the couple were driven to the train station as well-wishers threw rice and cheered. The many tenant farmers had lined the driveway to wave to the newly married couple. Sofiya saw Noah in the line of people, and her heart warmed. "How lovely that they all came to wish us well," she said to Edgar.

"They should," he said. "Without us, they'd have no livelihood."

Sofiya thought his remark was dismissive, then decided not to let it ruin her day. Perhaps he was as tired as she felt and feeling a bit crabby.

That evening, the train arrived in New York City, and a cab took them downtown to the Algonquin Hotel. They were greeted by the staff like royalty and escorted up the lift by no less than the head concierge.

"What a beautiful hotel," Sofiya exclaimed as they stepped off the elevator and followed the man to their room.

"It is. I always stay here when I'm in town," Edgar said.

"It's close to all the best places. I don't exactly agree with the owner's view of prohibition, but everyone who is anyone comes to this hotel."

Sofiya watched her new husband as he spoke. It seemed being among influential people was important to him. She wondered why but didn't ask. She figured he'd explain himself in time.

They had a large double suite with two bedrooms and a comfortable sitting room. The windows looked out over the cityscape, which was lighting up as dusk fell. After Edgar thanked and tipped the concierge, he joined Sofiya at the window and smiled.

"Exhilarating, isn't it?" he asked, placing his arm around her waist. "I'd live full-time in the city if I could. My parents would hate it if I did, though. Someday, I plan to buy a penthouse apartment here so I'll no longer have to stay in hotels."

"The Dakota is nice," she said. "The apartments are lavish, and the view is incredible."

"I've heard that from others," he said. "But for me, being downtown is where it's at." He looked at her then and kissed her sweetly on the lips. "It's been a long day. Why don't we dress for dinner and eat here in the dining room tonight? We have the whole week to enjoy everything the city has to offer."

Sofiya went to her room and changed into one of the many evening dresses she'd brought along. She was thankful Edgar had felt the need to give them their own bedrooms. Changing in front of him would have felt awkward. Perhaps once they'd been together for a time, that uneasy feeling would go away.

When she appeared in the sitting room, Edgar had already dressed in his tails and was waiting with a drink in hand. "I always have my own drink along," he said, grinning. "And I'll have them bring a bucket of ice up to chill the bottle of champagne I brought from home. For later, of course." He winked.

Sofiya tried to smile, but she was nervous about later. She was grateful he'd thought to bring champagne. It might help calm her nerves.

They ate a delicious meal in the lavish dining room as acquaintances of Edgar's stopped by to say hello. No liquor was served 'under the table' here, as the owner, Frank Case, was entirely against alcohol, Edgar explained. "It's a wonder that so many literary and actor types come here daily to meet up when they can't have a drink."

Sofiya realized it was the fact that so many of those famous and talented people came here daily that impressed Edgar. It made her wonder why a man like him, who was successful in his own right, would find it necessary to be on the fringes of other successful people.

After dinner, they danced to a few slow tunes before heading up to their suite. By now, Sofiya was nearly shaking, wondering how the rest of the night would go. Even though she'd worked at Miss Nora's, she was still in the dark about relations between men and women.

"I'll let you dress for bed before I join you," Edgar said as he placed the champagne bottle in the ice bucket. He kissed her chastely on the cheek. "Don't be nervous. It's just me."

His words calmed her. She had gotten to know him well as a person and a family man over the months, and she didn't fear him. But still, the anticipation made her stomach flutter.

Sofiya pulled the pins from her hair and let it fall down her back. Her hair was nearly to her waist and was very thick and heavy. She put on the light blue silky negligee and filmy robe that Amelia had helped her pick out on a shopping trip in downtown Syracuse. Sofiya had wondered aloud if it was too risqué. Amelia had said they were all the rage for young women, but now Sofiya felt nearly naked in it. "Well, that's the point, isn't it?" Amelia had said, giggling, when Sofiya had pointed that out. Taking a deep breath now, Sofiya tried not to be self-conscious as she pulled down the duvet and blankets on the bed.

There was a knock on her door, and she nearly jumped. "Can I come in?" Edgar asked.

"Yes," she said, sitting down on one side of the bed.

Edgar came in the room wearing his dressing gown and slippers, rolling in the ice bucket stand. He had two champagne glasses in one hand. When he looked up and saw Sofiya sitting there, he stopped mid-step. A small smile came to his lips, and his eyes lit up. "You look lovely."

"Thank you." Sofiya fingered the robe, not knowing what to do or say.

Edgar sat down beside her and ran his fingers through her long hair. "I had no idea your hair was so long. It's gorgeous." He stood again and reached for her hand. "Come," he said, leading her to the dressing table. "Sit down and let me run the brush through your hair."

This surprised Sofiya. It was the last thing she'd thought he'd do. She sat in the chair in front of the mirror and handed him her brush.

Smiling at her in the mirror, Edgar began to gently brush out her hair in long, smooth strokes. The rhythm of his brushing her hair relaxed her, and Sofiya closed her eyes, remembering how her mother used to do this when she was a child. She'd brush Sofiya's hair each night before bed, one hundred strokes, and it had helped her relax and fall asleep.

"Are you feeling less anxious?" he asked as he continued to run the brush down her mane.

"Yes," she said, opening her eyes. "My mother used to do this each night when I was a child."

"Someone once told me that brushing a woman's hair relaxed her. I find it very soothing to do. I'm surprised you haven't cut it all off like so many women are doing these days," Edgar said.

"My mother would have been horrified if I'd even thought about cutting it," Sofiya said. "I guess I'm caught between Victorian sensibilities and the modern days. I'm sure it would be easier to manage my hair if it was shorter."

"You'd look lovely either way," Edgar said. He set the brush down on the table and gave her a kiss on the cheek. "I'll open the champagne."

He did, and they sat on the bed and sipped from their glasses. Only a small table lamp was on, giving the room a soft glow. "To us," Edgar said, lifting his glass.

Sofiya clinked his glass with hers. "To us," she repeated. She felt the bubbly liquid warm her as she drank it.

At last, Edgar took her in his arms and kissed her until their kisses grew more passionate. He caressed and held her close, slowly making her feel more comfortable in his arms. Edgar was gentle and sweet, and by the time they consummated their union, Sofiya no longer felt nervous but instead felt loved and cherished.

* * *

The next day, Edgar brought Sofiya to Tiffany and Company and told her to choose whatever suited her fancy.

Sofiya was overwhelmed as she walked up and down the aisles of gorgeous jewelry. "I wouldn't know where to begin," she said, looking up at Edgar.

He laughed. "What about pearls?" he asked the salesman that waited on them. "A long strand. I see they're all the rage." The salesman brought a tray of strands of pearls from fourteen to twenty-six inches long. Edgar picked up the longest strand and placed it over Sofiya's head. "These are perfect. You can wear them long or make them a double strand."

Sofiya fingered the smooth iridescent pearls. "They're beautiful. I love them."

Edgar grinned proudly. "We need matching earrings." He pointed out a pair of dangling earrings made of platinum with two large pearls on the ends, two aquamarine stone set on each earring, and tiny, shimmering diamonds. "What do you think of these?" he asked Sofiya.

"They're gorgeous," she said.

"Perfect. They match, plus they have your birthstone in them. Wrap them up along with the necklace," Edgar told the salesman. He grabbed Sofiya's hand and pulled her to the section where colorful rings were. "You need a birthstone ring as well," he said, studying the sparkling gems. "There. That one."

Sofiya looked with wonder at the ring he'd pointed out. It was the largest oval-cut aquamarine stone she'd ever seen with diamonds all around it set in white gold. "It's beautiful, but you really don't have to buy me all of this," she said. She knew jewels were expensive, especially aquamarine.

"Of course, I do. My wife will have only the best," Edgar said proudly.

The salesman handed Sofiya the ring, and she slipped it on

her right hand. Surprisingly, it fit perfectly. "It's incredible," she said with wonder.

"It was made for you," Edgar told her with a broad smile. "My wife will wear the ring. Please wrap the other items."

The salesman was more than happy to do as Edgar asked. Edgar excused himself a moment to pay for the jewelry, then returned with a small bag that he pocketed in his coat. "Now you'll have new jewelry to wear to the opera tonight," he said, kissing her on the cheek.

"It's all so beautiful," she said, still stunned. "Thank you."

He patted her hand after she'd slipped it through the crook of his arm, and they walked out into the chilly streets of New York.

The following two nights were the most beautiful Sofiya had ever spent. The first night she dressed for the opera, and they attended with her wearing her new jewelry and a lovely black dress with a black lace overlay. Upon realizing that Sofiya didn't own a mink stole, Edgar ordered one to be delivered by one of the best stores in town, and she wore it that night. The next night they ate dinner at a lavish restaurant and then danced to the big band late into the evening. Each night ended with them together in her bed, making love in the sweetest way.

On the fourth night of their stay, Edgar suggested they eat at the hotel restaurant and then go somewhere a little more risqué. "Wear your most modern dress and the new jewelry," he told Sofiya. "We're going to dance the night away."

Sofiya wore her royal blue dress with the matching headband that had the peacock feather attached. Both the dress and headband had glass beads that sparkled under the lights. She wore the mink stole instead of her wool coat. With her headband and new jewelry, she looked much like a flapper, except her dress wasn't as short or slinky as a flapper would wear. But she felt beautiful because she could tell that Edgar thought she was when she walked out into the sitting room.

"You look perfect," he told her. "Absolutely stunning."

Sofiya had never felt beautiful before, let alone stunning but being loved by a man who thought she was helped build her self-confidence.

After eating a delicious dinner, Edgar escorted Sofiya out to a taxi, and they rode to the downtown area. It was dark out, and the air was brisk. It felt like it would snow. He instructed the driver to stop at a small restaurant, then helped Sofiya out of the cab.

"I hope we're not eating again," she said, chuckling. "I don't think I could eat another bite."

"No, no. We're going upstairs." He led her to a door on the side of the building, and they walked up a darkened staircase.

"This is a bit creepy," Sofiya said, feeling a chill run down her spine.

"Don't worry, dear. Just wait and see." They reached the top floor, where there was a large metal door. Edgar rapped on the door in a tune-like fashion, and it opened, spilling out the sounds of music, laughter, and a woman singing.

"Enter," the large man at the door said. Once inside, Sofiya was amazed at what she saw. The room looked like it could be a posh restaurant with a band, dance floor, and glittering chandeliers high above. Except this place looked disheveled. Tables were strewn everywhere, and the people had a wild look about them. Everyone was dressed to the nines—women in glittery dresses and men in suits and tails—yet everything looked askew to Sofiya. Women and men danced with abandon in front of the band as others stood in groups talking loudly, their cigarettes dropping ashes on the polished floor. To the right was a long bar with mirrors behind it, and it looked like they were serving every type of alcoholic beverage imaginable.

"Welcome to the Cattail Speakeasy," Edgar told Sofiya, smiling broadly. "Where there can never be too much fun."

"Edgar!" The bartender yelled and waved. "Now, the party will finally begin."

Edgar laughed and guided Sofiya to the bar, where a group of men and women parted to let them through. "Champagne for everyone!" Edgar bellowed to the bartender. "I'm now a married man."

The entire room cheered, and everyone crowded around Edgar and Sofiya to congratulate them. A woman's drink spilled on Sofiya's dress, and someone's cigar ashes nearly burned her mink. Sofiya hadn't been prepared for the onslaught of people, but Edgar became animated from all the attention. Champagne corks popped behind the bar, and trays of glasses were poured. Everyone clamored to get a glass. Sofiya pushed her way out of the group and found an empty table to sit at.

Edgar found her there a few minutes later, bringing her a glass of champagne. "I thought I'd lost you," he said, smiling. "Isn't this the best?"

The music had started up again, and people were once again dancing, talking loudly, and drinking with abandon. Sofiya wasn't used to being in such a place, and it was hard for her to be excited seeing everyone behave erratically. "It's quite different," she said, not wanting to ruin what Edgar obviously found exciting.

People kept coming over to Edgar to talk, and a few women in flapper dresses hung on him in the most inappropriate way.

This was so foreign to Sofiya that she didn't know how to react. She'd been raised to be a proper lady, and that was something she couldn't change overnight.

"Let's dance," Edgar said, grabbing for Sofiya's hand. His cheeks were ruddy from the heat of the room and far too many drinks.

"I don't know how to dance that way," Sofiya said, terrified that he'd pull her onto the floor.

"You'll learn," he said. "Come on. It's fun."

"Edgar. Please," she began, but then a woman came by and grabbed Edgar's arm.

"Come on, honey. Dance with me," the woman said.

He happily followed her to the floor, and they began moving in ways that Sofiya had never seen before. She was only nineteen years old, but among all these rowdy people, she felt like she was three times her age.

After a time, on unsteady feet, Edgar returned to the table where Sofiya sat.

"Can we go back to the hotel now?" she asked.

"Sure, doll," he said, slurring his words.

Sofiya had never heard Edgar speak that way before, and it frightened her. He'd always been the perfect gentleman. How would he behave once they were alone?

They found a cab and made it back to the hotel where Sofiya had to lead him to the lift to go up to their room. Once there, to her relief, Edgar staggered off to his bedroom. She went to her own, changed, and crawled into bed, praying he wouldn't join her. Thankfully, he didn't.

The next morning, they had breakfast brought up to their room. Edgar looked a little green but ate his food while Sofiya sipped her tea.

"I'm sorry you didn't enjoy the speakeasy last night," Edgar finally said. "I thought you might like to let loose for a change."

Sofiya chose her words carefully. "It was an interesting place, but not what I'm used to. My upbringing to behave like a lady didn't prepare me for such a place."

He stared at her over his cup of coffee. "All the women there were brought up the same way as you. But they want to let go of the old conventions and enjoy life a little. Don't you think you're a little young to be stuffy?"

His sharp words hurt. "Stuffy? I'm sorry you think of me that way."

Edgar set down his cup and sighed. "I'm sorry. I didn't mean to insult you. My head is killing me." He stood and walked over to her, placing a kiss on her head. "That was cruel of me. I married you because you're a lady, and I shouldn't have taken you to a place like that." He walked over to the sofa and sat back, rubbing his temples.

"Aren't you afraid of getting caught going to a place like that?" Sofiya asked. "They're illegal, aren't they?"

Edgar gave a short laugh. "It's not illegal to drink alcohol, it's illegal for the place to purchase and sell it. That's why there are so many places like it all over the country. The feds can bust up a place and put the owner in jail, but the patrons can go on their merry way. I'm in no danger of going to jail—at least not in a place like that."

Sofiya frowned, wondering what he meant by that. But she didn't press him.

The rest of their stay in New York was tame compared to that night. They ate at nice places, visited museums, and even strolled around Central Park, visiting the menagerie of wild animals there. Edgar was the perfect gentleman the entire time.

Sofiya chose to forget the night at the speakeasy and enjoyed the rest of her wedding trip.

They returned home the next week and took over the rooms on the west side of the house. Edgar's room was already on this end, and Sofiya was given the connecting room to his. They each also had their own bathroom and shared a sitting room where they could relax. Edgar set up accounts for her at all the best stores in Syracuse and told her she could buy whatever she needed for herself or to decorate her bedroom. Never, even back home in Russia, had Sofiya been allowed to spend so much money on herself. She didn't abuse it, however, because she still respected the value of money.

The Christmas holiday was celebrated in the most extravagant manner in the Burton house, and Sofiya was amazed at the gifts that were exchanged among the family. She had purchased gifts as well, with Amelia's help. To her surprise, Edgar had given her a beautiful set of drop diamond earrings that even Mrs. Burton gasped at when she saw them. Everything was so lavish that it was hard for Sofiya to wrap her head around it. Only a little over a year ago, she'd been a maid for a madam of a brothel, and now, here she was, living a lifestyle that would fit a queen. As Sofiya continued to write letters to her Maman about her life, she constantly said how thankful she was for her new family, her husband, and the good life he'd given her.

By January, she was most thankful for the baby she was pregnant with.

CHAPTER TWENTY-NINE

Addie

Thanksgiving Day, Addie, Zach, and Katie had dinner at Laurie's house with the girls. Katie felt completely at home with them by now after the many weeks of group sessions. The girls were all blossoming in their own ways, succeeding in the paths they'd chosen. They were a good example for Katie, who was also moving forward in the right direction.

As December began, Addie worked on the last bedroom upstairs. All she had left to work on after that was the upstairs hallway. Zach had painted the outside of the house in late summer and was now working on a few other projects like the gutters. He also had to check the roof for any damage. Other than that, they would be finished.

Addie walked around the house one day for inspiration on how to decorate the hallway. She could paint it, but she really wanted to do some type of period wallpaper. But what color?

In truth, Addie didn't want to finish the house. When she did, it would mean it was time to sell and move on, and she dreaded that. She'd come to love this house and its history. She liked Gail next door and loved the big yard outside. She also liked that Sofiya had once been here. Addie had never been sentimental about a house before, so this was a new feeling for her.

Addie finally decided on a burgundy wallpaper with flowers for the hallway upstairs and ordered it. While she waited for it to arrive, she sanded and stained the wainscotting and moldings and also sanded and stained the floor. She bought two thick burgundy patterned rug runners for the floor and polished the light sconces that hung on the walls.

A week before Christmas, Zach pulled out their Christmas tree and ornaments and set it up in the parlor. Not surprisingly, Addie collected antique ornaments, and Katie marveled at all the pretty decorations.

"These are so beautiful and fragile looking," Katie said. "I'm afraid of breaking them."

"They're meant to be used," Addie said. "I love how they used to make ornaments. So much beauty and detail."

They also placed garland on the fireplace mantel with lights strung through it. Addie attached shiny ornaments to it too and placed two large glass holders with red candles on the mantel.

"We should run garland up the staircase rail," Katie said excitedly. "It would be so pretty."

Addie enjoyed seeing the excitement in Katie's eyes. "Sure. I'll have Zach pick more up tomorrow, and we can do that."

"What would you think of inviting Laurie and the girls over for dinner so they can see how beautiful the house is?" Katie asked. "I know Laurie would love to see it."

Addie smiled. "That's such a great idea. Maybe we could have them over Thursday night before the Christmas weekend."

"I'll call Laurie right now and ask," Katie said. "And I'll

help with everything, so it isn't a lot of work for you."

As Addie watched her run to the kitchen, she couldn't help but smile. This was Katie's first Christmas since being rescued from trafficking, and Addie was happy to make it her best Christmas ever.

Laurie and the girls accepted their invitation, so Addie splurged and bought steaks and shrimp that Zach could cook on the grill. Addie and Katie spent a day in the kitchen baking Christmas sugar cookies that they frosted, brownies, fudge, and carrot cake for dessert. They had such a fun time together doing these traditional things.

"I haven't done this in a long time," Addie said. "I forgot how much fun it is."

"And how yummy it all is," Katie said, eating another cookie.

Zach had pulled a sofa and chairs out of storage for the parlor and borrowed a long folding table and chairs from a friend for a dining room. They covered it with a new red tablecloth and used the old silverware Addie had bought from an antique shop years ago. Their plates and glasses weren't fancy, but Addie knew the women wouldn't care. Being together, celebrating the holidays was more important than fancy tableware.

On the day of the party, Addie wandered around the rooms, looking at the decorations. She was reminded of Sofiya's first Christmas working for Miss Nora and how she'd had to decorate for the holidays despite being unable to enjoy them. Addie hoped the ghosts of the past had long been put to rest and that she'd turned this place into a house that would long enjoy happy memories.

That evening, Addie and Katie placed the shrimp in a pan filled with garlic butter and seasoned the steaks. There was also a tossed salad, glazed carrots, fresh buns, and mashed potatoes. Katie wore a dress she'd found on the sale rack at Target. She was being very careful with the money she earned, saving it for a car. Addie wore one of the vintage dresses she'd bought at a second-hand store, and Zach wore his jeans but added a shirt and tie.

"Oooh. A tie. Now that's fancy," Addie teased him.

"Say another word, and it comes off," he warned playfully.

Laurie and the girls arrived, and the place was filled with voices and laughter. Laurie had invited her longtime boyfriend, Joseph, who Addie had met only a handful of times. He was a tall, slender man with short, cropped hair, deep brown eyes, and a warm smile.

"It's good to see another man in the house," Zach said, greeting Joe. "I'm generally the only one."

"I know the feeling," Joe said.

Zach quickly recruited Joe to help him man the grill, and the women went into the parlor to chat.

"This house is so big!" Izzy said. "And beautiful. Look at that fireplace!" Her brown eyes lined with kohl grew wide as she gazed around her.

"Is the woodwork original to the house?" Wanda asked, running her hand gently over the wainscoting. She'd piled her naturally red hair on her head and wore an emerald-colored dress that reminded Addie of Sofiya.

"Yes, it is," Addie said. "I sanded and stained a lot of the woodwork and some I didn't have to. I put up new wallpaper in here and in some of the bedrooms. It's been a lot of work."

Laurie had been quietly looking around and peeked into the dining room. "There's so much room here. Do we have time for a tour?"

"Sure," Addie said.

All the girls followed as Addie and Katie took them on a tour downstairs and then up to the bedrooms.

"This staircase is amazing," Latisha said, running her hand over the curved stair rail. "It's like something out of an old movie."

"Yeah, an old scary movie," Tonya added, shivering.

Addie laughed. "It's all in how you perceive it. I love old houses, but I know some people think they're scary."

"Are there any ghosts in here?" Melanie asked, her blue eyes wide.

They had just entered the master bedroom. "Not any I've met yet," Addie said. "But it has a long history. There could be."

Melanie moved closer to Katie. "I hope not," she said.

Addie showed them all the bedrooms, pointing out things about each room she'd refinished or replaced, and also told them which lights were original. "Imagine how old these are," she said, pointing to one of the bedroom lights. "They were originally made for gas, then were changed over to electric. People didn't waste expensive items in those days."

The girls wandered around the upstairs, each trying to decide which room she'd choose if they lived there. Laurie and Addie watched them from the end of the hallway, laughing.

"I love this house," Laurie said. "You've done such a great job on it."

"Thanks," Addie said. "Once I finish the hallway wallpaper up here, it's pretty much ready to sell. I hate seeing it go, but we can't live here forever."

Laurie looked thoughtful. "I wish I could afford it. I could help so many more girls with a bigger place like this. But I love my house, too."

"You could have both," Addie said. "And hire people to manage this house or your other one."

Laurie looked at her like she was crazy. "That would be amazing, but I could never afford it. Even as a non-profit, I'd still have to come up with the money to buy the house. And even with grants and fundraising, there'd never be enough money to make payments."

Addie thought about that a moment. "What if you had investors? Like you say, there isn't a monthly income or anything, but this house will sell for a lot of money today or in the future. What if a couple of people help you buy it as an investment, and when, or if, you sell it, they get their profit then?"

Laurie laughed good-naturedly. "Where would you find people like that? They'd have to be rich to wait years for a return on their investment."

"True. It's a thought, though."

They went downstairs after that, and everyone followed Addie and Katie into the kitchen to help. While Zach and Joe grilled the steaks and shrimp, the girls helped mash the potatoes, make a vegetable tray with dip for the table, and got their own sodas to drink.

"I love this house," Melanie said. "There's so much room. And this kitchen is beautiful."

"Yeah. We all fit in it," Latisha quipped.

When the food was ready, they all found a spot at the table and began to eat. Addie watched as the girls and Katie talked, joked, and giggled, and her heart warmed. It was so nice to be able to give these girls a fun Christmas after all they'd been through. At one point, she caught Laurie's eye, and they smiled at each other. Addie knew she was thinking the same thing.

After dessert, everyone went into the parlor again to sit and relax. Wanda suggested they play a game, and Addie dug out a couple she had stashed away. They played Mad Gab in teams, and soon everyone was laughing as they tried to figure out the words each other were saying.

Later, after the girls had all thanked Addie, Zach, and Katie and piled into the van Laurie drove, Laurie hugged Addie goodbye. "Thank you for this. It was a great night for the girls. And me."

"For us too," Addie said. She waved goodbye to Laurie and Joe as they headed down the walkway to the van.

"That was fun," Katie said as the three of them cleaned up the kitchen. "Thanks for doing it."

"Thank you for helping," Addie said. "I had a great time too."

Later, as Addie and Zach headed up to bed, they heard music playing from Katie's room across the hallway.

"She's really coming into her own," Zach said. "She seems happy."

"She is," Addie said.

"We'll have to flip a big house again so she can come with us," Zach said as he changed for bed. "I'm sure it'll be a while before she can move out on her own."

Addie stared at him in wonder.

"What?" he asked. "Why are you looking at me so strangely?"

"You're amazing, you know that?"

"I'd like to think I am," he teased.

"The fact that you're okay with letting Katie stay with us, even after we sell this house, is so sweet," Addie said.

He shrugged. "We can't throw her out. She's doing so well,

we need to keep her safe a while longer."

Addie walked over and wrapped her arms around him. "Thanks for being so sweet. Your parents raised you right."

"Well, remember that when we spend Christmas Eve over at my parents' house," he said, making a face.

Addie knew he was being silly. She got along well with his parents, and his mother had even invited Katie to come to Christmas Eve.

The next day, Addie searched online about starting a safe house for trafficked teens and what it took to set up a non-profit. She understood now what Laurie meant when she'd told her that it wasn't easy to get the funds to support a safe house. But Addie still thought it might be possible to get investors to buy the house for that purpose. The more she pondered it, the more she wanted to do it. Addie knew she couldn't run a safe house, but she could invest in one.

They had a wonderful Christmas celebration at Zach's parents' house and again on Christmas Day at home. Katie had bought them each an inexpensive but practical gift, which Addie loved. Addie and Zach had bought her a new backpack for school and filled it with pens, notebooks, and other things she'd need. She loved it and couldn't wait to start college after the new year.

On New Year's Eve, Katie went to Laurie's house for an overnight party the girls put on, leaving Addie and Zach alone to spend the evening together. They went out for an early dinner, then sat by the fire in the parlor watching old movies until midnight. Once the clock struck twelve, they opened a bottle of champagne and toasted to the new year.

"A new year and a new house," Zach said, clinking Addie's glass.

She smiled and then gasped when she started to take a sip. In the bottom of her glass sat a diamond ring. "What's this?"

"It's for you," he said. "And don't freak out. I know you aren't ready to get married, and we don't have to be engaged. I just wanted to give it to you on the off chance that you'll at least call it a promise ring."

She laughed. "What are we, twelve years old?" She fished out the ring and wiped it with a napkin. "It's beautiful."

"It's not an antique because I didn't want to give you a ring with a history that might be bad," he said. "But I thought it looked like your style. Simple, but elegant."

She slid it on her ring finger and stared at it for a long time. It was a simple solitaire diamond set in white gold. She loved it. "Are you sure you want to do this?" she asked.

Zach hugged her. "Completely sure. Even if we're just engaged forever, I can live with that. I already know I want to spend my life with you. I just wanted you to have this as a promise."

"Thank you," Addie said, kissing him. "I love it. I really do. But please don't ask me to set a date, okay?"

Zach crossed his heart. "Never. Only if you want to."

As Addie gazed at the ring, she had to admit being engaged, even if they never married, was nice. Maybe she was finally ready to move forward after all.

CHAPTER THIRTY

Sofiya

O nce Sofiya announced she was pregnant, Edgar paid less attention to her. He was gone more often on his business trips to New York City, and when he was home, he slept in his own bed. At first, Sofiya was relieved he no longer wanted to sleep with her because she had been so sick the first four months. But soon, it settled down, and she was hungry all the time, and thankful she could finally keep food down.

Sofiya spent her days with Adelaine and Amelia, reading, doing needlework, and visiting with an endless line of women who came for tea time. She had Noah drive her to Marion's house often so she could visit her dear friend, and sometimes just asked him to take her on drives around the countryside because she was so bored at the house. Occasionally, she helped Adelaine, who insisted she call her mother, work with the plants in the conservatory, but the heat made her nauseous, and she'd have to lie down. Sofiya had never been a shrinking violet, but the pregnancy did tire her out.

Sofiya spent as much time as possible outside, walking

around the property in the spring and summer. Amelia joined her at times, but preferred sitting in the shade to actual physical exercise.

"We'll have to find a wet nurse for you, and I think we'll need to hire another nanny. Ours is so busy with the kids, and I think it would be too much work for her," Amelia said one day in late summer as they were sitting outside in the garden.

"A wet nurse?" Sofiya knew what one was but hadn't decided if she'd nurse her child or not.

Amelia looked shocked. "You certainly can't nurse the baby yourself," she said. "Ladies don't do that. Edgar would be shocked."

Sofiya sighed. She guessed she should do as her sister-in-law had and not make waves. But she was determined to be more involved with her child than Amelia was with her children. Sofiya's maman had been very hands-on with her, and Sofiya felt that was the best way to bond with her baby.

By the time August came to a close, Sofiya was quite large. Being short-waisted, there wasn't much room for the baby as it was. Her ribcage always hurt when she sat, and she thought for sure the baby was pushing on all her organs. But the doctor continued to tell her she was doing well and to rest the last month since she was so big.

"You don't want your ankles to swell up," he told her.

Sofiya felt like she was wearing tent dresses, but she was relieved that styles were looser now, and she wasn't expected to wear anything restrictive. She spent a lot of time lying in bed or relaxing in her sitting room with her feet up. When she did see Edgar, it was generally at the dinner table or as he passed through the sitting room on his way to bed.

"How is our baby doing?" Edgar asked one evening as he

walked into the sitting room. Sofiya had sat down in her dressing gown and had her feet up as instructed while she tried to concentrate on a book. They were alone, so Edgar had no choice but to acknowledge her.

"The doctor says we're doing fine," she told him, feeling suddenly shy around Edgar. He hadn't spent time alone with her in months, let alone spoken much to her. She'd felt so rejected and alone all these months, but Amelia had said it was natural for the husband not to bother his wife while she was pregnant. Since Sofiya wasn't versed in these things, she took her sister-in-law's word as true.

"Well, let's hope he's a healthy little boy," Edgar said, already walking away.

"Or a healthy little girl," Sofiya said.

Edgar stopped and turned back toward her. "Cross your fingers it's a boy. Otherwise, you'll have to do this all over again."

Sofiya frowned involuntarily.

"You're as big as a cow," he said. "Do you really want to get this big again?" He chuckled to himself as he disappeared into his bedroom.

Sofiya was stunned by his words. Had he meant to insult her? True, she was quite large, but she was carrying his baby. It seemed like such a cruel thing to say. As she thought it over, she decided that maybe he was just uncomfortable around her in her condition. Many men were. It may have been said in nervousness.

At the end of September, as the trees turned to glorious shades of red, orange, and yellow, and Sofiya thought she couldn't stand to be pregnant for one more minute, she went into labor. The doctor was called, as was Edgar, who was in

New York at the time. After hours and hours of labor, Sofiya gave birth to a little six-pound, two-ounce boy. She'd lost a lot of blood and was worn out, but as she held the little bundle in her arms, her heart filled with more love than she'd ever felt for another human being.

"We'll name him Edgar," her husband said, having made it home in time for the birth. "The third in the family."

Sofiya looked up at him with tired eyes. "Edgar Henri Burton," she said. "I want him to have my father's name as his middle name."

Edgar studied her a moment, then smiled. "Of course. It's a fine name."

Right then, Sofiya decided she'd call her little boy "Eddie" instead of Edgar. Edgar was too formal for such a little baby.

Sofiya was told to stay in bed for at least a week, and since she was so weak, she didn't fight it. A wet nurse was hired, and Sofiya had hired a second nanny just before Eddie was born. They'd set up a second room in the nursery just for the baby. Sofiya hated that it was so far away from her bedroom but hadn't been given any other choice.

Even though she couldn't leave her bed, Sofiya insisted little Eddie be brought to her after his feedings so she could hold him. The nanny complained at first until Edgar surprisingly intervened, and the nanny stayed quiet so she wouldn't lose her job.

"I'm not sure why you want the baby brought to you so often, but if that's what you want, that's what you'll have," Edgar told Sofiya when he came into her room to see the little boy. "He is awfully cute, though. I guess I can't blame you."

"Thank you for standing up for me," Sofiya told him. She was surprised at Edgar's interest in the baby but also pleased.

After he'd ignored her over the past nine months, she'd thought he'd ignore the baby as well.

"You gave me a son," he said tenderly. "You deserve to have what you want."

After she felt better and could join the family for meals again, Edgar surprised her with a sapphire necklace and earrings. "Our baby's birthstone," he told her. "It's fitting as a gift for you to celebrate his birth."

The gift had brought tears to her eyes. Edgar could be so kind and yet sometimes so cold. She wished she understood him more.

After the first few weeks, the newness of his son wore off, and Edgar resumed his weekly routine of going away to New York for several days a week. Sofiya didn't miss him. She enjoyed spending time in the nursery with her baby boy. While the weather was warm—despite grumblings from the new nanny—Sofiya took the baby for walks in the pram around the garden. Often, Amelia and the children would join her. Jonathon was six now, and Edina was four, and they listened well to Amelia and Sofiya, so it was fun to have them along. Sofiya knew that winter would soon come, and they'd all be stuck indoors, so she enjoyed the nice weather while she could.

Marion visited the little baby often after his birth and continued to be a regular fixture in the house for Friday night dinners and afternoon teas. She was so happy for Sofiya. She'd given little Eddie a silver rattle with his name and date of birth engraved on it and had also crocheted a sweet little blue sweater for him with matching booties and cap. "I feel like I'm an honorary grandmother," she told Sofiya.

"You're as much a grandmother to my child as my own maman would be," she told her friend. Sofiya felt very close to

Marion, especially with her parents gone.

As the weeks passed, Sofiya half expected Edgar to return to her bed, but he never even hinted at resuming their physical relationship. While part of her felt relieved, the other half wondered why he'd lost interest in her since she'd become pregnant and given birth. It was such a personal topic, though, that she didn't want to ask Amelia what she thought.

By Christmas, Eddie was three months old and was the cutest, chubbiest baby. He smiled and gurgled and watched the world around him with big blue eyes. He still had little hair, but Sofiya knew it would come in with time.

Edgar was home for the holidays, although Sofiya thought he was resentful about it, and he sometimes came into the nursery to see Eddie. Sofiya was changing his diaper when Edgar entered one day, and the little boy squealed and wriggled when he saw his father.

"He's a chubby one, isn't he?" Edgar said as he watched Sofiya dress their son. "He must take after his mother."

His comment cut Sofiya deeply. Since having the baby, she hadn't been able to lose the extra weight, and she'd been conscious of it. Even Amelia had hinted that Edgar liked thin women. But Sofiya had never been like the skinny flappers who hung out in the speakeasies, and she'd never be that way. Yet, backhandedly calling her fat hurt her.

"He's a healthy baby," she shot back protectively of both Eddie and herself. "You wouldn't want him to be skinny."

Edgar had just chuckled and gone on his merry way.

The Burtons hosted a large Christmas Eve celebration, inviting long-time friends and neighbors. The entire house was lavishly decorated with a tall, decorated tree in both the foyer and the parlor. Food was served on the best china, and wine was poured in crystal glasses. Other alcohol was available to guests despite prohibition.

Sofiya had purchased a new dark blue velvet dress for the occasion and wore her sapphire necklace and earrings. None of her old clothes fit her anymore, so she'd had to buy several dresses. She hoped to lose the baby weight but knew it would take time.

Sofiya never felt very comfortable at the big parties the Burtons hosted, and that evening was no exception. A few of the older women asked her about the baby, and she enjoyed telling them about little Eddie, but otherwise, she felt like an outsider. Women her age seemed so silly and immature, especially the unmarried ones. They stood around and drank and giggled like ninnies, flirting with the young men who attended. And unfortunately, Edgar was right in the middle of all that, complimenting all the pretty, thin ladies and giving them his complete attention.

"Don't mind him," Amelia said halfway through the party. Amelia had too much wine by this time and wasn't filtering her words. "He's always thought of himself as a ladies' man. Now that he's married, these young girls won't take his flirting seriously."

Sofiya was embarrassed just the same that her husband ignored her and spent his time around the single women.

As midnight approached and many of the guests were leaving, Sofiya made her excuses and left the party to go up to her room. She hadn't seen Edgar and didn't know where he was, nor did she care. She peeked in on little Eddie before walking down the hallway to her suite of rooms. That was when she saw a disheveled young woman leaving a room and hurrying down the hallway past her.

Sofiya reached the door to the sitting room, realizing the door the woman had exited was the door to Edgar's bedroom. Anger boiled up inside her, but shame also crept its way through her. How dare he disgrace her this way in their own rooms?

She entered the sitting room and headed to her bedroom. Before she could shut the door, she heard Edgar laughing behind her. Turning, she saw him in the sitting room, pouring himself a glass of whiskey. His shirt was unbuttoned, and his shoes were off. He looked a mess.

"I saw her leaving your room," Sofiya said, surprising herself. She was the last person to initiate a confrontation. "She's a bit too young for you, don't you think?" Sofiya was only twenty, probably the same age as the girl, but she felt much older.

Edgar's smile turned into an angry glare. "At least she's not a cow," he said, looking her up and down.

Sofiya's heart fell to her stomach. She couldn't understand why this man who only a year ago proclaimed his love for her could be so vicious. She turned and entered her room, shutting the door behind her. She wouldn't let him see the hot tears that ran down her cheeks or the pain he'd caused her. Falling on her bed, she cried softly. Why had he married her if he wasn't in love with her? How had she misread him? She'd thought he loved her and would love her more once she gave him a son. Now, she felt shamed by the very man who had vowed to love and cherish her forever.

Pulling out the paper that she wrote letters on, Sofiya poured her heart out to her Maman, wishing she were alive and could ease her pain.

What have I done? she thought as his cruel words continued to fill her head.

* * *

Once the holidays were over, Edgar left again for a week at a time, and Sofiya was relieved to see him go. She held her baby even closer, wondering what was in store for them in the future with such a cruel man running their lives. She knew she'd protect Eddie in any way possible. Edgar would never hurt their child as he'd hurt her.

January 1922 was a cold, blustery month leaving the women with no choice but to stay inside, warmed by the fire. Along with spending hours each day with Eddie, Sofiya also wrote letters to Mrs. Jarvi and Alina. Mrs. Jarvi had quit her job at Miss Nora's and found employment in a home with a nice family. Alina had given birth to a baby boy that they'd named Carlton Clinton. *"Clint didn't like the idea of a junior in the family, so we used his name as the middle name,"* Alina wrote. *"I'm so happy with my little girl and boy, as you now can understand. What a joy children are."*

Sofiya agreed with her dear friend. Eddie was everything to her.

In late January, Sofiya received a note from Marion that she'd been feeling poorly and hoped to see her soon. Worried about her friend's health, Sofiya asked Noah to drive her to Marion's home. Once there, she was disturbed by how sick Marion was.

"She's been quite ill, barely eating and having trouble breathing," Mrs. Prescott told Sofiya in a hushed voice. "I always have warm broth and tea ready for her, but she barely eats a bite."

Sofiya could tell the housekeeper was worried. "How long

has she been ill?"

"For about two weeks. It started as a chill and a little cough, but she finally took to her bed a few days ago, complaining that her joints and head ached."

"Has a doctor seen her?" Sofiya asked.

"Yes. Twice," Mrs. Prescott said. "He said to keep her warm and urge her to eat. He feels it's just a cold and will pass." She shook her head. "But she's getting thinner by the day and weaker. I'm not sure what to do now."

Sofiya took the woman's hand and patted it. "Hopefully, it's only a cold. I'll see if I can get her to eat more. Would you bring a small cup of broth?"

"Yes. Anything to help her get strong again."

Sofiya knocked softly on Marion's door and entered her room. Marion was lying in bed in the semi-dark room, her pillows raised to ease her breathing. "Marion. It's Sofiya," she said as she neared the bed.

Marion's eyelids fluttered open, and she focused on Sofiya. "Ah, dear. It's so nice to see you," she said weakly. "I'm sorry I wasn't up to greet you. It seems I've caught a chill."

Sofiya pulled a chair up closer to the bed. "Are you feeling any better today?"

Marion took a deep breath, then coughed. Sofiya offered her a sip of water from the glass on her nightstand. Marion's breathing sounded ragged even after her cough had subsided.

"I'm just a bit tired," Marion said finally. "I'm having trouble breathing, but the doctor said it would clear eventually." She tried to chuckle, but it came out as a cough. "I don't believe he knows what he's talking about."

Worried, Sofiya asked, "Should we call a doctor from the city? Maybe another physician can help you."

Marion reached out her hand, and Sofiya gently held it. "Don't worry, dear. I'm sure I'll be fine. I just need a little rest."

Mrs. Prescott came in with a teacup of soup. "Are you feeling any better, Marion?" she asked.

Marion tried to smile. "How can I not feel better when my two favorite people care so much?"

Sofiya and Mrs. Prescott shared a worried glance before Sofiya responded. "Can I get you to eat a little chicken broth?" she asked, picking up the teacup.

"I can try." Marion attempted to scooch up in bed. Mrs. Prescott helped her and fluffed her pillows.

"Can I bring you anything?" Mrs. Prescott asked Sofiya.

She declined, and the housekeeper left.

Sofiya was able to get Marion to take a few sips and then gave her a teaspoonful of medicine that the doctor had left. Seeing that she was tired again, Sofiya helped her get comfortable, then told her that she'd be back again soon to check on her.

Sofiya spoke to Mrs. Prescott before leaving the house. The housekeeper was as worried as Sofiya about Marion's health.

"I think I'll ask Mrs. Burton if we can have a doctor from New York City come and check on her," Sofiya said. "Her breathing is so ragged. Have you tried a poultice on her chest?"

Mrs. Prescott said she had but would be happy to try anything Sofiya thought would help. She told the housekeeper of the poultice she'd used to help the girls during the Spanish Flu epidemic. Mrs. Prescott said she'd try it that night to see if it would help soothe Marion's breathing.

Once home, Sofiya told Adelaine about Marion's illness and asked if she knew of another doctor who could help. Adelaine did and called a friend in New York City who would contact their doctor and see if he'd take the train up to see a patient.

Over the next few days, Sofiya went to see Marion daily, but she was growing sicker each day. The doctor did come up and check her. His diagnosis was she had pneumonia. He suggested bringing in a nurse who could administer poultices and medicine, although he admitted there was nothing they could do but wait it out.

"I'm afraid at her age, the chances of survival are slim," the doctor told Sofiya and Mrs. Prescott in the hallway so that Marion couldn't hear. "The best you can do is treat the symptoms and make her comfortable. And pray."

The two women decided to hire a full-time nurse to help Marion, and they took turns overseeing the nurse. It was the best they could do for their friend.

Mrs. Prescott moved into the house, and Sofiya came each day to sit with Marion to give Mrs. Prescott a break. But despite their care, Marion slowly faded.

Sofiya told Adelaine that Marion wasn't getting better and now was the time to see her just in case she passed. Adelaine was quite upset, and she and Amelia visited Marion while Sofiya was there.

After their visit, Adelaine broke down in tears in Marion's parlor. Mrs. Prescott brought them tea and gave them their privacy.

"She and I have been good friends for years," Adelaine said, wiping her tears with a handkerchief. "I can't believe we're going to lose her."

Sofiya comforted her and Amelia, who was also having a hard time. "I'm glad you had a chance to see her. We're praying she might still recover, but the nurse says it's not realistic."

After they'd left, Sofiya went in to sit with Marion again.

She was surprised when Marion awoke and spoke to her.

"I'm happy you found someone to care for you," Marion said in a whisper, her voice ragged. "I can leave knowing you're well taken care of."

Sofiya reached for her hand. "You've been such a kind friend to me. I hope you know how much I appreciate all you've done for me."

"I do know. You deserve a good life, dear. I hope you have one." Marion's eyes closed, and she fell into a deep sleep.

Tears filled Sofiya's eyes. She was in a loveless marriage in a place where she knew few people. Marion was the only person she'd felt close to. Adelaine and Amelia were kind to her, but she didn't feel the warmth from them that she had from Marion. She would miss her friend so much.

Two days later, Marion succumbed to pneumonia as Sofiya and Mrs. Prescott sat by her side. Both women cried openly over losing their close friend. Once again, Sofiya had lost someone important to her, and her heart was broken.

CHAPTER THIRTY–ONE

Addie

When Katie came home on New Year's Day and saw the ring on Addie's finger, she screamed with delight. "You two are engaged!"

"Wait, no," Addie said. "Not engaged, exactly. We're just practicing."

Katie sobered. "Practicing? Like, practicing being engaged?"

Addie laughed. "Yeah. It sounds stupid. Zach did propose, but it's open-ended. And I do love the ring. Maybe if I get used to being engaged, I might get married someday."

"Well, I'm still excited for you," Katie said. "And I love the ring!"

With the holidays over, Katie started college. Addie was worried about her on the first day, but Katie came home happy and excited about her two classes.

"The crowded hallways weren't a problem?" Addie asked her.

"They probably would have been," Katie said. "But I didn't use them. I walked outside between classes so I didn't get stuck in a scary situation."

"That's a great idea," Addie said, proud of her. "Baby steps."

Katie laughed. "That's exactly what Laurie says."

"I'm sure she taught it to me," Addie said, laughing also.

The vintage-style wallpaper arrived, and Addie went to work, finishing the upstairs hallway. It was a bittersweet time for her. She hated saying goodbye to this house, and she wished she could turn it into a safe house. As she cut and placed the wallpaper, she thought about all the young women who'd worked in this house for Miss Nora, stuck in a life they couldn't escape. She thought of how Sofiya and Alina had left and found new lives. Alina had been happily married, but Sofiya had been unfortunate enough to marry a man who, for some reason, didn't love her. Both had started their lives in America in this house, and now Addie had remodeled it for new people to enjoy. Wouldn't it be amazing if the one-time brothel redeemed itself as a safe house for trafficked teens?

A knock at the kitchen door brought Addie out of her thoughts, and she ran downstairs to answer it. Katie was at school and then working at Gail's the rest of the day, so she wondered who it could be. To her surprise, it was Gail standing at the door.

"Hi, Gail. Come on in," Addie said. "What's up?"

"I'm so sorry to bother you," Gail said. "I see you've been working. But Katie told me today that you are almost finished with the house, and I just couldn't stand it any longer. Can I be so bold as to ask for a tour?"

"Uh, sure," Addie said. "Let me wash my hands first. I was just putting up wallpaper in the upstairs hallway."

"I know I'm intruding, but I'm dying to see the house," Gail said. She looked around the kitchen. "This is beautiful. I love the quartz countertops, and the cabinets are perfect for this house. What did you do with the little room off the kitchen?"

Addie showed her that they'd made it into a laundry room and pantry. "This room used to be a maid's bedroom in the early 1900s," she told Gail. "Can you imagine how hot it would have been right here next to the kitchen?"

Gail looked at her curiously. "I had guessed that's what it once was, but how did you know?"

"To tell you the truth, I chose to buy this house because of some old letters I found in an antique store. A young teen girl and her friend lived here when it was a brothel. One worked upstairs, and the other worked in the kitchen. It's quite a story."

"Goodness," Gail said, looking shocked. "I'd heard that this might have been a brothel decades ago, but no one knew for sure. I'm surprised there was one here, though. This has always been a high-end neighborhood."

"It was a brothel for rich men, by the sounds of it. I suppose they quietly supported it so they could stay away from the brothels by the river," Addie said.

"That's so interesting," Gail said. "Tell me more."

Addie took Gail on a house tour while telling her some of Sofiya and Alina's story. By the time they finished the tour, Gail was mesmerized by how much Addie knew of the home's past.

"You've done a beautiful job with the house. I hope you'll be able to get your money back when you sell it," Gail said. "A duplex or fourplex may have been a better idea."

"I know," Addie said. "But I couldn't cut up this lovely home. There are getting to be fewer left around here."

"That's for sure."

Addie invited Gail back into the kitchen for a soda or coffee, and she accepted. As they sat at the kitchen counter, she hesitated, then decided to jump right in. "How do you think it would go over in this neighborhood to turn this home into a safe house for trafficked teens?"

"Oh, my." Gail stared at her a moment, digesting the question. "You mean a place for teens to rebuild their lives after having been trafficked?"

"Yes," Addie said. "There is such a great need for those places. I have a friend who runs a house not far from here, and I thought this would be the perfect place for such a house."

Gail tapped one of her long fingernails on the coffee mug. "Well, I'm not sure. I'm on the HOA's board, and to tell you the truth, many of the homeowners around here are very protective of the neighborhood."

"I suppose they'd think it would lower the value of their homes," Addie said.

"Maybe. I'd have to see how one is run and how it affects a neighborhood."

"You know, teens who get away from that life do so because they want to rebuild their lives. They didn't choose it to begin with—most were kidnapped or unwittingly brought into it and ended up stuck. It's not because they were troublemakers or law breakers," Addie said.

"I guess I'm not very well versed in teen trafficking," Gail said. "But I do know it's a big problem around here." She took a sip of her coffee. "Are you seriously considering selling this house to someone to use it as a safe house?"

Addie took a breath and let it out slowly. "I'm seriously considering investing into turning this house into a safe house. If I can get a few more people who'd be interested in investing in such a project, that is. But I know I'd have to get approval from the neighborhood and zoning authority first."

"I know a lot of people on the zoning board," Gail said. She chuckled. "I know a lot of people on a lot of boards. Can I ask you a question?"

"Yes."

"If you were me, would you be scared about having a safe house next door?"

"I completely understand how you feel. But honestly, knowing what I know about them, I wouldn't worry about having one next door to me," Addie said.

Gail looked thoughtful. "You said you have a friend who runs a safe house. Is there a chance I could meet with her and see exactly what it is?"

Addie hoped her face didn't register the surprise she felt. She'd thought for certain that Gail would be completely against it. "Yes. I'm sure she'd love to show you around."

Gail smiled. "Great. Set it up, and I'll be there." She stood. "Thank you for letting me tour the house and confiding in me about your plans. It's not that I'm against such a thing—I really think it's admirable. I just need to do a little research if I'm going to talk the rest of the community into one here." She said goodbye and headed out the door.

Addie stood there wondering what had just happened. Had she actually committed herself to turning this place into a safe house?

Zach came in from the garage a while later. He'd been staining the last of the molding for the hallway and needed a break. "I saw Gail leaving earlier. Did she finally get her tour?"

Addie chuckled. "She did. And I think she got much more than she'd expected." When Zach gave her a puzzled look, Addie began to fill him in on what had just happened.

* * *

Two days later, Laurie welcomed Gail into her home to give her a tour and tell her everything she wanted to know about running a safe house. Addie and Katie accompanied her as well. Laurie showed her their meeting room, the kitchen they all shared and helped to keep clean, the bedrooms upstairs, and then the third floor, where they ran a 24/7 hotline.

"We have volunteers for the hotline, but I put in hours too," Laurie said. "I also run the group meetings that are required for all the girls. Everyone who lives here is also required to work at a job or go to school. That is once they feel safe enough to go out in public."

"How do the girls find you?" Gail asked.

"Some find us through the hotline. Others are referred. If they have a drug or alcohol problem, that's addressed first in rehab before coming to live here. All my girls are well-behaved because if they aren't, they are sent to live at another facility."

"That's wonderful," Gail said, looking impressed. She met Latisha and Izzie, who were curious about the new guest.

"I love your nails," Latisha said, making Gail smile. "I'm going to beauty school and hope to work in a salon by next year."

"That's great," Gail said. "You'll have to let me know where you work, and I'll come in for a manicure."

As Laurie walked Gail out with Addie and Katie following, Gail asked, "What is the success rate for the girls? Do they all end up okay, or do some end up back on the streets?"

"My girls have a one-hundred percent success rate," Laurie said proudly. "But I know other places where some end up back on the streets. That's why it's important to have a place where there is constant communication and encouragement."

Gail looked thoughtful. "If Addie's house became a safe house for teens, would you be involved?"

"If Addie is successful in finding investors who could afford to have no return on investment for years, then yes, I'd run the house along with other employees," Laurie said, much to Addie's surprise.

"Okay." Gail turned to Addie. "If you decide to move forward with this, let me know. I have a lot of influence around town. And I also would like to be an investor."

"Really?" Addie was stunned. "You realize that the only way you'd get your money back is if the safe house closes and the house is sold."

"I do realize that. But I see the need for more of them, and you're right. Your house is the perfect size for a safe house. It's a good investment no matter what happens. It's an investment in our young people, and who can argue with that?"

Gail took off, leaving Laurie, Addie, and Katie on the porch, staring at each other.

"Did we just commit to opening another safe house?" Laurie asked.

"I think so," Addie said. "If you're up to it."

Laurie laughed. "Well, we still have a long way to go, but why not? I'll do what I do best. I'll start applying for grant money to run the other house. But you'll have to talk the neighborhood and zoning committee into letting you open one in that neighborhood."

"I can't believe this," Addie said excitedly. She hugged Laurie and Katie joined in on the hug.

"I'll do whatever I can to help," Katie said. "This is such a great idea."

Addie thought it was too. She only hoped that Zach would be on board too.

* * *

"Is this really what you want?" Zach asked Addie after she told him that Gail was on board. "Can we afford to do this?"

"I think we can," Addie said. "We wouldn't be involved in the day-to-day running of the house. We'd just be investors. If I can find one or two more people to invest, we could get two-thirds or three-fourths of our money back. That should be enough for us to buy another house to flip."

"That's a big if," Zach said.

"I know it is. But just think of it. Turning this house, a house that was once a brothel where women were bought and paid for each night, into a safe place for trafficked teens. Wouldn't that be amazing? I think Sofiya would be proud."

Zach smiled. "I think she would be too."

"Are you on board?" Addie asked, biting her lip.

"You know I always am. We'll make our money on the next flip."

The next day Laurie called Addie. "I did some searching, and I can apply for a few government grants to help pay for the house. There are no guarantees, though. Can you give me an amount on how much you would need to keep your business afloat, and then I can see what I can do?"

"I can do that," Addie said. "Are you seriously considering this?"

"Yes. I can't think of anything else but this now. It was always a dream of mine to help more teens, and this is a start. Also, Joseph said he'd pitch in with some money to be an investor. Isn't that great? It isn't a lot, but he said he can afford to help buy the house and not worry about the money."

"Wow! That's amazing."

"I also talked to two women I know who work in a larger, state-funded safe house, and they would love to come work for us if we can get the funding," Laurie said. "They apply for grants for their own wages now anyway, so they figured why not do that for our place? They gave me the links to those grant applications too."

"It sounds like a lot of work," Addie said. "Are you up for it?"

"Yes. But before we do any of it, I need to know if your neighborhood will approve it," Laurie said. "I can send some of my neighbors to a meeting to vouch for us if necessary. Just let me know."

"Okay. I'll go talk to Gail and get the ball rolling." Addie paused a moment, letting it all sink in. "This is crazy, isn't it?"

"Yes, it is," Laurie said. "And exciting. We'll be making a difference. Think about that and how far you've come. That's the most exciting part."

Tears filled Addie's eyes as she hung up. Laurie was right. While she kept thinking this was for Sofiya, the truth was, this was for her. It was her way of thanking all the people who believed in her.

She called Gail. "Okay. It's a go if we can get the neighborhoods' approval," Addie said. "And if you're serious about investing in it."

"Wonderful," Gail said. "I'm so excited about this. Would it be okay if I do an estimate on what your house is worth now so we can see what you'll need to sell it?"

"Yes. I'd appreciate that. And I'll be leaving some equity

into the house too, as an investor."

"Great. I'll also approach the HOA members and talk to each of them before we have an official meeting. I can be pretty persuasive when I want to be," Gail told her.

Addie laughed. "I'll bet you can be."

Addie took a moment to let everything sink in. Then she got to work.

Chapter Thirty-Two

Sofiya

Marion's funeral was a modest affair with several local friends attending. Letters and telegrams came from around the world from friends Sofiya had met, expressing their condolences. Edgar came home from the city to attend, and the entire Burton family sat in the front pew of Marion's church. They were as close to family as Marion had.

After the service, Marion's lawyer asked Sofiya and Edgar if they would attend the reading of the will. Sofiya noticed Edgar's face lit up when he heard they were invited.

"Would Marion have left us her money?" he asked Sofiya.

Angrily, Sofiya answered, "I have no idea, nor do I care. I just lost my dearest friend."

"Of course," Edgar said, looking somber.

Mr. and Mrs. Prescott and Edgar and Sofiya were invited back to Marion's house, where the lawyer would read the will. They met in the parlor where Mrs. Prescott served them tea.

"I know you are all mourning the death of your dear friend, so I will make this brief," the lawyer said. "Mrs. Dawson's will has many recipients, but she was adamant that you hear this personally from me." He pulled out several sheets of paper, put on his glasses, and began to read.

"Mrs. Dawson bequeaths ten thousand dollars each to Mrs. Sofiya Burton and to Mr. and Mrs. Prescott in appreciation of your friendship."

Mrs. Prescott gasped, and Sofiya was stunned. Ten thousand dollars. She would never have dreamed Marion would give her so much.

"Mrs. Dawson also bequeaths her emerald necklace, earrings, and ring to Mrs. Sofiya Burton, her pearl necklace, earrings, and ring to Mrs. Ardith Prescott, and her ruby necklace, earrings, and ring set to Mrs. Adelaine Burton. She would also like to have Mrs. Amelia Carlton choose a piece of jewelry from her collection as a remembrance," the lawyer said.

"All of her remaining possessions will be sold, and the money will be allotted to the various charities and foundations that Mrs. Dawson has listed," the lawyer continued. "She has left this to me to distribute. Mrs. Dawson has asked that Mrs. Prescott and Mrs. Sofiya Burton help go through her personal items and prepare them for sale."

"That's quite a lot to ask of you," Edgar whispered, but Sofiya shushed him.

"I don't mind doing it," she told him.

"You may stop by my office any time after today for your inheritances. I trust that Mrs. Prescott and Mrs. Burton will distribute the proper jewels to the rightful owners."

Everyone stood and thanked the lawyer before he left. Sofiya and Mrs. Prescott went to Marion's room to pick out the jewelry that was bequeathed to them, and Sofiya boxed up the rubies for Adelaine.

"I can bring Amelia later this week to choose a piece she'd like to remember Marion by," Sofiya told Miss Prescott. "And I can come by to help whenever you're ready to pack up Marion's things."

"Thank you," Mrs. Prescott said. "I'll wait for us to do everything together so there will be no one to accuse us of taking anything that doesn't belong to us."

"I trust you completely," Sofiya said. "Please don't believe otherwise."

The two women hugged goodbye, both understanding how hard Marion's loss was on the other. It was like losing a mother.

Edgar escorted Sofiya to his car. When he got in, he said, "I'll stop by the lawyer's office tomorrow and have the money transferred to our bank."

"Shouldn't I be there with you? I don't have an account set up at your bank," Sofiya said.

"Don't worry about it," Edgar said, brushing her off. "I'll take care of it."

Sofiya was so emotionally spent from the past few days that she didn't think much of it.

The next few days, she and Mrs. Prescott packed up all of Marion's personal items. They inventoried the leftover jewelry for the lawyer after Amelia had chosen a piece she loved, and they also inventoried the furniture. There were also piles of personal letters and photos they weren't sure what to do with.

"Are there no relatives at all?" Sofiya asked Mrs. Prescott. "I'd hate to see these go into the trash bin."

"Maybe the lawyer knows of someone who'd like these. A distant niece or nephew possibly?"

When Sofiya came upon the photo of Marion and her husband that she'd carried along with her during their

European trip, she showed it to Mrs. Prescott. "Do you think it would be okay if I take this? I'd like a photo to remember her, and she did treasure this one so much."

"Please, keep it. I'd rather you have it than some stranger just tossing it away," Mrs. Prescott said.

Finally, the house was in order and ready for an estate sale. Sofiya and Mrs. Prescott left the house together for the last time.

"It'll be strange not coming here to work anymore," Mrs. Prescott said, tears filling her eyes. "I hope the house is bought by a nice family who will treasure it."

"Me, too," Sofiya said. They hugged for the last time in front of the grand house. Sofiya's life was so different from Mrs. Prescott's, and she knew they'd probably never cross paths again. "Thank you for all you've done. I know Marion loved you dearly," Sofiya said.

"And you, too," Mrs. Prescott said. "Marion loved having young people around her, but you were the one she cherished the most. I'm glad you two went together to see her friends one last time."

They finally parted ways, two women connected by one incredible woman that they both would miss for the rest of their lives.

* * *

After Marion's passing, Sofiya's life continued as it had before. She spent a significant amount of time with little Eddie in the nursery and passed the rest of her days with Adelaine and Amelia, sometimes sitting in on luncheons or teas the ladies hosted. Edgar continued to ignore her while at home, which was very little since he spent most of his time in the city.

Spring finally came, and Sofiya was able to get outside with Eddie and the other children. Once again, they went on walks, and she'd sit and watch the children play in the fresh grass. She'd lay down a blanket, so little Eddie could roll around and try to crawl. Jonathan and Edina were patient with the baby and would roll a small ball to him or share one of their favorite stuffed animals.

One evening before dinner, as the family enjoyed drinks, Christian made a snide comment about Edgar buying an apartment in New York City and was no longer staying in hotels. Sofiya's ears perked up when she heard that.

"I suppose he grew tired of staying in hotels downtown," Edgar Sr. said. "I can't blame him. He's very successful with his business, and buying a place is a good investment."

"Oh, that's what we're calling it?" Christian said, snorting. Sofiya could tell he'd had one too many drinks.

"Hush," Adelaine said gently. "It's Edgar's business, not yours."

Sofiya turned to Amelia and whispered, "What did Christian mean?"

"Oh, he's jealous that Edgar can run around and do as he pleases," Amelia said quietly. "Edgar had told Christian he came into a windfall of cash, and that's how he paid for the apartment." She smiled at Sofiya. "Lucky you. You'll have a nice place to stay when you visit the city."

Sofiya didn't think she was lucky at all. The only windfall she knew of was her inheritance from Marion, and Edgar had promised her he'd put it aside for her. She'd wanted it to be saved for Eddie.

On Friday night, after dinner with the family, Sofiya

cornered Edgar in their sitting room. "Christian said you bought an apartment in the city. Did you use my money from Marion to purchase it?"

Edgar frowned. "Christian has a big mouth."

"Did you?" Sofiya asked again.

"What if I did?" Edgar asked, loosening his tie. "Real estate is always a good investment."

"But it was my inheritance," Sofiya said angrily. "I wanted to put it away for Eddie."

Edgar walked over to pour himself another whiskey. "Your inheritance is my money. You have no need for a bank account. I pay for everything. My business income is what's keeping this house together and paying everyone's bills."

"I understand and appreciate that," Sofiya said. "But you had no right to spend the money Marion gave me."

Edgar's eyes flashed. "I had no right? I have every right," he bellowed. "Do you know how hard I work? Do you even care what it costs to keep everything going around here? You can buy whatever you like for yourself and our son, and I don't complain. You live in a big house, have all the food you like, and never have to worry one moment about earning the money. So, if I were you, I'd keep my mouth shut and enjoy the luxury you live in."

Sofiya was taken aback by his ranting. She spoke in a soothing voice, hoping he would calm down. "I'm sorry you feel that way. It seemed that between your father's business and your own, the family was doing well. I didn't know the stress you were feeling."

Edgar snorted and took a long drink. "My business is the only one that's keeping this family afloat. My father's land and tenant farmers are barely breaking even since prohibition. I'm the one who came up with the business that keeps the family house running and everyone living a high lifestyle."

"I had no idea," Sofiya said. The way Edgar threw money around, she hadn't thought it was a problem. "I'm not even aware of what it is you do."

"Do you want to know what I do? Put on a pair of walking shoes, and I'll show you." He waved for her to follow him after she'd quickly put on a pair of shoes and a coat. They headed down the back staircase to the kitchen and walked out the back door. She followed him out in the dark, the glow of his flashlight leading the way. After a time, they made their way to a large barn that Sofiya had never gone into and had thought was no longer in use. Edgar opened a door and then flipped on the lights.

Sofiya looked inside the barn. There were a dozen trucks and several large cars in there.

"You see all of those?" Edgar said, not waiting for her reply. "There's a little island off the east coast that's owned by the French. Every night, boats come from there bringing cases of whisky, rye, and wine, made in Canada, Scotland, and France. I have a dozen small boats that go out there three times a week and fill up. Then they come down the river where these trucks are waiting. From there, the trucks and cars take the products to bars and speakeasies all over the northern part of this state."

Sofiya stared at him, her eyes growing wide. "You're a bootlegger?"

His chest puffed up. "I like to think of myself as a businessman. There was a need, and I filled it."

"But it's illegal. Aren't you afraid of getting caught?" Sofiya asked.

Edgar laughed. "I have the Fed guy around here in my back

pocket. He's not telling anyone. He enjoys a drink as much as the next guy."

Sofiya suddenly felt sick to her stomach. Her husband made his money illegally—and bragged about it. Everything she'd bought for herself and Eddie was purchased with tainted money.

"What's the matter with you?" Edgar asked. "You said you wanted to know."

"I did," she said, feeling disgust for Edgar creep over her. "Do your parents know what you're doing?"

"My father does. He keeps out of it. Don't say anything to mother or Amelia. They don't need to know."

Edgar snapped off the barn lights, and they walked back to the house in silence. Sofiya had nothing to say to her husband. He'd lied to her about loving her, and now she'd learned he'd do anything to earn money. She didn't even want to look at him.

As they entered their rooms, she turned and headed to her bedroom.

"I don't regret what I'm doing to support this family," he said to her back. "We would have lost this house and the property if I hadn't stepped up. I'm proud of myself."

Sofiya stopped and let that sink in, then slowly closed her door. The money meant nothing to her. She'd be just as happy living in an apartment with a loving husband and her son. Now she understood what the most important thing was to Edgar—money. Not her. Not Eddie. That realization hurt her more than any words he could have flung at her.

CHAPTER THIRTY—THREE

Addie

O nce Addie and Laurie had set the ball in motion, things moved quickly. Gail spoke to a few of the neighbors about having a safe house in the neighborhood, and she reported back that the response was fifty-fifty.

"They like the idea of helping teens rebuild their lives, but not necessarily in their neighborhood," Gail said. "I get what they're saying, but they haven't talked to you and Laurie yet, so you just might be able to change their minds."

A neighborhood meeting was set, and flyers were distributed. Addie also was able to get on the agenda at the next zoning commission meeting after filling out tons of paperwork.

"What can I do to help?" Katie asked Addie.

"I just need you to continue to work hard with school and your healing," Addie told her. "I think that's enough pressure to be under."

"But I really want to help you succeed at this," Katie said. "This is so important."

"If I think of something, I'll let you know," Addie said.

"But for now, we need the neighborhood to agree before we can do anything."

The night of the neighborhood meeting, Laurie and Addie were nervous. The meeting was taking place in Addie's house, so everyone could see it was the perfect place for a safe house. Laurie's current girls said she could use their stories as examples of successful teens. Katie attended the meeting also for moral support.

Twenty-two members of the HOA attended the meeting. They toured the house and sat down with refreshments in the parlor to listen to Laurie speak. She told them about her college degree in psychology and then about the years she has owned a safe house for trafficked teens. Two neighbors from her neighborhood attended as well, and each spoke about not having any issues with the girls who lived in the house.

"These teens come to us wanting to change their lives," Laurie said. "Some are traumatized, most have PTSD, but I work with them and slowly get them used to living in the regular world again."

"Don't many of the trafficked teens become hooked on drugs?" A woman in her fifties who lived across the street from Addie's house had asked the question.

"Yes. Many do," Laurie said. "But I don't accept teens until they've completed rehabilitation for drugs or alcohol. My teens stay clean, or else they have to go to another facility."

"Is it really that easy for the teens to change their lifestyle?" another woman asked. "What if they relapse or have an emotional breakdown or something. That could be dangerous."

"It's only a danger to them, not to the neighborhood," Laurie said. "These kids want to build a new life. They get their GEDs. They go to college. Or they get a job and contribute to society. They aren't looking to rejoin that life again."

Addie studied the crowd and could tell they weren't completely satisfied with the answers. She'd been sitting next to Zach, so she squeezed his hand for strength, cleared her throat, and stood.

"I was a trafficked teen," she said loud and clear. The entire crowd stared at her. "I was a runaway teen who was conned into *the life* at fourteen years old. At seventeen, I took a big chance and ran. Luckily, I met a wonderful person who took me under her wing and taught me how to remodel houses. Then I met Laurie," she smiled over at her friend. "And she helped me deal with PTSD and my fear of strangers. I run my own business, I pay taxes, and I have no desire to ever get involved in *the life* again. I'm a success story."

Everyone, even Gail, stared at her, looking shocked. Gail finally stood and walked over to her. "I had no idea," she said. Much to Addie's surprise, Gail hugged her.

"You'd be surprised at how many survivors there are," Laurie said, standing up. "I'm a survivor. I was also a trafficked teen. But look at me now. I have a college education, and I help other teens."

Gail had stood back and again looked shocked. The entire crowd was quiet.

Katie stood. "I was recently saved by Addie from trafficking. I'd been in *the life* for three years. I came from a broken home and was vulnerable. That's who traffickers prey on. Vulnerable girls and boys who have no one to protect them. Addie literally saved me from my captor, and now I'm going to college and working a part-time job. We're not criminals. We're victims. But with a safe house, victims can become active members of society."

Addie's heart swelled as she listened to Katie. She hadn't expected her to tell her story, and if she'd known, she would have discouraged her. But here she was, putting her life out there for these people to judge her to help her and Laurie start this new safe house.

Gail looked the most shocked of everyone. She walked over to Katie. "I'm so sorry that happened to you. You're a very brave young woman." She reached out her arms, and Katie walked into them. Watching the two hug brought tears to Addie's eyes.

Addie went to sit with Zach again, and Katie sat beside her as they let Gail take over the meeting.

"I'm so proud of you," Zach whispered to Addie. She smiled up at him, wiping away tears.

"Well, I, for one, have heard enough success stories to say I'm one-hundred percent in on this house being a safe house for trafficked teens," Gail said. "In fact, I'm willing to help sponsor the program by investing in the house. You all know me in this neighborhood. I'd be the first one to worry about house values and safety. But I see no reason this would have a negative impact on our community."

With that, Gail called for a vote. Of the twenty-two people attending, twenty voted yes to allowing the house to be used as a safe house. Addie and Laurie exchanged smiles. They were on their way.

After Addie and Laurie had thanked everyone for coming, and the house cleared out, Gail stayed to talk with them.

"We'll have to give it a day or two to see if anyone else registers a complaint. If not, you're cleared to move ahead once the zoning committee agrees," Gail told them. She grinned. "And I'm sure we won't have any trouble with them."

"Thank you so much," Addie said. "We couldn't have done

this without you."

"No. Thank you for opening my eyes to this. I'm so happy to be a part of it." Gail turned to Katie. "That couldn't have been easy to do tonight. I'm so proud of you." She hugged Katie once more, then left.

After another round of hugs and a few tears, Laurie left too. Addie turned to Katie.

"You didn't have to do that, but I'm so proud of you for telling your truth." She hugged the young girl.

"I'm proud of you both," Zach said, circling his arms around them. "Group hug."

They all started laughing.

* * *

The zoning commission voted unanimously to allow them to run a group home in the area. The fact that the neighborhood had voted yes had helped.

Laurie would open the house under her current non-profit status, but she was still waiting for replies to funding grants she'd sent in. Gail had estimated the home's value and said she could fund one-third of the cost. Addie had been shocked.

"Are you sure? That's a lot of money."

"Yes, it is," Gail said. "But what good is money if you only hoard it? I want to know my money is helping people."

Addie and Zach decided they'd take only what they needed to remodel another house, and the rest of the money would be used to buy furniture for the safe house. If any of Laurie's grants came through, then that money would go toward paying Addie and Zach for the house plus expenses to start the program.

To everyone's surprise, several of the neighbors put on a

spring dance and dinner fundraiser at their golf club and raised thousands of dollars for the new safe house. When they handed Laurie the check, she cried.

But the biggest surprise of all was when Addie's mentor, Valerie, called her and said she'd like to invest a huge amount of money into the project.

"I'm so proud of you for all you've accomplished, and now for this," Valerie told her. "We can afford to help fund the safe house. It's an investment into our youth, and what better investment can there be?"

Addie had always known how generous Valerie was, but this was more than she'd ever have expected from her. "You saved my life and helped me start over," she told Valerie. "You are already a hero in my eyes. But this, this is so amazing. Thank you."

"I will always be thankful for the day you came into my life," Valerie said. "Helping you only made my life fuller."

When Addie told Laurie of Valerie's investment in the project, her friend sighed with relief.

"Thank goodness for her. Now, we have enough so you and Zach can continue your business, and we can hire the two women to help manage the house," Laurie said. "I'm still hoping for some of the grant money to come through, but at least we can start even sooner than I had hoped."

Soon, under Laurie's supervision, they purchased beds and other furniture, linens, living room furniture, a dining room table, and everything else the house would need. Addie, Zach, and Katie helped with the buying and setting up of the house to save money.

"It looks like it's time to search for a new house to flip," Zach told Addie one night after they'd spent the day putting together IKEA furniture for the bedrooms.

"What? Are you already tired of building dressers, tables, and chairs?" Addie teased.

"Well, as much fun as that has been, we need to start making money again," he said. "After we build all the furniture."

"Have I told you how much I love you?" Addie asked.

"You can never tell me enough." Zach grinned.

CHAPTER THIRTY-FOUR

Sofiya

The seasons came and went as Sofiya lived on in her sham of a marriage with Edgar. After Eddie turned two, Adelaine hinted at the possibility of Sofiya having another child soon, but Sofiya knew that wasn't possible. Edgar had nothing but contempt for her. She had no idea why he'd married her in the first place, other than to have an heir and then be free to do as he pleased.

The only bright spot in Sofiya's life was little Eddie. He grew so fast that she could barely keep up. She spent hours in the nursery with him during the winter months, playing and reading to him. When he turned three, she began teaching him his numbers and letters. Eddie was a bright boy who loved to learn, and by three and a half, he could count to fifty and say his alphabet. He enjoyed storybooks and had memorized the ones he loved best. In the summer, he enjoyed playing outside with his cousins, kicking the ball around, swinging on the old wooden swing that hung from a large oak tree, and tumbling about. He was growing into a happy, loving boy, and Sofiya was thankful that he was more like her than his father.

Rumors spread around town that Edgar had a woman living openly in his New York City apartment, and when those rumors came to Sofiya through Amelia, it didn't surprise her. Edgar had already proven he was a terrible husband, but she felt trapped. Leaving would mean taking Eddie away from the only family he'd ever known and to an uncertain future. Staying, however, was getting harder for her to bear.

"Why do you let Edgar get away with his horrendous behavior?" Amelia asked her one day as they sat outside in the shade of a tree while the children played.

"What do you propose I do? Leave him? I certainly can't tell him what to do," Sofiya said. "He supports Eddie and me. I have to be thankful for that. Believe me, it's a difficult world out there, especially for a single woman with a child."

Amelia was so upset with her brother that she told her mother what was happening, and in turn, Adelaine admonished her son. When Edgar came home for the weekend, he cornered Sofiya in their rooms.

"Why did you complain to my mother? What is so wrong with your life that you had to tell her our personal business?"

Sofiya was taken aback. He had whiskey on his breath, and even though he wasn't a tall man, he'd backed her in a corner to intimidate her. "I've never spoken to your mother about our relationship," she told him with as much dignity as she could manage. "I don't know what you're referring to."

His eyes narrowed, but he backed up a step. "Someone told her I have a mistress set up in my apartment and that I ignore you, and you're so angry you're considering leaving me."

Sofiya was shocked. "I never said those words to anyone, least of all your mother."

Edgar swore and went to refill his drink. Sofiya turned to leave to dress for dinner, but he stopped her with his words.

"Since everyone is so interested in my personal business, then yes, I do have a woman living with me in New York," Edgar said. "A much prettier, thinner woman than you who is happy to fulfill my every need." He laughed, a tight, evil sound. "But I'll never admit that to anyone else, and I'll say you're a liar if you repeat it."

He may as well have thrown a knife at her back, it hurt that much. Sofiya slowly turned and stared at him. "Why did you marry me? Why did you pretend to love me? If you aren't happy with me, why am I here?"

He came closer with a drunken grin on his face. "I never wanted to marry you. It was all my mother and sister's idea. The very first time my mother and father met you, they thought you were so special. 'Sofiya's the type of woman you should marry,' my mother had said to me. All they wanted was a respectable daughter-in-law to give me an heir. They were never interested in what I wanted. They'd never agree to let me marry someone I chose. So, I married you to make them happy."

Sofiya's heart dropped. She fell into a chair, unable to believe he could be that cold. She had hoped he'd cared for her in the beginning, but now she knew their son was not conceived from love. It hurt her to think she'd been used as a broodmare.

He laughed. "Oh, please. Did you really believe I ever loved you? I don't remember ever telling you I did."

Sofiya thought back through the time he'd courted her and even their marriage and honeymoon. She couldn't think of one time he'd said he loved her. How could she have been so stupid to marry a man who had never proclaimed his love? Sofiya stood, feeling weak at the knees. "If you don't love me, then you should let me go. I can't live the rest of my life knowing my husband had only used me."

He sneered at her. "Oh, no. It doesn't work that way. You'll never leave me, and you'll definitely never take my son away from me. I'll see you dead first before I'll let you shame my family by leaving me."

"Are you threatening me?" Sofiya asked, shocked that he'd go that far.

"Let's just say I'm telling you how it is."

Sofiya turned and went to her bedroom. She now knew where she stood in this house. She wasn't sure she could live out her life in a loveless marriage being supported by a man who earned his money illegally. Once again, she'd been pushed into a corner just as she'd been at Miss Nora's house. But this time, she had a reason not to give up. She had Eddie. And she'd do whatever she had to do to protect him.

* * *

As time went on, Sofiya grew more and more resentful of her treatment by Edgar and the way people in town looked at her with pity in their eyes. Edgar was no longer just flaunting his lifestyle in New York City. Now, he was spending time in Syracuse, going out nightly to speakeasies and coming home smelling of booze and the cheap perfume of other women.

"Are you enjoying my company?" he asked one morning on the way down to breakfast. "I promised my mother I'd spend more time at home. She mentioned something about us having a second child."

Sofiya was repulsed. The last thing she wanted was for him to touch her. "I was just fine with you spending your weeks in the city," she said. "At least the people here didn't know exactly what you were up to. Now, everyone knows you're out until all hours of the night."

He grabbed her arm and squeezed tightly. "Yes, but at least I come home to you, my dear," he said, mocking her.

Sofiya shrugged him off. "Don't do me any favors."

Adelaine acted as if all was well with the world, ignoring that her son was making a spectacle of himself every night in town. She was thrilled to have him home.

"You know, dear," Adelaine said to Sofiya one morning after breakfast as the three women spent time in the morning room. "Sometimes men just need to get things out of their system. Edgar will eventually realize how lucky he is to have a dedicated wife and son. Maybe if you have another child, he'll settle down."

Sofiya was appalled at her mother-in-law's words. She saw Amelia cover her mouth with her hand to stifle a laugh. It was all so insane. How could Adelaine think it was okay for her married son to be out sewing wild oats? It was demeaning to Sofiya.

Edger finally grew tired of Syracuse's nightlife and once again returned to the city for his fun and games. Sofiya's life continued, finding joy in her growing son.

When Eddie turned five, the family hosted a large party for him, which demanded Edgar's attendance.

"Well, it won't be long before young Edgar will be ready to go off to boarding school," Edgar Sr. said. Sofiya was stunned. She'd thought Eddie would attend school in Syracuse.

"We won't really send Eddie off to a boarding school, will we?" she asked her husband when they were alone. "Your father said he'd go to one in New York City when he's eight."

Edgar shrugged. "I don't see why not. Maybe this town's schools are fine for Amelia's children, but our son will have nothing but the best. All the good schools are in the city."

Over the next few days, Sofiya grew frantic. She could manage staying in her marriage as long as she had Eddie, but if he were sent off to school, then she'd no longer be needed. Would Edgar find a way to get rid of her? She didn't want her son to grow up to be like Edgar—entitled and heartless. She wanted to raise her son with love, just as her parents had raised her.

Sofiya wasn't sure how she'd do it, but she knew that for the third time in her life, she had to escape. She just needed a plan.

* * *

Over the next few months, Sofiya made plans to leave. Except for a few pieces of jewelry and the jewels her mother had given her, she had absolutely no way to fund her escape. And she didn't want to take any of the jewelry Edgar had given her as gifts. She wanted nothing from him. She'd keep her wedding and engagement ring to sell, but that was it. Sofiya felt she'd earned that from the pain he'd caused her.

Edgar never gave her any cash. All her purchases were made with credit in the stores where he'd set up accounts. And she couldn't go to a local jewelry store to sell her ring. Word would get back to Edgar immediately.

Sofiya had to reduce herself to stealing cash a little at a time. Edgar always had money in the pockets of his pants and jackets and often laid it out on his dresser or nightstand when he changed clothes. Her plan was to go in his room before breakfast and before the maid cleaned his room and take a dollar or two at a time. Not enough for him to notice. It was risky, but it was all she could do.

Winter passed, and by spring, Sofiya had a small pile of dollar bills hidden away. She had no idea if it was enough to buy two train tickets. Sofiya finally found enough courage to go into Edgar's room in the middle of the week to dig through the pockets of his suits for more cash. If a maid caught her, she'd say she was checking his suits for any necessary repairs.

She snuck into his room and went to his dressing room. He had multiple suits, so she started checking the pockets, unsuccessfully. As she pushed aside a group of suits, her eye caught something metal in the back of the closet. Looking closer, she was surprised to see a small safe.

For a moment, Sofiya pondered why he'd have a safe in his closet. Edgar had never offered to put away her jewelry for safekeeping. Then, it dawned on her. He earned money illegally. He couldn't put his earnings in the bank without questions about how he'd acquired it. He probably stored the cash here and gradually ran it through the bank to pay his bills.

Sofiya got down on her knees to study the safe. She'd never opened one herself, but she'd seen people open safes at hotels. She knew she needed at least three numbers, but what numbers would Edgar use?

She tried using Eddie's birthday, but nothing happened. She tried Edgar's birthday, but that didn't work either. She tried their wedding date and even her birthday, but again, it didn't open. Frustrated, Sofiya stood, moved the clothes back to hide the safe, and left the room.

All afternoon, Sofiya pondered the numbers Edgar would use. She went back to his closet and tried the birthdays of Adelaine, Edgar Sr., and Amelia. When those didn't work, she began digging through his dresser draws for any kind of hint. There was a small writing desk in Edgar's bedroom, so she opened the middle drawer and looked inside. A pile of bills sat in the drawer, with the address of what she assumed was his apartment in New York City.

Sofiya stared at the address. The number of the apartment was 211. That was a number no one in the house would know. She hurried back to the closet and tried it. The safe clicked, then opened.

Peering inside, she was shocked to see piles of money. Sofiya pulled out one stack. One-hundred-dollar bills were banded together. She pulled out another pile and then another. They were all stacks of one-hundred-dollar bills. There were thousands of dollars in this safe, more money than she could have ever imagined.

Sofiya wasn't greedy. She just needed enough money to get her and Eddie away safely. She assumed Edgar would know how many piles he had in the safe, so she couldn't take an entire stack. So, she slipped out six one-hundred-dollar bills, each from a separate pile. He would never notice they were missing unless he counted each banded stack. Then she placed the money back inside and closed and locked the safe.

Two days later, Sofiya waited until long after everyone had gone to bed to go get Eddie from the nursery. She knew his nanny slept soundly, so she had no problem waking him and taking him to her room. Earlier in the day, she'd taken some of his clothing on the pretense they needed mending. These were now packed in a bag along with her own clothing.

"We're going on an adventure," she told her son. "But we must be quiet so we don't wake anyone." She helped him dress in warm clothing and a coat, then they both crept down the back staircase and through the kitchen.

Sofiya's heart was pounding the entire time as they made their way to the garage. She had studied how Noah started and drove the car, but she wasn't sure she could manage it herself. There was no way they could walk the long distance to the train depot. She knew there was a midnight train to Chicago, and she needed to get there in time.

Sofiya had Eddie sit in the back seat and covered him with a blanket, then placed her bag in there as well. She opened the large garage door, then got behind the wheel. She was relieved to see the key was in the car, so she turned it like Noah did to spark the battery. Sofiya hit the starter with her foot, and the car motor came to life. She prayed the noise couldn't be heard in the house.

Suddenly, a light blinded her, and a voice asked, "Mrs. Burton? What are you doing?"

Sofiya's heart beat wildly. She squinted and realized that Noah was standing there, shining a flashlight on her.

"I...I didn't know you were still here," Sofiya said. That's when she noticed he was half-dressed, his suspenders hanging loosely around his legs. He looked like he'd jumped out of bed.

"I live above the garage," he said. "I heard the engine start and thought someone was stealing a car."

"I'm so sorry," Sofiya said. "I didn't mean to wake you."

Noah shined his light on Eddie in the backseat. "Hey there, Master Eddie."

"Hi, Noah." Eddie smiled back at him.

"Is there somewhere I can drive you?" Noah asked, turning back to Sofiya.

Tears rolled down her cheeks. What had she been thinking? She'd never be able to get away from here without someone seeing her.

"Mrs. Burton? Are you okay?" Noah sounded concerned.

"I need a ride to the train station," she said. "I thought I could do it myself. It's imperative that no one ever know."

He frowned as he stared at her, but then realization filled his eyes. "I see. Well, let me get my coat, and I'll take you. No one needs to know."

Sofiya slid over in the seat as Noah slipped the suspenders over his shoulders and left a moment to grab a coat from a hook on the wall. He returned with a newsboy cap on his head instead of his chauffer's hat and got behind the wheel.

"I take it you're going on the midnight train?" he asked.

"Yes."

"I can buy the tickets so no one recognizes you," he said.

They took off into the night. Noah kept the car lamps off until they were well out of range of the house, then turned them on.

"I'm sorry I got you involved," Sofiya said to Noah. "I hope you don't lose your job for driving me to the station."

Noah thought about this a moment. "There may be a way for no one to know," he said. "Don't worry about me. I'll come up with something."

"Thank you for being so kind to me all these years," Sofiya told him.

Noah smiled. "It was my pleasure. I'll miss driving you places."

Sofiya's heart warmed at his words. Noah had been so young when he first started driving her around. At least, he'd seemed young. He was probably her age, for all she knew. She'd been young then too. Now, she felt old and worn out.

They arrived at the train depot, and Sofiya gave Noah the

money for two train tickets. He purchased them, then returned.

"Here you go, Mrs. Burton," he said. "Don't worry about anything here. I won't tell a soul."

"Thank you for your help," Sofiya said, taking Eddie's hand. "I wish you all the best. I mean that."

Sofiya was so touched that she hugged Noah. She remembered the day Carter had helped her leave Miss Nora's, risking his job just as Noah was doing now. "I wish you all the best, too," she said. Then she and Eddie boarded the train.

"Has our adventure started?" Eddie asked after they were seated in a private sleeping car.

She smiled at her son. "Yes. It has." As the train left the station, Sofiya prayed Edgar wouldn't come after her and that she was once again free.

Chapter Thirty-Five

Sofiya
May 1927

Sofiya hadn't been sure where she would go, but once she was in Chicago, she bought two tickets to Portland, Oregon. She knew the city, and even though it hadn't been kind to her the first time, she hoped she could start anew there.

They arrived at Portland Union Station on a chilly May morning. As Sofiya and Eddie stepped off the train, she was reminded of the day she and Alina had arrived in Portland ten years before. She was no longer a young, naïve girl, though. This time, her eyes were wide open in the ways of the world, and she knew how to keep herself and her son safe.

Sofiya chose one of the many cabs waiting for fares and asked the older cab driver to take her to tenth and Irving Street. He helped her and Eddie inside the cab and then took off.

Sofiya had pondered where she'd go the entire train trip and had decided to stop at her old friend Olga Jarvi's home first. She thought that Mrs. Jarvi might know of a nice place she and Eddie could rent until she found her own house.

The driver pulled up in front of a small white house with a tiny lawn and a white picket fence around the yard. Sofiya paid him and stepped out. The neighborhood was quiet, and the homes were all sizes, the Jarvi house being the smallest. It looked cute and inviting, and even though Sofiya had never been there, she felt like she was coming home.

Sofiya knew that Mrs. Jarvi's husband had passed away recently and that she worked for a nice family up on twenty-fifth street. She hoped Mrs. Jarvi would be home as she knocked on the white wooden door.

Mrs. Jarvi opened the door and looked at Sofiya with wide eyes. "Am I seeing you for real? Or am I imagining you?"

"I'm here for real," Sofiya said, and the two women hugged each other tightly.

"Oh, my goodness," Mrs. Jarvi said as she pulled back and looked down at Eddie. "Is this your son? He's grown so big."

Sofiya introduced Eddie to Mrs. Jarvi. "She's an old friend of mine," she told her son.

He said hello, and Mrs. Jarvi shook his little hand. "I'm so happy to meet you, Eddie. Come in out of the cold. It's been so damp here lately."

They walked inside the small house. There was a tiny entry-way with hooks on the wall for coats and a rug to set wet shoes and boots. After they'd removed their coats, Mrs. Jarvi directed them to the kitchen in the back of the house.

"I had the oven on earlier, so it's warmer in there," the older woman said. "And I just made cinnamon rolls. Come have one."

They sat at the wooden kitchen table as Mrs. Jarvi bustled about getting plates and cups for coffee. She poured Eddie a cup of milk to go with his roll. The little boy dug in, enjoying the gooey sweetness of the roll.

"I hope I'm not keeping you from going to work," Sofiya said.

"No, no. I only work there three days a week, and this is one of my days off. I had thought Carter might stop by this morning, so I'd made the rolls."

"Carter? You still see him?" Sofiya asked. Mrs. Jarvi hadn't mentioned that in her letters.

"Yes. He's a dear. He came to my husband's funeral, and since then, he stops by once a week to see if I need any help. He's married now, and they live a few blocks from here. He works as a porter at the train station. He's been such a great help."

"Oh, I'd love to see him," Sofiya said.

"I'm sure he'd love to see you too, dear."

Eddie had finished his roll and milk, and his eyes were drooping.

"Poor boy," Sofiya said. "He didn't sleep well on the train. He was too excited."

"Let's let him nap in the guest room, and then we can talk," Mrs. Jarvi said. She showed them to the room and left so Sofiya could tuck her son in. He was asleep in seconds.

"Thank you," Sofiya said as she reentered the kitchen. She looked around the small room. "This sure brings back memories. Us sitting in the kitchen having rolls and coffee with Harry. Those were the only good times living at Miss Nora's."

Mrs. Jarvi refilled Sofiya's cup. "I still haven't heard what happened to Harry. His father grew ill and couldn't keep up the business, and they closed it down. I don't know if they are even in town anymore."

"I'm sorry to hear that," Sofiya said.

Mrs. Jarvi gave her a warm smile. "Now tell me, how on earth did you come to be here?"

Sofiya sighed. Mrs. Jarvi knew her well enough that she didn't have to lie. She told her the whole story of how she'd married a man who didn't love her, but she hadn't known that until after Eddie was born. The taunts, the threats, and finally, learning that they'd send her son away to boarding school to learn to be arrogant like them. "I couldn't take it any longer. So, I left. Edgar is a terrible person. He only cares about money and doesn't care what he does to earn it. He can never learn that I'm here, though. He'd kill me if he got his hands on me."

"Oh, dear. That's terrible. I had so hoped you'd found your happily ever after," Mrs. Jarvi said.

"I'd thought I had. But I have Eddie, and that's what matters most to me," Sofiya said. "I'm hoping I can find a decent-sized house to run a boarding house. That way, I can be home for Eddie but still earn money."

"Well, that's not a bad idea," Mrs. Jarvi said. "This town keeps growing, and men come from all over to work. Do you have the money to buy a house?"

Sofiya nodded. "I have some jewelry I can sell. I think it'll be enough to get something. Until then, I need to look for a room to rent. I was hoping you'd know of a boarding house that takes children."

Mrs. Jarvi smiled at her. "You'll do no such thing. I have an extra room if you don't mind sharing with Eddie. You two will stay with me until you find a house. I have a nice yard he can play in, and it's a safe neighborhood."

"Oh, I couldn't impose like that," Sofiya said. She hadn't expected her friend to take them in.

"It's not an imposition," Mrs. Jarvi said. "I'd love to have you two here for a while."

Sofiya was about to protest again and then thought better of it. It would be nice to be around someone she knew in a place where she felt safe. "Thank you. I'm actually relieved to be able to be with a friend."

Mrs. Jarvi smiled and patted her hand. "We have so much to catch up on. It'll be a nice change to have you and little Eddie around."

The next day, Sofiya and Eddie took the trolley to the downtown jewelry store that Mrs. Jarvi recommended. She'd heard that the man bought jewelry and was honest about the price. Eddie had fun riding the trolley with his mother since he'd never ridden one before.

When she entered the jewelry store, Sofiya took a quick look around. Holding Eddie's hand so he wouldn't touch anything, she studied the wedding rings for sale, but unfortunately, there were no prices attached.

"May I help you?" A heavyset man who looked to be in his forties and wearing a brown suit came around the counter and smiled at Sofiya.

"Yes. I was looking to sell a piece of jewelry," Sofiya said, suddenly embarrassed. What would this man think of a woman selling her wedding ring?

"I see." He glanced down at Eddie. "Hello, young man. How are you today?"

"Hello," Eddie said, smiling up at him. "I just rode a trolley."

"Really? Well, I'm sure that was fun," the jeweler said.

Eddie nodded enthusiastically.

"If you'd follow me, please," he said to Sofiya, "I can look at the piece you're selling." He led her to an office, let her go inside, and then followed her in, leaving the door open. Sofiya sat in a chair across from his desk, and Eddie sat in the chair next to her.

Sofiya handed him the small box that held her engagement and wedding rings. She watched as he used an eyepiece to study the diamond in the engagement ring and the smaller diamonds too.

"This is a lovely set," he said, looking up at her. "I see by the markings it was purchased at Tiffany & Company in New York City."

"Yes, it was," Sofiya said.

The jeweler glanced from her to Eddie, then back at the ring. "I can offer you one-thousand dollars for the set," he said.

Sofiya thought about the price. She had no idea how much Edgar had paid for the rings, but it sounded like a lot of money. "I'll need to purchase a plain gold band to wear," she said.

He nodded. "I understand. A woman with a ring feels safer than one without. I'd be happy to let you pick one out at no extra charge."

Sofiya nodded. "Then it's a deal."

"Wonderful. What name should I put on the receipt?" he asked.

Sofiya hesitated. She didn't want to use her married name anymore. And she couldn't be known by Henderson, either, because it would be easier for Edgar to find her. She decided to use her maiden name. Surely, no one here would know that her maiden name was attached to the Romanov family.

"Mrs. Sofiya Hanikoff," Sofiya said.

"Fine. I'll get your money. Please feel free to look at the rings while I do," he told her. "I'll have my assistant help you."

They left the office, and Sofiya kept Eddie by her side as she looked over the choices of gold wedding bands. She chose a plain one, and the assistant helped her with the correct size. The jeweler returned and handed her an envelope and Eddie a small lollypop.

"Thank you for your business," he said. "My name is Daniel Markheim. If you have anything else you'd like to sell, I would be interested in seeing it."

"Thank you," she said, then left the building. Sofiya wasn't sure if she'd received a good price, but she had money to get her through the next few months, and that was all that mattered.

* * *

Living with Mrs. Jarvi—who told Sofiya to call her Olga—was easy and comfortable. Olga loved having Eddie around and was always baking him cookies or some type of treat. On the days Olga worked, Sofiya prepared dinner so she could rest when she came home. Sofiya also contributed to buying the groceries and helped pay the electric and gas bills. She would have felt terrible if Olga was carrying the load for them.

For the first few days, Sofiya scanned the newspaper ads for houses for sale. There were always several. She and Eddie took walks up and down the hill, looking at the houses listed, but nothing seemed right. They'd be too small for a boarding house or so run down that she'd have to put too much work into them. Sofiya didn't mind fixing up a house, but she couldn't afford to put on a new roof or fix a sagging porch. Finally, she decided to try one of the real estate offices she'd seen advertised in the newspaper.

She went to the office closest to Olga's house. Olga was

home that day and offered to watch Eddie, so Sofiya went alone. The day was warm and sunny as Sofiya walked the few blocks to the office. She felt happy and carefree for the first time in years. If she could only find an affordable house to buy, everything would be perfect.

She stopped in front of a small brick building with a large window with Roger Williams Real Estate written on it in big gold letters. It looked like a respectable business, so she walked inside.

The woman behind the front counter stood as Sofiya entered.

"Good morning," she said with a bright smile. "How may we help you today?"

The woman was short and stocky with brown hair and eyes, and in an instant, Sofiya recognized her. "Mabel?"

Mabel looked startled a moment, then her smile widened. "Sofiya? Oh, my goodness. It is really you?" She came around the counter and hugged her. "I thought for sure you'd left town."

"I had," Sofiya said as the two women parted. "But after all these years, I'm back. And you work here. That's wonderful."

Mabel winked at her. "I told you I'd be okay."

Sofiya smiled. She remembered the day Mabel left the house. She was happy things had worked out well for her. "I came here today looking for a house to buy."

"Wonderful," Mabel said, going back around the counter. "What exactly are you looking for?"

Sofiya told her the type of home she needed so she could run a boarding house. "Do you have anything like that available?"

"Well," Mabel glanced behind her where there was a private office. "Mr. Williams is the real estate agent, and you'll be working with him. But I do know of the perfect house if you can stand to live there again."

Sofiya's brows rose. "Again?"

"You do know that Nora Petrov disappeared a couple of years ago, don't you?" Mabel asked. "She just up and left, and no one has seen her since. She owed several years of back taxes on the property and just abandoned the house." Mabel glanced behind her again. "Of course, the neighborhood was ready to run her out of there anyway."

"Really?" Sofiya said, wondering what that had to do with her.

"Yep. Nora's house is up for sale at a good price. Fully furnished. That's nine bedrooms, one large one for you and then eight you can rent. It would be perfect for a boarding house. And it's in a nice neighborhood, too."

Sofiya's mind was spinning as she thought of all the possibilities the house on Marshall had. It was large, and it had a good-sized dining room and parlor. But could she live there after all the terrible things that had happened?

"It's priced at six-thousand dollars," Mabel said, looking at a folder on her desk. "You'd probably want to change the wallpaper and drapes in the parlor and master bedroom to look more respectable, but otherwise, it's not bad. What do you think?"

"Maybe I can look at it," Sofiya said. "And any other houses that may be similar?"

Mabel smiled. "I'll get Mr. Williams and have him show it to you." She gathered up a couple of folders to take back with her. "You know, someday I'm going to sell houses. Mr. Williams won't let me right now, but I'll wear him down, and he will eventually. I'm not stopping at being just a receptionist."

"I believe you can do anything you set your mind to," Sofiya told her. And she believed it wholeheartedly.

Mabel stood a little straighter. "Thank you. I always did like you." She winked and headed to the back office to tell Mr. Williams he had a customer.

Mr. Williams took Sofiya on a tour of the Marshall Street house. It was a surreal experience for her to walk around it now, all these years later, knowing she no longer had to fear Miss Nora. The house was in pretty good shape, and so was most of the furniture. As Mabel had suggested, she'd probably want to tone down some of the decorating to make it more like a home and less like a brothel. The kitchen could use a few upgrades, and all the beds would need new linens, blankets, and comforters. But overall, for the price, it would be the perfect house.

As Sofiya wandered into the little room that was once her bedroom, her heart went out the the young girl she once was. The girl who'd been naïve about the world around her and soon learned that it could be a scary and terrible place. But standing there now, as an adult who'd learned how to make her own way in the world, she could see the room, and the entire house as it could be, not as it was.

The realtor took her to see two other houses for sale, but they both were more expensive and only had four bedrooms. She would never make enough money with homes that small.

"Can I get back to you in a day or two?" Sofiya asked Mr. Williams. "I need to speak to my banker." It was a lie, of course. Sofiya didn't have a banker. Her only potential income lay in the false bottom of a cigar box.

"Of course," he said, looking excited about a potential sale. "Let me know as soon as you're ready."

Sofiya returned to Olga's house that afternoon just in time

for lunch. After Eddie had finished eating and gone outside to play in the backyard, Sofiya told Olga her idea.

"Really? That house? Are you sure?" Olga asked. "I would think that place would give you nightmares."

"I thought so too," Sofiya said. "But after I'd walked through it, I realized it was just a house. Nora's gone, the girls are gone, everything that made it a terrible house is no longer there. It's like it's been waiting for someone to save it and make it whole again."

Olga raised her brows. "Does the house need saving, or do you?"

"Good question," Sofiya said. "Maybe we both do."

A slow smile came to Olga's lips. "It's a good place for a boarding house. Especially if it's already furnished. And it's in a nice neighborhood up on the hill, so you could charge a little extra."

"Do you think it's a good idea? Mabel figured I'd need to buy all new linens and comforters, plus change out some of the wallpaper. The kitchen could use a bit of an update, too. And I'd need to buy a dining room table. But still, it's better than having to furnish an entire house."

"Wait? Mabel?" Olga asked.

Sofiya laughed. "Oh, yes. I left that part out. Mabel is the receptionist at the office. Can you believe it? I'm so happy for her."

Olga laughed along. "Well, good for her. I hope all the girls moved on to better lives."

"So, what do you think?" Sofiya asked.

"I think it's a good idea. If you can get the money, that is. And I'll help you clean the house and get it ready. This will be fun." Her eyes lit up with excitement.

"I couldn't possibly ask you to work on the house," Sofiya protested.

"You didn't ask me. I offered. And if you think you're going to do that all by yourself, then think again. How else will I spend my days off? Just sitting around here?" Olga said.

Olga agreed to watch Eddie while Sofiya went to secure funding for the house. Sofiya went to her room and lifted the cigar box from a dresser drawer. Taking out her comb and brush, she opened the false bottom. There, underneath the letters she'd never sent, wrapped in hankies, lay her mother's emerald necklace and diamond earrings and the lovely emerald jewelry Marion had given her. Sofiya knew her mother's emerald necklace would be worth much more than Marion's, so reluctantly, she lifted it out of the box and carefully placed it in her purse.

"Maman will understand," she said softly.

Taking the trolley, Sofiya went downtown to the jewelry store where she'd sold her rings. When she entered the store, she saw only the assistant who'd helped her choose a gold band.

"Is Mr. Markheim available to speak with?" Sofiya asked.

The young gentleman nodded and went to get the owner. Mr. Markheim emerged from the back room while slipping on his suit jacket.

"Good afternoon, Mrs. Hanikoff," he said, smiling at her. "It's so nice to see you again. How may I help you?"

"I have another piece to sell if you're interested," Sofiya said.

His blue eyes lit up with interest. "I would very much like to see it. Please, come to my office."

He let her go inside first and again left the door open. Sofiya trusted a man who had a sense of propriety. He waited until she was seated before sitting behind his desk.

"I see the little man is not with you today," he said.

"He's with a friend. I'd like to keep this item between us if you don't mind." Sofiya lifted the precious necklace from her bag and unwrapped it. The emeralds glittered under the office lights. She carefully handed them to Mr. Markheim.

"These are exquisite," he said, staring with wonder at the emeralds. He picked up his eyepiece and studied the stones closely. "Amazing," he said softly. When he turned the necklace over and examined the clasp, his eyes lifted to Sofiya.

"This is a Russian piece from the House of Fabergé," he said, looking shocked.

Sofiya's heart pounded. "How can you tell?" She was shocked he'd known where it came from.

"This hallmark." He pointed to the small, stamped engraving on the clasp. "It's the initials, AH. That would be for August Holmstrom or his son, Albert Holmstrom. Both created pieces for the late Tsar Nicholas II." He studied Sofiya as if he'd never seen her before. "Where did you get this necklace?"

Sofiya tried not to fidget under his stare. The worst thing that could have happened to her was happening this very minute. She'd known nothing about hallmarks on jewelry. If she had, she never would have tried to sell this piece. Trying to remain calm, she said, "My father gave it to my mother as a gift. But we lived across the gulf in Helsinki. Not in Russia."

The jeweler continued to watch her. "Your father must have been a wealthy man to purchase such a necklace. Even many years ago, it would have been quite costly."

"My father had inherited some money," she said. If she told the truth, he'd know she was lying. Her father did not earn a large salary as a university professor, but Tsar Nicholas shared a portion of his yearly income with members of the royal family, each amount depending upon their status. That was why her father could afford a few luxuries.

Mr. Markheim dropped his eyes to the necklace again. "Yes. Of course, the House of Fabergé sold to people other than the royal family."

Sofiya quietly let out the breath she'd been holding. But Mr. Markheim again set his gaze on her.

"It's none of my business, and I'm sorry to intrude, but I get the feeling that you haven't felt safe for a time. Are you safe now?" Mr. Markheim asked, looking concerned.

"I am," Sofiya said, feeling relieved.

He smiled. "I'm happy to hear that." Mr. Markheim studied the necklace once more. "This piece is worth a lot of money, and I want to be fair with you. No one sells such an heirloom if they don't need to. I can offer you eight thousand dollars. I'm afraid that's the best I can do."

Sofiya nearly gasped. She wondered if she'd heard right. "Eight thousand?"

"Yes. The fact that it's a Fabergé piece from one of their best craftsmen is what makes it worth more than just the stones and gold," he told her.

Sofiya was elated. She'd not only be able to pay for the house in full but have enough extra to buy the things she needed to update it. And she'd still have money to live on until she started renting rooms. "Thank you for the generous offer. I'll take it."

Mr. Markheim smiled broadly. "Wonderful. Just so you know, this is the kind of piece I will sell at auction, not locally. It will not be sitting in the store window."

"That's good to know," she said. It was a relief that no one locally would know where it had come from.

"They've never been found, have they? The girls and the young boy," Mr. Markheim asked, watching Sofiya again.

Sofiya stared at him a moment until his question sunk in. She realized he was asking about the princesses and Alexei. She shook her head sadly. "No. I don't believe they've been found."

"Such a shame," he said. "They didn't deserve to disappear."

"I agree," Sofiya said.

Mr. Markheim stood, and so did Sofiya. "I'll get your payment for you," he said. He placed the necklace carefully in the middle drawer of his desk and locked it. Then he escorted Sofiya out of the office.

Excitement grew inside Sofiya as she waited for her money. Now, she could buy the house and begin to earn an income. She could support Eddie on her own—legitimately. She and her son would be safe. She silently sent up a prayer to her maman for ensuring she had a way to take care of herself.

CHAPTER THIRTY-SIX

Addie

Tears streamed down Addie's cheeks as she read Sofiya's account of buying the very house that she was in right now. All along, Addie had thought she was the one redeeming the house from its sordid past. But Sofiya had come back and done it first. And now, Addie was going one step further. Not only was the house being redeemed, but it would also rehabilitate lives.

Zach rolled over in bed and watched her with sleepy eyes. "What's happened? Is Sofiya okay?"

Addie laughed despite her tears. "She came back. She bought this house in 1927 and transformed it into a legitimate boarding house. Here all along, I thought we were saving the house. But she already had."

"But we are saving the house," he said. "No one wanted it. We're giving it life again."

Addie wiped her tears. "I wasn't complaining. I'm just astonished at how life works. This house called to me, and it called to Sofiya too. All of this was meant to be. I don't care if that sounds crazy, it's the truth. She was meant to come back to it, and I was meant to find her letters and her house. Don't you just love that?"

Zach smiled and reached for her. "I do. And I love you for your generous spirit. I was worried about the money, but everything will be fine. This house will help young people change their lives, and it's all because of you. And Sofiya."

She loved Zach so much. He understood her completely and didn't make fun of her for her crazy vibes and feelings.

"I want to dedicate this house to Sofiya," she told Zach. "We can get a little plaque and call it the Sofiya Hanikoff House. Don't you think that's a good idea?"

"Hanikoff? I thought her name was Henderson."

Addie laughed. "I guess I should catch you up on everything."

The next day she told Laurie about her idea of dedicating the house to Sofiya, and she thought it was a great idea.

"Women have been suffering at the hands of all types of abusers for centuries. It's only fitting that it be named after the first woman to turn this house around," Laurie said.

They planned for the first of March to be the day they'd open the doors to the safe house. Addie and Laurie decided to have an open house for the neighborhood that first day, and they'd dedicate the house to Sofiya. As word got out about the safe house's opening, the local newspaper called Laurie to ask for information and published an article about it. Before they knew it, agencies from around the area were calling and asking if they could come and tour the house as well.

"This is crazy," Laurie told Addie. "I hadn't expected so much attention."

"It's wonderful," Addie said. "Maybe others will want to do

this. Wouldn't that be great?"

As the time drew near for the house to open, Zach and Addie got serious and began searching for their next flip. Addie found a cute Victorian row house on SW Montgomery Street that was in need of some tender loving care. The moment she saw it, she had to have it.

"Another house you need to save?" Zach asked after they'd toured it.

"Another house I want to save," Addie said. "And it's perfect. With four bedrooms and two bathrooms, Katie can still live with us while we remodel, and it's still not too far from her college."

The price was perfect, too, so they bid on the house and bought it.

When Addie told Katie they'd found a house, the younger girl grew quiet.

"Hey. I thought you'd be happy for us. Unless you don't like the idea of living in a mess again," Addie said.

"Are you sure you want me to stay with you and Zach?" Katie asked. "I could stay at Laurie's or be a resident at the new safe house."

They were sitting in the kitchen, and Addie moved her chair closer to Katie. "Is that what you want? To live with Laurie or to stay here? I just want you to be happy."

"I love living with you and Zach, but I don't want to be in the way," Katie said.

Addie smiled. "You're not in the way. We want you to stay with us for as long as you want."

"Really?" Katie asked.

"I wouldn't say it if I didn't mean it," Addie said.

Katie broke out with a huge smile. "Then I really want to

come live with you guys."

Addie hugged her then, happy she'd chosen to stay with them. She already felt like family to Addie, and she hoped Katie felt the same way.

Their new house closed a week before the open house, and the three of them packed up their things and moved over to the Montgomery house.

"This is cute," Katie said. "I can't wait to see what you do with it."

Addie couldn't wait to see how they transformed this house too. It would be work, but she loved every minute of what she did.

* * *

Later that week, as Addie was putting some finishing touches on Sofiya's house, Gail came by.

"I just got the abstract from the old owners," Gail said excitedly, waving the old document in the air. "I wanted you to be the first to look through it."

Zach was in the room above the garage, setting it up to be used as the Hotline office, so Addie called him on his phone to come into the house. She wished Katie were there, but she was in school.

"What's up?" Zach asked, coming into the kitchen.

"The abstract," Addie said excitedly. "I thought you'd want to be here when I look for Sofiya's name."

The other two waited as Addie sifted through the document's old pages. "Look," she said, pointing to a spot on a page. "Nora Petrov is listed as the owner until 1927, although it says the bank took it over before that. And here's an addendum stating that she sold part of the property next door in 1925." Addie turned the page, and there was the name she was searching for. A chill ran up her spine as she said, "Sofiya Hanikoff. She purchased the property in 1927."

"There it is in black and white," Gail said. "It's proof that the letters you're reading are true. Isn't that amazing?"

Addie nodded. She was too choked up to speak.

Zach placed an arm around her. "We should write your name inside it as the owner of the house with this year on it. Everyone should know that you were the one who found Sofiya's story."

She looked up at Gail. "Should I? It wouldn't be a legal document."

"I think you should," Gail said. "You bought it and brought it back to life." She pulled a pen out of her suit jacket pocket. "Go for it."

Addie went to the last page of the document and wrote her full name, Zach's full name, and the date they purchased the house. Then she added the date it would become a safe house and listed Laurie, Valerie, Joe, and Gail as part owners. "There. We're all on it," Addie said.

"It's a shame they don't use these anymore," Gail said. "They're a wealth of information."

"Say? What year did Sofiya sell the house?" Zach asked.

Addie hadn't thought to look. She went back to the page with Sofiya's name, and it stated she'd sold the house in 1965. "Wow. She owned it all those years. That's amazing."

"Boarding houses started to go out of fashion in the late 1960s," Gail said. "Plus, she would have been in her sixties, right? She was probably ready to retire."

"I haven't read the rest of her letters. There aren't many

left," Addie said. "I should finish them before we dedicate the house, so I have the full story."

Gail said goodbye and left through the kitchen door. As Addie watched her, she thought of the multitude of times Sofiya had walked through that very door while she lived here.

"What are you thinking?" Zach asked. "You sort of zoned out for a minute."

She sighed. "It's hard not to think of all the people who've passed through this house and how their lives changed. I hope Sofiya reveals more about what happened after she started the boarding house and what happened to Alina and even Mabel. I guess I want a happy ending for all of them."

"Isn't that what we all want?" Zach asked. He smiled, kissed her cheek, then headed back to the garage.

"I never thought that was what I wanted," Addie said quietly as she watched Zach walk across the backyard. "But I'm beginning to want it more and more."

CHAPTER THIRTY-SEVEN

Sofiya

Sofiya purchased the house and soon was so busy working on it that it made her head spin. When she'd returned to Olga's house after obtaining the money, she'd been delighted to see Carter there. The two hugged, and then Sofiya told him her news.

"Well, that's a mighty big change," he said. "But a good one. If you need help, Miss Sofiya, don't be afraid to ask. I will be happy to help you with the yard or anything else you need fixing."

Sofiya took him up on his offer. Soon, Sofiya, Olga, Carter, and his wife, Everly, and even little Eddie were all working on the house. They cleaned everything, from the wood floors and rugs to the windows and curtains. Sofiya and Olga picked new, lighter wallpaper for the parlor and bought new draperies. The transition was remarkable. The room looked nothing like the party room it had once been.

They also changed the wallpaper in the master bedroom and placed a twin bed where Nora had once had a sofa so Eddie could have his own bed. Any furniture or woodwork in the house that needed painting or staining was done by Carter, and Everly was a wiz at sewing curtains for all the bedrooms. By the time they finished the house, it looked like a respectable boarding house.

Sofiya cooked a turkey dinner with all the fixings for everyone when they'd finished to thank them for their hard work. "I know this doesn't repay you for everything you've done, but I am so grateful to all of you," she told her friends. "And if I can ever do anything for any of you, please don't hesitate to ask."

"Oh, you may regret that one, Miss Sofiya," Carter said, making everyone laugh.

Sofiya made a couple of other changes too. She decided to change Eddie's full name to Edward Henri Hanikoff. He'd always been called Eddie, so he didn't know his first name was actually Edgar. Eddie had asked a few times about his father and his cousins and grandmother, and although Sofiya felt terrible about it, she'd made excuses about why they hadn't seen them. Eddie had become so immersed in their new life and their new friends that he'd stopped asking, and she hoped it would be years before she'd have to explain the truth to him.

The day came when Sofiya placed a sign on the lawn announcing Rooms for Rent, and in smaller letters, it stated Single Gentlemen Only. She never wanted anyone to think this house was a brothel, so she felt it would be more respectable if only men lived there. She also placed an ad in the newspaper. It wasn't long before she had one, then two, then five men rent rooms. One young man was attending the local university, and the other four worked at respectable jobs. Before she knew it, all the rooms were rented. Sofiya was thankful that she now earned enough to keep a roof over her and her son's heads and earned money as well. She'd never grow rich this way, but as long as she could support herself, that was all that mattered.

Sofiya's life was a busy one. She served breakfast to the men at seven each morning and made lunches the men could take to work for those who paid a little extra each month. Dinner was at six sharp, but she was always willing to keep a plate heated for someone who worked later. The men were responsible for keeping their rooms clean, and Sofiya gave them clean bed linens once a week. In the winter, they were given a bucket of coal a week for the fireplace, and if they needed more, they had to pay extra. Sofiya expected them to clean out their fireplaces each week before she refilled their pails with coal.

For the most part, the renters were gentlemen and followed the house rules. One man came home drunk one time too many, so Sofiya asked him to leave. When he refused, Carter came and made him go. She was thankful to have Carter in times like those to keep her safe.

Sofiya enrolled Eddie in school that fall since he was almost seven years old. She was relieved when he said he loved attending school and making new friends. She was also sad because this was his first step toward independence.

One afternoon in October of 1928, Olga stopped by on her way home from her job, looking grim. She had a folded newspaper tucked under her arm.

"Is something wrong?" Sofiya asked. She made Olga a cup of tea and brought out a plate of cookies. Sofiya always made treats for dessert since the men seemed to enjoy them.

"I think you need to see this," Olga said, handing her the newspaper.

Sofiya sat down and opened the paper. In the bottom corner of the second page was the headline:

Syracuse Speakeasy Raided: Five Men Shot Dead.

She quickly scanned the news article. When she saw Edgar's name as one of the men killed, she gasped.

"I'm sorry, Sofiya," Olga said. "It seems his illegal activities caught up with him."

Taking a deep breath, Sofiya read the full article. Edgar had been at the speakeasy downtown when it was raided. He was known as the person who sold liquor to the owner, and they targeted him, so he shot back. They shot him several times before he fell to his death.

"What an awful way to die," Sofiya finally said. She had no emotion for him whatsoever, but she felt bad for his mother, sister, and father. They had always been kind to her, and she would never have wished this on them.

"What are you going to tell Eddie?" Olga asked.

"I'm not sure. I think I'll wait a bit and then tell him his father died suddenly at home. I'd never want to tell a child something like this," Sofiya said. Someday, she'd have to tell her son the truth—all the truths she'd kept from him—but not now. She wanted him to have a happy childhood.

"I'm sure that's for the best," Olga said.

Sofiya swallowed hard. "Sometimes, I'm not sure what is best. My life is filled with secrets, and each one weighs me down a little more. I hope that someday I can share them all and be free of them."

Olga studied her a moment with her brilliant blue eyes that had not faded as she'd aged. "We all carry secrets, dear. Some of us more than others. It cannot be helped. I hope yours don't weigh you down too much."

Tears filled Sofiya's eyes as she reached for the older woman's hand. "I'm so happy I came back here, and I have you in my life. Without my mother, I have no one to help me through the tough times. But I have you and your wisdom, and I cherish that."

Olga smiled at her. "Thank you, dear. I cherish you and Eddie like family too. It's good we have each other."

Sofiya waited a few weeks, then found the right time to tell Eddie that his father had passed away quietly back home. "I'm sorry we didn't see him before that," she told her son. "But remember that he loved you and cherished you dearly."

Eddie didn't seem very upset, which didn't surprise Sofiya. Edgar had spent very little time with his son and was rarely home. She figured Eddie barely remembered him. In truth, Sofiya was relieved that she was no longer tied to Edgar Burton. She could move forward with her life without worrying that he might come looking for them and take Eddie away. Of this one secret, she was finally free.

* * *

The winter had seemed long to Sofiya as she worked hard but finally, when March came in 1929, she was ready for spring. One afternoon as she swept the front porch, she noticed a man wearing a long overcoat walking up the hill with the aid of a cane. Hoping he was coming to see the room she had for rent, she straightened the flower dress she wore and dusted off her apron. Sofiya was always too busy to worry about her appearance, but she didn't want to appear sloppy to a potential renter.

The man stopped in front of the house and stared up at it. Sofiya realized he was much younger than she'd first thought, and he wore a nicely cut wool coat. When he didn't come closer and continued to stare, she walked down the porch steps and onto the walkway.

"Is there something I can help you with?" she asked. She noticed how tall the man was, and when he took off his hat, his combed-back hair was blond. She took a step closer. "Are you looking to rent a room?"

At that moment, the man looked into her eyes with his light blue ones. Sofiya gasped, and a chill ran up her spine.

"Sofiya?" he asked. His voice sounded as if he could hardly believe it was her.

"Harry?"

He smiled wide and hurried as fast as his limp allowed. They stood there, inches apart, gazing at one another.

"Is it really you?" Sofiya asked, studying his face. He did look the same, yet older. His facial features were more defined, but his kind eyes were exactly the same.

"I can't believe you're here," he said. "Can I hug you?"

Sofiya didn't reply, she dropped her broom and wrapped her arms around her beloved old friend. "It's really you," she said between sobs. "I thought I'd never see you again."

Harry held her tightly. "I felt the same way."

Finally, they parted, and Harry bent down with the aid of his cane to retrieve her broom. "I had read in the newspaper that this house was now a boarding house. I had to come to see for myself. But I never imagined that you'd be here."

"I own it," Sofiya said, smiling.

"You do?" A hearty laugh filled the air. The same laugh Sofiya remembered so well.

"Come inside," she said. "Sit in the kitchen like the old days and tell me how you've come to be here."

"Gladly," Harry said.

They spent the next two hours catching up while drinking tea and eating cookies like kids. Harry explained how he'd been hurt in the war and had stayed in Europe for a long time afterward and had several surgeries to save his leg.

"I wasn't in a good place, mentally," he said. "I didn't have the heart to contact my parents and tell them I was wounded. I stayed in London, then Paris, for so long, I thought it would be best if they just forgot about me. It took me a long time to get into a good frame of mind and realize that I was ready to come home."

"Paris?" Sofiya asked.

"Yes, and you know what happened there? I actually believed I saw you at the top of the Eiffel Tower. I was hurrying toward the lifts to catch the next one down, and I literally bumped into a young woman who looked so much like you. But I told myself it was crazy and continued to the lift. I thought I was losing my mind. Why on earth would you be in Paris?"

"Did you have a full beard then?" Sofiya asked, holding her breath.

Harry's face sobered. "Why, yes, I did. I had one the entire time I was in Europe. How did you know?"

"Oh, my goodness. It was you," Sofiya said. "I had thought for certain it was you, but then I thought I was going crazy. I was the girl at the top of the Eiffel Tower."

Harry could hardly believe it. He listened intently as Sofiya told him how she'd escaped Miss Nora's grasp and traveled with Mrs. Dawson. Then she told him about how she'd met Edgar Burton, married him, and then learned that he didn't love her.

"He was just using me to give him an heir that his parents approved of. It was awful. When he made it clear that I was not important to him and that he'd kill me if I ever took his son away, I knew I had to leave. So, I ran again, but this time, it wasn't to protect myself, but to protect my son."

"I'm so sorry," Harry said, reaching for her hand. "Is there any chance he could come after you?"

She shook her head and explained that he'd been killed in a speakeasy raid. "He wasn't a good man. He was greedy and only cared about his own happiness. I wouldn't have wished him dead, but truthfully, I was relieved."

"I don't blame you," he said sympathetically.

Eddie came through the door then with his schoolbooks in hand, and Sofiya introduced him to Harry. "He's an old friend of mine," she explained to her son.

After a few more minutes, Sofiya reluctantly said she had to start dinner for the guests. "Please eat dinner with us. Then we can catch up afterward."

"Oh, I'd love to, but I need to get home," Harry said.

It hadn't occurred to Sofiya that Harry might be married with children of his own. "I'm so sorry. I shouldn't have taken up all your time." She dropped her eyes.

Harry seemed to read her mind. "I need to get home to my parents," he said. "I'm not married, but my mother is expecting me. Can I stop by tomorrow, and we can talk some more?"

Sofiya smiled and nodded her head. "Yes. I'd like that."

After Harry left, Sofiya went to work cooking dinner. For the first time in months, she was so happy that it didn't feel like work. She couldn't wait to see Harry again.

* * *

Throughout the next few weeks, Harry and Sofiya filled each

other in on all the things that had happened to them over the past ten years. Harry explained how he'd returned home to find his father had closed the bakery because he'd had health issues. Harry suggested they open a new bakery, but one that supplied grocery stores. After talking with several stores in the area, they had enough clients who remembered how wonderful their baked goods were and wanted to buy from them.

"It multiplied from there," Harry said. "My father and I started it with my mother's help, but almost immediately, we had to hire help, and then our small building was no longer large enough, and we had to get a bigger place. After four years, we have a large warehouse where we bake and package our products and have several trucks to distribute them. My father can rest when he needs to and work when he feels well. It's been incredible."

"I'm so happy for you," Sofiya told him. She was proud of all he'd accomplished in such a short time. She'd always known he was smart and a hard worker.

Every time that spring and summer when they got together, they talked for hours. Eddie grew to like Harry, and sometimes the three of them would go on outings around Portland to the zoo, the park, and even to the waterfalls on the Columbia River. Sofiya and Harry spent many evenings after dinner sitting on the bench under the old oak tree in the backyard, talking about their past and the future.

It was on that bench that Harry described how he'd injured his leg in the war and had been so scared he might lose it. He said he was lucky that a doctor in London took an interest and worked tirelessly to save it. "It's not perfect, and sometimes it aches if I've been on it too long, but I can walk, and that's all that matters," Harry told her.

With each passing day, Sofiya was falling more in love with Harry. She met his parents and adored them immediately. They were kind and loving, and she could see how proud they were of what Harry had accomplished. They visited Olga at her house, and she was so thrilled to see Harry that she cried. Carter, too, was happy the young man had made it through the war and had come home.

On a balmy evening in August, sitting under the oak tree, Harry proposed. "I promise to love and care for you and Eddie for the rest of my life," he said. Through tears of joy, Sofiya accepted. This was all she'd ever wanted out of life—a man who truly loved her and a home they could share.

They were married in the backyard on a beautiful September day in 1929 with their friends and family in attendance. Even the male boarders were there to wish the couple well. Eddie had grown to love Harry like a father, and that made Sofiya very happy.

The couple had decided to keep running the boarding house, and Harry continued running his business as well. When the stock market crashed in October of that year, the young couple didn't worry too much. But as the country slowly fell into a financial depression, Harry and Sofiya held strong. They kept their businesses running by being frugal and never giving up hope that the country would pull out of it. They'd been through war—they could withstand this too. Sofiya believed that no matter what happened, as long as she continued to own her home, she would be fine in the end.

No matter what was happening in the world, Sofiya had found happiness with Harry. She had the family she'd always dreamed of. The family her mother had hoped she'd have some-day. And that meant more to her than anything else in the world.

Finally, Sofiya was ready to give up her secrets. Maybe not to the world or to her family yet, but she needed to write one last letter to her dear departed mother. Only then could she move forward with her new life, no longer carrying a heavy load.

Sitting at her desk, she wrote the words she'd needed to say all these years.

CHAPTER THIRTY-EIGHT

Addie

Addie read Sofiya's last letters with tears in her eyes. Sofiya and Harry had found each other after all those years and had their happily ever after. Her heart filled with joy for them. She was sure they still had hard times ahead of them through the depression and then World War II, but she knew they'd survived it. After all, Addie had the abstract that showed they'd owned the Marshall Street house until 1965, so she knew they had made it through those difficult times.

But it was the very last letter that touched her heart. She wondered if Sofiya's son had ever read it. Or if any of Sofiya's family had read it since it had been written in French. Had she taught Eddie to read French? While Addie had learned so much about Sofiya's life, there were still so many unanswered questions.

When Addie told Zach about the last letters, he was as amazed as she'd been.

"Imagine finding Harry after all those years," Zach said. "They were truly meant to be together."

His words stayed with her as they prepared for the upcoming dedication of the safe house. Addie believed in kismet. She believed in coincidences, karma, and destiny. She also believed in love at first sight. She knew that many people thought those things were silly, but she took them seriously. Addie knew she'd been meant to find Sofiya's letters so that they'd lead her to the Marshall Street house. And now, turning it into a safe house had been her destiny too. So, if she truly believed in all those things, why didn't she believe she and Zach were meant to be?

Addie had been fighting the truth for so long, she forgot to just let life lead her. Zach was her destiny. She'd loved him from the first time they'd met, and she loved him more each year they were together. What was she waiting for?

The night before the dedication, Addie and Zach sat at the old wooden table in their new house, going over plans for the remodel. Looking up at Zach, Addie stared into his warm brown eyes and smiled.

"What?" he asked once he'd noticed she'd been watching him. "Do I have pizza on my face?"

She laughed. "No. I just want to tell you that I'm all in."

Zach frowned. "All in? You mean with the remodel? I hope so because we own this mess."

Addie laughed again, then reached for his hand. "I'm all in. With you. With our relationship. Even with this remodel. Everything." She flashed the engagement ring at him. "And this. If you're still asking, then yes, I'll marry you, Zachery Walker."

Zach looked stunned. Once he realized what she'd said, his face broke out into a big smile. He reached for Addie and drew her to him. "I'm still asking," he said, inches from her face.

"And the answer is yes," she said.

Zach kissed her in a way that made Addie feel she'd made the best decision of her life.

* * *

March first arrived, and Addie was ready with a speech in hand, and Sofiya's plaque hung proudly on the front of the house beside the door. They had a large turnout from the neighborhood and people from all over Portland who were interested in the new safe house. Visitors toured the home, read the information pamphlets, and enjoyed the refreshments. Finally, it was time for Addie to speak.

Everyone came outside onto the lawn as Addie stood on the front porch with Zach, Valerie, Laurie, Joe, Gail, and Katie by her side. Nervously, Addie began.

"Thank you all for coming to help us dedicate this new safe house for trafficked teens in our community. You will never know just how important a place like this is and how life-changing it will be to those who will benefit from it." She continued speaking, talking about Sofiya, who had once lived in the house when it was a high-end brothel, and how she'd returned and transformed it into a respectable house again. She told the crowd how she'd found Sofiya's letters and how they had led her to this house. And then, she shared a little about her own experience as a trafficked teen and how the help of others saved her life.

"Women have been exploited since the beginning of time," Addie said. "This isn't anything new. Sofiya and her friend Alina were exploited a hundred years ago in this very spot. What we're doing here is helping to bring awareness and, hopefully, one day will help to stop the violence against all women and men of every age. Because our society cannot afford to continue this cycle for another hundred years.

"So, with great honor, I'd like to dedicate this safe house in honor of Sofiya Hanikoff."

The crowd cheered and applauded as all of Addie's friends hugged her.

"We did it," Addie said to Laurie. "This is an amazing day."

"Now the work begins," Laurie said, laughing.

Addie knew that was true. Already, their staff was preparing for the arrival of two girls who had just been saved from a trafficker.

People continued to wander around, and soon the crowd thinned out. Addie had come outside on the porch to pick up any cups or plates left behind when she saw an elderly gentleman in khakis and a dress shirt walk slowly up the sidewalk.

"Hello," he called, still a few paces from the porch. "Am I too late for a tour?"

She smiled. "Not at all. Please, come inside and look around."

He stepped up on the porch and gazed at the plaque with Sofiya's name on it. Then he smiled and followed Addie inside.

Addie let the gentleman look around while she helped Zach and Katie pick up trash and clear the table of leftover goodies from the parlor. As the gentleman came downstairs, Addie walked up to him.

"Do you live in the neighborhood?" she asked.

"No, I don't. I read about the dedication today in the newspaper. I wanted to come see it," he said.

"I'm so glad you did," Addie said. She raised her hand to shake his. "I'm Addie Cameron."

"Well, it's nice to meet you," he said, shaking her hand.

"You're the young lady who remodeled the house, aren't you?"

"Yes. Well, me and my partner in crime," she said, smiling.

Zach walked over to join them. "That would be me. I'm Zach." He shook the man's hand.

"You both did a wonderful job. The house looks exactly the same, yet fresh and updated," he said.

Addie stared at him. "Have you been here before?"

He chuckled. "I'm sorry. I didn't introduce myself. My name is Herold Hanikoff. I'm Sofiya's grandson."

Addie felt her mouth drop open. "Really? You're Edward's son?"

He nodded. "Yes. His youngest son. He named me Harold after his stepfather, Harry. Although, he'd been more like a father to my dad. My eldest brother died in the Vietnam War."

"Oh, I'm so sorry," Addie said. She was trying to wrap her head around what was happening. "So, you knew Sofiya?"

"Oh, yes. She was a very kind and loving grandmother. As a child, I ran all over this house. And when I was a young teen, I'd come and help her and Grandpa Harry. They were amazing people."

"I have a million questions for you," Addie said, making Zach laugh.

"Well, I'm afraid I could only answer questions about her as she grew older. To tell the truth, no one in our family knew anything about her past. It's been quite a mystery," Harold said. "When I saw you were dedicating this house to her, I had to come hear what you knew. I'd be so interested in learning more about her."

"So, you didn't know about the cigar box filled with letters?" Addie asked.

"No. I never saw anything like that. My father cleared out

her personal things after she passed. I was away at college at the time."

Addie and Zach looked at each other. She knew they were both thinking the very same thing. She turned to Harold. "I have something that belongs to you," Addie said, smiling wide.

EPILOGUE

Sofiya

January 1, 1930

Dear Maman,
I am at last safe and happy. Everything you desired for me has come true. I've married a wonderful man who truly loves me, and I know we will be together for life. I have a lovely home all my own and am able to earn money while my dear Harry runs his very successful bakery business. Although times are tough right now, we're doing fine. We have a roof over our heads, an income, and a great love for each other—and that is all we need.
And, of course, I have the best gift in my dear son, Eddie. He is growing so fast, Maman. He is nine years old and has taken a great liking to Harry, which warms my heart. I hope he grows to consider Harry as his father, as my dear husband is the best influence a boy could have.
I must tell you, Maman, that Alina and her husband, Clint, are doing well, as are their beautiful children, Floriana and Carlton. Clint's father isn't well, and there is talk that they will return

to Portland to run the family business. I would so love to have my dearest and oldest friend by my side once again.

I thank you, Maman, for all the love you gave me, and I know now that it had to have been the most difficult decision for you to send me so far away, knowing you might never see me again. Your love and sacrifice brought me here, and I'm grateful every day. I wish you and Père were here too. I miss you both so much.

This is my last letter to you, dear Maman. I no longer need to put my thoughts to paper as I now have a partner in life who I can share everything with. I have kept my promise to you, Maman, to keep my true identity secret so that I might be safe. I understand now why you wanted me to lie about my past. I haven't even shared it with my dear husband, Harry, although there are times I wish I could. But out of respect for you, I will not.

I will keep these letters hidden away until the time of my passing. Only then will my Eddie know the truth about my past and his birthright. So, in my last written words to you, dear Maman, I will break my promise so that Eddie may know the truth.

Edward Henri Hanikoff, you are a descendant of the Romanov family, cousin to the last great Emperor of Russia, Tsar Nicholas II. My father, Henri Hanikoff, was cousin to Tsar Nicholas on his mother's side. More than that, they were great friends who enjoyed spending time together discussing all matters of topics. While, to my great distress, it has been learned that Tsar Nicholas was executed along with the Tsarina and all their children, there are still a great many Romanov cousins alive today. I hope you will seek them out and learn more about your heritage.

And now, with that said, I can finally put my last secret to rest.

I will forever love you, dear Maman.
Sofiya Hanikoff Meyer

My great-grandmother (left) and her friend
who traveled with her to America (right).

AUTHOR'S NOTE

This novel is a work of fiction, but it is also based on real-life events. My great-grandmother and her good friend arrived in Portland, Oregon, from Finland sometime around 1913, both in their late teens. I have a multitude of photographs from her early years there and then as a traveling companion for an elderly woman, yet no story to back them up. She never told anyone about when and why she came to America and had never shared the photos with her family. It wasn't until she passed that the photos were found. And, of course, as a writer, my imagination took the story from there.

My deep love of Portland comes from my own best friend and her family who live there. We visited them as often as we could and got to know the area well. Out of all my great-grandmother's photos, I had one that distinctly tied her to the area—a 1915 postcard sent to her from a friend that had her address on it. Back then, that address would have been a house just a block or two from the Willamette River. Today, hotels, businesses, and condominiums fill that area. Because I wanted Addie to find the same house Sofiya had lived in, I had to move the place up many blocks. But as I said—this is fiction—so I could place it wherever I needed to.

While this isn't my great-grandmother's story, that is where the concept came from. I added in events that occurred during Sofiya's time—like the Spanish Flu pandemic, World War I, and of course, the abdication and murder of Tsar Nicholas II and his family. So many historical facts are sprinkled in this story. Facts that I had to dig relentlessly for and some that even surprised me. As with all my historical novels, half the fun is the research.

I hope you enjoyed Sofiya's story. I spent so much time with her that she actually feels like family. In the following pages, I'm including what I believe happened to some of the important characters in the story—because I've found that enquiring minds need to know. And it's fun.

Thank you for reading this story and all the other stories I've written if you've had a chance to. I waited a long time to start my writing career, and it's been such a rewarding experience. I appreciate every one of you.

Deanna Lynn Sletten
May 28, 2022

This photo inspired the picnic scene in the book.

What Happened to the Characters?

Because I know you want to know...

Harry and Sofiya lived happily over the next forty years, enjoying watching Eddie grow into a man and then spending time with their two grandsons. Their first scare was when Eddie served in World War II, but they were thrilled when he returned home and married. The second saddest moment in their lives was when their eldest grandson, Edward Jr., was killed in the Vietnam War. They sold both the bakery business and the boarding house in 1965 and retired. The couple purchased a smaller home in Gresham and spent their time traveling around the United States. Harry passed away in 1973 at the age of seventy-four after a long fight with cancer. Sofiya died quietly in her sleep in 1975 at the age of seventy-four. Sofiya had left a note to save her jewelry for Harold in the hope that someday he could pass it on to his daughter or son.

Alina and Clinton lived in Ketcham, Alaska raising their two children until 1935, when they returned to Portland so Clint could take over the entire business from his father. Alina and Sofiya remained close friends until their deaths, and their children also became good friends. Because Alina wasn't comfortable going to the boarding house due to all the unhappy memories there, Sofiya always visited her at her home. Both Alina and Clinton lived good lives and died in the early 1980s within days of each other.

Mrs. Olga Jarvi remained friends with Sofiya until she died in 1945. To Sofiya, she was like a second mother. Her estate was split between Sofiya and Carter. Sofiya thought of her often throughout the years after her death and was always thankful to have known her.

Mabel Harper continued to work in real estate and, in 1936, finally received her license as a real estate sales agent. In 1938 she joined the Women's Council of Realtors because women were not yet allowed to join the National Association of Realtors despite there being over three-thousand women sales agents across the United States. She purchased the business she worked for and went on to open three more offices around Portland. Mabel never married or had children. She worked hard and loved what she did.

Nora Petrov walked away from the Marshall Street house in late 1925 because she couldn't pay the past due taxes. With nowhere to go, she found a job in a bar on the waterfront, catering to patrons for whatever they desired. Her heavy drinking continued, and after she'd been found stealing cash from the bar, she was thrown out on the streets. She found a small shack by the riverfront and called it her home, finding alcohol or money wherever she could get it. Nora died drunk and alone in the shack, with no one missing her. In 1955, during a cleanup of the waterfront, a skeleton was found in a dilapidated pile of wood that had once been a shack. She was buried in an unmarked grave in Portland. (Did you really think I'd give her a happy ending?)

Carter and Everly worked hard and lived a happy life. Carter retired from the railroad in 1957 at the age of seventy with a nice little pension. Everly, who had a sewing business at home, also retired that year at the age of 65 to spend more time with her husband. They had saved their small inheritance from Olga Jarvi and were able to take several small vacations around the United States. Both continued to be close to Sofiya and Harry until their deaths. Carter died peacefully in his sleep at the age of 85 and Everly followed him ten years later.

Addie and Zach married on a beautiful spring day in the backyard of their Montgomery Street house with friends and family in attendance. They had decided, for the time being, that would be their forever home, and Katie could live with them until she was ready to be on her own. The happy couple continues to flip houses, although Addie has slowed down because she's expecting a baby girl in the fall.

Katie Abrams found she enjoyed attending college, and after her first year, she applied and was accepted to the University of Portland in downtown Portland. It was a big change for her, but she continues to attend group meetings at Laurie's house, which have helped her greatly. Katie has declared her major in Social Work and hopes one day to help others the way Laurie and Addie helped her. She also continues to live with Addie and Zach and cannot wait until the birth of their first child.

About the Author

Deanna Lynn Sletten is the author of THE ONES WE LEAVE BEHIND, THE WOMEN OF GREAT HERON LAKE, MISS ETTA, MAGGIE'S TURN, FINDING LIBBIE, and several other titles. She writes heartwarming women's fiction, historical fiction, a murder mystery series, and romance novels with unforgettable characters. She has also written one middle-grade novel that takes you on the adventure of a lifetime.

Deanna is married and has two grown children. When not writing, she enjoys peaceful walks in the woods around her home with her beautiful Australian Shepherd, traveling, photography, and relaxing on the lake.

Deanna loves hearing from her readers.
Connect with her at: deannalynnsletten.com